DAUGHTERS OF THE MOON

DAUGHTERS OF THE MOON

BOOK ONE

goddess of the night

BOOK TWO

into the cold fire

BOOK THREE

night shade

LYNNE EWING

HYPERION
New York

This edition, 2010
5 7 9 10 8 6 4
ISBN 1-4231-3450-8
G475-5664-5-13191
Library of Congress Cataloging-in-Publication Data on file for individual titles.

Visit www.hyperionteens.com

THIS LABEL APPLIES TO TEXT STOCK

For Alessandra Balzer with deep gratitude.
These books would not have been possible without
her unlimited enthusiasm and encouragement.

BOOK ONE

goddess of the night

PROLOGUE

In ancient times, it was said that the goddess Selene drove the moon across the sky. Each night she followed her brother Helios, the sun, to catch his fiery rays and reflect the light back to earth. One night on her journey, she looked down and saw Endymion sleeping in the hills. She fell in love with the beautiful shepherd. Night after night she looked down on his gentle beauty and loved him more, until finally one evening she left the moon between the sun and the earth and went down to the grassy fields to lie beside him.

For three nights she stayed with him, and the moon, unable to catch the sun's rays, remained dark. People feared the dark moon. They said it brought death and freed evil forces to roam the black night. Zeus,

King of the Gods, was angered by the darkness and punished Selene by giving Endymion eternal sleep.

Selene returned to the moon and drove it across the night sky, but her love was too strong. She hid Endymion in a cave; and now, three nights each lunar month, she leaves the moon to visit her sleeping lover and cover him with silver kisses. In his sleep, Endymion dreams he holds the moon. He has given Selene many daughters to guard the night. They are powerful and beautiful like their mother, and mortal like their father.

CHAPTER ONE

VANESSA CLEVELAND cursed silently as she walked down the street. She couldn't shake the puzzling feeling that someone was following her. How could she forget it was the dark of the moon?

Overhead, low, thin clouds crept around the red-tile roofs and brought the ocean's cold. The cold didn't come to her all at once, but slowly and gently. She started to shiver and wasn't sure if it was from the cold or fear.

Vanessa had passed two houses when a soft scuttling sound made her stop and turn. The breeze picked up, and a bunch of dead leaves scraped down the sidewalk toward her. She felt a surge of relief and smiled. She tried to focus on something pleasant to keep her mind off her fear.

She thought of Michael Saratoga. His wild black hair hung in thick curls on his shoulders. He had strong, angular features, a sexy smile, and soft, dark eyes. She had liked him since the beginning of the school year when she first met him in Spanish class. But she had never imagined he would like her. Even now, fear of jinxing what might be forced her to push that sweet thought away. He made her feel all fire and ache down to her bones. That was good. That was also very bad. How could someone as different as she was ever expect to do a normal thing like have a boyfriend?

Abruptly she was aware that someone was on the street with her. She looked behind her. She expected to see a person in a bathrobe walking a dog, a wad of plastic sacks in hand, or a homeless person trudging down the middle of the road pushing a shopping cart.

But the street was empty. Was it the dark of the moon that was making her so jumpy?

She tried to concentrate on Michael again

and not think about the creeping shadows that seemed to be pressing closer with each step. Michael had asked her to dance eight times tonight at Planet Bang in Hollywood, and he would have spent more time with her if Morgan Page hadn't kept pulling him out onto the dance floor. Michael liked to dance, and Morgan danced better than she did.

She tried to remember the feel of Michael's cheek, his hand on her waist, his—

Something moved in the corner of her eye. She turned sharply. Whatever it was had slid across the shadows and then was gone.

She bent down and took off her heavy, wedge-soled shoes. The heels felt solid and lethal in her hands. She took two steps back and scanned the street. Then she knew. Relief broke through her fear. Her best friend, Catty, must be trailing her. Why hadn't she thought of that before? It wouldn't be the first time Catty had tried to scare her, thinking it was funny.

"Catty," she said. "I know it's you, come out." She spoke loudly, but a fine tremor had crept into her voice.

No one answered.

"Catty," she started again. Her voice was soft now, a whisper filled with fear.

She peered into the dark that clung to the side of a house. What had been there was gone. Had it only been an illusion of the dark?

Finally, she turned and started walking again, her bare feet steady on the cool cement. Her mother had warned her how dangerous it was for a girl to be out alone in Los Angeles at night. Now anger filled her and made a knot in her throat. It shouldn't be dangerous. Girls had a right to enjoy the night, to run wild under the moon and stars, not stay home huddled behind bolted doors.

Anger quickened her pace and made her brave. She gripped her shoes tightly. When she got to the corner, she stood defiantly under the steady glow of the street lamp. She waited a long time in the amber light. If it were someone with evil intent, a gangbanger, mugger, or desperate homeless person, they would have attacked by now.

She thought of Michael again, his hand on

her cheek. Had he been leaning down to kiss her when Morgan pulled him away?

Something skipped through the darkness. Something trying hard not to be seen. She was certain it was real this time, no trick of light and shadow. She turned to run and tripped over a tricycle lying on its side. Her shoes fell from her hands and scattered. The handlebar pushed painfully into her stomach.

The tricycle hadn't been there before. She would have seen something that size. Someone had crept behind her and placed it there. But how and when?

She left her shoes, pulled herself up, and ran. She didn't scream. A scream stole too much oxygen. She ran with savagery, her arms pumping at her sides. Already she could feel the arousal in her molecules, a soft and pleasant tremble. She could give in to her special power, but it was too chancy. She had a horrible feeling that what was happening to her now was somehow connected to her strange ability. She had always feared that one day someone would discover her secret.

If one person discovered the truth, she

would be hunted down, taken to some cheesy place like Las Vegas, and put on display. Then a new terror struck. Maybe the person skulking behind her was trying to frighten her into using her power. Perhaps a video recorder watched her, the owner hoping to capture the unthinkable on tape and sell it to the highest bidder.

Whoever it was was getting closer. Footfalls pounded softly in the grass behind her, gaining. She didn't glance back to see who it was.

Her molecules grew more excited, pinging to be free of gravity. She imagined herself, invisible, running through her clothes, her stalker stopping to pick up the organza peasant dress. Too risky.

Stay, she thought, stay. She had to concentrate to keep her molecules together. Her body longed to give in to the stretch of bone and muscle, and dissolve into a million fragments.

Then another sound made her heart wrench.

Other footsteps joined those of the person chasing her. More than one person this time, maybe more than two. Could it be even worse than she had first imagined?

What was her mother going to do when she found out her daughter was a freak? What would kids at school say? High school was hard enough without this, too. All she'd ever wanted was to be like everyone else.

She heard someone speaking. Then she realized the words were tumbling from her own lips in a high, keening pitch. What was she saying? Some forgotten prayer her mother had taught her when she was a child?

Her lips formed the strange words again. *"O Mater Luna, Regina nocis, adiuvo me nunc."*

Besides English, she knew only a little Spanish. These words were definitely not Spanish or English. Where had they come from?

From the corner of her eye, she saw a hand reach for her.

The words gathered on her lips again, hard and strong. She spit them out. *"O Mater Luna, Regina nocis, adiuvo me nunc."* The power of the words filled her as she spoke.

And then her chasers were gone. She kept running, afraid to trust what she knew was true. She was alone.

At the next block, she stopped and turned back. She rested her hands on her knees. Her breath came in gasps that stung her lungs. The street behind her was empty.

A trio of lawn flamingos stood in front of her. She stepped across the wet lawn and pulled on the serpentine neck of the first bird. The body tore free from the legs. She tossed the pink plastic bird aside and heaved the iron legs from the ground. The iron rods felt good in her hands.

She walked backward for half the block. She was only two blocks from Melrose Avenue now, and that meant people. She turned and ran toward the comforting traffic sounds, the garish neon lighting. The smells of Thai spices and northern Italian spaghetti sauces swirled deliciously around her as she barreled into the throng of kids crowding the sidewalk.

She stopped near a bus stop and stared back at the street from which she had fled. Four boys and a girl sat on the bus bench. The boys wore the uniform of modern primitives. Silver hoops pierced nipples, eyebrows, nose, and lips. Tattoos curled in languid lines around their necks and arms, and black leather vests flapped against their naked white chests like wicked pelts.

"Who you fighting?" the tall boy with the ratted black hair asked. He stared at her hand.

She glanced up. She held one flamingo leg like a javelin, aiming, her muscles taut, ready to strike.

She smiled to reassure the boy. He stepped back and stumbled off the curb. His eyes looked as if he saw something in Vanessa's face that frightened him.

"Go haunt another corner," the girl said.

Vanessa left them staring after her and started down Melrose. Her feet stepped in the black powdered grime that covered the street. She hated to think what foul things were gathering between her toes.

At home, the porch light blazed a welcome and covered the small craftsman-style house in a halo of gold light. The twisted olive tree stood rigid near the front walk. She crept to the side of the house and hid.

When she was sure no one had followed her, she walked to the back door, opened it, and stepped onto the back porch. She dropped the flamingo legs on the washing machine. The metal made a loud clank.

"Vanessa," her mother called.

She walked into the warm kitchen. The smells of coffee, glue, and pencil shavings wafted around her. A large bulletin board hung on the wall above the table. Her mother called it her inspiration board. A fanfare of sketches and bold-colored swatches were tacked to it now. She worked as a costume designer for the movies.

"You're late," her mother said and rushed to her. There was more fear in her eyes than anger. Her brown hair looked as if she had raked worried fingers through it. With cold hands she touched Vanessa's cheek, and then held her tightly. "I was worried about you. I hope you didn't walk home. You know how I feel about that."

"I got a ride," she lied. "Catty's mother picked us up."

Her mother shook her head. "Catty's mother wouldn't care if you stayed out all night." She didn't approve of the way Catty's mother let Catty run wild.

"I'm sorry I'm late," Vanessa said. She felt genuinely bad that she had caused her mother so much anxiety. "Planet Bang closed at *one* A.M., not midnight."

"On a school night? You know that's too late."

"I'll make sure I check the time next time."

"If there is a next time," her mother muttered.

"Mom, everyone goes to Planet Bang on Tuesday night. Tuesdays and Fridays are the only nights kids under twenty-one are allowed."

She stopped and followed her mother's stare. Her feet were black with city dirt, one big toe bleeding.

"For goodness sake, Vanessa, what did you do with your shoes?" her mother blurted out.

"The new shoes hurt my feet," Vanessa started another lie and stopped. Why did it seem like all conversations with her mother started or ended with lies? "I forgot them at Planet Bang. I'll call and see if someone found them."

"From now on I'm going to pick you up. This is not going to happen again. Ten-thirty is late enough for a school night. You should be in bed."

"All right." Vanessa stepped to the sink and poured herself a glass of water.

"Did anything happen tonight that you want to tell me about?" her mother said, suspicion rising in her voice.

"Nothing." Vanessa sipped the water. It tasted metallic and filled with chlorine. She spit it out.

"Something's wrong if you're drinking tap water," her mother said. "You'll poison yourself." She poured a glass of water from the cooler in the corner and handed it to Vanessa.

Vanessa swallowed the cool water, then stared at her mother. She had never thought of telling her mother the truth, but she had never felt so close to being exposed before this. What would her mother do? Maybe her mother had special powers of her own and had been waiting all this time for Vanessa to bring it up.

"Mom, are you . . ."

"What?"

"You know . . . different? I mean, besides the clothes." Her mother dressed on the cutting edge of fashion, wearing clothes before anyone even knew they were in style. That was her job. But sometimes it was embarrassing to have a mother so overly trendy. She had been wearing high-waters and pedal pushers two years ago, when everyone just thought her pants were too short.

"A psychic once told me I didn't march to the beat of a different drummer," her mother explained. "She said I had a whole band marching behind me."

"No, I mean really different." Vanessa's chin began to quiver. "Like in the freak category."

"Oh, honey." Her mother embraced her. "It's perfectly normal to feel like you don't fit in. It's part of growing up. You don't need to worry. Look at how popular you are at school. You get lots of telephone calls and invitations to parties."

If her mother only knew how much of her real self she had to keep hidden. Maybe kids at school liked her now, but what if they knew the truth?

"I have to do a lot to fit in, Mom." It wasn't self-pity. It was fact. "Kids aren't very accepting of someone who is really different."

"What's so different about you? You're pretty. You get good grades."

Did she dare tell her? Did she have a choice? If her life was in danger, maybe her mother could help. "Do you remember the night when I was a little girl and I woke up crying from a nightmare?"

"Which night? There were so many."

"The night you thought I was playing a game of hide-and-seek?"

"Yes—I found you sleeping in the bathroom and carried you back to bed."

"I wasn't hiding."

"What were you doing, then?"

"I was . . ." she stopped.

"Yes?"

She looked at her mother. How could she tell her that she had been invisible?

"I was . . . That was the night I found out . . ."

That had been the night she woke from a nightmare and couldn't see her body in the pale glow of the night-light. She had been terrified, and afraid to tell her mother. She had thought she had done something bad. Her mother had heard her crying and ran into her room. She had lifted her arms to be comforted, but her mother couldn't see her. That had frightened her even more. While her mother was searching the house for her, her molecules had come back together, but they had come back wrong. Her face had looked different. She had locked herself in the bathroom then, knowing her mother could never love her now. Sleep had finally taken her, and when she woke in the morning back in her own bed, she had looked normal.

"Vanessa, what did you find out that night?"

"Nothing. It's not important."

Her mother lifted her chin and looked into her eyes. "You're shaking."

"I just wish . . ."

"Tell me."

"I just wish I could be like everyone else."

"Is that all? Trust me, it's better to be an individual and to have your own idiosyncrasies." Her mother sat back at the table. "There's life after high school. Don't try too hard to blend in and be like everyone else. Kids who do lose something important." Her mother continued reciting what Vanessa called Standard Lecture No. 7.

She left her mother talking to the wall and went upstairs to the bathroom. She washed her feet. The water turned black and swirled down the drain.

Then she took a bath, put on pajamas, and went to her bedroom. She loved her room. She had window seats and shutters, flowered wallpaper, and a bed with too many pillows. Her mother called the decor "romance and drama," and said the room looked like it belonged to a fairy princess.

She turned on her computer and clicked on a program called Sky Show that she had purchased through *Astronomy* magazine. A thin slice of moon came on the screen. She looked at the date. According to the program, today should have been the first crescent moon, a time when she should have felt adventurous and filled with curiosity.

But the program had made an error. It was the dark of the moon tonight. Those three nights when the moon was completely dark and invisible from Earth had always had a strange hold on her. She felt nervous then, as if some part of her sensed danger. Catty's mother said superstitious people believed the dark moon brought death and destruction, and freed evil forces to roam the night.

A breeze ruffled the curtains. She hadn't left her window open. Maybe her mother had opened it. She shut the window and locked it, then sat on her bed and stared at her computer.

The door to her room opened. Her mother walked in.

"I came to kiss you good night," her mother said. "Why does it feel so cold in here?"

"My window was open. You didn't open it?"

"No, but that explains the draft I was feeling all night."

"My program's messed up. Did you play around with my computer?"

"Computer?"

"Right." Vanessa shook her head. "Silly idea."

Her mother kissed her quickly and started to leave.

"Mom?"

"Yes?"

"Do you know what this means?" She tried to repeat the sound of the words she had spoken earlier. *"Oh, Mah-tare Loon-ah, Re-gee-nah no-kis, Ad-you-wo may noonk."*

"That sounds like Latin." Her mother smiled. "That's what you did when you were a little girl."

"Speak Latin?"

"No," her mother said. "Hold your moon amulet that way."

She glanced down. After her father died, her nightmares had become stronger. Always the same dream—black shadows covering the full moon and then, like a specter, taking form and chasing her. She always woke clutching the silver moon amulet she wore around her neck. She was gripping it now.

"Good night, sweetheart." Her mother kissed the top of her head and left the room.

Vanessa stared at the night outside her window. Where would she have learned Latin? She knew it had to be connected to her power. If it weren't so late, she'd call Catty. Now she'd have to wait until tomorrow to find out if Catty had ever uttered words that she didn't understand.

She crawled under the covers. The cotton

sheets were sun-dried and ironed and filled with the smell of sunshine. She breathed in the fragrance and glanced back at her computer. For the first time she noticed her alarm clock with the luminous hands. It was turned toward the wall. She got up and turned it back to face her. Then she noticed her wristwatch. It was turned facedown. Odd. Maybe Catty had been playing around and left a calling card. She'd have a serious talk with her tomorrow and tell her that this time her jokes had gone too far.

CHAPTER TWO

CATTY AND VANESSA sat at the counter inside the Johnny Rockets diner. The smells of bacon and onions hung in the warm, thick air. Conversation whirled around them in a mad tangle of laughs and squeals, but only the thunder of motorcycles taking off outside was loud enough to drown the loud sing-songy music from the fifties and sixties.

"I swear I didn't go into your room last night." Catty's brown hair fell in perfect spirals around her face. When she tilted her head, the curls caught the sunlight pouring through the window.

"Someone turned my clock around," Vanessa said.

"Why would I turn your clock around?"

"Just to show me you had been there." Vanessa looked at her. "It wouldn't be the first time you had done something like that."

"But I was at Planet Bang with you." Catty had a slight smile that curled on her lips even when she frowned.

"I thought maybe you had tweaked time." She had hoped it had been Catty. "Who was in my room if it wasn't you?"

"Maybe no one," Catty pointed out. "Maybe you're creeping yourself out. You could have been nervous while getting ready. So you knocked over your clock and set it up facing the wall without noticing."

"Maybe," Vanessa agreed, but the nagging feeling that someone had been in her room wouldn't leave her.

"I can't believe you were so scared that you almost told your mother the truth about . . . you know." Catty flipped through the song titles in the Seeburg Wall-O-Matic. She picked up the nickels the waiter had left for the vintage machine, dropped two in the coin slot, and punched in a set of numbers. "Would you have told her about me, too?"

"No," Vanessa said. "Just me."

Charlie Brown boomed from the speakers, competing with the sizzle of hamburgers frying on the grill. A crowd of bikers walked in and straddled red seats at the counter.

"What would she have done?" Catty asked. "It's not something a mother expects to hear. 'Hey, Mom, did you know I can be as see-through as a ghost? Wanna see?' I mean, not see.'" Catty laughed so hard the bikers turned and smiled at her.

Vanessa wiped the drop of chocolate running over the Johnny Rockets red emblem on the glass. "I'm not kidding, Catty, it wasn't just the dark of the moon. Someone was following me."

"I know one way we can check it out." Catty dug her spoon into the whipped cream on top of the shake.

"No," Vanessa said firmly. "I told you. Never

again. Not after last time." The truth was, Vanessa found Catty's power frightening.

"You always say that, and then you end up changing your mind."

"I guess. Want my tomatoes?"

"Last night made you all messed up." Catty took the tomatoes and tucked them into her burger.

Vanessa didn't want to talk about last night anymore. It was better forgotten, like a nightmare. "I looked for you at school today."

"I was hopping time," Catty said. She picked up a French fry covered with chili and cheese and pushed it into her mouth.

"You got to stop doing that! You're missing too many tests."

"My mother doesn't care."

"But you should." Sometimes Vanessa felt jealous of Catty's relationship with her mother. Catty's mother didn't care if she missed school, because she knew Catty was different. She also wasn't Catty's biological mother. She had found Catty walking along the side of the road in the desert between Gila Bend and Yuma when Catty was six years old. She'd planned to turn her over to the authorities in Yuma, but when she saw Catty make time change, she decided Catty was an extraterrestrial, separated from her parents, like E.T., and that it was her duty to protect her from government officials who would probably dissect her. She brought Catty to Los Angeles, knowing that in a city where anything goes, a child from another planet could fit in.

Catty had only two memories of the time before she was six. One of a crash, the other of a fire. Both were only flashes of memory and didn't reveal much about her past. When her power was strong enough, Catty planned to go back to the time before she was six.

Vanessa rolled down the paper wrapper that swaddled the hamburger. She opened her mouth wide and bit down. Mayonnaise, pickle juice, and mustard ran down her chin.

The waiter came back. "How's the hamburger?" he asked.

"Great," Catty said and let a piece of tomato fall from her mouth.

The waiter laughed and picked up the tomato from the counter, then walked away.

"You are so gross!"

Catty punched her playfully. "Vanessa, I'm just trying to get your mind off last night. You probably had some dog running after you, or a homeless person who likes to play games. Let's go back and see."

"No."

"Why not?" Catty persisted, sipping her shake.

"You know why. I'm too afraid we'll go back some time and get stuck."

"So what? All you'd have to do is relive the time. It would be fun. We'd know what was going to happen."

"You don't know if that's how it really works."

"That's because I've never gotten stuck," Catty pointed out.

When Catty had first tried time traveling, it had only been in short bursts. Then she had learned that if she concentrated she could make hops in time up to twenty-four hours into the past or the future. Catty figured if she lost her power and couldn't return to the present, she would just relive a day or, if she had jumped time into the future, lose a day. Vanessa wasn't so sure. There was also the tunnel, the hole in time they had to go through. She was terrified of getting stuck there.

"I don't know why you worry so much," Catty said, taking another bite.

"Forget it. It was probably a homeless person, like you said." Vanessa insisted. "I don't need to see."

Catty spoke with her mouth full. "We should check it out. To be sure."

Vanessa plucked a French fry from the globs of melted cheese and chili. She twirled it in the raw onions and slipped it into her mouth.

"You remember the first time you took me traveling?" Vanessa said with a smile.

"Yeah," Catty giggled. "You about broke my eardrums in the tunnel."

They had been watching TV after Catty's ninth birthday party, waiting for Vanessa's mother to pick her up. Catty wanted to show her something special. Vanessa had thought it was another birthday present. Instead, Catty had grabbed her hand, and a strange heaviness crackled through the air. The fine hairs on her arm stood on end before the living room had flashed away with a burst of white light. Suddenly, they were whirling downward through a dark tunnel. The air inside felt thick enough to hold. She could barely breathe. Her screams bounced back at her until the sound became deafening. Just when it had grown unbearable, they fell with a hard crash back into the living room. Only, the living room was different now. Sunlight came through the windows. Wrapping paper and ribbons were scattered over the gray-green rug. Then they had peeked into the dining room, and Vanessa had seen herself, sitting at the table eating cake and ice cream. She had been too shocked to scream again. Catty stole into the kitchen, and returned with two pieces of cake, and before Vanessa could ask her what was going on, they were back in the hated tunnel with its thick, sucking air and bad smells. Instead of landing in the living room, they had landed five blocks away on someone's front porch.

"I got in so much trouble." Vanessa shook

her head. "My mother thought I had wandered off." She couldn't tell her mother what had really happened. Her mother would never have believed her, anyway.

"But the cake was worth it," Catty said.

"You ate my slice," Vanessa smiled. "I was crying because the tunnel scared me so much. Remember?"

"It's not like you didn't get even."

"You deserved it," Vanessa teased. "You were always getting me in trouble." Vanessa had planned for weeks, practicing with her teddy bear until she could make it invisible with her. Then one Sunday while they were playing in Catty's backyard, she had hugged Catty and scrunched her eyes in concentration until she felt her molecules pinging. She had opened her eyes. Catty was becoming a dusty cloud. The cloud swirled around, and Vanessa had seen a look of utter astonishment on Catty's face before she became completely invisible. Success! Her plan had worked. Vanessa's molecules had exploded outward in complete delight. At first Catty had buzzed around the backyard like a balloon losing its air. Vanessa couldn't see her, but she could feel her air currents. But then she had started to get cold and wanted to become visible again. Vanessa wasn't as practiced as Catty. An hour later, even with total concentration, she had only managed to make parts of them visible. When Catty saw her hand floating, unattached to her arm, she had started crying. That had made Vanessa more nervous. It had taken her hours to get them back together, whole and right.

Catty nudged her. "You should use your gift more often. Practice makes perfect and all that."

But Vanessa had felt so badly about what she had done to Catty that she had sworn never to use her power again. Since then she had tried to control her molecules, but in times of intense emotion, her molecules had more power than her ability to restrain them and the light from a full moon seemed to fuel their change.

"Hurry up and eat," Catty prodded her.

"Why? We've got plenty of time."

Two minutes later, Catty put her hand on Vanessa's shoulder. Her eyes were dilated as though a powerful energy were building in her brain. Vanessa glanced at Catty's watch. The minute hand started moving backward.

"Don't," she begged. "This will be the third time we've left without paying."

"But they won't know. As far as they'll know, we never came in. It will be last night for them."

"But we've still eaten their food without paying for it."

Catty rolled her eyes. "The food didn't *exist* yesterday, so why does it matter?"

"It just feels wrong, and I told you I didn't want to go back, anyway."

The hands on Catty's watch stopped moving.

"You need to go back and see that nothing was there, or you'll never stop thinking about last night."

"I won't," Vanessa said. "Besides, Morgan just walked in."

"So?"

"She's been around too many times when we've switched time. I think she suspects something."

"Morgan doesn't suspect anything. She can't."

"I know she can't, but she's been asking

questions," Vanessa said. Catty was sure that when she went back in time, people had no sensation of returning to the past. But Vanessa thought people sensed the changes in the length of an hour, the confusion of memory, and a rash of déjà vu.

"Besides," Vanessa added. "I told her we'd go over to the Skinmarket with her."

"Why do you want to hang out with her when she tried to take Michael away from you?"

"She didn't try to take Michael away. She's a better dancer than I am, and Michael likes to dance."

"I don't want to hang out with her," Catty complained. "She makes me feel like I'm not clean enough."

"That's just your imagination."

Vanessa reached for her soda. As she put her hand out, Catty clasped her wrist. The hands of the watch started spinning backward.

"No!" Vanessa screamed as "Love Potion Number 9" began playing on the Seeburg.

The bikers turned and stared at her. Morgan waved, and her lustrous hair swung out as the air pressure changed.

Vanessa dropped the hamburger and clutched the strap of her messenger bag. Her skin prickled with static electricity. A white flash burned reality away, and the diner roared from them with the speed of light.

That was the last thing Vanessa remembered as she fell into the tunnel with Catty. She kept her eyes closed as they spun downward, and her stomach lurched. She hated the smell and feel of the air. Without looking, she knew Catty was watching the backward-spinning hands on her glow-in-the-dark wristwatch. When they arrived at their time destination, she'd put all her concentration into stopping the flow of time, and they'd fall back into time and reality.

They landed on a lawn with a heavy thud.

She looked up. The smells of onions and frying hamburgers still wafted in the air around them, but it was dark now, and they were on the street where she had walked the night before.

"You've got to work on the landings," Vanessa groaned and pulled herself up.

"I told you, a fall is the only way out."

Vanessa looked around. The night was silent

except for the occasional scrape of palm fronds overhead. Then, in the distance, she heard soft, running footsteps and the rapid, pounding steps of the person who had chased her.

"Let's go see who it was," Vanessa said. "I mean, who it *is*."

"Right," Catty agreed.

They bolted and ran wildly down the street. The cool evening breeze stung their faces. Their footsteps pounded softly on the dew-wet pavement. Vanessa knew at once that the second set of footfalls she had heard the night before were those that she and Catty were making now.

A block ahead, she could see herself, barefoot and running rapidly. Someone was chasing her. It was impossible at this distance to identify her pursuer, who was dressed in black and wearing a cap.

She heard herself shout the strange prayer in the language she didn't understand.

At the same time her pursuer glanced back. The person must have seen them, but Vanessa couldn't be sure. Suddenly, the person darted across a lawn and into the shadows.

"This way," Catty said.

Vanessa followed her to a shortcut between two houses and into a narrow alleyway. She whispered. "Do you think whoever it is saw two of me?"

"If so, they'll never chase you again."

Vanessa almost laughed, but she was too breathless and excited with anticipation to see who it was.

They ran down the alleyway to the next block, then crossed another street.

"Whoever's following you should be around here someplace," Catty whispered.

They crouched low and stepped cautiously down the alley.

Without streetlights, the backyards were darker, the shadows deeper. Vanessa peered over the fence. She didn't see anyone, but she heard the soft, padding steps of someone trying hard to be quiet.

They ducked and hurried along a length of fence to a garage. She looked around the corner of the garage. A shadowy figure ran across the back lawn to the next house.

She motioned to Catty, and they stepped silently forward. When they got to the next house, they gazed over a row of garbage cans into the tomblike quiet in the yard beyond. If her pursuer had been there, the person must have heard their movements and hidden.

Catty nudged her and pointed.

A thicker shadow formed between the house and a twisting cypress. It looked like someone was standing there. Vanessa was sure the person was looking directly at her even though she couldn't see the eyes. And then the shadow whispered, *I'll find you later when you're alone.* She wasn't sure she'd heard it, as much as felt it like a soft rustling across her mind.

Panic seized her.

"Did you hear that?" Vanessa asked.

"What?"

"Take us back, Catty. Now!"

CHAPTER THREE

VANESSA FELT HERSELF jerked away. Her neck whipped backward, and then the night zipped away with a sudden flash and roar. Vanessa clutched Catty's hand as they spiraled through the tunnel. Her stomach wobbled with nausea, and she knew if they didn't stop soon she was going to lose her hamburger.

They landed with a hard knock. The air left her body. Pain spun thin and sharp inside her skull. She closed her eyes against the harsh fluorescent lighting.

A buzzing sound filled her ears. She soon realized it was laughter.

"Dang! Girls," someone shouted and the laughter grew. She struggled to open her eyes.

She was vaguely aware that Catty was squealing and calling her name.

"Catty," she whispered. This time Catty's voice penetrated her aching head.

"Vanessa, we're in the boy's locker room and the water polo team just finished practice."

Water polo? She was still in a dreamlike trance. Michael was on the water polo team. She'd get to see him. That made her smile. "Michael."

New laughter echoed off the walls. "She wants to see you, Michael."

Her nose touched something wet. She looked down. A wet blue Speedo lay in the chlorine-smelling water near her face. Her head shot up. The boy's locker room!

As quickly as she had looked up, she looked down again. A scream caught in her throat.

"Catty!" she yelled. Keeping her head down, she stood. She was never going to forgive Catty for this landing,

"Here." Catty was giggling in pure delight.

Vanessa found Catty, yanked her hard, and

pulled her through the throng of naked boys.

"Did you get to see what you came looking for?" someone said.

Embarrassment made her molecules dis-arrange. "Not now," she whispered.

A shrill whistle made the laughter stop. Vanessa spread her fingers. Coach Dambrowsky plodded into the locker room, his tennis shoes squishing water. His forehead and nose were sunburned.

Vanessa ducked around him, her hands in front of her face. He must have sidestepped because she ran into his soft stomach.

"Excuse me." She tried to worm past him.

"Wait a minute!" He grabbed at her arm. His fingers whipped through her disorganized molecules. "What the—?"

This time he caught Catty.

"You two are busted," he said and brushed flecks of dandruff from his blue sweatshirt.

Catcalls filled the locker room.

"You girls should be ashamed of yourselves. Don't you have any modesty?" Coach Dambrowsky scolded.

"If we were boys in a girls' locker room you'd

snicker and pat us on the back," Vanessa argued from behind her hands. She spread her fingers to see how angry he looked. The sunburn had turned crimson. He was pissed.

"Let's see, who do we have here?" Coach licked his thumb and pulled pink demerit slips from his pocket. "Let me see your face."

Vanessa slowly brought her hands down.

Coach looked surprised. Was her face disarranged?

She glanced at Catty. She could tell by Catty's expression that she looked fine. She took a deep breath. How was she going to explain this to her mother?

"Vanessa Cleveland. Of all the girls in the sophomore class, I expected more from you."

He looked at Catty with a dour face. "And Catty Turner." He didn't seem surprised that Catty was there. He handed a slip to each of them. "Demerit slips, girls."

"It's a nice color of pink." Catty smirked.

"Yes, sir," Vanessa mumbled. Head down, she ran back, picked up her messenger bag from a puddle of water, and hurried outside.

Catty waited for her at the door.

"I can't believe you brought us back here," Vanessa said. "What's everyone going to say? They'll think we snuck in there."

"So what?" Catty wadded her demerit slip and tossed it away. "It's not like I did it on purpose."

"Catty, you'll just be in more trouble," Vanessa said. "You can't throw away your demerit slips."

"We wouldn't have demerit slips if you'd let me tweak time a little. Want to?"

"You can't always use your power to get us out of trouble. You rely too much on changing time to duck responsibility."

"Who made you my mother?"

"Sorry." Vanessa adjusted the bag on her shoulder. "But it's dangerous."

"Dangerous?" Catty acted as if they'd never had this conversation before.

"What if you get stuck in the tunnel?"

"If something went wrong I'd just fall out. It's not real. It just feels like I'm going faster than the speed of light."

"Maybe." Vanessa leaned against the sun-soaked wall. It was as hot as a fire brick and felt good against her throbbing head. She wasn't as convinced as Catty. The tunnel felt like a real place to her. The times she had ventured a peek, it seemed to stretch to infinity. "Did you ever think that maybe that's the world we belong in? That somehow we got stuck in some kind of time warp? Maybe that's why your mother found you walking along the side of the road."

"That would explain me, but what about you?" Catty stood next to her. They had tried many theories to explain their powers. The time warp was just another one.

"I'm afraid you could get stuck in that world."

"That's crazy," Catty said. "Won't happen."

"Just promise to be careful, or I'll get mushy on you and tell you how much you mean to me."

Catty punched her gently. "Stop. I've got it under control. Loosen up, all right?"

Vanessa looked at Catty. She felt something dreadful gnawing at her.

"So who do you think was following me?" Vanessa pulled her sunglasses from her pocket.

The fall had cracked the lens. She tossed them into her bag.

"I think you've got a mystery man. Someone with a crush on you."

"A secret admirer?" Vanessa joked.

"Half the boys at school have crushes on you."

As if to prove her point, two seniors walked by, swinging skateboards.

"Hey, Vanessa," one said.

"Looking good," the other added.

"Hi," Vanessa waved.

"See," Catty pointed out.

"I'm just friendly." Vanessa shrugged, and then she remembered what had really bothered her about the night. "Did you hear anything?"

"No. What did you think you heard anyway?"

"I thought someone said, 'I'll find you later when you're alone.'"

"I didn't hear that," Catty mused. "But if I had, I would have been freaked!"

Vanessa lifted her face, and with the late afternoon sun beating down on her, it was impossible to remember how dead scared she had felt the night before. The terror had slipped away in a drowsy way, like smoke after a fire.

"A mystery man," Vanessa repeated softly.

"Definitely," Catty said. "At first he was probably too shy to approach you, some loner walking home from Planet Bang, then he gets up his nerve to talk to Vanessa Cleveland, the most popular girl at La Brea High—"

"I am not."

"Be quiet, it's my story. He goes to talk to you and you panic and run away. Now he's got to chase you down to tell you he's sorry he scared you. Then he turns and sees us, and now he's really embarrassed so he hides. I wonder who it is?"

"Someone like Michael Saratoga," Vanessa whispered as last night slipped deeper into memory. "I hope it's Michael."

"You talking about me?" a voice said.

Her eyes flew open.

Michael walked over to her. He wore a short-sleeved T-shirt. Barbed-wire tattoos circled his tan arms. He had just come from the boy's locker room and his hair was still wet. His dark round eyes made her think of an ancient sun god trapped in L.A.'s urban nightmare. She liked the way his eyes looked at her. His lips curled around perfect white teeth. She wanted those lips to want her. Her molecules hummed. Could he hear her desire like a soft growl rushing through her spreading molecules? Damn invisibility. Maybe if she thought of the upcoming geography test, her molecules would stay.

"Hi, Michael." She tried to keep the excitement out of her voice.

He stepped closer, and a whiff of spicy deodorant and chlorine enveloped her. She breathed deeply.

He sniffed. "You smell like onions."

She smelled her hands. The aroma of the onions from the Johnny Rockets chili fries clung to the tips of her fingers. "Sorry." What magic did those dark eyes have to make her apologize?

"I like onions."

"Me, too," she said. "I didn't see you after school."

"I had water polo practice." Michael smiled. "I guess you saw me there."

She felt the blush rise to her cheeks, and then

thought, so what? He should be the one blushing. She smiled with an insolence her mother would have scolded her for. She knew he was blushing behind his dark cheeks by the way he shifted his feet and cleared his throat.

"You want to hang out on Saturday?" he asked.

"What do you have planned?" Was this a date? She stomped her foot, trying to make her molecules obey. Don't go invisible now.

"Something special." The tips of his fingers brushed across the fine hairs of her arm. Her stomach fluttered and her molecules tingled with delight.

"Sure."

"See you Saturday, then," he said. "I'll pick you up at seven." She watched him walk away, his backpack bouncing against his shoulder.

CHAPTER FOUR

VANESSA AND CATTY walked across the school lawn. New worry started buffeting her happiness.

"What will I do if Michael tries to kiss me?"

"I don't know, open your mouth a little, I guess."

"I'm serious," Vanessa scolded. "What am I going to do? Just looking at him makes my molecules vibrate. The last time I tried to have a boyfriend, I couldn't control it. I never even got one kiss."

"Let your molecules sing," Catty said. "Maybe he'll like it. Besides you don't know it will happen this time. Have you been practicing with your power like I told you?"

One look and Catty knew she hadn't. "When you're alone you need to make yourself invisible," Catty explained. "Visible, invisible. Just like exercises. How else are you going to learn how to control it? You should practice every day."

"That won't help me now. What if my molecules go off on their own?" Vanessa wondered. "What if I scare him? Maybe he'll think I'm a ghost or something evil."

"You should appreciate your gift more. I mean, just think what you could do with it. I know what I'd do."

"What?"

"I'd spy on people and copy answers to all the tests. You waste it."

"All my problems seem to come from what you call a 'gift.' I wish we could be like everyone else."

"Speak for yourself. I like what I can do," Catty said. "You want a Coke?"

The fact that they were freaks never bothered Catty as much as it bothered Vanessa. Maybe it was because Catty's mother encouraged her to use her power.

"No, thanks." Vanessa sat on a cement bench facing a bank of outside lockers. "I'll wait for you here."

She looked down at the amulet that hung around her neck. She seldom took it off, but she unclasped it now and studied the face of the moon etched in the metal. Sparkling in the sunlight, it wasn't pure silver but reflected pinks and blues and greens. Maybe who she was had something to do with this moon charm that was given to her at birth. Catty had one, too. That's how they had first noticed each other at the park in third grade. They had been playing soccer on opposing teams, chasing the ball down the field. When they saw the silver moon dangling from each other's neck, they'd stopped running and let the ball go out of bounds.

"Where'd you get that?" Catty had asked, ignoring her jeering teammates.

"I got it as a gift the night I was born," Vanessa said. "Where'd you get yours?"

"Don't know. I've always had it. I never take it off."

"Me, neither," Vanessa said.

The referee blew her whistle and the game continued, but Vanessa couldn't focus on the ball. She kept turning to look at Catty. Twice she kicked the ball out of bounds, and once she collided with one of her own teammates.

Afterward the two teams went out for pizza. She and Catty shared a double-cheese pepperoni with pineapple and anchovies. They had been best friends ever since. It had taken longer for them to share their unique talents. What Catty called their gifts.

Maybe it wasn't a gift, but a curse, and if she got rid of the charm, her strange ability to become invisible would also go away. But she felt too uncomfortable when she took it off. She wondered why that was.

CHAPTER FIVE

CATTY CAME BACK with a Coke and sat next to Vanessa.

Morgan Page ran up to them. She dropped her purse and swirled. "What do you think?" She wore a bare, breezy sundress. It was too skimpy for the school dress code, so she wore sleeves over the halter sundress during classes. Now she shed the sleeves and showed off her solar-glow tan, the best in the school. Expensive salon highlights added luster to her already perfect hair. She picked up her purse and pushed her yellow shades into her hair.

"Where have you been? I walked all the way to Johnny Rockets looking for you. I must be glistening with sweat."

Catty leaned into Vanessa muttering, "She's got to be the only person in the world who thinks her sweat is pretty."

Morgan didn't hear Catty over her own running talk. "I swear I saw you two sitting at the counter. I thought we were supposed to meet at Johnny Rockets."

Vanessa gave Catty a quick, angry look.

Morgan watched them with curiosity.

"You couldn't have seen us," Catty said. "We were in the boys' locker room."

She elbowed Vanessa. Vanessa held up her demerit slip as proof.

Morgan couldn't be lured away from her questioning. "I could have sworn I saw you two munching on burgers, and then you were gone."

"We weren't there," Vanessa insisted.

Morgan stopped. She eyed the silver moon charm in Vanessa's hand.

"That would go perfectly with my dress." She reached for it.

Vanessa quickly clasped the necklace around her neck.

"You always wear it," Morgan said. "Don't you ever get tired of it?"

"Sometimes, I guess," Vanessa lied, and wished she hadn't. She didn't want Morgan to think the amulet was something she would ever lend out.

"I saw you talking to my hottie."

"Who?" Vanessa asked.

"Michael, of course. Was he asking about me?"

"Michael asked Vanessa to go out with him," Catty informed her smugly.

Morgan seemed upset, but only for a moment. She smiled and pulled the yellow shades back on her perfect nose. "So you're going out with Michael."

"Yes." Vanessa felt a little embarrassed.

"Be careful."

"Be careful of what?"

"You know, he conquers the land and leaves it desolate."

"Translation?" Catty's eyebrows raised.

"He makes like he's all vulnerable and sensitive so you start trusting him and then he takes advantage," Morgan responded knowingly.

"How can he take advantage if you don't let him?" Catty demanded.

"Guys have their way. Sometimes they think it's their due."

"Michael doesn't seem—"

"That's my point exactly," Morgan continued. "That's how he gets away with it. And I bet you haven't even kissed."

"So what?" Catty was exasperated.

"You'll see," Morgan warned.

"I didn't know you liked him," Vanessa said.

"Please," Morgan snorted. "I call every good-looking guy my hottie. He's nothing special."

Vanessa sensed that Morgan was upset, maybe even jealous, but before she could say more, Morgan's radar picked up someone else.

"There's Serena," Morgan said. "She's such a freaky dresser."

Serena Killingsworth walked toward them, carrying her cello in a brown case. Her short hair, currently colored Crayola-red, was twisted into bobby-pin curls. A nose ring glistened on the side of her nose. She wore purple lipstick, red-brown shadow around her green eyes, and a smile that seemed to hold a secret. She was new at school. Vanessa liked her look and especially admired the way she seemed so oblivious to what other people thought about her.

"Hey, Morgan." Serena set down the cello. Her chartreuse fingernails worked the combination on her locker.

"She's such a walking rummage sale," Morgan whispered disapprovingly.

"I like it," Vanessa said.

"I like it, too," Catty agreed.

Morgan sighed. "Okay, she has her moments. But she's got a bad addiction to the bizarre."

"How could you know that? She's only been in school a few weeks," Vanessa argued. "I heard her family moved here from Long Beach so she could take classes at UCLA along with her high school classes."

"Having brains doesn't mean you're not weird," Morgan said, casting a sly glance at Catty. "Her best friend is on probation, some gang girl from East L.A."

"That doesn't mean anything." Irritation buzzed inside Vanessa.

"I hear they stay out all night. I bet they're into some kinky stuff."

Serena opened her locker and cast an amused look at Morgan.

Morgan pulled peach hand lotion from her purse and spread it over her arms. "Too bad her brother's such a surf nazi. What a loss. He's the kind of guy you'd like to spend the night with. But the only thing he's looking for are waves. What is it with this town, anyway? Do all the gorgeous guys just wake up one morning and decide they're too good for women?"

"Don't you think there are other things to worry about?" Catty was losing her patience.

Vanessa gave her a quick look. She wasn't in the mood to referee another fight between Catty and Morgan.

Morgan didn't seem to hear her. "Collin is as cute as Michael," she continued. "Almost. I don't know how he got such a freaky sister. Hey, why don't you ask Serena about Michael if you don't believe me?"

"Has she dated him?" Vanessa asked.

Morgan laughed dismissively. "I can't believe you don't know."

"What?" Catty and Vanessa said together.

Morgan leaned in closer. "She's a fortune-teller. She can answer your questions about guys. She charges twenty dollars a pop. But I swear it's worth fifty."

"How did you find out so much so quickly?" Catty was amazed.

"I ask," Morgan nodded wisely. "She's read my fortune twice already."

"She probably just tells you what you want to hear," Vanessa scoffed.

Morgan shook her head. "It's spooky. I swear. With her tarot cards, it's like she knows things no one can know. Don't ask her anything you're afraid to find out because you might not like the answer. And you have to go alone. That's her only rule. You need to go see her, Vanessa."

"Why?"

"She'll tell you just how bad your broken heart will be; some girls never recover from Michael Saratoga."

Vanessa didn't think that sounded like

Michael. He was polite and sweet, and she liked his gentle humor. He never told raunchy jokes, or made vulgar comments like so many of the guys at school did.

Serena picked up her cello and walked over to them. "Were you one of those girls, Morgan?"

"What girls?"

"You know, one of the girls who never recovered from a broken heart?" There was a sparkle in Serena's green eyes.

"Damn," Morgan's eyes narrowed. "See what I mean?"

"How did you know what we were talking about?" Vanessa asked.

"I have acute hearing," Serena said.

Morgan gave her a dirty look.

Serena stuck out her pierced tongue, showing off the stainless-steel barbell.

"Cool." Catty had already pierced her belly button. Vanessa wanted to but hadn't had gotten up the nerve yet.

Morgan wrinkled her nose in disgust. "Germ central." She walked away, but she kept casting backward glances as if she were afraid Serena was going to put a curse on her.

"Here." Serena handed Vanessa and Catty each a piece of paper. "My home address. Come by any time you want your fortune read. And come alone." She picked up her cello and started toward the bus stop. "Catch you later."

Catty tossed her paper on the ground. "Too endlessly weird. On a scale of one to infinity, she gets infinity plus a billion. I don't believe anyone can see into the future."

"That sounds strange coming from you." Vanessa glanced at her watch. "We're supposed to meet my mother, and with your insane time travel we're going to be late."

"I'll just take us back an hour," Catty started.

"No." Vanessa stopped her. "We're going to do it the old-fashioned way. We're going to walk and I'm going to get yelled at for being late."

Vanessa stared at the paper Serena had given her as she and Catty walked up La Brea Avenue toward Melrose. Was what Morgan had said about Michael true? She tucked the paper in her pocket.

CHAPTER SIX

FRIDAY AFTERNOON, campus security roamed the hallways and parking lot at La Brea High School, trying to stop surfers, skaters, gangsters, and ravers from cutting the rest of the school day and starting an early weekend.

"Come on," Catty called. "They'll never catch us if we sneak off campus through the back field. I've done it a million times."

Vanessa hesitated. "But we'll get suspended if they catch us."

Catty giggled and pulled Vanessa forward. "Whoever thought of suspending students for cutting classes? It's exactly what they wanted in the first place."

"It goes on your permanent record."

"Don't you want to ask my mother if she knows what those words mean, the ones you said the other night?" Catty smiled persuasively.

"I can wait till after school."

"I told you she's busy tonight. Now's your only chance."

"All right." Vanessa sighed.

"Great," Catty said. "Let's hurry."

They ran down the narrow weed-filled corridor between the gym and music building. Grasshoppers and moths scattered in front of their feet. A trill of flutes and the honk of a tuba came from inside the music room.

At the end of the buildings, they stopped and scanned the football field. It was empty.

"Walk slowly," Catty warned. "If security calls us, just turn back and pretend we didn't hear the bell. Or . . ."

"Or?" Vanessa said.

"Or just make us invisible."

"Right," Vanessa mumbled sarcastically, and glanced behind them. Her heart thumped against her chest. Catty was always talking her into doing things she knew were wrong, like staying out late, cutting classes, and making prank calls.

They squeezed under the wire mesh fence and hurried down a side street to La Brea.

"There, see? Not so hard." Catty grinned as they headed down La Brea Avenue toward Third.

The Darma Bookstore was between Polka Dots and Moonbeams Dress Shop and Who's on Third? café. Brass bells on long leather cords tingled in harmony when they pushed through the door. Smoky incense curled sinuously around them and filled the air with a pungent scent.

"Hi, Mom," Catty called.

The store always gave Vanessa a feeling of peace and security. Water bubbled from fountains set in stone planters near the door and the chanting of Tibetan monks flowed from speakers set in the wall. Books, packages of candles, incense, prayer beads, crystals, and essence oils lined white shelves in neat arrays.

Catty's mother, Kendra, pushed through the blue curtains separating the back room from the store.

"You got out of school early," she said with a smile and winked. She was tall and bony, with a narrow face and long brown hair streaked with gray. She wore a stunning purple dress that flowed around her when she walked. The sleeves were long and touched the tips of her fingers. A pair of red-framed reading glasses dangled on a chain around her neck and clicked against the rose crystals she wore. She believed in the healing energy stored in crystals. Today she also wore the pouch given to her by a traditional doctor on one of her trips to Botswana.

She hugged Catty, and then put both hands around Vanessa's face and kissed her. She smelled of sesame oil, camphor, cardamom, and cinnamon. She rubbed the spicy concoction into her temples several times during the day to stimulate her senses.

She looked at Vanessa a long time. Vanessa always had the feeling that Catty's mother was trying to detect something different about her.

"I was just making ginger tea. Let's go in the back. It'll help detoxify your body and digestive system."

Catty rolled her eyes. "Mom, don't you have anything that regular people like?"

"I just grated the ginger and the milk is warm," Kendra went on as if she hadn't heard Catty's complaint. "You'll love it."

They followed her through the bookcases to a small kitchen in the back of the store and sat down at the oak table. Pictures of UFO sightings and a huge poster of deep space taken from the Hubble telescope hung on the walls.

"Did you girls have a good day at school?" Kendra asked, and started to pour them each a cup of milky ginger tea.

Catty put her hand over the top of the cup. "Don't you have any cocoa mix?"

"The ginger tea is better for you."

Catty rolled her eyes.

Vanessa smiled. She liked Catty's mom.

Kendra sighed. "All right." Then she looked at Vanessa. "I suppose you want hot chocolate, too?"

"Yes, please." Vanessa studied the picture of a fuzzy flying saucer hovering over the desert in Arizona.

Kendra reheated the milk in the microwave, then spooned cocoa into two mugs. She poured milk over the cocoa and brought the mugs back to the table and sat down.

Vanessa opened her messenger bag and pulled out a piece of paper on which she had carefully written the words she had spoken on the night she was being chased. She handed the paper to Kendra. "I was wondering if you knew what this meant."

Kendra put on her reading glasses. Her lips moved as she read the words to herself.

"These words just came to you?"

Vanessa nodded.

Kendra examined the words closely. "The words are misspelled, but even so, I know it's Latin. It appears you were praying to the moon to protect you." She smoothed the paper and ran her index finger under the words as she read, "O Mother Moon, Queen of the night, help me now."

Vanessa put down her cocoa, unable to speak. She lifted her moon amulet with trembling fingers and stared at it.

"Mother Moon," she repeated, then she

looked at Catty and saw she was reacting the same way.

"Freaky," Catty said.

"Oh, it's not so strange." Nothing ever seemed to surprise Kendra. "You and Catty have always had a connection to the moon. I suppose you could have seen this prayer in a book a long time back, memorized it, forgot it, and then said it in panic. Now if the moon had helped you, *that* would be strange."

Vanessa nodded, but she was sure she had not read this prayer before. She stared at the words she had written on the folded piece of paper. Why had she prayed to the moon to protect her?

CHAPTER SEVEN

SATURDAY, VANESSA waited impatiently outside her house for Michael. She wore a pale green sundress and sandals that she had bought with her mother in a boutique on Robertson Boulevard. Her mother had been thrilled she had wanted to shop with her. Now Vanessa worried the dress looked too desperate, with its thin straps, bare back, and short skirt.

Too bad, she decided. Why was she so worried, anyway? She enjoyed the silky run of material over her skin.

The sun's last fiery rays dusted the tops of the palm trees with gold as a Volkswagen bus painted with psychedelic pink-and-orange flowers like an old hippie van turned onto her street. The headlights came on, and the van drove slowly toward her. The van stopped in front of her and Michael leaned out the window.

"Hi," he said with a slow, lazy smile. She felt herself getting lost in that smile, those eyes and lips.

"Hi." Her molecules buzzed slow and easy.

He turned off the engine, crawled out, and walked around to the passenger side door.

"You like the van? My dad couldn't part with it, so he saved it for me," he said and opened the van door.

"Nice." She admired it, but her thoughts were not on the van.

She climbed in and settled nicely, her bare back pressed against the warm seat. Inside smelled of spicy foods and beach tar. His surfboard lay on wadded towels in the back.

He hesitated before he closed the door.

"You look pretty." But his eyes said she looked more than pretty. He took her hand and kissed the fingers, still gazing at her.

Waves of energy rushed through her, stirring her molecules into a risky dance. Her hands and neck tingled. She took a slow easy breath. "Thank you."

The van door slammed.

The thought of being alone with him made an indolent smile cross her face. Her stomach muscles tensed, skin tight. Her nervous fingers were unable to stay still. She grabbed the sides of the seat to steady herself as he got in the van.

"I want to take you to the Hollywood Bowl. Do you like music?"

She nodded and watched him look at her. His eyes said he wanted to devour her. Good, she thought, and pushed Morgan's warning away.

"L.A. Philharmonic," she said as the van pulled away from the curb. She let the wind rush through her hair.

A purple crystal hung from a black satin string draped over the rearview mirror. Vanessa touched it. It felt oddly smooth and then it almost seemed to move in her hand. She pulled her hand back.

"It feels alive, doesn't it?"

She nodded.

"It was a gift from my grandfather," he said, and seemed pleased she had noticed it. "It's for courage and patience. A patient heart needs courage to endure."

"I wish I'd known my grandfather," Vanessa commented. "It's just my mother and me. My father died when I was five."

"What happened?" He spoke softly.

"He was a stunt coordinator on a movie," she explained. "Something went wrong and one of the helicopters crashed. I remember seeing it on the news, but I was too young to understand it was real. I thought he was just making another movie. I mean, he had taken me to so many movies where he had rolled a car or jumped off a building. And he was always okay. But this time, he never came home."

He waited a moment to speak as if he were imagining what life would be like without his own father.

"My family's a big mess of people," Michael said finally. "Cherokees and Lebanese. You'll have to come to one of our family get-togethers."

Was he planning their future?

"Grandpa tells great stories. You'll really like him. He gets frustrated with me, though, because I don't believe all his stories. They're just ancient legends, but he acts like they're fact."

She wondered if his grandfather knew any stories about invisible girls.

Michael turned left and followed a narrow winding road into the Hollywood Hills. At the crest of the hill the houses no longer had yards. Front doors opened onto the corkscrew street. He parked the van in front of a sprawling house perched next to the curb and jumped out.

Disappointment blossomed inside her. He wasn't taking her to someone's home, was he? A party? He had definitely said the Bowl. She wanted to be alone with him, not competing with a crowd.

He opened her door and took her hand.

"I thought you said we were going to the Hollywood Bowl?" she asked.

"It's a surprise," he answered. "I hope you don't mind a walk."

She looked down at her beaded sandals.

"No," she lied, and hated that she hadn't worn oxfords.

He took the picnic basket from the back of the van, then holding her hand led her down a tight cement walk between two houses. They squeezed around a line of palm trees and a Doberman panting behind a chain-link fence.

"Be careful," Michael took a step down a rugged ridge, then turned and helped her off the cement slab and into the underbrush. They walked through dense shrubs. Leaves and grass scraped her legs. They continued downhill under houses built on stilts. Then the houses gave way to chaparral and fire road. He ignored the sign that read NO PUBLIC ADMITTANCE.

"My grandfather told me about this place," he said. "Back in the forties, airplanes used to buzz around the Bowl, so they had spotters, guys with powerful binoculars, stationed on the hills to take the license numbers off the airplanes. Grandpa was one. He loved music and that was the only way he could afford to come to the Bowl."

He pulled her through bushes with waxy coated leaves. A swarm of gnats flittered around her face. She tripped and tumbled against his back. She didn't try to right herself. She enjoyed the feel of him, the sweet soap smell. She let her cheek rest against him.

"You okay?" He turned to her.

The tips of her fingers brushed along his chest. She was sure the twitching molecules in her legs were half-invisible now. Too bad. He couldn't see in the dusk. Kiss me, she thought and lifted her face.

He leaned closer. His warm breath touched her quivering lips.

"Come on," he whispered. "You don't want to miss the beginning." He started forward.

"Damn." Vanessa cursed to herself as she waited for her molecules to reassemble.

"Hurry," he called.

Vanessa followed after him. She could hear the sounds of an orchestra tuning up now. Oboes, bassoons, and flutes followed by a lazy rumble of drums. The sweetness of violins filled the night air, bows scraping strings, and finally the lower-pitched cellos joined the song.

"Sounds like we're just in time." Michael

stepped out on a small ledge. A pole flaking with red rust stood on one side of the shelf. He tapped it with his finger. "The spotter used to attach the binoculars to these poles." He kicked away leaves and stones, then pulled a blanket from the basket and spread it.

"It's a perfect view." Vanessa looked down at the white shell-like building cradled in the natural amphitheater. They were perched high above the concrete bleachers in the rear.

"Have a seat." Michael sat down.

She sat on the blanket, stretched her legs in front of her and kicked off her sandals.

"I should have told you to wear your hikers," Michael began. "I just thought . . ." He shrugged. "Normally you wear real sturdy shoes. At least they feel solid."

She thought of the dance and flushed with embarrassment. Had she stepped on his feet? She let out a sigh and wiggled her toes, then glanced to the west. Her breath caught. A thick crescent moon, hanging low, appeared as the last rays of sunlight drew a broad line of orange-red below the indigo sky. To add an exclamation point to the moon's appearance, the music began. *Da Da Da Dum.*

One star appeared, then another as if summoned by the fervent music.

"Okay, ready?"

She pulled her gaze away from the night sky and looked at him. Her stomach fluttered with nervousness. She was actually alone with Michael. How many times had she fantasized about this?

He opened the basket and pulled out three red luminarias. He lit the candles inside. The flames flapped fitfully in the breeze. Shadows throbbed and twitched until the flames settled.

"I love candles." Vanessa didn't know that Michael was so romantic. She was happy that he was.

He placed two plates on the blanket.

She looked at him, surprised.

"Bread, cheese, sparkling cider, and my own tomato salad made with olive oil, garlic, and basil." He pulled out paper plates. Then, a little embarrassed, he added, "I hope you like it."

"I know I'll love it." She couldn't believe

Michael Saratoga had actually prepared a meal for her.

She took in his beauty, there in the candle's glow. The music surrounded her and she wondered if he was going to kiss her.

She lay back, her arms folded behind her head and looked at the unhidden desire in his eyes. She smiled. Anticipation made her skin feverish. Her molecules flared. She closed her eyes and enjoyed the feel of it. The night had taken on a dreamlike quality, and even the evening breeze was gentle and caressing across her arms and legs.

"My grandfather says the moon is the greatest gift from the gods."

She glanced back at the sky. "Why is that?" She had always felt the same way but had never understood it.

"God put the moon in the sky to remind us that our darkest moments lead us to our brightest."

"Never give up hope," Vanessa finished quietly.

"Grandpa says that's what the phases of the moon teach us," Michael said. "The moon goes from light to dark, but always back to light."

A laugh came from the hillside behind her, so soft it was like a rush of air. She felt it more than heard it. Her back went rigid and she sat up with a start.

Michael had not heard it. He still gazed at the moon.

She glanced at the shifting shadows behind them.

"What?"

"Nothing." She looked back at him and smiled. Maybe it had only been a cat's meow, or a rustle of a coyote attracted to the smell of food. She laid back on the blanket.

Michael moved closer. She could feel the warmth of his body radiating from his skin. "Here, try the Kasseri cheese." He placed a chunk of cheese on a piece of bread and handed it to her.

She felt too nervous to eat but took a bite anyway. The rich flavors filled her mouth.

"You really like it?" he said.

She nodded. "It tastes great."

He stared at her lips. Was he staring at bread crumbs caught in her lipstick? Or cheese stuck to her teeth? She brushed her hand over her mouth and licked her tongue across her front teeth.

"And the music?" he whispered.

"All of it. It's perfect."

He was silent for a moment, just looking at her. When he spoke, the words were quiet. "I love it here," he said. "I've been coming up here alone. It's better if someone is with you."

She smiled and nodded. "I'm glad to be here."

"I've always loved music," Michael explained. "If the only thing you got going for you in high school is your looks and your athletic ability, you could be a has-been by the time you graduate. You've got to have something more to pull you into your future. I've got music."

"What do you play?"

"Guitar and piano," he said. "I'll play for you sometime."

"I love guitar music. My father played a little. He'd strum and I'd pretend to be a famous flamenco dancer." She stopped. She hadn't told anyone about that before.

Michael smiled. "I bet you were cute."

She shrugged, embarrassed. Why had she told him that?

"This is great," he said. "I'm glad you came with me. I was afraid to ask you out. I thought you'd say no."

"Me?" she felt a jolt of delight.

He leaned back on his elbow. "You." His voice was soft.

"I was hoping you'd ask me out," she confessed.

"Yeah?" He looked at her intently. "Then I wish I hadn't waited so long."

She closed her eyes. "Me, too."

The music was incredibly beautiful, all flowing notes and joy. She felt his warm breath on her cheek. When she turned, Michael's face was next to hers. She smiled. He placed his lips on hers. Her breath caught, and then her mouth opened slightly as she felt his tongue. Her molecules danced in pleasure and bounded outward. She tried to pull them back, but the kiss was too powerful. The intensity surprised her. His hand slid down her arm. Then he leaned back and looked at her, his brown eyes soft and longing. She felt a little flustered, not sure what she should do next.

She glanced down. Under the candles' glow, her feet looked like dancing dust, spinning to the music. Her legs had a glittery, transparent quality. Damn invisibility. What if he saw? Quickly, she lifted her hand to his cheek and held his face. She wanted another kiss. She concentrated all her thoughts on making her feet and legs whole again.

"Was that all right?"

"Very all right." She wished she had thought of something clever to say. What did other girls say?

He leaned over, and as he moved his hand to place it around her, he brushed across her breasts. She sharply drew in air. Her molecules collided with cold pain that sent a shiver through her body. So Morgan was right.

He jerked his hand back. "Sorry," he said quickly.

He seemed sincere, but Morgan had warned her. Maybe he brought all his dates up here, acting like each was the only one special enough to share this romantic evening. Then he would use his charm to seduce them.

Her thoughts were broken by hard laughter coming from behind her, still barely audible above the music, but definitely laughter this time.

"Your hand was in the way," Michael kept trying to explain.

Didn't he hear the laughter? She hushed him. There it was again. Was someone mocking them?

Suddenly, an irrational fear seized her. She looked into the shadows under the scrub oaks and felt a terrible need to be away from where they were.

"I said I'm sorry," Michael insisted and reached for her hand.

"Let's go," she said abruptly and stood.

He seemed baffled. "Look, it was an accident."

"I know." She scanned the foliage. She wished they hadn't come to such a deserted place. It felt too dangerous to climb back the way they had come, but even more dangerous to stay where they were.

"Are you angry?" he tried again.

"No," she said too sharply. "But I want to leave."

"All right." He seemed resigned. He picked up the candles and blew out the flames.

Darkness gathered around them, thick and complete and alive.

Maybe they could go down the side of the canyon to the concrete seats. Maybe that way would be safer.

"Come on." She slipped into her sandals.

"Don't you want to go to the van?"

She put her fingers to his lips to quiet him. That's when she heard it, a faint rustle of dry grass followed by the snap of a twig. Something was trudging down the hillside.

"Something is there." Michael finally heard it. He stuffed the blanket into the basket but left the food and the luminarias on the ground.

Tuesday night, when she had sensed someone watching her, she had felt stark fear. But now a new feeling overrode her fear. She felt an irresistible need to protect Michael. Where had that come from? He stood a foot taller than she, with rock-hard muscles. He played water polo, surfed, did all the guy things, but she suddenly felt the Amazon stir inside of her, an instinct that had been dormant all these years. She grabbed his hand.

"Can we leave by going down the hill?" Her voice was steady.

"Yeah, but we'll get in trouble. Illegal access to the Bowl."

"It's better than . . ." She didn't finish the sentence. She started walking, pulling him behind her. What he saw as trouble, she saw as salvation. If someone saw them creeping down the terrain and thought they were trying to sneak into the Bowl, the person might alert the security guards, who would rush to meet them. They would no longer be alone.

"Vanessa," Michael whispered. "It's probably a coyote. They're all over the hills. Or a skunk. Some wild animal must have smelled our food, but it won't attack us."

Then why are you whispering? she wanted to say. From the jagged tone of his voice she knew he didn't believe his own words. Whatever ran stealthily in the dry brush was not a wild animal.

Something blundered down the hill, no longer trying to hide its approach.

She jumped in front of Michael to protect him from whatever was ready to crash through the bushes. At the same time Michael bent down to pull her behind him. Their heads collided in a clap of pain. They fell and tumbled down the side of the canyon, scraping knees and palms.

A dried scrub oak stopped their fall.

"You okay?" Michael said and helped her stand. His hands traced her face and arms as if he didn't trust her to tell him the truth.

Her hands stung and her head pounded. She felt a trickle of blood on the inside of her mouth.

"I'm okay," she panted. "You?"

"Just scrapes."

"We better go." She reached for his hand again. He pulled back.

"If we keep trying to protect each other, we'll kill ourselves."

"We're not far enough away yet." Vanessa didn't let him pull his hand away this time. She grabbed it and held tightly.

Something tramped down the side of the canyon above them.

"I'll follow you then." He let her lead.

She stepped onto hard baked earth and slid on loose gravel. He grabbed her arm and pulled her to him, his body hard against hers. She wanted to kiss him, to feel his hands on her back. But another sound made her wrench free. How had it caught up to them so quickly? She whipped around and stood between Michael and the foliage.

"Come on," he chuckled. "If it's a skunk, you'll be sorry."

The closer they came to the cement bleachers, the more comfort she felt. But no security guards ran to meet them.

She and Michael sat in empty seats near the back. She was sweating, her mind too stormy to let the music wrap around her. She kept turning and staring into the fierce shadows on the hillside behind them, but she no longer sensed danger, not with seventeen thousand people in the audience.

But the evening was over, the magic gone. She wanted to leave.

She turned to say so to Michael. He seemed upset. She felt suddenly embarrassed that she had made him come down to the bleachers the way she had. How could she ever explain why she had needed to flee?

"Great," he said sarcastically. "Stanton's coming over here."

"Who?" Even as she asked she saw a boy dressed in black walking toward them, his hands in his pockets. His shaggy blond bangs hung in his face. He kept flicking his head as if he was trying to whip the hair out of his eyes.

"What a lowlife," Michael muttered.

"Is he from our school?"

"No, he hangs out with a pack of losers in Hollywood."

Stanton was good-looking, but there was something strange and foreboding about him. His eyes were so blue they seemed luminescent. How could she see the blue so clearly in the dark? Her body thrummed, alert and watchful, as if something portentous was about to happen.

"Hey, Michael." Stanton stared at Vanessa as if awaiting an introduction. He sat down next to her. His body pressed against hers.

"I'm Stanton," he said. His gaze lingered over

her body as if she had invited him to look and take all the time in the world. His blue eyes made her wish she had worn jeans and a turtleneck.

She snapped her fingers in front of his eyes. "My face is here." She spoke with deliberate venom in her voice. Another time she might have let it pass, but her emotions felt raw after the trek down the side of the canyon.

Stanton looked in her eyes and smiled with one side of his mouth. He seemed to enjoy her reaction.

Michael stood. "Come on, Vanessa, we have to leave before the crowd." Was he jealous?

"I was just saying hi." Stanton grinned as if Michael's jealousy fed some need inside him.

Michael walked quickly, his face a scowl. Once they were away from the concert, they hiked to his van in the hills.

Michael helped her into the van, then went around and climbed into the driver's seat. He looked at her curiously. Under the streetlight his face tottered between looking angry and seeming frightened.

"Did you feel it, too?" she asked.

"You mean when we were being chased?"

"No, I'm talking about Stanton," she said. "Something's weird about him."

"You noticed it? The way he gets all happy if he makes other people uncomfortable or angry or—" He stopped. Was he going to say jealous?

"Yes." She looked directly at him.

He started the engine. They drove back to her house in silence. Michael parked with a slam of the brakes, then got out, opened her door and walked her up to the porch.

"I better get going." His eyes were dark and intense. Then he ran back to his van.

Where's my good-night kiss? she wanted to scream. She unlocked the front door as his van pulled away from the curb. She didn't turn to wave good night, because she was too afraid he wouldn't be waving back.

CHAPTER EIGHT

THE HOUSE WAS DARK inside and still smelled of her mother's late-night coffee. Vanessa climbed the stairs. A spill of light from her mother's bedroom covered the hall runner. She stopped at the door. Her mother had fallen asleep reading, an empty coffee mug on the nightstand beside her. She walked to the bed. The fragrance of her mother's hand lotion and face creams filled the air. She wanted to curl against her mother as she had when she was a little girl.

Mom," she said softly. Her mother did not stir. She pressed her cheek against her mother's and let it rest there a long while.

Finally, she took the book, set it on the nightstand, switched off the light and went down the hallway to the bathroom. She turned the spigots. Hot water rumbled into the tub. Then she caught her reflection in the mirror. Dirt streaked her face, but it was something more that made her stop and stare. Her eyes looked wide, haunted, different. The pupils dilated, the lashes longer, darker. What was happening to her?

She bathed quickly, put on PJ's from the hook on the bathroom door, and hurried back to her bedroom. She started to turn on the light, but caution made her stop. She crept to the window and closed the shutters against the night, then switched on the small lamp on her desk. She looked at her computer and scanned her room to see if anything looked disturbed.

The door to her bedroom stood open. The dark hallway loomed before her. She took three quick steps across the room, shut the door, and locked it. When was the last time she had done that? Even knowing her mother was down the hallway did not comfort her now. Finally, she called Catty.

A sleepy voice answered the phone.

"Can you spend the night?"

"Now? What's going on?" Catty mumbled, her voice still sluggish with sleep. "What time is it?"

"I don't know. Midnight maybe. Can you come?"

"Yeah, I guess," she said. "How am I going to explain it to my mother?"

"Your mother never needs an explanation." Vanessa looked behind her. Why did she feel so edgy?

"I don't know," Catty hesitated.

"Take a cab. I'll pay."

Vanessa waited at the front window, impatiently watching cars drive past her house. Finally headlights turned down the street, and an orange-yellow taxi pulled up to the curb. Catty climbed from the cab. She held a tackle box in one hand and an artist's pad under her arm. Her messenger bag dangled from her shoulder. She wore bunny slippers and a tan trench coat over her pajamas.

Vanessa ran outside and gave the driver fifteen dollars. He waited until they were inside before he drove off.

Vanessa locked, then bolted, the front door. When they were in her room, she spoke. "Do I look different?"

Catty's mouth fell open. "What did you do with Michael? Tell me all about it. Every detail."

Vanessa flopped on her bed. "Nothing happened with Michael, other than I acted like a fool. Someone followed me again tonight. I don't look different to you?"

"You look tired is all. Someone followed you with Michael there?"

Vanessa sat up and cuddled a pillow against her. "I acted like some freaky Amazon woman."

"He saw your true self? So what? I bet he liked it."

"I don't even know why I did it. I felt like I had to protect him. He's probably never going to speak to me again."

"Then you don't want him. Did you see who was following you?" Catty set her bag down, opened the tackle box, and took out several charcoal pencils. She sat on the floor with her artist's pad as Vanessa explained everything that happened, from the walk down the canyon wall to the strange look in Michael's eyes when he didn't give her a good-night kiss.

"We could go back, you know, and see who was following you."

Vanessa sat cross-legged on her bed. "That's not why I asked you over. I was . . . I didn't want to be alone."

"Maybe it's date anxiety. You've never been afraid of anything before. You've only had these strange feelings since Michael started acting like he liked you. Maybe they're panic attacks."

Vanessa laughed. "I don't think you can call the way he makes me feel a panic attack. You think he likes me?"

"Yes." Catty nodded firmly.

"Did you bring anything to eat?"

Catty pulled a glass pan covered with aluminum foil from her bag. Vanessa could smell the rich chocolate before Catty removed the crinkling aluminum foil.

"The dateless made fudge," she said, and handed the pan to Vanessa.

Four pieces were already missing.

Catty looked at her. "Maybe you should tell

your mother. I mean, it could be some pervert or something. Your mom would know how to handle it."

"Tell her I think someone is following me because I can make myself invisible?"

"It's not like you can't prove it," Catty pointed out. "Sit in the light so I can sketch you."

Vanessa sat in the overstuffed chair next to her bed. Catty's pencils scratched across the paper.

"I think we should go back while it's only a few hours in the past and see who was there," Catty declared.

"Yeah, and end up falling down the canyon. Sorry, your landings make it too dicey."

Catty didn't argue this time.

"Maybe I should visit Serena. She might see something in her tarot cards. Morgan said she was good."

"You don't think she can really tell fortunes, do you?" Catty drew Vanessa's hair in long swirling lines.

"You're right. The best thing to do is talk to my mom." Vanessa watched Catty draw her face, pouty lips, the dimples in her cheeks. Catty was too quiet, which meant she had something more on her mind. Finally she stopped drawing and looked up.

"Did you ever think my mother was right?" Catty said finally. "Maybe we did come from another planet and the spaceship crashed. That would explain the two memories I have."

"The crash and the fire."

"Maybe we survived both, and the moon is like a guidepost that tells us how to get home, only we don't understand it yet because we're still in a sort of larvae state."

"Great, that's all I need. You mean we haven't grown our green antennae yet?" Vanessa joked. She started to laugh, but then she thought of the changes she had seen in her eyes when she looked in the mirror an hour ago.

"Maybe together our powers can take us home."

"Your mother's theory only works if I was adopted," Vanessa said. "And my mother has assured me with gory descriptions of ten ugly hours of labor and twenty-two stitches that I was not."

"But what if—" Catty stopped drawing. "What if something happened to her real child?"

"Like aliens ate it?"

"I'm serious." Catty frowned. "Maybe there was an alien mother who gave birth that night, and a nurse got confused."

Vanessa stared at her. "I look like my mother. You've said so yourself."

"What about the necklaces? Maybe they're like a homing device." Catty started smudging the charcoal drawing with her finger, then stopped and stared at Vanessa. Vanessa knew by the look on Catty's face that she didn't want to hear what she was going to say next. "It might explain who's been following you."

"How?"

"Government agents. The ship might be repaired now. And they're going to send you back to your own planet but they have to make sure you're the right person."

Vanessa thought about it. How would she survive on a different planet? Even if that was where she belonged. "I don't want to leave. My home is here."

"But, Vanessa, if it's true."

"It's not—"

"Just if. If they come for you, don't let them leave me behind." Catty was serious.

"If," Vanessa said. "If it is true, I promise."

"Thanks." She paused a moment. "I keep having this awful dream. In it these shadowy people are trying to reach me. I can't see their faces. I wake up, and it feels so real. Maybe the others are using telepathy to contact us, but our skills are too rusty to pick up their message."

"Stop," Vanessa whispered. "You're frightening me."

"Sorry," Catty said.

"Maybe we should try to get some sleep."

"Okay," Catty agreed.

Vanessa turned off the lights and opened the shutters. She and Catty crawled into bed and stared out the window at the night sky.

"I wish we only had normal problems like everyone else," Vanessa said.

"Me, too. It'd be fun to just worry about school, zits, and boys."

"I worry about that. It's not fun."

"Yeah, it's not fun for me, either," Catty said. "I wish I knew why we're so different."

"Freaks of nature," Vanessa whispered and wondered how she could ever have a boyfriend. Maybe it was better not to try.

"It's hard sometimes," Catty added. "If you weren't here, I'd be so alone, probably smoking pot with lodos on the back lawn at school."

"Yeah," Vanessa said. "I'd probably be a shy little mouse with a stack of books in front of my face and no friends." She pushed back tears crowding into her eyes. "I'm glad you're here."

"Ditto on the mushy stuff." Catty pulled her covers tight around her.

As she was falling asleep, Vanessa decided to visit Serena tomorrow. It was her last hope before confessing everything to her mother. Maybe Serena could look at her tarot cards and tell her who had been following her and why.

CHAPTER NINE

SUNDAY EVENING VANESSA walked up the tinted stone walkway of a large Spanish colonial revival house. Faded ceramic frogs and trolls sat under the spiked paddles of a prickly pear cactus. The wind blew, and purple-red bougainvillea flowers rained over her.

She started to knock on a large wood door, when it opened.

"Hi," Serena greeted her. "I'm glad you came." She wore Hawaiian-print bell-bottoms and a pair of clogs painted fairy-tale red with blue flowers. She looked like a pixie, the way her hair was moussed with glitter on the ends.

"Let's sit in the kitchen," she said. "The light is better there."

Vanessa stepped inside and waited for her eyes to adjust to the dimness. Then she followed Serena down an unlit hallway. Their footsteps echoed through an imposing dining room that felt cold and never used. Finally, they pushed through a swinging door into a yellow kitchen that smelled of freshly baked cookies.

A raccoon sat on the kitchen table on top of papers that were scattered around a laptop computer. A cello rested against a long counter. Its varnished wood reflected the warm kitchen lights. Vanessa had expected to see anarchy symbols and smell incense, or maybe worse.

"I practically live in here," Serena explained. She seemed nervous to have Vanessa visiting. She picked up a pile of papers. "This is Wally."

The raccoon stood on its hind legs, then climbed off the table and scuttled flat-footed away from Vanessa.

"I got him on a camping trip. His mom deserted him, same as my mom deserted me, so my dad let me keep him. Have a seat."

Vanessa sat down.

Serena went to the counter next to the sink. Wally followed on her heels, his bushy ringed tail in the air like a flag. She tossed the raccoon a cookie, then brought a plate of chocolate chip cookies to the table. "Here, have one. I just made them."

Serena didn't look like the kind of person who would bake. Vanessa picked one, had a moment's hesitation wondering what might be in the cookie, then saw Wally chomping daintily away and took a bite. It was rich and buttery. The chocolate melted in her mouth.

"It's good." She wished she hadn't sounded so surprised.

"I'm glad you like it." Serena smiled. "Sometimes I think about becoming a chef. Well, if it weren't impossible."

"Anything's possible." Where had that come from? She sounded like her mother. Standard Lecture No. 9.

Serena shook the spangled bracelets on her arm. "I guess my life is pretty much planned for me."

Vanessa felt sorry for Serena. Too many kids at school had parents who drew road maps for their lives.

"It's not what you think," Serena added quickly. "Dad's pretty cool. It's other things."

Vanessa started to ask like what, but before she could ask, Serena spoke.

"What do you want to drink? Soda? Coffee? I'm having milk."

"That sounds good."

Serena poured two glasses, then came back to the table and sat down across from Vanessa. She shuffled her tarot deck, then placed it in front of Vanessa. "Think of your question while you divide the deck into three piles with your left hand."

Vanessa took the worn deck and shakily separated it into three stacks. She wondered if the cards would be able to tell her who was following her. When she glanced up, Serena had a peculiar look on her face and her eyes seemed dilated the way Catty's became before they time-traveled.

"What?"

Serena shook her head. "Sorry, I was daydreaming." She took the deck, gave Vanessa a sly smile, then turned over the first card. "Ace of cups. Love affair. Don't worry about Michael. He likes you. It's genuine."

Vanessa tried to smile, but worry kept pulling at her. Did she dare ask Serena about her real problem? An odd sensation rippled across her mind. It wasn't unpleasant, but it felt peculiar, almost like the feeling she sometimes had after completing a difficult algebra problem. She glanced up. Serena was staring at her again.

"You know," Serena began carefully, "if you have other problems, I might be able to help with those, too. I mean, we could ask the cards."

"I've got a problem," Vanessa whispered.

Serena clicked her tongue piercing against her teeth and waited. "You want to tell me about it?"

"I can't."

Serena continued to stare at her. Why did her pupils seem so large? She blinked and her eyes looked normal again.

"Well, maybe the cards can help you if you just think about your problem." Serena turned over the next card, but she didn't seem to concentrate on it—her eyes kept returning to Vanessa.

"Do you see something bad in the cards?" Vanessa asked nervously.

Before Serena could answer, the back door opened. The salty smell of the ocean drifted into the room. A boy walked in, his sandals flapping against the back of his heels. His face was sunburned, his nose peeling, and his lips still had traces of white zinc oxide. Lines from dried salt water traced around the back of his deeply tanned neck. His sun-bleached hair fell in his blue eyes and down his back in a shaggy ponytail.

"This is my brother, Collin," Serena said. "Vanessa's a friend from school."

"Hey," Collin nodded, but he barely looked at Vanessa.

"Hi." Vanessa could see how Morgan would have a crush on him.

"Anything for dinner?" He walked over to the stove.

"Macaroni and cheese," Serena said.

"Where?"

"The oven."

He took the casserole from the oven. Steam rose into his face. Collin set the casserole on a trivet, then took a spoon from the dishwasher and dug in.

"It's hot," Serena called out.

He bit anyway. "Hot!" he yelped, and danced around. Wally scampered under the table.

"Collin's a surfer," Serena said adoringly, as if that explained everything.

"The macaroni is great," Collin yelled. He scooped some onto a plate and left the kitchen. The sound of MTV came from someplace deep in the house.

Serena turned back to Vanessa. "He's pretty cool for a brother, actually. Morgan had a big crush on him for a while. But I think she's had a crush on everyone, especially Michael."

Vanessa sighed and wondered if she even had a right to date Michael. After all, Morgan was her friend and—

"Don't worry about it." Serena interrupted her thoughts. "Collin says Morgan doesn't have boyfriends, she takes prisoners. She's really possessive. So maybe she didn't have a relationship with Michael like she thinks she did."

Vanessa still felt bad. Had Michael taken advantage of Morgan? Was she too embarrassed to tell Vanessa everything about it? Maybe Michael had—

"She never had a real date with him." Serena spoke in a soothing voice. "She saw him at a party and they got together."

"How do you know so much?"

"I listen." Serena smiled. She shuffled the cards. "Let's start again. Think of your question. You need to be specific for the cards to work."

"Okay," Vanessa said.

"Ready?" Serena snapped the cards. "Divide the deck into three stacks again."

Vanessa nodded and thought, Am I in danger of having my secret discovered? Then she divided the cards into three stacks.

Serena gazed at her, her green eyes fiery. Again Vanessa had an odd feeling, this time like a whisper of wind roving around her mind. It was relaxing. She started to close her eyes.

Serena slapped the first card on the table.

Vanessa opened her eyes with a start.

"The knight of cups," Serena said. "He's always a bearer of important news or an invitation to social events." She grinned. "He also brings new developments in love. Are you sure you're not thinking about Michael?"

"Yes." Vanessa tried to concentrate on the two different nights when she felt as if someone had been following her.

"Maybe you should be more specific."

"How would you know if I was specific or not?" Vanessa asked.

"I can't know." Serena giggled. "Just in general people aren't very specific. It's easier for the cards to work if you add in all the details."

Vanessa shrugged and thought of the night with Michael at the Bowl; then she looked at Serena and stopped. Serena's pupils were enlarged again, and she was staring. Vanessa winced. That feeling in her mind was strong this time. Maybe she was getting a migraine. She rubbed her temples.

An odd look gathered on Serena's face as if she saw something that amazed and puzzled her.

"What do you see?" Vanessa asked, the balls of her fingers working her scalp.

"Nothing," Serena said; but her voice filled with wonder and she seemed excited about something. Then she turned the next card. "Damn," she muttered, and her mood seemed suddenly dark.

The card showed the image of a moon with the face of a woman. Two yellow dogs barked at the night sky.

"I think this one was out of order." She started to push the card back into the deck. "Let's go to the next."

Vanessa grabbed her hand and took the card. "What does it mean?" she said nervously. She didn't really believe in fortune-telling, but it frightened her the way Serena was acting.

"The card means an unforeseen danger. Something is not as it seems." She looked at Vanessa long and hard. "It means you should be cautious. Very cautious."

"Why?"

Serena clicked the piercing in her tongue against her teeth. "It's complicated."

Vanessa waited.

"According to the card, you're looking for answers, and the information you'll receive will be difficult to believe, so you'll put yourself in danger. You'll have confused feelings and not be sure what to do, but you can't run from this problem. The only way is through it."

Serena looked down at the cards. She turned over the next and let out a small gasp. Before Vanessa could catch her, she stuck the card back in the deck. Her quick jerky movement toppled her glass of milk.

"Sorry." She ran to get paper towels. She brought them back to the table.

Vanessa helped her sop up the milk. "What did the last card say?"

"Nothing, I didn't even really see it before I spilled the milk."

Vanessa knew she was lying. She had looked too frightened. She had seen something in the cards. And why did she keep staring at Vanessa? Maybe Morgan was right.

Serena tossed the wet towels in the trash, then came back to the table. "So do you want to watch some TV, or go down to Ed Debevic's and watch them dance on the counter? I love their hot fudge sundaes."

Serena was talking too quickly. What was she afraid of? Surely she would tell her if she thought she was in danger.

"You didn't tell me what you saw in the last card," Vanessa said. "The one that frightened you."

"Oh, that." Serena tried to laugh but it came out sounding fake. "I would have told you all the usual stuff that everyone thinks fortune-tellers make up anyway, about a happy life and all that."

But Vanessa knew she was hiding something. "Are you sure there wasn't more?"

Serena seemed nervous. "No, I'd tell you if there was more," she said. "Come on, let's go to Ed Debevic's. It'll be fun."

"I can't tonight. I promised Mom I'd be home early." Vanessa pulled a twenty-dollar bill from her jeans pocket. She handed it to Serena.

Serena started to take the money, then stopped. "I can't charge a friend. Just don't tell anyone else I didn't charge you. Telling fortunes is a cool way to make extra cash."

"Thanks." Vanessa tucked the money back in her pocket. "I'll see you tomorrow."

"Yeah." Serena walked her to the back door.

Vanessa hurried down the drive to the front of the house, then stopped and looked back.

"Freaky," she whispered. She knew Serena was holding something back, but why would she? Was it something about Michael? Or Morgan? She felt heartsick.

She turned and bumped into a girl with long black hair. The girl gasped and took a step backward. She looked like a gangbanger, in black cargo pants and sport tank. Homemade tattoos covered her back and arm. She was thin with large brown eyes that seemed afraid of something she saw in Vanessa's face.

"What?" Vanessa said.

"*Ten cuidado,*" the girl whispered. "Be careful."

That made Vanessa more uneasy than if she had snarled.

"Sure," Vanessa muttered uncertainly and began the long walk home. She decided that she shouldn't see Michael anymore. Her heart twisted at the thought. But that took care of one problem, at least. Then she could concentrate on finding out who was following her and why.

CHAPTER TEN

MONDAY MORNING Michael was standing on the concrete steps at school when Vanessa and Catty arrived. He wore khakis and Birkenstocks. His tumble of black hair curled against a white T-shirt. He waved, and adrenaline shot through Vanessa with a sweet pleasant tingle. What was it about his smile that made her body turn traitor to her mind and crave his touch?

"Come on." Vanessa pulled Catty back the way they had come.

Catty looked up. "Maybe he's looking for you."

"I'm done with him."

The look in Catty's eyes told her that she didn't believe her.

"I'm too embarrassed to see him," she begrudgingly admitted. "Besides, I can't have a boyfriend. There's no way it can work out. I can't even kiss him without going invisible."

Catty glanced back at the cement steps. "If he were my boyfriend, I'd find a way."

By noon, heat, smog, and automobile exhaust had settled over the city. Security guards stood at the front gate checking off-campus passes, but kids loitered on campus. The air was too hot and sultry to walk up to Okie Dog or Pink's or sit at Kokomo's in Farmers' Market. Morgan lounged under a tree, fanning herself with an algebra test and sipping a Big Gulp through a straw. Vanessa and Catty joined her.

"Won't this day ever end?" Morgan said. "It feels like it's been going on forever."

Morgan motioned with her chin at something behind them. "Why is Serena following you?"

Serena gravitated toward them and sat in a shady spot near the building.

"She's not following us. She wants to get out of the sun like everyone else." Vanessa opened her bottle of carrot juice.

Serena wore jeans hemmed with red feathers. FLOWER POWER was written on the front of her green tank top. Pointy rhinestone glasses kept sliding down her nose, and her hair was curled in tight ringlets.

"She'd be pretty hard to miss," Catty said. "We would have noticed her."

The hot day had made everyone restless and kids were starting to squirt each other with bottles of water. Steam rose from the puddles.

"I saw her." Morgan wrapped her hair on top of her head. "She's been hanging behind you all day. Weird little goat. You should say something to her."

"Leave her alone," Vanessa snapped.

"Oh, *please,*" Morgan bit back with a spark of anger. "Since when does she need you to protect her?"

"Morgan," Vanessa started, but stopped. It wasn't worth arguing.

"Maybe she's the one who's been following

you," Catty whispered, and unwrapped a peanut butter and jelly sandwich that had melted through the bread. She wrapped it back up and wadded it into a ball for the trash. "It's too hot to eat."

"So how was the big date?" Morgan said. She took a piece of ice from her Big Gulp and held it against the back of her neck.

Vanessa didn't answer.

"I warned you about Michael." Morgan shook her head. "You're not sexperienced. I won't hold it against you. But you shouldn't dive in over your head."

"Why do you keep saying that? I thought the sexual revolution was about choice," Catty said. "How can you hold that against anyone?"

"Give it up." Morgan tossed the ice cube away.

"Well, it does seem like you want to make Michael sound bad," Vanessa accused her. "He was really nice."

Morgan gave her a bitter look. "Whatever." She stood suddenly. "This day is dragging. I'm going to the nurse's office so I can go home. Heat exhaustion." She walked off.

"What's her deal?" Catty said.

"I don't know." Vanessa wondered if Morgan was still upset about Michael.

"Why are you still friends with her, anyway?"

"We used to have really good times together, don't you remember?"

"No. She never liked me, and now she's got to bust an attitude on everyone."

"Catty—" Vanessa had something else she wanted to talk about. Something important.

"Yeah, what's up?"

"I've made a decision," Vanessa said. "Mom doesn't work tomorrow. I'm going to stay home and tell her about . . . you know. Maybe she can help me."

Catty frowned. "Are you sure?"

"I don't know what else to do. Besides, I'd rather she hear it from me than see me go invisible on the nightly news."

"All right," Catty agreed, but her voice was dry with anxiety.

A noise startled them. Serena gathered her books and ran across the hot blacktop. She slipped past the guards at the front gate, and didn't stop when the guards yelled after her for her pass. Kids standing against the chain-link fence applauded her audacity.

"Cool," Catty said.

"Why didn't she get a pass?" Vanessa wondered.

"Must've been in a hurry." Catty shrugged. "Let's go see if a classroom is open where we can cool off."

The day stretched on forever. Morgan was right. It felt like someone had bent reality and made classes twice as long. By the end of the day Vanessa was worn out. She trudged across the empty basketball courts, her sweater tied around her waist and shirt open to the third button, when someone called her name.

"Hey, Vanessa." Michael ran up to her, his face flushed. "I've been trying to catch you all day." He touched her arm. A drop of sweat trickled down his cheek.

She tried to pull her breath in slow even draws. She didn't want him to see her nervousness. She almost made an excuse to flee, but the sweetness of his smile closed her mouth and made her stay.

"I'm sorry about what happened at the Bowl." His eyes drifted to the third button on her shirt, then pulled away. "I was pretty rude after."

She thought he'd be angry about the way she had acted. But he thought he had ruined the night. She wanted to cheer. "I had a great time," she said.

"Yeah?"

She cleared her throat. "I loved the music."

He shifted his books and put an arm around her. When his hand touched her waist, new heat rose inside her, a fire for something forbidden.

"Stanton pushes my buttons," he said as they walked across the basketball courts. "It's like . . . do you think someone can be evil?"

"What do you mean?"

He seemed a little embarrassed. "It sounds crazy, but the guy creeps me out."

"Like how?" she asked. But she couldn't pay attention. Her mind drifted to thoughts about his hand on her waist. What would it have felt like if his hand had brushed over her at the Bowl, and it hadn't been an accident, but invited?

"He pushes me, like he wants to make me

mad. Usually he can't get to me, but when I saw the way he looked at you right in front of me, something happened inside me. At first I thought he liked you, too, but then I knew he was flirting with you because he'd heard how much I like you."

"Me?" Her stomach fluttered.

He smiled, and his eyes said *you*. "The last time I really liked someone, he tried to take her away from me. I figured he was the one who was spying on us. I was so furious that all I wanted to do was drop you off and go back to have it out with him."

"You went back?"

"I started to, then I realized . . ."

"What?"

"That's exactly what he wanted. So I didn't." He guided her away from the bus stop toward the students' parking lot.

"You think he was following us?"

"I wouldn't put it past him," Michael said. "So I acted like an ass. Forgive me?"

"Yes." She smiled. And then they were at his van.

"Can I give you a ride home?"

"Okay," she said. Her heart beat wildly. Was this another chance for a kiss?

He smiled and opened the van door. She untied her sweater and rolled it into a ball on top of her books, then climbed in. The air was tight and hot inside. The plastic seat burned her back through her blouse.

Michael got in and started the van. She rolled down her window and let the velvet breeze cool her face. He babbled on about school, his guitar, and surfing. She sank lower in the seat, listening to the song of his voice. Sweet melody, don't stop.

The van parked and her eyes opened. They were in front of her house already.

"Don't get out yet," he said.

She paused.

"I really like you, you know, because you're so different."

Her heart flipped. If he only knew how different.

"You're so mysterious." His eyes smiled slyly. "I like a mystery to unravel." Then he leaned over. He stopped when he was close enough to kiss her and waited, as if he were asking for permission. She closed her eyes. His lips, warm from the heat, rested on hers, and then he pulled away.

She didn't want him to stop.

"I really like you, Vanessa," he said, his face still close to hers, his breath caressing her cheek, and then he kissed her again. Soft, gentle, sweet. His hand touched her knee. Her body tingled, longing for more. The tip of his tongue traced over her lips. His other hand slipped lazily to the back of her head. His fingers traced through her hair. Her body was spinning. The molecules stirred. She shouldn't let him kiss her again. She did.

His mouth pressed harder. She knew what was happening, but she continued to kiss him anyway. At the last possible second she jerked back and hoped her face wasn't drifting into a whirl of golden light. She glanced in the side mirror. A face stared back at her, gratefully whole and complete.

"You haven't been kissed before, have you?"

"Of course I have," she said defensively. She felt embarrassed; her first kiss had been with him at the Bowl. "Lots."

He only smiled. But she didn't see it. She was too focused on looking at feet that were no longer there, only flecks of gold whirling on the floor mats. She threw her sweater over her legs. The sleeve snapped his eye.

"Ouch." He bent down and held his eye.

"Sorry." She felt like an idiot. "I must be coming down with a cold. I feel so chilled suddenly. I better go." She propelled what remained of her body out of the van. Her sudden movement left him unbalanced. He fell forward.

"Vanessa," he called out.

She turned back for one last quick look.

"I don't care if you've never been kissed before," he said, still holding his eye. She didn't answer because she wasn't sure she could speak. Her throat tickled, and sometimes as she became invisible she didn't have all the abilities she had when she was solid. She dropped a pencil and didn't stop to pick it up. Her hand was missing. She ran as fast as she could, hoping he didn't see the way her body was unraveling into a trail of dust. She darted behind the olive tree in the front yard, then sprinted through the lilies and onto the porch. She flung open the front door. Her arms vanished. Her books crashed to the floor and scattered.

She whirled to the front window and floated there, no more than a sinuous vapor. Anyone looking in the window from the outside would see only dust motes caught in a bar of sunlight. She looked back at Michael, afraid he had seen too much.

He started the van and drove slowly away.

"Good-bye, Michael." The words came out like a sigh of wind. A boyfriend would never be part of her life. Even a kiss was too complicated. She looked down at her hands. They were starting to come into focus now. Gradually, the heaviness of gravity began to pull her back into form.

She was going to spend the rest of the afternoon feeling sorry for herself. Why shouldn't she? There was no way she could continue to see Michael. If only there was a guidebook she could purchase to explain the laws of invisibility. Did such laws exist?

Tears started to form in her eyes when someone grabbed her from behind. Her molecules snapped together with a jolt of pain.

She shrieked, mouth open, until air had drained from her lungs.

CHAPTER ELEVEN

"WHEN DID YOU become a screamer?" Catty asked. "It's such a girlie-girl thing. I think you broke my eardrums." Catty hit the side of her head like a swimmer trying to dislodge water.

"You shouldn't sneak up on me, not with everything you know has been going on," Vanessa snapped.

"Sorry."

"It's not your fault," Vanessa said, regretting her anger. "I started to go invisible when Michael kissed me."

"So you're not totally done with him?" Catty teased with a smug smile.

"It's over. How can it not be?"

"Do you want it to be?"

"No." Vanessa's emotions were a knot of confusion in her stomach. "But what would he do if he opened his eyes and saw a ghost hanging on his lips? He'd probably die right in front of me."

Catty laughed, then bit her lip to stop. "Sorry," she said. "But if you think about it, it does sound funny."

"Nothing's funny about his kisses," Vanessa said. She felt herself go fuzzy thinking about the dreamy way he made her feel. "What am I going to do?"

"Kiss him in a really dark room?"

"You're no help."

"Maybe I am," Catty insisted. "If we travel back to Saturday night, I know I can make a pin-point landing so we won't fall down the canyon wall. I've been practicing all day, skipping back an hour at a time, then forward a little, then back. My landings are perfect now. I landed inside your house at the exact time you got home."

"That's why the day seemed so incredibly long," Vanessa said, and sprawled on the living room couch. "How many skips did you make?"

"I don't know, twenty." Catty grinned and slumped beside her. "All right, thirty-two, but I wanted to get it right . . . the landings, I mean."

"Next time practice in the night when the rest of us are sleeping. Do you know what it feels like to spend thirty-two hours in classes on a hot day?"

"But you don't have a memory of it."

"No," Vanessa argued, "but that explains why everyone was so dragged out by the end of the day."

"No doubt," Catty sniggered. "Next time I'll make sure you're with me."

Vanessa shook her head. She didn't think she had the energy for that either.

"So let's go back to Saturday night."

"But now it's too far in the past." Vanessa raked her hands through her drooping hair. She needed a shower and a nap.

"I figured that out, too."

Vanessa was doubtful.

"I'll leapfrog," Catty spoke rapidly. Her hands made semicircles to demonstrate the leaps.

"I'll go back twenty-four hours, then another twenty-four hours, until we're there."

"It must consume a lot of energy."

"I'll rest tonight. We'll do it tomorrow."

Vanessa chewed the side of her lip. Her real worry was the tunnel. She hated its rank musty smells and the dizzy feeling it gave her. "Your mom said there was probably a good reason why you couldn't go back more than twenty-four hours."

"What does she know?" Catty shrugged. "She's never time-traveled."

"Her explanation made sense to me." Kendra thought there was some natural law that stopped Catty from going too far into the past because the farther she went into the past, the more likely something small and seemingly insignificant could change the future in big ways.

Catty shook her head. "I've thought about it. Everyone thinks time is like a river. But I don't think so. I think time occurs all at once. We just experience it like a river because that's the way we've been taught to think about it. Really, it's more like a huge lake, all time existing at once. And my skips back and forth, that's all part of it, too. So I'll never do anything to change what has happened because if I were going to, I already would have, so I'm not." Catty thought a moment. "It's safe to go back."

"Maybe it is safe, but I don't want to do it."

"Please. Let's try." Catty jumped off the couch, animated again, and nearly collided with the door as it opened. Vanessa's mother walked in carrying three bolts of glittering blue silky material.

"Hi, girls," she said. "Catty, I hope you can stay for dinner. It's been such a wonderful day. I accomplished so much. Why can't every day be like this one?" She walked through the living room back to her worktable in the kitchen, her heels tapping on the wood floors.

"See, some people liked it." Catty grinned. "So how 'bout it? We'll time it so we'll come up behind the person who was spying on you and Michael." She made wild gestures like she was capturing the person.

"Forget it." Vanessa dismissed the idea. An uneasiness spread through her. "And promise me you won't go back alone."

"Sure," Catty said too easily.

"I mean it. At least let me think about it for a couple days. I don't want you to go alone." Maybe if she could make Catty wait and they went far enough into the future, Catty wouldn't try her dangerous leapfrog plan.

"I really promise," Catty insisted, but her eyes glanced too quickly away. "I've got to go anyway. I have homework to catch up on."

Catty left and Vanessa went back to the kitchen. Her mother was cutting tissue paper. She made patterns for the dresses she had sketched that were hanging on the wall.

"Pretty." Vanessa admired them.

"Where's Catty?" her mother said, and snipped the tissue.

"She had to go."

"Without eating?" her mother asked. "Was she upset?"

"Homework," Vanessa explained. "Mom, you're not working tomorrow, are you?"

"I have the day off. I'll be sewing, but gratefully at home. No more measuring sweaty actresses."

"I thought maybe we could have the day together."

She put the scissors down. "Sounds wonderful."

They ate mixed green salads and poached salmon for dinner. Vanessa wasn't really hungry. She felt like she'd eaten two dinners already. She wondered if Catty was practicing again, or simply nudging time to give herself an extra hour for homework.

Vanessa watched her mother cut the salmon into perfect flakes and spear them into her mouth. She loved her mother, but she wondered if her mother would feel the same way about her if she knew the truth about her only daughter. Would she still sit at the foot of her bed to keep the nightmares away as she had done to comfort Vanessa after her father had died, or would the truth fill her with a nightmare of her own?

"I love you, Mom," Vanessa whispered.

Her mother looked up, startled. "I love you, too, Nessy."

"Well, good night, then," Vanessa said. She cleared her dish and put it in the dishwasher.

"Good night," her mother called after her.

She took a bath and decided to do her homework and go to bed early. By the time she plopped on her bed, she was so tired she couldn't fall asleep. She stared at the luminous hands on her clock. She must have drifted off, because when she stirred again, her room was cold.

She rolled over and snuggled deeper under the covers. As she started to fall asleep she saw the curtains billowing gracefully out from her window. She had locked the window, hadn't she? Maybe a Santa Ana had ripped down from the desert and blown the windows open.

That's when she saw the shadow in the chair next to her bed. It looked like a person. This time, she was determined not to be scared. Finally to prove to herself that no one was there, she reached her hand out from underneath the warm covers to touch the shadow.

Cold fingers grabbed her wrist.

CHAPTER TWELVE

VANESSA JERKED HER hand back and sat bolt upright in bed, staring at the cloudy shape of the intruder. A scream scrambled up her throat and died.

"Serena?" Vanessa cried.

"Sorry," Serena said. Her tongue piercing clicked nervously against her teeth. She moved her head, and in the dim light falling through the window, with her hair spiked and her face shining, she looked like a forgotten fairy from some arcane legend.

Vanessa caught her breath and pushed the palm of her hand against her chest. Her heart pounded as if she had almost tripped over a precipice.

"I thought you were sleeping." Serena's words were soft, like a lullaby. "I was trying to figure out a way to wake you up without scaring you."

"If you didn't want to scare me, why didn't you use the doorbell?" Irritation wrapped in tight coils inside her.

"I had to talk to you," Serena said. "It's really important, and I didn't want your mother to know I was here."

Vanessa pulled the covers tighter around her. "Couldn't you just call next time, or talk to me at school?"

"I tried at school, but I needed to talk to you privately."

"You should have tried harder," Vanessa said, her heart still beating rapidly. Maybe this was what Morgan had been talking about when she said Serena was weird. "What's so important?"

Serena hesitated as if she was trying to find a way to put her thoughts into words. "I'm sorry if I upset you Sunday night."

Vanessa sighed and shook her head. "Believe

me, you could have waited until school tomorrow to tell me that. How did you get in here, anyway?"

"How?" Serena seemed surprised. "Your window, of course." And then she giggled in disbelief. "You mean you've never used your window to sneak out?"

Vanessa thought of the times she had left her room late at night under the steady light of a full moon. If Serena ever saw her do that, the sight would jam her giggles down her throat.

"You have snuck out." Serena leaned close to her. "But there's something different about the way you leave your room, Vanessa."

"What do you mean?" Vanessa asked, and wondered how Serena could know what she had been thinking. And then another panicked thought came to her—had Serena seen her?

"Tell me. It's really important. I need to know." Serena grabbed Vanessa's arm, the fingers icy cold. "What is it about you, Vanessa, that makes you so different from everyone else? I need to know more about your secret."

A sudden fear pushed into Vanessa's thoughts. How could Serena know there was anything different about her? Unless . . . the thought came as quickly as lightning struck. "It was you. You've been following me. Why? Don't you know how much you've been scaring me?"

"No." The word hit in one staccato beat and hung in the air between them. "It wasn't me," she added softly. "And stop calling me weird. I hate that."

"I didn't say the word."

"I know," Serena answered quickly, "but you were thinking it."

"You can't know what I'm thinking," Vanessa said, more to herself than to Serena.

"If I prove to you I can, will you go with me?"

"Where?"

"Just promise to go with me if I can prove to you that I can read your thoughts."

"Sure, why not? Like people can do that," Vanessa said sarcastically, and thought, *A dog has brown spots.*

Serena stared at her. "This isn't fair. I can't do it if you're giving me something that has no emotion attached to it. No content!"

"All right, here's another." Vanessa thought of the number seven.

"You're trying to trick me." Serena seemed really frustrated now.

"I'm not!" Vanessa said too loudly, and hoped she didn't wake her mother. She stumbled from the bed and turned on the fluorescent lamp near her computer. White light flooded the room with a buzzing sound. "I don't want you sneaking into my room ever again, and I really think we should wait and talk tomorrow. We could meet at Urth Caffé after school, okay?"

Serena sat back on the chair, green eyes reflective, and studied Vanessa like a cat.

A jolt of energy suddenly filled Vanessa's head. The sensation confused her at first. She tried to close her thoughts, make her mind blank.

Serena squinted. The feeling stopped. Then Serena opened her eyes and the feeling returned like the slap of a cold wave. It felt like Serena was rampaging through her mind, examining stored memories. Impossible. It had to be a headache, some strange flu, a virus. She was beginning to feel dizzy and nauseated.

"Stop!"

Serena seemed to draw back, although no movement was perceptible.

Vanessa sat on the edge of her bed and stared at her. "You can read minds." But even as she said the words she started to disbelieve. People can't do that, she thought. It's probably the cold and being awakened with such a start. Or she hypnotized me. Why?

"Sorry." Serena licked her lips. "I hope I didn't scare you too much. I had to be sure. I needed to know you weren't a trap."

"Trap?"

"It happens now and again. I get deceived," Serena explained.

Vanessa started to speak again, but the way Serena was looking at her made her words fall away.

"You're in danger," Serena said.

The fine hairs on the back of Vanessa's neck bristled.

"You know who's been following me?" she asked.

"Yes." Serena's voice was solemn. "I know."

"Who?" Vanessa asked. She felt a rising impatience not only with Serena but with herself. How could she believe this? If Serena knew who it was, then it was probably Serena who had been following her.

"I can't tell you."

"Why not?"

"That's for someone else to do." Serena stood. "I'm supposed to take you to her."

"You mean now?"

"Of course now. Why else would I have climbed up the side of your house and through your bedroom window to tell you you're in danger? I could have done that on the phone, or slipped you a note at school. You have to meet someone, and she wants to do it now, before you say anything to your mother."

"How do you know I was going to say anything to my mother?"

"You told Catty at lunchtime." She started pacing, her shoes made a steady beat.

"You couldn't have heard."

"Of course not, I read the thought before you spoke it. Hurry. My friend Jimena's waiting around the corner. We've got a car and we'll drive you." She started for the window as if she expected Vanessa to follow her. She straddled the windowsill and turned back.

"Come on," she urged. "Get dressed. Hurry!"

Vanessa hesitated. "If you knew when I was over at your house, why didn't you tell me then?"

"I couldn't. I had to check first. I had to make sure you weren't one of them."

"Who?"

"Never mind," Serena said. "You'll know soon enough if you get dressed and come."

Vanessa fell back on her pillows.

Serena read her thoughts clearly.

"It's not a dream, Vanessa," Serena told her. "There's no waking up tomorrow. This is happening."

"What is happening?" Vanessa asked. "Tell me."

"I can't tell you. I can only take you to the person who can explain it all to you."

Vanessa stared at Serena, poised on the window ledge like some mysterious fairy. She could go with her. Her mother would probably never know, but there was something else to consider. Morgan had said Serena had a reputation for liking the bizarre, and maybe this was part of it. How could she trust her? Maybe Serena was the person who had been following her. Of course, she would deny it if Vanessa asked her. And even the strange feeling that Serena had penetrated her mind could have been some form of hypnotic suggestion, especially with the way she had stared at her . . . the way she was staring at her again now.

"You need to trust me." Her voice was taking on a gentle, almost pleading tone. "Please. "

Vanessa wanted answers. She needed to know who was following her, but still she hesitated. "Can't we wait and do it tomorrow?"

"It has to be tonight." Serena sighed. She stared out at the night sky. "The moon is up. You'll be safe."

"What does the moon have to do with it?"

Serena smiled and stretched her arms. "Doesn't the dark of the moon make you feel uncomfortable? And the full moon make you feel strong? Do you look forward to seeing the moon rise the way some people love to watch a sunrise?"

Before Vanessa could answer, she turned to her, eyes on fire, and said, "I do."

Vanessa hesitated but only for a second. "I'll get dressed."

"Great!" Serena said too loudly.

Vanessa knew it was wrong. She thought she would probably regret it, but she hurried to the closet and yanked a pair of jeans from a hanger. The hanger fell to the floor and skidded across the room. She almost had the jeans pulled on when she heard her mother.

"Vanessa," her mother called.

There was a soft padding of bare feet on the runner in the hallway.

"Damn." Serena quickly climbed out the window as the door to Vanessa's bedroom opened.

Vanessa struggled out of the jeans and kicked them back in her closet.

"Vanessa, what's going on? I heard voices." Her mother walked into the room. "Did Catty sneak over here again?"

"No," she said.

"I told you, Catty can spend the night

anytime, but I need to know." She slammed the window shut.

"But it wasn't Catty!" Vanessa tried to say. "It was Serena."

"Don't lie to me, Vanessa. I know it was Catty again. You two just can't keep running around at all hours of the night. You're on restriction. No Planet Bang tomorrow night or Friday."

Vanessa moaned in protest.

Her mother turned off the light and left the room as quickly as she had come.

Vanessa climbed back in bed and pulled the covers around her.

Outside the roar of a car engine filled the night. The pounding beat of hard music followed. She wondered if that was Jimena and Serena, mission failed, on their way to wreak havoc in some other part of Los Angeles.

It took her hours to fall asleep. Did Serena really know someone who could answer her questions? Or was Morgan right? Was Serena just odd? When she fell asleep, she dreamed of a woman riding the moon across the sky. Her pale hair caught the light of the sun, and the long curls became iridescent rainbows that wrapped the world with love and peace.

"There's someone you have to meet," the woman in the dream said. "Hurry."

But Vanessa's feet were frozen. Shadows seeped into the dream then. Opaque clouds hid the moon, and Vanessa found herself trapped in another nightmare.

CHAPTER THIRTEEN

LEAF BLOWERS AWAKENED Vanessa early the next morning. She dressed quickly in yellow drawstring pants and a lacy camisole over her bra, then pulled on a sheer blouse with dragons crawling down the shoulders. She slipped into sandals with butterflies, grabbed her messenger bag, and hurried downstairs. She left a note on the kitchen counter for her mother. She apologized about last night and told her she had changed her mind and decided to go to school.

Then she walked to Catty's house. She told Catty about Serena's late-night visit while they made breakfast burritos with red and green chili peppers, eggs, and cheese, and drank *champurrados,* a frothy mixture of water, cornmeal, chocolate, and cinnamon. When they were done, an early morning breeze flapped the white curtains over the soap suds and dirty pans in the sink.

"No wonder Morgan calls Serena the Queen of Weird," Catty said. She sat cross-legged at the breakfast counter, still in her pajamas, and twisted the ear on her bunny slipper.

"Maybe she has the answer." Vanessa spooned more hot sauce onto her burrito.

"How can you trust her? You don't even know her."

"She seems nice enough." Vanessa took a bite of burrito.

"You say that about everyone."

"Well, she does."

"Look, Vanessa, everyone likes you because you're so nice to them, but I think this is one time when you should be less nice and not so trusting. What if Morgan's right?"

Vanessa sighed, then tossed the last of the burrito into her mouth. A jalapeño pepper burned its way down her throat. She reached for the *champurrado* to put out the fire. "Get dressed," she ordered. "It's getting late."

"You go on," Catty said. "I'm not feeling well. I think I overdid it with the time-travel yesterday."

"You want me to stay with you?"

"No. Get notes for me, okay?"

"Sure." Vanessa picked up her bag.

Catty followed her through the living room to the door.

Vanessa started to leave, but apprehension made her stop. "Maybe I should stay with you." She spoke over the rising smoke from sandalwood incense that burned near the door.

"Go on," Catty urged. "I'm going back to bed. I wouldn't be much company." She held her head down and stared at the bunny slippers, as if she didn't want Vanessa to see her eyes.

"You sure?" Vanessa said.

"Yeah, go."

That was the last time she saw Catty.

CHAPTER FOURTEEN

VANESSA DIDN'T KNOW how she got through the rest of the week. How could she do homework, take tests, or even flirt and smile with Michael when Catty was missing? The teachers said Catty fit the profile of a runaway. How could they say that when they didn't really know her? None of them did. A policewoman had come and gone. So had a protective-services worker from the county. Each had questioned Vanessa at school and then slapped their notebooks closed as if to say, just another runaway.

On Friday, after school, Vanessa sat on the cement bench where she normally waited for

Catty. The day had been hot and now the smog was as thick as tar, and made sky and trees a hazy yellow-brown. The air smelled metallic. She lifted her hair off her neck, hoping the stagnant air might evaporate the sweat.

The thought that had been pushing at her all day finally entered her mind. Catty wasn't powerful enough to leapfrog a week into the past. If she had successfully made the journey back, then Vanessa wouldn't be sitting here in the sticky air. She'd be back at the Bowl reliving her date with Michael. Catty wasn't coming back because she couldn't. Vanessa had a sudden flash of Catty floating in the tunnel, unable to break free.

She heard footsteps and looked up. Michael walked toward her.

"I heard Catty still hasn't come back," he said. "Are you okay?"

She shook her head. "We've been best friends for so long I can't even believe all the ways I miss her."

He sat down beside her and his arm circled her back. "Do you want me to give you a ride over to Catty's house just in case she's come back?"

"Thanks."

She picked up her messenger bag, and they drove over to Catty's house. No one answered the front door. She and Michael went around to the backyard. Wind chimes and hummingbird feeders hung from the eaves, and pink oleander blossoms brushed lazily against the redwood fence. She crossed the patio and knocked on the sliding glass door, then held her hands around her eyes and peered inside. The sun set behind her and the last rays colored the dining room with fire.

They walked back to the van, holding hands.

"I wanted to take you to Planet Bang tonight," Michael said, "but I didn't know if you'd want to go."

"I'm grounded. My mother won't let me tonight, but even if she said it was okay, I'd feel funny going out, not knowing where Catty is."

"I thought that's what you'd say, but I wanted to ask anyway." He didn't hide the disappointment in his voice. "Come on, I'll give you a ride home."

"I promised I'd meet Morgan at Urth."

"I'll give you a ride."

"Thanks, but I need—"

"Time alone." Michael put both arms around her. "Catty didn't like rules much. I think she's run away. Maybe she didn't tell you because she didn't want you to talk her out of it." His tone implied that Catty wasn't coming back. "I'm sorry."

"I know," she said. She was grateful for the understanding she saw in his eyes.

"If you change your mind and your mom will let you go out, then give me a call, okay?"

"Yes."

"Promise?"

"I promise." She smiled. Michael made her feel so good.

He climbed in his van and she watched him drive away. Then she walked over to the Urth Caffé near the Bodhi Tree book store.

Morgan sat alone at a small table near the window. She sipped tea from a huge cup. The steam curled around her face.

"Hi." Vanessa sat down.

"Any luck finding Catty?" Morgan said. She took another sip of tea.

"No. She wasn't home."

"She wasn't at the rose garden at Exposition Park either."

Vanessa must have looked surprised, because Morgan answered her. "Well, I thought maybe she had boy trouble and went someplace to think." She shrugged. "I ditched afternoon classes and took the bus. I like to go there."

Vanessa wondered if she had gone there to think about Michael. She didn't think she really went there looking for Catty.

Morgan stared at her hands. "I can't believe her mother didn't even call the police. That's so like Catty's mother."

"The school called them." Vanessa spoke defensively. Catty's mother had probably driven over to Griffith Observatory again this evening to see if she could spot a spaceship and wave goodbye to her daughter.

"We should do something." Morgan caught Vanessa's look and shrugged. "So maybe I didn't like Catty, but I hate what's happened to her. I'd want everyone to keep trying to find me."

Serena walked into the cafe. She was wearing gold platform shoes and overalls spray-painted with graffiti. Serena saw them, waved, and came toward their table.

"Why is she always following you?" Morgan said, exasperated. "You'd better watch out for her."

"Hi," Serena greeted them. "I was just picking up some books at the Bodhi Tree. I'm glad I saw you here. I've been trying to catch you all week, Vanessa."

"I've got to go." Morgan stood abruptly. "If I'm going to Planet Bang tonight, I've got to buy something to wear." She gathered up her things.

"Bye, Morgan," Serena said.

Morgan ignored her and hurried out.

"I heard about Catty." Serena sat down. "Is Catty different like you? She is, isn't she?"

"Look, I'm feeling really bad right now about—" Vanessa stopped. She had almost said "about losing a friend." The words felt too final to say. She thought of Catty spinning down the tunnel for eternity. Hot tears rimmed her eyes.

"You didn't lose her," Serena comforted Vanessa. "I hope not yet, anyway—if you'll come with me, maybe my friend can help."

"I'm sorry you think this is another chance for a practical joke," Vanessa spat out. All she could think about was Catty caught in the tunnel. She pushed back her chair, grabbed her bag, and walked to the door.

Serena's heavy platforms clumped on the wood floor behind her.

"If Catty were my friend and someone told me they knew someone who could help, I wouldn't hesitate," Serena called out.

Vanessa paused, chewing on the side of her cheek. Serena was right. She didn't have a choice. She had to go with Serena if there was any chance the person she knew could help bring Catty back.

"All right," Vanessa said, but she still felt unsure.

Serena smiled broadly. "Jimena is parked down the street."

They walked across the small parking lot, then down the block. A blast of music filled the night and made her heart vibrate with the beat. The music came from a blue-and-white '81 Oldsmobile. The girl she had seen in front of Serena's house on Sunday night leaned against the car. The wind whirled her black hair around her face. She wore Daisy Dukes, athletic shoes, and a fuchsia T-shirt. Her long dark legs were crossed in front of her.

Serena opened the car door on the passenger side. "Jimena, this is Vanessa. Vanessa, Jimena."

"Hey," Jimena called.

"Is she going to drive?" Vanessa asked over the music.

"Sure," Serena said.

"She looks kind of young to be driving," Vanessa said nervously.

"Jimena's fifteen. Her brother lets us borrow his car."

"You got to know how to drive if you're going to jack cars," Jimena said with a wry smile and climbed inside.

Vanessa hesitated.

"Come on, I quit the life," Jimena yelled back at her. *"Te lo juro."*

Vanessa thought of Catty. She really had no choice. She threw her bag in the back and crawled in after it. Serena climbed in the front.

Jimena started the engine. The sound of the

mufflers thundered off the road and shattered the night. The car shrieked around the corner and the rear end fishtailed.

Serena and Jimena squealed with joy.

Vanessa wished she had listened to Morgan now. She rubbed her forehead. What was the world coming to when Morgan was offering good advice?

The traffic light ahead turned yellow, then red. Jimena blasted through the intersection as the oncoming traffic started to move. Horns honked. Tires skidded.

"We almost had an accident," Vanessa shouted above the music, and yanked her seat belt into place with a snap of metal.

"The light was yellow." Jimena floored the accelerator. The driver of a Jeep honked at her and a woman in a Corvette leaned out her window and screamed profanities.

"Aren't you afraid of getting stopped by the police?"

"In Los Angeles? Who are the *placas* gonna pick? Everyone breaks the law," Jimena said. "Besides, I can outrun them."

The awful gnawing in Vanessa's stomach got worse.

"You'll totally get used to this," Serena explained cheerfully.

"No doubt," Vanessa muttered.

"Don't be so scared," Serena said and leaned over the seat. A silver chain fell from her overalls. A moon amulet dangled at the end of the chain. It looked identical to the ones Catty and Vanessa wore. Was it just a weird coincidence? Maybe there was a shop in Venice Beach that specialized in moon charms.

She started to ask Serena where she got the amulet when Jimena slammed on the brakes. There was a terrible squeal of tires. Vanessa gripped the seat and squeezed her eyes, waiting to become a tangle of flesh and metal. When nothing happened, she opened her eyes. Jimena and Serena were both staring at her.

She leaned forward to tell them she had changed her mind, but the car shot out again. Inertia pushed her back with a quick snap of her neck. How had she let Serena convince her to go with them? It only proved to her how absolutely desperate she felt. But overriding all her doubts was a strong foreboding that something important was about to happen that would change her life forever.

CHAPTER FIFTEEN

THE CAR SCREECHED around the corner and stopped in front of a small gray apartment building near Cedars-Sinai Medical Center. Waves of disappointment rolled over Vanessa. She thought she was on the verge of discovering something earth-shattering. She had at least expected a dark alley off Melrose and some threatening punker in five-inch platform boots with silver studs jutting dangerously from leather clothes.

Jimena shut off the engine. The music stopped. Vanessa rubbed her head against the silence ringing in her ears.

Serena opened the car door. "Come on," she coaxed. "You'll like Maggie."

Vanessa climbed from the car. The sweet scent of night jasmine enveloped her. Jimena walked over to the security panel and buzzed an apartment. A loud hum opened the magnetic lock.

Vanessa followed Serena and Jimena into a mirrored entrance. She glanced at the reflection, three girls with nothing in common, an odd combination.

"Who am I going to meet?" she asked.

"Maggie Craven," Serena told her.

"She's retired history teacher," Jimena added.

"How can she help me find Catty?"

They smiled and pulled her onto an elevator. The metal doors closed, and the elevator trundled up to the fourth floor.

"Look, maybe I shouldn't have come," Vanessa hesitated.

"Too late," Serena said.

They each took one of Vanessa's hands and pulled her off the elevator, then walked her down a narrow balcony that hung over a courtyard four stories below. Ivy entwined the iron railing.

Before Jimena could knock, the door opened.

"Welcome, welcome." A thin, short woman smiled. She wore flowing white pajamas that looked like a kimono. Her long gray hair curled into a bun on top of her head. She hugged Jimena and Serena. Then she touched the moon amulet hanging from Vanessa's neck.

"My dear, dear child, I've been searching for you a long time," she said. Her warm, caring eyes looked so deeply into Vanessa's that she thought the woman was inspecting her soul. "You're here now. That's all that matters."

Maggie motioned them to come inside and they continued down a narrow hallway to a living room and kitchen. Candle flames and oil lamps lit the apartment. Simple haunting music of four notes played from a stringed instrument Vanessa couldn't identify.

"Do you like tea, my dear?" Maggie said.

"Really, I just wanted to ask about Catty and then go."

Maggie pulled out a chair. "Sit, please."

Vanessa sat at the small table. The tablecloth

caught the light from the oil lamps and candles and gave the impression that it was spun with gold and silver threads.

Maggie scooped five teaspoons of loose tea into a white teapot. The round face of the pot looked like the face of the moon. She added boiling water from a kettle on the gas stove.

"Milk?" Maggie held up a small white pitcher. She didn't wait for anyone to answer but poured a little into the bottom of each cup.

"Now we'll wait a moment for the tea to brew." She looked at Vanessa in a loving way. "I'm so glad you've finally come to me. I have so much I need to tell you, but where to start? That's always a difficult decision."

"You know what happened to Catty?" Vanessa said.

Maggie smiled at her and set the strainer on top of a cup, poured tea, and handed the cup to Vanessa. She repeated the same for Serena, Jimena, and herself.

Vanessa drank the tea. It tasted of cloves and honey and something bitter.

"This is great tea." Vanessa sipped again. She

hadn't realized how thirsty she had been until she was staring at tea leaves on the bottom of her empty cup. "Now, what about Catty?" she asked.

"More tea, my dear?"

"Yes, please. What kind is it?" She handed her cup to Maggie. Already her urgency about Catty was melting away. She began to relax.

"Perfect tea for the occasion," Maggie said.

In the candle glow Maggie's face seemed to transform. She looked young, and her eyes, something in them looked so familiar. Vanessa blinked. Maggie looked younger still, and her hands were definitely those of a young woman. Why hadn't she noticed that before? She wasn't old.

Maggie refilled Vanessa's cup and handed it back to her. Then she pulled pins from her bun. She shook her head and ran her hands through her hair. Luxurious curls fell to her shoulders. Vanessa could see now that her first impression had been wrong. Maggie's hair wasn't gray, but the pale blond of shimmering moonbeams, and silky. Why hadn't she seen how beautiful Maggie was before?

"There now, has my tea relaxed you,

Vanessa?" Maggie asked. "After centuries of experience I find it works best to give a little herbal tea before I talk the truth, something to help you see with your soul, not your eyes."

Vanessa blinked. The walls had given way and the apartment was a windswept vault dominated with the classical colonnades of antiquity. She blinked again and the four walls of a small apartment returned.

"Tu es dea, filia lunae." Maggie glistened when she spoke, as if an aura of pure luminosity curled around her. The words seemed similar in cadence to the words Vanessa had spoken when she was being chased.

"What language is that?" Vanessa said in a drowsy sort of way.

"Latin." Maggie smiled.

"I know some Latin words." Vanessa tried to repeat the words as she remembered the sounds, but her tongue twisted sluggishly in her mouth. *"Oh, Mah-tare Loon-ah, Re-gee-nah no-kis, Ad-you-wo may noonk."*

"Yes." Maggie seemed concerned. "You've used this prayer?"

Vanessa nodded, feeling bewildered and totally dizzy. "How can I know Latin?"

"You were born with it," Maggie said. "You know ancient Greek as well."

"I'm sure I don't." Vanessa giggled.

"It seems I've found you without a second to spare if you've already been forced to use the prayer." Maggie looked at Jimena and Serena. "It was easy to bring Jimena and Serena to me because their dreams were open. You must have nightmares, Vanessa."

"Yes," Vanessa whispered.

"It happens now and again, but I'm afraid it's not a good sign. It means the Atrox has already discovered who you are and entered your dreams. That's why it was nearly impossible to speak to you in your sleep and bring you to me. Thank goodness Serena found you."

"Did you say something about an Atrox?" Vanessa couldn't have heard her clearly. The tea was making her feel so strange.

"Not an Atrox. The Atrox," Maggie whispered. "The primal source of evil. Since creation it has been jealous of the world of light and tried to destroy it."

Maggie considered the shadows clinging to the corners of the room. "The Atrox is always around, sending shadows like tentacles to be its eyes. Tell me, dear," Maggie continued. "Have you noticed any inexplicable shadows following you?"

Vanessa thought of the unnatural way shadows had frightened her when she was a girl alone in her room, but before she could answer, Maggie lifted her hands. Silver tendrils pulsated from her palm to the corners of the room and scattered the shadows hovering there.

Maggie stared at Vanessa. "To put it as simply as I can, Vanessa, there are evil forces in the world. The Atrox controls them and the Atrox wants to destroy you."

"Destroy me?" she whispered and began to tremble. "Why me? I'm just—"

"Tu es dea, filia lunae. You are a goddess, a Daughter of the Moon."

"Goddess?"

"Yes." Maggie smiled. "When Pandora's box was opened, countless evils and sorrows were released into the world. But the last thing to leave the box was hope, the sole comfort for people during misfortune. Only Selene, the goddess of the moon, saw the demonic creature lurking nearby, sent by the Atrox to devour hope. She took pity on Earth dwellers and gave her daughters, like guardian angels, to fight the Atrox and perpetuate hope. That is why you are here, Vanessa, to keep hope alive."

"How?"

"By stopping the Atrox, of course."

"I'm going to fight the Atrox." Vanessa would have laughed if Maggie hadn't looked at her so gravely. "What happens if the Atrox wins?"

"The end of the world as we know it."

Vanessa felt fear spread through her.

"I'm going much too fast for you, my dear," Maggie said. "Sip your tea."

Vanessa looked at the tea and felt a flood of relief. It must be the tea. There must be something in it that was making her feel so strange. Drug dealers weren't all young and streetwise. Hippies aged. The tea must be a powerful hallucinogenic. None of this was real. Hopefully, the effects would wear off so she could walk home. The whole thing seemed silly now.

"There's something in the tea," Vanessa declared. "It's making me see things. It made you look different and the apartment, too. And I'm imagining you saying these crazy things." She started laughing then, but no one joined her.

"It's a simple herbal tea from Tibet." Maggie sounded puzzled. "Why would I drug you when I need to warn you about the Atrox and the Followers?"

"Followers?"

"The victims of the Atrox, the Followers," Maggie explained. "The Atrox steals their hope, sucking it from their soul. Then they become predators themselves, stealing hope from others, trying to replenish their own and feel alive again. But their hunger is never satisfied. They become masters of deceit. They look like anyone, you or me, but they hate the moon because it is a symbol of Selene and represents goodness. Under a full moon, their eyes turn phosphorescent, and even ordinary people can sense their evil."

"So why aren't people aware of them?" Vanessa argued. "If they can see their eyes and sense their evil, there should be squads of police fighting them."

"A woman sees a glint of yellow in a stranger's eye and rather than trust her instincts, she thinks it's her imagination. It's amazing how far people will go to deny what is all around them." Maggie sipped her tea, then continued. "The Followers also hate timepieces, not digital ones, but watches with hands and, of course, sundials. Anything that reminds them of their eternal bond to evil. It won't stop them like a crucifix is reported to stop a vampire, but it will cause them to start."

Vanessa thought back to that first night when she had felt someone following her. Her alarm clock had been turned toward the wall and her wristwatch had been turned upside down. Could one of the Followers have climbed into her room and changed her computer program to make her think it was the crescent moon so she would walk home alone in the dark? It could just as well have been Serena or Jimena who had climbed into her room. Serena had done it once. Why not twice?

Maggie continued, "And they can never harm a person who does a genuine act of kindness toward them. Evil is so unprepared for that. But then, I suppose few people have ever acted kindly toward them."

Vanessa didn't want to hear any more. It was definitely bye-bye time. Maybe Maggie had been a teacher who had gone mental from the stress brought on at school. Perhaps Serena and Jimena had cruelly thought that Vanessa would find this sad woman's trouble entertaining. She glanced at them and felt a chill settle over her. They looked deadly serious.

"Can I use the rest room?" Vanessa asked. She'd use it, then come back, make excuses, and go.

"Of course, my dear," Maggie handed her a candle.

"I'll just turn on the light." Vanessa started to excuse herself from the table.

"I don't have electricity."

"Oh." Vanessa was startled. "I'm sorry you had your electricity shut off."

"The electricity wasn't shut off," Maggie said

indignantly. "I never had it turned on. I don't believe in electricity. I avoid it when possible. It destroys the magic of the night."

Vanessa looked around her. For the first time she noticed the utter lack of electrical appliances; no microwave, no television, no dishwasher or refrigerator.

"Electricity and certain other so-called conveniences have caused modern populations to lose touch with their deeper intuition, not to mention what they can't see. Electricity." She formed the word as if it left a bad taste in her mouth. "In ancient times people saw the magic in the night. The day, too. But today? How many people do you know who can really see? I can't understand why people insist on ignoring the beauty of the mythical world. How many times do teachers say it's imaginary? Or parents?"

Vanessa shrugged, took a quick step back, and stopped. Her knees felt too shaky to hold her. She sat back in the chair with a thump.

Maggie leaned over, blue eyes tense, and spoke quietly. "The greatest strength of the Atrox is that modern people no longer believe the demonic walks amongst us. So you see why it is so important that you defeat it."

"Me?" Vanessa said. "I'm going to destroy it, like vampires, with a stake?"

"Not like vampires." Maggie shook her head. "I'm talking about an evil more ancient than Transylvania's undead. The spirit who tricked Lucifer into his fall."

"You want me to fight that?"

"You have no choice. That is what you were born to do and it is my responsibility to guide you and to help you understand your powers. Your breed is descended from unconquerable warriors. Remember their courage and never dishonor them."

Maggie seemed to sense her disbelief. "My proof, dear, is in your gift."

"Gift?" Something twisted inside her. Her heart beat quickly and she couldn't breathe.

"Your ability to become invisible." It was a statement.

Vanessa felt herself plunging into a whirlwind of emotions. She had always wanted someone to explain her strange ability to her, but she had always thought the answer would come from science; a failed government project, a strange overdose of radiation, some experimental medicine her mother had taken while she was in the womb. She could even accept being from outer space more easily than this. A goddess? Weren't they supposed to be sweet and lovely and make flowers bloom beneath their feet?

Vanessa stood and grabbed her bag. It couldn't be true. It wasn't true. But even as she was trying to deny it, another part of her mind was recalling the shadows and the nightmares. If it were true . . .

"It can't be true," she shouted. And then she ran.

She hurried down the fire stairs and out into the cool night. She didn't believe any of the ramblings about the Atrox and its Followers, so why did a cold fear grip her chest?

"Goddess." she let the word linger in her mouth. She didn't feel divine. She had zits and cramps and worried about people liking her. She looked up and saw the moon creeping over the buildings.

"Mother Moon," she whispered. She felt awestruck. Could it be? But if it were true, if she were a goddess, then that meant the Atrox was also real. And its Followers, were they somewhere nearby? She turned and looked at the shadows hovering around the cars and trees. She had never felt so alone and afraid in the night before.

CHAPTER SIXTEEN

AN HOUR LATER, Vanessa walked into the kitchen. Her mother was at the worktable drawing lotus flowers, vines, and paisleys on a sketch pad. A mehndi cone lay on the table next to a plate of cut lemons.

"Hi, baby, what do you think?" Her mother held up her hand. She had painted her nails bright red and decorated the skin with a black design. "I can't decide if I like the geometric designs or the ones I'm working on now." She picked up a white cone. "Let me draw the new ones on your hand."

"Don't you know how to make chocolate chip cookies?" Vanessa yelled. Her emotions had been clashing inside her since she left Maggie's apartment. Frustration and anger had won and had been building as she walked home. Now her whirling emotions exploded into the room. "That's what mothers do. They do things to comfort their daughters."

"Vanessa." Her mother sounded more worried than offended. "What is it?"

Vanessa dropped her bag and slumped into a chair at the table. All week, she had wanted to tell her mother about Catty. She had planned to several times this week, but every time she started, it felt too much like closing the door to the tunnel. If her mother knew, then it would be true.

"Mom, we need to talk."

"Did you and Catty do something weird again? She's been getting you into trouble since you were both eight years old."

"No, we didn't do anything *weird*," Vanessa said.

"But you mooned—"

"Mom, we didn't do anything."

"Well, it's pretty embarrassing when your daughter has to appear in court because she showed her buttocks in public."

"Mom, do we have to repeat these old arguments again?" Vanessa said with a heavy sigh. "This is really important."

"All right."

"Mom, what would you do if you found out something about me personally—"

Her mother broke in. "There's nothing I could hear about you that would change the way I feel. You're my daughter. I love you."

"Mom, I'm . . . I'm very different from what you think I am."

"Let's talk about it. We have chocolate chip cookies. How long has it been since we ate cookies and hot cocoa?"

"You can't make everything okay with cookies and cocoa. I'm not a kid anymore."

"I wasn't trying to make anything better. I thought it would be nice. We could have a long talk."

Vanessa stood. "Maybe later. I think I'll sit outside." She didn't want to sit around moaning over her problems. She needed a solution. Serena had said she was going to take her to see someone who might help her find Catty. Instead, the visit had added to her worries.

Her mother looked at the window over the sink. The moon shone huge and ivory yellow through the kitchen window. "You've always loved the moonlight. It seems to relax you."

Vanessa looked outside at the moon. "Do you think there is a goddess of the moon?"

"Oh, several," her mother answered.

"No, I mean for real."

"I was answering for real." Her mother pushed back her chair, then walked over to the sliding glass door, opened it, and stepped out on the patio. The night jasmine filled the cool air with its sweet fragrance. "God must have many spirits to help. We call them angels because that's what we learned to call them when we were little. But there must be many divine beings who act as God's messengers. I think there's room for a goddess or more. When you look at the beauty of the moon it's easy to believe." Then her mother turned and looked back at her. "Vanessa, why are you crying?" She gently wiped the tears from Vanessa's cheeks.

"Mom, where did you get this moon amulet?"

"It was a gift from a woman at the hospital the night you were born. I thought you liked it. You wear it all the time."

"You didn't question her?"

"Well, no. She was a sweet little thing and she fussed over you. She said you reminded her of her own child. I didn't see any harm in taking it and it seemed to make her so happy that I did."

"Did she tell you her name?"

"Maybe. I don't remember. What's wrong, Vanessa?" Her mother looked concerned and put her hand on Vanessa's shoulder.

"Nothing really," Vanessa lied. "Just regular stuff, and I'm tired." She wandered into the yard.

"Vanessa, tell me. Something's troubling you." Her mother started after her but stopped suddenly as if she sensed Vanessa's need to be alone. "Don't get too cold," she said with worry in her voice.

Before she slid the patio door closed, Vanessa spoke. "Mom, I'm sorry. I didn't mean to yell at you."

"I know," her mother said quietly, and closed the sliding glass door.

Vanessa sat in the lounge chair near the hibiscus. The milk of moonlight bathed the trees and lawn with pale magic. She leaned her head on the pillow. Tears streamed down her cheeks.

In the gibbous moon's glow, her molecules became restless, urging her to give in, become invisible, and float over the city. She shouldn't. Not tonight. She was too anxious, her thoughts too mixed. Focus was impossible.

Her skin began to prickle. Ripples like tiny waves washed down her arms. Her heartbeat raced.

"Don't," she pleaded. Her body disobeyed her. A chill rushed through her and her molecules began to spread. She glanced at her hands.

"Stop," she ordered. But her fingers refused her command. The tips of her hands became fuzzy. She blinked. She could no longer see fingers or palms, only feel their essence. The clothes next to her body became invisible, their molecules aroused by the forcible change of her own. Then her body levitated, as light as air, the transition complete. She floated to the kitchen window. Her mother sat at her worktable drawing designs she would paint on movie stars.

Her mother turned suddenly and looked out the window. "Vanessa?" she said as if she felt her daughter's closeness. She looked quickly around the kitchen, then shrugged and went back to drawing.

Vanessa glanced back at the lounge chair. Her sandals and blouse were still there, not enough to make her mother worry or wonder. What could she do about it anyway? Her mind was jangled, unable to concentrate and pull the molecules together. She would have to wait until they came together on their own.

She drifted into the night air, rising higher and higher. A breeze carried her as gently as a bedtime song. The moonlight permeated her molecules, bathing them with hope. Catty would return. She felt sure now. She continued on, riding the night air. Maggie and the strange tea party fell further and further into a blur of memory.

She was near Sunset and Vine when a sudden gust hit her hard. She hadn't been prepared for a change in wind. Before she could collect herself and dive for shelter, another rush of air caught her. Her molecules scattered in two directions. She concentrated hard and almost had them back when a blast whistled into her and spun her into a dangerous vortex. A strong uprising wind split her apart.

Cold seeped into every cell. Even with total concentration she could no longer feel all of her body. Toes, knees, and femurs were gone. Not invisible, just no more. Panic set in. This had never happened before.

Wind thrashed and whipped. Another gust slammed her into the palm trees that lined the street. The palm fronds slashed between her remaining molecules and swept them in different directions. Her mind became confused. Her eyesight blurred, then left.

Silence and darkness cradled her.

CHAPTER SEVENTEEN

THE MUSIC WAS FAINT at first. The beat struggled to find her. Had she been unconscious? The music grew louder and pulsed through every cell. Her molecules gathered. The cadence seemed to regulate her heart. It was becoming strong again. Her eyesight returned. She was no more than long thin bundles of cells, but at least now the cells were absorbing oxygen through osmosis. The side of a building protected her from the raging Santa Ana winds.

She hovered, a transparent veil high over the heads of kids waiting to go inside Planet Bang. It was teen night again. She recognized some of the kids in line.

A gust of wind screamed down the side of the building and blew her through the entrance. It was dark and hot inside and smelled of sweat, cigarette smoke, and musky colognes.

She wavered over the freestyle dancers. The strobe light flashed and cut their dance into freeze-frame clicks. The boys stomped close in a savage circle. They shouted their crew name with the beat and waved handkerchiefs to flaunt their colors. Blue lasers swept over the girls on the periphery of the circle, hips rolling in soft, smooth spins.

Club kids stood near the deejay, dressed in outrageous costumes of turquoise feathers and sequined velvet. Couples stopped and admired their outfits. The club kids posed and danced in their private Mardi Gras parade.

Other kids lolled in dark corners, zombied out. They'd probably paid some homeless guy to buy liquor for them in a corner shop.

Vanessa was lower now, eye level with the dance crews. The pulse of the music beat through her. Her feet found the rhythm and she started to dance, close with the girls. She lifted her hands. She liked the heat and sweat of dancing. She followed the lead of the dance crew, hips in line, and thought of Catty dancing with light sticks and Christmas tinsel.

A hand touched her back. She hadn't realized she had become visible.

She turned abruptly. Morgan stood behind her, all smiles.

"Hey, I didn't know you were allowed to come here after what happened last week." She wore a zip-up top, a silver pull ring dangling seductively at the base of her throat.

"I'm not."

"Cool." Morgan grabbed Vanessa's arm. "You're dropping that goodie girl attitude. I like your outfit. It's a Mom-would-die-if-she-saw-me choice." Vanessa glanced down. She was wearing the lacy see-through camisole over her bra. Her yellow drawstring slacks had thankfully made the trip, but she was barefoot, except for her toe rings.

"This place is definitely a blues buster," Morgan said. "Staying home and crying is a waste of time. All it does is make your nose red and your eyelids puffy. Let's meet those guys over there in the corner."

"I'm not staying," Vanessa turned to go.

"Why'd you come, then?" Morgan took her hands and pulled her across the floor. "Your hands are as cold as ice. Why are you so nervous? Is Michael coming?"

"No, really, I've got to get home. I'm grounded."

"That's a new one," Morgan commented. "Then how did you get here?"

"Long story."

"Right, you're checking up on Michael. I know the game. Look over there." She motioned with her head.

Seven boys stood in the dark away from the reach of the strobe lights. The tallest leaned into the flash of white light as if he knew they were talking about him. It was Stanton.

"Any one of those boys could love me to death," Morgan said. "How can there be so many cute boys I haven't met yet? Isn't life fabulous?" Her voice was a little too frantic, like she was trying to chase the sadness away.

"Maybe you should be careful," Vanessa warned. She wasn't in the mood to say hi to Stanton or any of his friends.

"Those boys look like they need someone to tame them. I'd just be doing my duty."

"Morgan, do you ever think of anything besides boys?"

"Sure, clothes and style. I must be doing something right, haven't you noticed?"

"What?"

"Look at how many girls are wearing a tassel of mini-braids like I wore last week. Imitation is the sincerest form of flattery."

"Yeah, if that's important," Vanessa muttered.

"It's everything." Morgan pulled her through a line of dancers to the smoke-filled corner.

"I think I'll start a diet tomorrow." Morgan kept watching. "It'll change the way I feel about myself." She pinched a nonexistent roll of fat on her thigh.

"Morgan, what century are you living in?"

"I'm just trying to get your mind off Catty. I'm *teasing*. You know I don't believe all that stuff I say."

"Then why do you say it?"

"It's expected," she said, and pointed. "There! That one. What do you think?"

Stanton popped a match with his thumbnail and lit a cigarette. His eyes never left Vanessa.

"I think we should go home."

"Because you have a boyfriend no one else needs one? Please. Look at the tall one."

"I know him," Vanessa said.

"Good." Morgan smiled. "That's the one I want. Introduce me."

Vanessa tried not to stare at Stanton, but she kept feeling her eyes drawn back to him.

A girl stood next to him. She had long maroon hair and wore a low-cut black dress. Something in her hand flashed dangerous silver. It was a razor blade. She lifted it to her chest and cut a jagged S, then looked up at Stanton with a coy smile.

She licked her lips and sliced a T into the pale white skin. Blood trickled down her breasts.

No one seemed alarmed. Vanessa felt sick. She barreled through the crowd and grabbed the girl's wrist to stop her from cutting the A.

Stanton took the razor from the girl, his fingers unafraid of the slicing blade. "Cassandra's into blood sports," he drawled, and dropped the blade into his shirt pocket.

Cassandra seemed to hiss and draw back. She stared at Vanessa, then quickly looked away, but not before Vanessa saw the bottomless black deadness in her eyes.

"She's a cutter," Stanton whispered, his lips too close to Vanessa's cheek. "She can't feel, so she cuts herself to escape it."

Cassandra smiled in a dreamy sort of way and patted at the blood with the tips of her fingers.

Morgan pulled Stanton away from Vanessa.

"I'm Morgan," she said, hanging on his arm. "Vanessa's best friend."

Stanton smiled at Morgan, but his eyes returned to Vanessa.

"Let's dance." Morgan pulled him back into shadows, too much desire and desperation in her face. She held her hands over her head. Her hips moved sinuous and slow. Stanton placed his hands on her waist. She looked shyly into his eyes, then her hands entwined the back of his neck.

Another boy with shadows in his eyes hopped over to Vanessa. She was instantly afraid of him. He appeared to be like any boy her age, but there was something creepy about the way he looked at her.

"You're Stanton's friend?" he said. "I'm Karyl." His eyes held frank sexual suggestion and kept returning to her see-through camisole. He brushed an uninvited hand down her arm. His skin felt dry and thin like lizard skin. He stared at her as if there was something Vanessa had that he wanted desperately.

She stepped away from him and bumped into another boy, tall with white-blond hair and black roots. He smiled at her, lips curved in a crooked sort of way. His nose hoops shimmered. The strobe light made his thin face look haunted. He put his arm around her waist, fingers digging into her side, craving.

She slapped his fingers.

He laughed. "Don't you like me touching you?" He touched her again, his hand dangerously bold.

She pushed him away. "Stop it."

He laughed again. So did Karyl.

She hated that they were making her feel so vulnerable.

"My friend Tymmie's got a longing for something," Karyl said. "I got it, too, a real bad hunger. Maybe a pretty girl like you can feed it."

"And maybe not." Vanessa started to walk away.

The boys circled around her, and then Cassandra joined them.

"Dance with me," she said, her body slinking around Vanessa as tight as a cat.

"No." Vanessa tore away from their hands. She barreled toward the dance floor where she had last seen Morgan dancing with Stanton. Karyl hurried beside her.

"You don't want me to go hungry, do you?" he said. "That wouldn't be nice. You seem like a nice girl."

"Get away!" Vanessa ducked under his arm.

He laughed and jumped as if she had blown him a kiss.

She slammed through the throng of dancers.

Cassandra stepped in front of her. Inch-long fingernails cut into her skin.

"Ouch." Vanessa jerked her arm away.

"Play nice." Cassandra let her bloody fingers glide down Vanessa's neck. "Karyl and Tymmie just want to play. So do I. Be our friend."

"You guys are lost in the K hole," Vanessa said with disgust. Planet Bang was strict about drug use, but kids took them in the parking lot. Stanton's friends were on Ecstasy or worse, Special K, the drug from hell.

Then she saw Morgan kissing Stanton. She yanked free from Cassandra and grabbed Morgan. Her zipper had been pulled down to her silky pink push-up bra. Her eyes looked dreamy.

"Let's get out of here," Vanessa whispered fiercely. "I think they're doing Special K. I don't want to stay and see the rest."

"You go on." Morgan looked up at Stanton. "I'm staying."

Vanessa couldn't abandon Morgan. She had a strange feeling that bad things were going to happen.

"I've got to go," Vanessa said again. "You coming with me, Morgan?" She didn't wait for an answer. She yanked Morgan away from Stanton and rammed through the dancers, pulling Morgan behind her.

She rushed outside into the cool night air. The wind whirled around her.

"What's your problem?" Morgan jerked away from her. "I never knew you were so jealous."

"I'm not jealous! Did you meet his creepy friends?"

"So they're druggies. He's not." Morgan shrugged and started back inside.

Vanessa seized her hand. "It's not safe."

She started to say more but something made her look behind Morgan. Stanton had stopped at the door. Now he gazed up at the night sky as if something in the black endless night was filling him with despair. Was it the moon that tormented him? She thought she saw his eyes flicker with a yellow light. It had to be her imagination.

Vanessa took a sharp breath. "Did you see?"

"Yes. He's beautiful, isn't he?" Morgan breathed. "What's with you?"

A hand touched Vanessa's shoulder. She turned quickly.

"Michael!" she jumped, surprised.

"You told me you were grounded," he said, his hurt and confusion barely concealed in his tight smile.

"She is," Morgan replied for her in a flirty way. "Isn't it great she's getting rid of her goodie-girl attitude?"

Michael ignored Morgan and looked at Vanessa. "I thought you didn't want to go out tonight anyway, because you were too upset about Catty."

"I didn't."

His eyes drifted to the entrance of Planet Bang. Stanton waved and smiled maliciously.

Michael glanced back at Vanessa, then back at Stanton.

"You could have told me the truth, Vanessa," Michael said in anger. "I thought you were a good person . . . I guess I was wrong." His words stunned her.

"I did tell you the truth." Vanessa felt desperate. "Things just happened."

"Why shouldn't she party?" Morgan added defensively.

Michael glanced at Morgan, then back at

Vanessa. "I guess I can see what happened." He motioned with his head toward Stanton, then he turned and walked away.

"Michael!" She ran after him.

He stopped and the look on his face made fear cut through her like a jagged blade.

"I didn't mean to come here tonight. I was going to stay home, but something happened that I couldn't control."

"Like Stanton came by," he said grimly.

She turned to Morgan. "Tell him!"

"Tell him what?"

"Tell him I wasn't with Stanton."

Morgan cocked her head and smiled at Michael with her eyes lowered. "Why would I tell him that?" Her hand slid up Michael's chest. "Did you come to dance with me, Michael?"

The music started again and Morgan swayed to the beat.

"Morgan!" Vanessa pleaded. "Tell him!"

"Oh, please." Morgan jerked away from her. "Take care of your own problems. I've got to go." She left, pushing through the crowd.

"Morgan is with Stanton." Vanessa tried

again. "I don't know why she wouldn't tell you."

Michael shook his head. He didn't hide the sadness in his voice. "Have fun, Vanessa."

She hated the hurt she saw in his eyes. A fierce pain spread through her as she watched him disappear in the crowd, but this time she didn't run after him. How could he think she had come here to be with Stanton? She glanced back at the entrance where Morgan stood with Stanton now. She flashed an arrogant smile at Vanessa before she took his hand and went back inside.

"Thanks, Morgan," Vanessa said bitterly.

"Hey." Jimena pushed through the crowd and ran up to her, breathless. "*¿Qué onda?*"

"We've been looking for you." Serena was following after her.

"I got a premonition when you left Maggie's," Jimena said. "I saw you at Planet Bang. Well, I didn't see you exactly, I saw dust sliding down the side of the building, but I knew it was you."

"I was just leaving." Vanessa started to walk away from them.

"Wait," Serena called. "As long as we're here, let's check out the guys."

"I gotta get home." Vanessa kept going.

"Not yet." Jimena smiled. "You have not checked out guys until you've checked them out with Serena."

Vanessa reluctantly stopped.

Jimena spread her hands through her hair. "Smile pretty."

"Why?" Vanessa asked.

Jimena elbowed her playfully. "Just do it."

Vanessa tried to smile, but her eyes kept scanning the crowd for Michael.

"That one." Jimena pointed to a tall guy with a goatee, dressed in an edgy mix of swing and hip-hop.

"He thinks we're hot," Serena said slyly.

"Well, I could tell you that without reading his mind." Jimena laughed. A song ended inside and the deejay started another. The new beat was quicker, louder, and vibrated through them.

"We gotta jump to this music." Jimena started to move.

Serena leaned into Jimena, their hips moving together. People in the crowd stopped what they were doing and watched.

"Come on." Serena grabbed Vanessa's hand.

"I can't."

"Sure you can." Jimena put her hands on Vanessa's hips. "Just move with us. It's like the bunny hop—"

"Yeah, bunny hop," Serena squealed.

"But closer."

"My hottie is looking again." Jimena smiled wickedly. "What's he thinking now?"

Serena laughed. It was infectious. "It's X-rated. Definitely."

"Take it up a notch," Jimena said. "Come on, Vanessa, bend your knees. Low. Yeah, girl. Now you look like a *nena pachanguera*."

"You can do it," Serena whooped. "Feel the music."

Vanessa felt embarrassed and stiff. She concentrated, trying to bend her knees and move her hips at the same time. It was different from dancing with guys. The muscles above her knees ached as they danced lower, then lower still. She glanced up. A crowd had gathered around them. She blushed.

She stopped dancing and pushed through the crowd. Serena and Jimena ran after her.

"We're going to make a hot dance crew," Jimena panted when she caught up to Vanessa.

"You get a premonition?" Serena asked.

"I don't need magic to know that." Jimena smiled again. "Any fool can see. We're *suave*."

Then they both looked at Vanessa with concern. "We better take Vanessa home," Serena said.

"I'll walk." Vanessa spoke quickly, thinking of the last car ride with them.

"No, it's safer if you go with us," Jimena insisted.

Moonlight glittered through the twisted branches of the jacaranda trees as they drove Vanessa back to her house.

CHAPTER EIGHTEEN

SATURDAY MORNING the sun burned through the gauzy haze, and gray sunlight fell across Vanessa's bed. She reached for the phone and punched in Catty's number. When the answering machine clicked on she hung up and climbed out of bed. She trundled downstairs in her pajamas. Her mother was already at work in the kitchen. Plastic beads and sequins were spread across the table.

Vanessa poured a cup of coffee, grabbed a croissant, and stared at the pottery on the window ledge.

The doorbell rang.

"Who could it be this early?" her mother said.

But Vanessa was already at the front door, pulling it open and hoping to see Catty on the other side.

Michael stood on the porch.

"Michael!" She took a step back, feeling foolish in pink poodle pajamas; then she remembered last night. What was he doing here?

"I didn't want to call," he apologized. "I was afraid you wouldn't talk to me on the phone, so I drove over."

"What is it?" she asked, feeling her stomach clench. Was he going to continue their fight?

He smiled shyly. "I was driving away last night and I saw you dancing with your friends."

She thought of the dancing she had done with Jimena and Serena and felt a blush rise to her cheeks.

He seemed to read her mind. "You looked good."

"I looked silly, you mean."

"No, really." He paused. "I watched you leave with them and then I realized you weren't there with Stanton."

She felt a wave of relief wash through her.

"But then I still can't understand why you went to Planet Bang without me. You told me you were grounded."

Vanessa looked down. How could she explain to Michael what had happened? She desperately wanted to say the words that would make it right. She chewed on her bottom lip. Why did he keep staring at her?

"I was grounded. I never planned to go there." She chanced a look into his brown eyes. "That's just where I ended up."

"Because you were still looking for Catty," he said.

"Well . . ." she started, but before she could finish he interrupted.

"It's okay. I understand. I should have figured it out last night. You and Catty were really close. But you should have told me. I would have understood." He looked into her eyes and smiled again.

She hadn't realized how bad she had felt about last night until this moment. Suddenly, she was happy again. Maybe things were going to work out. Her stomach muscles tightened in pleasure and she felt a distinct lightness in her chest and arms as her molecules swarmed in joy. How could he awaken so many feelings inside her?

"I thought maybe you'd want to drive around Hollywood this morning and see if we can find Catty. Lots of runaways hang out there."

She heard her mother's quick intake of breath. Had she been standing behind them the entire time, listening?

"Mo-*ther*!"

"Catty's run away?" her mother said, shocked. "No wonder you've been acting so strange. Why didn't you tell me? Oh, for goodness sake, Vanessa, you really should have. We'll all go look for her."

"We'd probably get a lot more area covered," Michael offered, "if Vanessa and I take Hollywood Boulevard and you look on Sunset."

"Good idea." Her mother rummaged through her purse. "I can't believe you didn't tell me, Vanessa. Why didn't Catty's mother call me? Of course she didn't call. What am I thinking? Does she even know Catty is gone?"

"Mom, please don't start." Vanessa rolled her eyes upward. "Please."

"I'll meet you at Musso and Frank's at noon for lunch. You should have told me, Vanessa. I just can't believe that Catty's living like a street rat. You know she can always live with us."

Then her mother was gone.

"I'll change and be right back." Vanessa hurried upstairs. How could she tell Michael or her mother that Catty was lost in time? They wouldn't find her where they were looking. She slipped into a funnel-neck sweater and spandex pants and ran back downstairs.

She and Michael walked up and down the streets in Hollywood, threading through thick crowds of tourists, gutter punks, homeless kids, and runaways. They stopped by the homeless shelter on Hollywood Boulevard and checked the bulletin board, then went to a drop-in kitchen and back out to the street.

After they had walked a few blocks, Michael stopped in front of the lines of people waiting to go inside Mann's Chinese Theater and turned Vanessa to face him.

"I'm sorry we can't find Catty," Michael said, and kissed the top of her head. His tenderness awakened a yearning inside her.

His arm circled her waist. When he finally kissed her lips, it felt electric. Her molecules swirled like a lazy whirlpool but when the quiver reached her bones the molecules bubbled up and out, faster and faster. She was dissolving. She opened her eyes. Already her hand was missing.

She yanked away from Michael's arms and ran.

"Vanessa!"

What had he seen?

CHAPTER NINETEEN

VANESSA CROUCHED behind tourists placing hands and feet in the cement movie star imprints in front of the theater.

Michael pushed through the crowd after her. "Vanessa, what is it?" Michael reached for her hand. It wasn't there.

She gasped and jumped behind the tourists taking pictures of Marilyn Monroe's imprints. She focused on making her hand reappear. It didn't.

"Vanessa?" Michael called, sounding worried. "Are you all right?" He caught up to her and tried to take her hand again, but she was afraid he'd discover it was missing. She took a quick step back.

Confusion gathered on his face. "What's going on?"

"I just wanted to see Marilyn Monroe's footprints," she lied, and jumped into the cement prints. Maybe if he looked at her feet he wouldn't see her missing hand. She risked looking in his eyes. Big mistake. She could feel her arm dissolving. What was it about him that made her molecules go so crazy?

He looked down. "Do they fit?" He reached for her hand again.

"Damn," she muttered, and jerked away. She ran back to the street.

"Vanessa?" Michael ran after her. "What's wrong?" He placed his arm around her, but she shrugged it away. She couldn't risk his touch. Not now. She could feel the tremble of the molecules in her shoulder, pinging in delight, begging for his touch to set them free.

No, she thought, this can't be happening. Was she going to disappear right before his eyes? She concentrated, *stay, please, stay,* and walked quickly, hoping the physical exertion might calm her molecules.

Michael walked in silence beside her.

Minutes later, they stepped over the chain circling the parking lot behind Musso and Frank's, then crossed the hot asphalt to Michael's van.

He helped her inside and crawled in after her. She couldn't tell from his face what he was feeling.

"Vanessa," he spoke slowly. "I get the feeling sometimes that you really like me."

"I do," she looked straight into his eyes.

"But then you do things that make me think you don't. Why did you run off when I kissed you? And why won't you let me hold your hand?"

"Well, it's just . . ." She sighed.

"I don't think you're that shy . . ."

"No," she tried again. "I'm sorry I acted that way."

He looked away from her. "I guess I made a fool of myself coming over this morning. I should have left things the way they ended last night."

"No, I'm glad you came over," she insisted with rising anxiety. "It's just that when I get really emotional I start to . . . well, I get nervous when you kiss me and I guess I do act strange." She hated the doubtful look she saw in his brown eyes. She could tell him the truth, but would he even believe her? There was no way.

Her molecules had settled now and she wanted him to take her hand and say everything was okay, but that's not what he did.

"Look, I see your mother coming. Maybe I should go and the two of you can have lunch alone."

"I'd really like you to join us."

"Thanks, but I think I'll go to the beach."

She waited, hoping he'd ask her to go. When he didn't, she added quickly, "We could have lunch first."

"Vanessa," he said quietly and she could feel the mix of hurt and anger in his words. "It's just not working."

She felt suddenly dizzy. "I thought you cared about me, Michael."

"I do," he whispered. "But I don't want a

girlfriend who runs away from me every time I try to kiss her. All I wanted to do was hold your hand. Maybe you don't like me the way I like you. It's okay. We can be friends if that's all you want."

Before she could say anything, her mother tapped on the window. "Hey, did you guys have any luck?"

"You better go."

"But, Michael—"

"Go on. We've said enough for today."

She climbed from the van, an achy throbbing in her chest.

"Isn't Michael joining us?" her mother said with a look of concern.

"No." Vanessa shook her head sadly and watched the van drive away.

CHAPTER TWENTY

BY THE NEXT FRIDAY the loneliness inside Vanessa was as big as a boulder. She missed Catty. Tears had been creeping into her eyes all week and if she hadn't been in the middle of Urth Caffé with everyone hanging around, she would have started crying again. The coffee and muffin smells reminded her of the crazy times she and Catty had there. She tried not to think of Catty wandering in the nightmarish land between times, but the thought came uninvited. She had a painful feeling that she was never going to see Catty again.

She set her café mocha on the table near the back window, then pulled her books and papers from her messenger bag. She doodled on a course outline, drawing the face of the moon. Then she opened her geography book. The words blurred.

Footsteps pounded across the wood floor. Someone jarred the table and her café mocha slopped over the side of the cup onto the map of Japan.

Morgan sat down. Her smile was like morning sunshine. She crossed her legs. She was wearing new chunky-heeled lace-up boots, her thighs golden and slim under a black mini.

"Hey, I've been looking for you," Morgan said breezily. "I'm going out with Stanton tonight, you want to go with?"

"I don't think so." Vanessa was still angry with her.

"It'll get your mind off Catty," Morgan said. "Look, you got to face it, she's not coming back."

Vanessa dabbed at the spilled coffee with her napkin.

"I know you miss her, but she ditched you," Morgan said. "She didn't even tell you she was running."

The disquieting tunnel flashed in Vanessa's mind. "Maybe she couldn't tell me," she snapped.

"Come on," Morgan cajoled. "I'm just trying to cheer you up. It's better to think she ran than to think—"

"Enough!" Vanessa shouted in a burst of anger.

Morgan was silent for a moment, then she held up her slim tan wrist. "Look." A silver watch dangled on it. "Stanton gave me this watch. He didn't like the one I was wearing."

"I liked your old one." Vanessa frowned.

"This one is digital," Morgan said. "He said I had to get modern."

"Morgan, maybe Stanton isn't really the guy you should be going out with."

"Jealous?" That seemed to please her.

"No." Was she? She had never warned a friend away from a guy. Why would she be? She still liked Michael. But she couldn't get rid of the uneasy feeling she had about Stanton. "Stanton hangs with some really strange people and—"

"Quit worrying about me. I like Stanton. He doesn't act like other high school boys. You know, how they have to be tough and have this attitude like they're so cool. He's different—dark and intense like a poet. I've never had a guy write a poem for me before."

Vanessa felt a sudden yearning for Michael. She wished she hadn't ruined things with him.

"Besides, it's nothing serious." Morgan looked down and waited a long time before she spoke again. "I need a guy in my life. I know that's not cool, but I can't help it. How could you understand anyway? You make friends in a snap, you're really popular and you've got the look."

"Me?" Vanessa looked up, surprised. "That's what everyone says about you."

A satisfied smile crossed Morgan's lips. "Thanks. So don't worry about me. It's a waste of time. I've got it all together."

Vanessa sighed. "Be careful."

"I don't need to be." Morgan looked outside. "He's so fine."

Stanton stood at the edge of the back parking lot, wearing jeans and a black shirt, hair blowing in his eyes. He was incredibly sexy in a wild and dangerous way. She could see why Morgan was attracted to him. Maybe he really did like her.

"Yeah, well, gotta fly," Morgan said. She almost knocked into Serena and Jimena as they walked into the café.

"Hey." Jimena walked over to her table. She had transferred to La Brea High on Tuesday. Maggie thought it was safer if they all went to the same school. Vanessa still didn't believe the things Maggie had told her last week. But she liked Jimena and Serena and had started to sit with them at lunch. After school they went to Pink's for chili dogs, Retail Slut to look at punk rock clothes, and Aardvark's Odd Ark so Serena could buy Hawaiian shirts. More than once, she'd had a strange feeling that she had known them a long time. Everything would be so good now, if only Catty were back. Well, and Michael. She wished she could think of the right thing to say to him.

Jimena handed her a roll with pink sugar sprinkled over the top.

"Here, my grandmother made *pan dulce*. Dunk it in your coffee," she said. "It's really good." She pulled two more from a brown paper bag.

Jimena had three dots tattooed in a triangle on the web of her hand between thumb and index finger. She caught Vanessa staring at it.

"I got that when I got ganged up. It's for *mi vida loca*." She smiled but there was sadness in it, then she pointed to the teardrop tattooed under her right eye. "I got this in a Youth Authority Camp. Means I've served time so all the little hood rats will know I'm one tough *chola*. I got caught up again but the judge gave me community service instead."

Vanessa didn't know what to say. Jimena understood. "You don't need to say anything."

Serena set two cups of café au lait on the table, then sat down. Her hair was parted on the side and slicked back, eyes and lips metallic violet. She looked pretty.

Serena smiled. "Thank you."

Jimena laughed at Vanessa's shocked expression. "You'll get used to Serena reading your mind."

Serena's green eyes stared at Vanessa and then she said in a low whisper, "I can't do it all the time, or the way I need to be able to do it, but I'm learning. Maggie's been teaching me."

"For me it just happens. *Wham*, like a brick in

the head," Jimena said, playfully hitting the side of her head with a clenched fist. Then she looked sad again. "The first time it happened . . ." She gazed out the window as if she were remembering something that still caused her pain. "I was seven, playing with my best friend, Miranda. All of a sudden I got this picture of Miranda in a white casket. Then Miranda touched me and another picture filled my mind. She was walking down Ladera Street. A car was going by. Shots fired. I can still see the white flash coming from the gun barrel. Miranda was killed. I saw everything. After that I wouldn't let Miranda walk down Ladera. It meant we had to go a block out of the way every day when we walked home from school."

"But it came true?" Vanessa asked softly.

Jimena nodded. "I didn't go to school one day. I had to stay home because I had the flu. It was around two-thirty, when kids were getting home from school. I heard the shots and then I knew." She looked away and brushed at her eyes.

"I thought I made it happen because of my premonition." She smiled but her chin still quivered. "Maggie told me I was seeing the future, not making the bad things happen. I don't know what I'd do without Maggie, but in the beginning it took me almost a year to believe everything she said. I mean, *goddess*?" She laughed now and the sad memories seemed to fall back into their dark secret places.

Serena tore her roll in two and dipped half in her coffee. "When I was young, I answered people's thoughts. Not all the time, but often enough so people noticed. I couldn't tell the difference at first."

"That must have shocked everyone," Vanessa commented.

Jimena laughed. "No doubt."

"Yeah, I must have really freaked them out. I know it upset my mom."

"Do you know everything a person is thinking?" Vanessa asked.

"No," Serena said. "Like the night you came over to have your cards read. I didn't know you were a Daughter at first. Then I saw your memories. First I was shocked, then I was excited. I couldn't wait to tell Maggie. I knew Maggie had been looking for you a long time. But then the cards started showing danger for you. Could you tell I was flustered?"

"I thought you saw something in the cards that you weren't telling me." What had she seen?

Serena gave her a curious look. "Just what I told you already."

"That I can't run from this problem?"

Serena nodded.

"After you left, we went over to tell Maggie," Jimena said. "She is one cool woman."

"How did you meet her?" Vanessa asked.

"In our sleep." They both laughed.

"I started having dreams about her when I was about five," Serena explained. "Then when I was around twelve she started asking me to meet her."

"Did you go?"

"After a few months I made Collin take me. He thought I just wanted to check out L.A. By then I was thirteen and he had just gotten his driver's license, so he was really happy to drive me anywhere." Serena took another bite of roll. "I didn't think she'd be there, but—"

"There she was," Jimena finished. "Me and

my home girls went to check out the address I saw in a dream."

"I never dreamed about her." Vanessa thought a moment. Her nightmares had always begun with black shadows covering the moon. And the other night she had dreamed of a woman riding the moon across the sky. The woman had said something before the shadows had seeped into the dream and hidden the moon.

"The Atrox must have sent you nightmares so Maggie couldn't talk to you in your dreams," Jimena mused.

"Maybe one of the Followers saw you go invisible," Serena added.

"A woman saw me once." Vanessa spoke slowly. "I was afraid she was going to tell my mother."

"But she didn't," Serena guessed.

"Yeah, 'cause she was one of them," Jimena said.

The nightmares had started after that. Was is just a coincidence?

"You want to go dancing?" Jimena asked. "We'll teach you some more moves.

Vanessa smiled. She admired girls who had enough nerve to dance the way they did. "You'll have to teach me *a lot*," she said, laughing. But suddenly she thought of Catty. How could she go out and have a good time when Catty was still missing?

"Actually, I better not," Vanessa decided. "I need to study."

"It's all right." Serena gave her a sympathetic look. "We can practice when Catty gets back."

Vanessa stacked her books and hurried outside. Tears came, uninvited.

CHAPTER TWENTY-ONE

VANESSA SAT AT HER desk, her geography book open to the same coffee-stained map of Japan. She couldn't tolerate sitting at home another evening knowing Catty was lost, even if it was in another dimension. There had to be something she could do. She wanted to go to the Hollywood Bowl and see if she could find any trace of Catty. Maybe she could find footprints. And then what? Even if she found a print, what could she do? Probably nothing. But the urge to return to the Bowl became greater as the minutes passed.

Her mother had always told her to follow her instincts. Intuition was an infallible guide. She slammed her book closed and crept to the top of the stairs. Voices and strained laughter came from the television downstairs. Her mother must have fallen asleep on the couch. It was late, past midnight. She didn't think her mother would check on her when she finally woke and staggered up to bed.

She went back to her room, pulled on a jacket, wrapped it tightly around her, and opened the window. She stood in the soft night breeze. The velvet darkness welcomed her. It was hard for Vanessa to make herself go invisible at will. Usually the feeling came, and she either fought it or gave in to it.

She closed her eyes. Silky moonbeams from the last quarter moon washed over her. She relaxed and stretched her imagination out to the stars. In her mind's eye she was in deep space, the blackness as warm and soft as a womb, then she came back to her body and again surged upward into the depths of the universe.

One by one her molecules lost their connection to gravity. They detached from each other with soft pings, until she was a gray mist, shimmering half inside, half outside her bedroom window. A cool breeze filtered through her body and she became one with the night.

She floated over the city. Traffic sounds, sirens, and horns seemed as far away as a dream. She sailed on a current of air over the Hollywood Walk of Fame, then caught a breeze up the hill, and hovered over the Hollywood Bowl. The concert had ended and workers were picking up trash.

She focused all her energy on tightening her molecules.

"Please let it work," she whispered.

Slowly she slid through the treetops and fell to earth, a trickle of vapor settling between eucalyptus trees and flat-leafed shrubs. Her molecules whisked together in a maelstrom that made her body sting. She stood, dazed with the pain for a moment, then stepped forward. Her feet crushed over dried leaves. Floodlights from the Bowl made long narrow shadows slant up the slope.

She stepped out on the ledge where she and Michael had sat. She picked up a paper plate, left behind in their haste. Ants crawled over the plate in single-line formation to steal the last stains of food in the paper. She stared at it and wondered if Catty had found it and held it, watching the ants as she did now, before she had fallen into a hole in time.

Something glowed in the tall dry grass near the edge. At first she ignored the sparkle. Then she stepped closer. Catty's watch lay tangled in the grass. Catty would never leave her watch behind. She had to see the hands to know which way she was traveling, past or future. Vanessa snapped the watch on her wrist. Another glint of light caught in the corner of her eye. Her heart lurched. Catty's moon amulet lay in loose gravel, the chain caught on a stone. She picked it up.

A twig snapped behind her. She turned quickly.

Stanton stood behind her, eyes intense.

She started to take a step back and caught herself. She balanced on the edge of the ledge. If she stepped back farther she would plummet to the cement seats below.

"I knew you'd come looking for Catty," he said, his voice as soft as the night.

"I thought you were out with Morgan," she said, trying to buy time.

"Morgan's here," he answered. "You shouldn't worry so much about your friend." He took her hand and pulled her from the ledge.

Her breath caught. With his face silhouetted against the dark, she knew why he was so curiously familiar.

"You?" she said as a cold knot of fear tightened in her stomach. "You followed me that night when I walked home from Planet Bang."

He smiled, eyes fervent. "Yes," he stated simply. "I've always been in the dark with you."

He pulled her closer to him. His head leaned down and he spoke against her cheek. Soft lips grazed her skin. "I can feel your heart racing. You shouldn't be afraid of me." His breath caressed her. "I've come to help you."

"Help me?" She glanced down. Catty's amulet glowed opalescent. Fiery pinks and blues shot into the dark.

"I've come to help you get Catty back."

"How?"

"Next Saturday, during the dark of the

moon, I'll take you to her."

"If you know where she is, why can't we go now?" she demanded.

"It must be during the dark of the moon," he explained.

"Why?"

He looked at her, then his hand gripped the back of her neck and forced her to look into his blue eyes. A black emptiness seemed to be voraciously trying to drag her in. His thoughts touched hers and then she knew. She pulled away. Everything Maggie had told her was true.

"Because my power is weakest then," she whispered in disbelief and wonder. "And you . . ."

"Yes." He nodded. "I am a Follower."

"You have Catty?"

"If you want her back, you'll go with me and surrender your power to the Atrox."

"My what?"

"Do you want me to say it?" he breathed into her ear. "Your invisibility."

She nodded.

"I'll be waiting around the corner from your house at the lost soul's hour."

"Which is . . . ?"

"Goddess, don't tell me you don't know?" He said *goddess* as if it were her rightful name.

Her hands started trembling. "I don't."

"The deepest part of night, two hours before it dawns."

She watched him walk away. The shadows closed around him. Disbelief mingled with her fear. This was crazy. What Maggie had told her couldn't be true, and yet it was.

She started up the hill. She hadn't gone far when she heard whimpering. At first she thought she was mistaken but the sound came again, a definite human lament. She pushed through gluey cobwebs and tripped over something large and soft.

"Morgan?" she whispered.

"Vanessa?" Morgan flicked on a flashlight hooked to her key chain. A tiny beam of light circled them. The air around Morgan felt thick with sadness. She looked as if she was about to cry, and then she grabbed Vanessa's arm and did. The tears fell warm on Vanessa's skin.

"Something's wrong," Morgan finally said

when she stopped crying. "I feel . . . so . . . empty."

"It's all right," Vanessa soothed, her own voice as thin as a ghost.

"I'm cold, so cold."

Vanessa took off her jacket and wrapped it around Morgan. Her skin felt rough with goose bumps.

"Did Stanton do something to you?" Vanessa asked when Morgan had finished crying again.

"Stanton?" Morgan echoed. She brushed her hand through her hair. Bits of leaves and dirt clung to her forehead. She didn't wipe them away.

"His friends—did they do something?"

"Who?"

Vanessa sat down beside her and put an arm around her. "Can you walk?"

"Maybe," Morgan said, but she didn't move. Even the smallest task seemed to require too much effort.

Vanessa stood, took her hand, and helped her to her feet. Dry grass and dirt covered her boots and thighs. "I'll take you home."

She and Morgan struggled up the steep slope. The wind had shifted and Vanessa could smell the salt spray on the damp air rolling in from the beach. She had a strange feeling that something had cut through the air and ripped a curtain between reality and another plane. And she had entered a shadow universe that few people see.

CHAPTER TWENTY-TWO

AN HOUR LATER, Morgan sat at the table in her mother's blue kitchen, a yellow afghan wrapped around her shoulders. Vanessa warmed a cup of milk in the microwave and set it on the oak table in front of her.

Morgan's housekeeper, Barushe, sat in a rumpled green robe at the opposite end of the table, staring at the wide plank flooring. Her round face said she was still trying to cast off the last remnants of a dream. Then she looked at Morgan and her kind eyes filled with understanding. She kissed the gold crucifix hanging around her neck.

"Can you call her parents and tell them they need to come home?" Vanessa asked.

"I'll call them." Barushe nodded and went to the phone.

Morgan sipped the milk. She held the cup with two hands like a small child and looked at Vanessa with a strange faraway stare.

Vanessa left through the back door. She followed the gray stone slabs around the swimming pool. The water echoed the moon's glow, adding gentle ripples to the reflection. She walked through the pool house. The scents of chlorine and wet bathing suits held the night until she opened the iron gate and stepped into the alley.

By the time she turned the corner to Maggie's apartment a line of deep gray pushed against the horizon, lifting the night. Men and women in bathrobes walked their dogs and sipped steaming cups of coffee.

She pushed the security button at the door to Maggie's apartment.

"Yes?" A voice came over the speaker.

"It's Vanessa."

The magnetic lock buzzed. Vanessa opened the door and hurried inside.

Maggie was waiting for her on the fourth-floor landing when the elevator doors slid open. She wasn't disguised as a retired schoolteacher this time. Her pale moon-blond hair curled around her head like a halo. She was more beautiful than Vanessa remembered.

Maggie smiled. "I knew you'd be back. Now, tell me what has happened that made you believe."

Vanessa told her about meeting Stanton and finding Morgan as they walked down the balcony to the apartment.

"Does that mean Morgan will become one of them now?"

"No, she can't become one simply by having hope taken from her," Maggie explained as she opened the door. "The Atrox doesn't come as a vampire does. Its victims must choose to be Followers."

Maggie and Vanessa entered the apartment.

"Unfortunately," Maggie continued, "evil is an easy choice once hope is gone. Without hope, people become desperate to escape the pain. They seldom see the rhythms in their own lives, how dark phases come before new beginnings. The victims seek the evil of the Atrox because anything feels better than the absolute nothing with which they are left. Violence confirms their existence and evil becomes their way of life. They can become very powerful and very dangerous. And, of course, the Atrox rewards their evil doings. Immortality is one gift it bestows. Now, sit down while I get us some chamomile tea."

Maggie came back from the kitchen, carrying a tray with a steaming teakettle and two cups. She poured hot water over yellow flowers in a strainer. "The dark of the moon is a time too dangerous for you to meet any of the Followers. I absolutely forbid it."

"I have to do something." Vanessa had thought Maggie would tell her all the secrets and send her charging back to rescue Catty.

"I know you're concerned for Catty. So am I. But you must take great care. These creatures of the Atrox are strongest during the dark of the moon when your power is weakest." She handed

Vanessa a cup of tea. "They have power to steal your thoughts, your dreams, your hope, and they can imprison you in their most evil memories. During the dark of the moon you won't be strong enough to resist their mind control."

Maggie sipped her tea, then added, "I must caution you—if they can stop one Daughter . . . eliminate her, then the power of all the Daughters is greatly weakened."

"But they already have Catty," Vanessa insisted.

"Yes, so there must be a reason the Atrox needs you," Maggie reasoned. "The Followers are probably holding Catty as a way to capture you. Perhaps, the Atrox has seen something in your future."

Maggie was thoughtful. "I had always thought it would be Serena because her power is so similar to that of the Followers. She can penetrate minds and see things people keep hidden even from themselves. But maybe . . . maybe it is you, Vanessa. Maybe you are the key, the one who will find the way to wipe out darkness permanently."

"Then why didn't they kill me before?"

"Kill you? No, my dear, the key can turn both ways. If you are the key, then you can be used to increase either the powers of the dark, or the light. If you are the key, the Atrox means to seduce you and have your soul."

Vanessa felt a chill pass through her. "How do I defeat it?"

"Simply by being on the side of good. It's water on a flame, when someone laughs or loves or sings with joy."

Vanessa wanted a simple answer. A silver bullet, a stake through the heart, something definite and precise, but could she do that? Kill? She hesitated a moment, then spoke. "I could never kill anything."

"No, of course not, we never use the tools of the Atrox. Violence only feeds the Atrox. The Followers grow stronger when people use the tools of the Atrox to fight. They become utterly invincible then, because you have unwittingly chosen evil as your defense. You are a force of good. You must always remember that."

"But how can I defeat something if I can't fight it?"

"With the power inside you. As a Daughter

of the Moon, you will know intuitively when the moon is full. So take heart, be brave. It will come naturally to you."

"Then I'm dead for sure," Vanessa mumbled. "Nothing has ever come easy for me."

"This month has a Blue Moon, a fairy night. We'll bring Catty back then. I promise. Now run along home and be safe. Take no chances while I make plans."

"But what will happen to Catty if I wait?"

"If they keep her long enough, I suppose she could willingly turn. But you must promise me that you won't do anything."

"I thought I was supposed to save the world from the Atrox?"

"Yes, but you are too vulnerable during the dark of the moon. And this Dark moon is especially bad coming in the tenth month of the New Millennium It is the Blood Moon. Very risky. Promise me!"

Vanessa hesitated. "I swear."

CHAPTER TWENTY-THREE

BY THURSDAY VANESSA was seriously worried about Morgan. She hadn't come to school, and today was the day they were supposed to sign up to decorate for homecoming.

After school, Vanessa stopped at a newsstand on Fairfax. She bought Morgan's favorite magazines and then caught the bus to her house.

Barushe answered the door. She had a strained look of fear on her face. "I'm glad you're here. Her parents can't come home until next week." She glanced up as if she expected Morgan to suddenly appear at the top of the stairs.

"How is she?"

"I'll show you," Barushe said. "Let me get her tea first."

Vanessa followed Barushe to the kitchen. She had fixed a tray with lemon tea and cookies.

"We'll use the back stairs." Barushe motioned with her head as she picked up the tray.

Vanessa followed her up the narrow winding staircase that led upstairs from the pantry next to the kitchen.

At the end of the hallway Barushe pushed a door open with her foot and led Vanessa into Morgan's bedroom. The first thing she noticed was the odd smell. Barushe had placed bouquets of wild mountain thyme in glass jars and strung garlic across the windows and around the iron bedpost. Barushe came from Romania. Maybe she thought Morgan had fallen prey to a younger evil, one for which garlic and thyme were charms.

Morgan lay in bed, a pink quilt wrapped around her in spite of the heat. Her hair was swept up in a knot on the top of her head, and without makeup she looked pale and childlike.

Barushe set the tray on the bed. "A friend has come to see you." Barushe glanced worriedly at Vanessa, then left the room quickly and closed the door behind her.

"Hi, Morgan," Vanessa said, her voice overly cheerful.

Morgan stared at her, eyes flat. "Hi." She turned her head and a strand of hair fell in front of her eyes. She didn't brush it away.

"I brought you some magazines." Vanessa placed them next to the telephone on the nightstand. The red digital light flashed thirty-two messages. That explained why Morgan hadn't called her back.

"You've got calls," Vanessa pointed out. "Don't you want to hear them?"

Morgan shrugged. "Whatever."

A reflection of sunlight caught Vanessa's eye. She looked down. A razor blade sat in the ring holder next to the telephone. She glanced back at Morgan. The covers were too tightly wrapped around her to see if she had tried to cut herself.

Vanessa sat on the edge of the bed.

"We missed you at school," Vanessa tried again.

Morgan didn't answer.

"Do you remember anything that happened?"

"I," she started, and then looked out the window before she continued. "I was dancing and . . ."

"And?"

"I think." She sighed. "I don't know what to think. What does it matter anyway?"

"I want to help you."

Morgan looked at her. Her dull eyes seemed unable to focus. Her hand reached out from the covers for the tea. Thin brownish-red scabs sliced down her wrist.

She saw Vanessa looking at the cuts as she sipped the tea.

"I can't cry anymore," she whispered, as if that explained the marks on her arm. She set the cup down and studied the ragged lines on her skin.

"Has Barushe seen the cuts?" Vanessa's uneasiness was rising. What had Morgan tried to do? Her concern quickly turned to self-blame; she should have come over sooner.

Morgan looked confused for a moment, then

a slow smile crept over her face. "Barushe keeps looking at my throat for puncture wounds." She tried to laugh but the sound came out wrong. "You think that's what she told my parents?" Morgan said. "Is that why they haven't come home? They think Barushe is being hysterical?"

"Why don't you call them?"

"Maybe later." Morgan sighed. "What's the use?"

Vanessa took Morgan's hand. The skin was wet and cold. "Remember when you talked to me about Catty over at Urth?"

Morgan shook her head.

"You said you'd want everyone to keep trying to find you if you were missing."

"So?"

"So I'm going to keep trying to find you until I get you back. I have a friend who might be able to help."

Morgan's eyes shined with tears and her chin quivered, but then her face hardened. Her lip raised in a show of contempt. "No one can help me."

"She can," Vanessa insisted. "Let me help you get dressed and we'll go visit her. She opened the closet door, turned on the light and walked in. The clothes were arranged by colors. Long shelves held shoes, sweaters, and purses. She grabbed a gray hooded sweatshirt and black flared pants and brought them back to the bed.

"Put these on," Vanessa instructed. "I'll go talk to Barushe."

Morgan looked at the clothes as if she didn't understand.

"Dress," Vanessa explained.

"Get my five-pocket carpenter's," Morgan ordered.

"You got it," Vanessa said, and smiled with confidence. If Morgan could think about clothes, she wasn't completely lost. She hurried into the closet pulled the denim pants from a hanger and brought them back.

Morgan took the pants and stared at the brass button, zipper, and tie as if she were trying to recall how to work them.

Vanessa hurried back downstairs. Barushe was waiting for her at the bottom of the stairs.

"I am so grateful you came to see her," Barushe said. "Her other friends—"

"Other friends? Who?" Vanessa was suddenly alert. Morgan was popular. She had lots of friends, but they weren't close friends who would worry about her absence at school.

"Tymmie and Cassandra," Barushe said. "I think the other one's name is Karyl." She made a face like she was tasting something sour. "I don't like them."

The doorbell rang.

Vanessa grabbed Barushe's hand. "Is that them?"

Barushe looked at her oddly. "I don't know. Maybe."

"Barushe." Vanessa was forming a plan as she spoke. "I don't think Morgan should see them."

Barushe was silent.

"I'm going to take Morgan with me."

"She can't leave."

"She shouldn't see them," Vanessa said again, and lifted her eyes toward the door. "I'll take her down the back stairs and over to a friend's house."

Barushe looked uncertain.

"Can you tell them she's sleeping? Please. Give me enough time to get Morgan away."

Barushe nodded but her eyes looked nervous.

Vanessa hurried back to Morgan's bedroom. She took Morgan's hand. "We're leaving."

Morgan looked at her blankly.

Vanessa tugged. "Come on."

Morgan followed reluctantly down the hallway to the back stairs. Vanessa could hear Barushe talking to Tymmie.

"No, she's sleeping." Barushe spoke with a slight tremor in her voice.

"We'll wake her up then," Tymmie replied.

"Like Sleeping Beauty," Karyl snickered.

"I better go see my friends," Morgan said in a dazed kind of way.

Vanessa pushed her out the back door. "Not now."

It was after seven when she finally had Morgan in Maggie's apartment. Maggie didn't seem surprised by Morgan's condition.

She sat Morgan in a chair and stood behind her. "They have stolen some of her thoughts, maybe, but at least she's not imprisoned in their memories. Her soul needs to visit the spirit-world for healing." Maggie gently touched Morgan's hair.

"Can you do that?"

Maggie smiled as if Vanessa had asked a silly question. "People do it every day in prayer. You go on now. I'll make sure she gets home."

Vanessa started for the door.

"Vanessa," Maggie called as she opened the door. "Remember your promise."

Vanessa nodded and left.

On the way home, she looked at her hands. They were trembling. Fear was a mild word compared to what she was feeling. She realized then that she had made her decision. She knew now what she had to do.

CHAPTER TWENTY-FOUR

SATURDAY NIGHT, Vanessa lay curled in her covers, waiting for her mother to fall asleep. She was going to meet Stanton. She didn't see that she had a choice. She had to defy Maggie. What if she waited and something happened to Catty? She couldn't let them do to Catty what they had already done to Morgan. And if they had already? That was even more reason to go now and rescue her. She threw back the blankets and crept down the hallway to the third bedroom where her mother stored the clothing she designed for movies.

She opened the door and walked inside. The room smelled of dust and mothballs. She flicked on a light and searched through the dresses hanging on racks. She held a scarlet sequin dress to her chest and posed in front of the mirror. Too hot. She put it back and took a black mini. Too dreary. Then a blue as pale as a whisper caught her eye. She took the dress. The material was silky and clinging. Perfect for a goddess. On the floor below the dress sat strappy wraparound high-heeled sandals that matched the blue.

She didn't understand why she needed to dress up to meet Stanton but the impulse to steal into the storage room had been rising in her since the sun set.

She took the dress and sandals back to her room, then sat on the floor and painted her toenails and fingernails pale blue. She drew waves of eternal flames and spiral hearts in silver and blue around her ankles and up her legs with body paints.

When she was done, she pressed a Q-tip into glitter eye shadow and spread sparkles on her lid and below her eye. With a sudden impulse she swirled the lines over her temple and into her hairline. She liked the look.

She rolled blue mascara on her lashes, then brushed her hair and snapped crystals in the long blond strands. She squeezed glitter lotion into her palms and rubbed it on her shoulders and arms. Last she took the dress and stepped into it. She turned to the mirror on the closet door.

A thrill ran through her. Her reflection astonished her. She looked otherworldly, a mystical creature . . . eyes large, skin glowing, eyelashes longer, thicker. Everything about her was more powerful and sleek and fairy tale. Surely this wasn't really happening. Maybe she would wake up and run to school and tell Catty about her crazy dream. But another part of her knew this was real.

She leaned to one side. The dress exposed too much thigh.

"Good." Her audacity surprised her. Another time she would have changed her dress. But why should she?

She took Catty's moon amulet from her dresser and placed it around her neck, next to her own. When the two charms touched, silver sparks cascaded from the metals and remained bright stars on her skin.

She grabbed the shoes, tiptoed down the hallway to her mother's room, and crept inside. She kissed her mother good-bye. The kiss remained visible on her mother's forehead, all rainbow and glitter dust.

Finally, she turned, back straight and strong, and walked through the still house and out the front door. She sat on the porch steps and put on her sandals. As she tied the straps, it came to her with a sudden shock. She had been preparing for battle like a medieval knight, or an ancient warrior, with ritual and ceremony.

She stood. She felt ready.

She strolled luxuriously down the dark empty street as if she owned the night. Her heels clicked nicely on the cement walk. She didn't feel self-conscious or fearful that people might see her. She felt good in her body, thrilled to belong in it. She whooped. It was a war cry. The lights in the house beside her flicked on.

Let them peek out their windows and see me, she thought.

Stanton had told her he would be waiting around the corner from her house the night she met him in the hills surrounding the Hollywood Bowl. She felt his presence before she even turned the corner.

Stanton stood silent against his car, his blond hair tousled in the night breeze. The car was sleek black metal, low to the ground, and spitting reflections from the street lamps. He glanced up when he saw her but didn't move. His blues eyes met hers, and she glimpsed something predatory in them.

He took three quick steps toward her. She tried hard to keep herself steady. She didn't flinch. She wouldn't let herself feel afraid. The air between them prickled with static electricity. He smiled and she thought for a moment he was going to kiss her.

"I didn't think you would come." His breath was sweet and warm and mingled with hers.

"I'm here for Catty."

She saw something in his eyes then. Was it disappointment? Maybe it had only been her imagination. He turned as if he didn't want her to look in his eyes and walked away from her, his slow easy steps echoing into the night. He opened the car door. She followed him and started to climb into the car but stopped. She saw her image in the car window. A goddess. Her breath caught, heartbeat quickened. She couldn't pull away from her reflection. It was as if the warrior goddess had emerged, and she looked less human, more dangerously beautiful. Stanton seemed to know what had stopped her.

"That's how I've always seen you," he said. "Since the first night."

Her head jerked around and she caught something in his eyes before they turned hard again. It wasn't her imagination this time. She definitely saw something gentle and caring.

"What do you mean by the first night? How long have you been watching me?"

"Awhile," he smiled mysteriously. He took her hand and helped her into the car.

Her dress was too short and rode up her thighs. Her long legs stretched in front of her, glistening with glitter and entwined with flames and hearts.

He jumped in the driver's seat, then turned the key in the ignition. The engine roared like slow, thick thunder. The car pulled away, and they drove toward the southeast side of Los Angeles. He merged into traffic on the Hollywood Freeway. Headlights cast light and shadow across their faces. They rode in uncomfortable silence, her body too aware of his presence. She took a deep breath, trying to calm herself and glanced at him.

"Is Catty all right?"

"You'll see soon." He cut in front of a speeding car.

"How did you . . ." she started to ask, but her mouth was so dry her words caught in her throat. She had to be braver. Finally, she asked, "How did you become a Follower?"

He glanced at her, then back at the freeway. "You don't need to know"

She took another long breath. "I was just wondering if someone did to you what you did to Morgan." There was too much challenge in her voice. She regretted it as soon as the words were spoken.

He grabbed her hand.

"Let me show you, then." He drew her to him, forcing her to look in his eyes.

His eyes were startlingly compelling. She tried to pull away. She grabbed the steering wheel. The car swerved. A car honked and three cars sped around them.

Against her will, she felt herself pulled into his memories. She struggled desperately, trying to resist the terrible force. Then his mind was in hers, but it wasn't as horrible as she had imagined. He seemed to be holding back as if he were afraid to frighten her. Then his memories flooded into her, coming so quickly they spun inside her, as if he had waited a long time to share them with someone. She clutched his hand tightly. She was afraid that if his hand let go she would remain lost in his memories. She saw a small blond boy hugging his grandfather's tombstone. The same boy running after his mother when she left him in the care of another couple. And the boy waving good-bye to a man in plate armor riding a prancing black horse. The sad feelings associated with the memories overwhelmed her. His fear and grief and loneliness. Then she felt something else. Something she was sure he had wanted her to see. He had been following her that night a month back, but not to harm her, he had wanted to warn her. Of what? He had stopped following her when he felt the shadows of the Atrox watching him.

She could feel his sudden hesitation now, his need to hide those feelings and memories from her. Then his hand let go and she was falling into a deep black hole. She tried to grab the car seat. Her hands swooshed through empty air. There was nothing but darkness around her.

She had been deceived so easily. Now she was lost. What had Maggie said? The Followers had the power to imprison you in their most evil memories.

She tumbled in the black void.

Then she landed painfully on a cold rock floor.

She stood. Behind her milky light fell through a small window in a damp stone wall. She looked outside. A turret was above her, below a moat. The rising stench from the moat waters made her gag. She was in a castle. She must have been transported back in time as well. Is this where they held Catty captive?

The great hall behind her filled with a soft whimper. Was it Catty? At least they would be together.

She followed the sound to a plank wood door. She pushed against the heavy wood. The door opened slowly with a soft groan. She peered inside. Gradually her eyes adjusted to the utter darkness. A small boy sat on a large bed, crying. He didn't seem aware of her presence. His eyes held something in the corner of the room.

She stepped to his bed. Unnatural shadows gathered overhead. Like black thunder clouds, the shadows surged and grew. Was that the Atrox? Suddenly, the shadows swept toward the boy. He shrieked and pulled the covers over his head.

Stanton might have deceived her and trapped her in another time, but she could still save this child. She pushed through the frenzied shadows and grabbed the boy. His body felt cold and thin as bones on an altar. She held him tight against her and ran.

The dark shadows swirled in anger, then

charged after her with a savage whip of air. She staggered. The boy screamed.

"Don't cry," she soothed. "I'll find a way to get us out."

She ran from the room with the crying child down a vast hall. The furor of the shadows shook the stone walls.

At the end of the hall she entered a dark stairwell. The steps were twisting, steep, and narrow. She kept her shoulder against the wall for balance and plunged downward. The boy sobbed in her neck. His tears ran down her back.

The shadows whipped down the stairwell with tumultuous fury, howling like a squall. She tripped and fell. A force greater than she could have imagined stripped the child from her arms. She struggled to stand. Her hands searched frantically in the dark for the boy.

His crying became farther and farther away. Then he was gone.

A demon-dark shadow eclipsed the others. She knew instinctively that it was the Atrox. It seeped into her lungs with complete coldness. She struggled to breathe.

A hand reached through the darkness and grasped hers. It yanked hard.

Suddenly she was back in the car, clasping Stanton's hand. She gasped for air. Had she only been lost in his memory? It had felt so real. What would have happened if he had not pulled her back?

"You tried to save me," he whispered. "That was the night the Atrox took me from my home. You were going to fight the Atrox." His finger wiped a child's tear from her neck and held it in front of her eyes as proof.

"I'm sorry I didn't save you." She kissed the tear on the tip of his finger.

He seemed overcome with emotion. He snapped his hand back and tapped the steering wheel.

"No one could have saved me anyway." He stared ahead of him, but when he spoke she saw a quick flicker of doubt cross his eyes. He seemed to be saying the words to convince himself.

He turned off the freeway into a dark and dangerous part of town. They were in an industrial area. Bleak warehouses lined the street.

"What happened that night?" she asked.

"That was the night I lost who I once was." His voice choked. "Now I can no longer remember the person I used to be."

"But why did it take you when you were just a boy?"

"My father was a great prince of western Europe during the thirteenth century. He'd raised an army to go on a crusade," Stanton said.

"So he left you alone."

"My father didn't go on a crusade to the Holy Land. It was a crusade against the Atrox. The Atrox knew that by taking me, it could stop my father."

Without being aware of what she was doing, her hand reached out to comfort him. She held his cold fingers. He looked at her with a different kind of longing then. Maybe no one had ever tried to comfort him before. He jerked his hand away as if her pity were too painful for him to endure. But before his hand left hers, a deeper knowledge seeped into her fingers. There was a part of him that wanted to escape his dark destiny.

"Maybe there is a way to reclaim your soul," she offered.

"It was my choice," he insisted.

"You can make another choice."

"You can't understand what it means to have lost hope, because you still have it." He seemed angry now.

"I'm sorry," she said quietly.

She thought he was going to cry, but instead he smiled. That was far worse. It was a sad imitation of a smile, devoid of warmth and joy.

"Party time." His foot slammed on the accelerator and the car skidded around the corner.

The new street was filled with cars and people waiting for the next band to play. Music blasted from car radios and heart-thumping stereos. Richter-scale blasts vibrated the cars' exteriors. Girls sat in car windows, waving and flirting and flaunting their bodies. Guys in low-crotch jeans and baseball hats with clique initials showed off their custom cars. Others cruised looking for girls, checking things out.

Stanton parked the car. He got out, walked around the car, and opened her door. He put his hands around her waist and lifted her out. Only then did she realize how incredibly strong he was.

He kissed her then, a surprise, but so gentle and sweet, she let him. She wondered if Persephone had fallen in love with Hades when he abducted her and took her to live in the underworld. There must be a way to rescue him from this, she thought.

He put his arm around her and shoved through the crowd of kids waiting to go back inside the warehouse.

At the entrance, two large security guards frisked boys and opened purses. They confiscated pencils and pens, anything that could be turned into a weapon.

"Everything out of your pockets," a huge security guard said to Stanton. "Anything I find left in your pockets is mine."

Stanton glared at the man. "I don't think so."

The security guard took a stunned step backward as if he had seen something in Stanton's eyes that made him afraid.

Stanton pushed around him and he and

Vanessa entered the warehouse. It was noisy inside and Vanessa could feel the impatience rising in the crowd, anxious for the music to start again.

Security guards righted white metal barriers and set them in front of the stage. A large sign hung above them: MOSHING AND CROWD SURFING NOT ALLOWED.

Catty stood between Cassandra and Tymmie. She didn't smile when she saw Vanessa. She looked quickly away. But not before Tymmie caught her look and followed it to Vanessa. He nudged Cassandra. The razor cuts on her chest were now covered with scabs. She looked at Vanessa with a hungry smile.

"How do I surrender my power?" Vanessa whispered to Stanton as the band ran onstage. The restless audience screamed and applauded.

"You don't," Stanton said and stepped away.

"I thought we were going to trade."

"Sorry."

"For what?" she asked.

"I lied," he said simply.

The music started with a piercing scream. The crowd crushed forward, knocking over two barriers. Stanton jumped back as the crowd surged toward the stage.

Vanessa was squished into the mob. Then she saw Catty. She struggled around bobbing bodies over to her.

"You shouldn't have come," Catty yelled. "Now they'll have you, too!"

Vanessa looked at the faces of the kids around them. Most of them were ordinary moshers, ravers, and punkers, but then she saw the angry faces of Cassandra, Tymmie, and Karyl staring back at her. Too late, she realized the plan had always been to destroy them both. It was so obvious now. Stanton had betrayed her. But why shouldn't he? What had made her trust him? Maggie had warned her.

Cassandra and Karyl pressed closer. She could feel their thoughts invade her mind, a spectacle of swirling terrifying pictures.

"Don't look in their eyes," Catty warned, and yanked her away.

The band went full speed into punk rock.

The crowd around them exploded into thrashing fists and jumping bodies, knocking Cassandra and Karyl away.

Security guards ran to the slam pit and tried to stop the hitting and shoving and head butting, but it was like trying to stop a train.

Vanessa grabbed Catty's hand as the fury of the crowd shoved them deeper into the mosh pit away from the Followers. A boy tore off his T-shirt and climbed on the shoulders of his friends. Hands grabbed him, held, touched, and pulled him across the heads of the audience, crowd surfing.

A girl climbed onto the stage, struggled around the security guards, and jumped into the crowd. Vanessa ducked as the girl landed on the sea of hands. Catty ducked too late. The girl's boot thumped Catty hard in the forehead.

Surrender, Goddess. The thought hit Vanessa with the sharp strike of a headache. She turned quickly. Cassandra, Karyl, and Tymmie were back. Karyl's eyes caught her and seemed to expand. She had a sudden mental image of Catty crushed beneath jumping feet. Karyl smiled, his eyes deep and mocking. Had he done that? She winced and the trance broke.

The music became a clash of air-ripping tones and head-splintering beats. The thrum of guitars and drums pulsated in Vanessa's head, but it was the other pounding inside her mind that frightened her. Karyl and Tymmie and Cassandra pushed into her thoughts. *Turn. Come back.* She crawled on the sticky floor through jumping, kicking bodies. She was only three feet from Catty now, an impossible distance.

Cassandra's thoughts grabbed Vanessa and twisted into her mind. *You're mine now, Goddess.* Cassandra sent the words screaming through Vanessa's head. She look at Vanessa and smiled, her pale face and garish makeup looked hellish in the flash of the strobe light. Vanessa tried to laugh. What had Maggie said about water on a flame? But she couldn't make her mind focus. She looked in Cassandra's blank eyes and saw tiny images of herself imprisoned in the black pupils. A cold electric feeling invaded her mind like tiny metal worms. Her fears and worries suddenly fell away. Only Cassandra's eyes and Vanessa's need to obey her remained.

Someone bumped into them and the two moon amulets hanging around Vanessa's neck slid against each other. Silver sparks flew from the metals, and Cassandra's eyes flashed with white fire as bright sparks burned into her skin. Vanessa blinked. The spell was broken. Her fear returned. She yanked away, lost her balance, and sprawled on top of Catty. She tried to protect Catty from the hammering feet.

A heavy metal guy in a black T-shirt and silver chains saw their trouble and attempted to help them up, but Karyl appeared from nowhere and head-butted him. The boy staggered back, clutching his forehead.

The music became louder and sent the audience into renewed frenzy. Girls unbuttoned their blouses and flashed the band.

Vanessa reached for Catty's hand. Maybe she could make them both invisible. She tried to concentrate but each kick sent new pain racking through her.

So much for the warrior, she thought and gave in to the hurricane of trampling feet.

Kids surfed the crowd and slammed about.

No one noticed Vanessa and Catty being trampled on the mosh pit floor.

Vanessa felt herself melting into the pain that tore through her body when a hand grabbed her and pulled her up.

CHAPTER TWENTY-FIVE

KARYL DRAGGED VANESSA away from the crowd.

"Failed goddess," he smirked. "Look in my eyes to save your friend."

She knew it was another lie, but she was too weak to pull away. His eyes held hers. She felt herself falling again. Another memory? It was different this time. She could feel hope ebbing from her. Was this what Morgan felt? An inhospitable cold swirled deep inside her and still she could not look away.

"Stop," she begged. She doubted Karyl could

hear her over the maelstrom of music. She continued to fall. Her lungs burned for oxygen. Her heart was on fire. She felt dizzy. The dizziness brought up tears and unhappy dreams from some hidden place behind her heart where she had tucked so many disappointments. Tears pushed into her eyes.

Then she heard someone calling, the voice barely audible, like a whisper on the wind. Impossible. It had to be her imagination. A voice in her mind was telling her not to look. It was Stanton.

If you look too long in his eyes, Stanton's voice whispered across her mind, *you'll be lost. He's stealing your life force, your hope.*

She closed her eyes.

"Look at me," Karyl ordered, shaking her.

She felt Karyl push away, and then Stanton took her in his arms.

"Come to my world," Stanton ordered. "It's the only way I can save you."

"Save me?"

"They will destroy you."

"But I'm the key. Don't they need me?"

"No, Vanessa, you're not the key," Stanton said. "It's a special night for the Atrox. If two Daughters of the Moon are destroyed during the night of the Nefardus moon, the power balance shifts in favor of the dark. The only way I can save you now is to make you one of us. Of your own free will, join me to save yourself."

At that moment, she wanted him and his world. Why not give up the struggle? It would be so easy. She shook her head. "What about the people I'm supposed to protect?"

"Save yourself," he repeated.

"I don't want a life like yours."

"I can't harm you, because you performed an act of kindness to save me when I was a boy," he said. "But I can't protect you from the others."

Karyl ripped her away from Stanton and he let her go without a struggle. She could feel Karyl in her mind like an electrical current and already part of her wanted to turn and gaze in his eyes and fall into that sweet dangerous peace.

With renewed energy and determination she fought the images Karl was pushing into her mind and pictured the full moon instead. She wasn't going to die like this. Power filled her body. She closed her eyes and let her mind expand to the ends of the universe. Her molecules loosened. She floated through his grasping hands.

She found Catty and became visible again. She didn't care who might see. She tore Catty's amulet from her own neck and pressed it into Catty's hand. It had been a long time since she had tried to make anyone invisible with her, and her powers were weak.

She held Catty's hand as the Followers pushed through the crowd toward them. She could feel Cassandra's thoughts clasp hold. And then Tymmie's. She was determined not to let them overpower her this time. Her amulet began to glow. Energy seared through her like a burst of flame. She pulled Catty up and stood as Karyl attacked.

"Vanessa," Catty warned weakly.

A strange light from the amulet struck Karyl's face and he instantly stepped back, surprised. What had stopped him? The amulet? Did it have powers?

Cassandra and Tymmie circled, a strange grin of torment on their faces.

"Why aren't they attacking?" Catty said.

Vanessa didn't answer. She couldn't. The power inside her felt too strong. It pulsed through every cell. Then an unearthly glow shimmered protectively around them and they rose like silver smoke into the air.

They floated over the crowd. As they neared the exit, something drew her eyes back to Stanton. He was charming and handsome in a threatening and seductive way. He stared up at her even though she was sure he couldn't see her. He had betrayed her, then saved her, only to betray her again. But looking at him now and seeing how sad he looked, she felt sorry for him. She thought of his offer. Did he love her? Too late she realized she shouldn't have looked back. She had lost her concentration. Her molecules clustered.

Catty became dense and slipped from her grasp. Her molecules reformed rapidly and she dropped toward the crowd. Vanessa tumbled close behind her.

They hit the crowd. Hands grabbed their arms, legs, and stomachs and carried them over the bobbing heads.

Vanessa prayed the swell of hands would carry them to the barricades and drop them into the arms of the waiting security guards. Then they could run backstage and out to safety.

But the hands carried them the wrong way, back to the Followers.

CHAPTER TWENTY-SIX

THE HANDS DROPPED Vanessa in front of Cassandra.

"Goddess." Cassandra said the word like a curse.

"Nice to have you back." Tymmie grinned, his eyes blank and deep.

They crowded around her, their thoughts pushing into her mind. She tried to escape through the mangle of pounding arms and feet, but when she saw Karyl clutching Catty, something sparked inside her. She flung herself at him. He stumbled backward, stunned. Too late she remembered Maggie's warning about using the tools of the Atrox. He turned and snickered. His thin face fired with a horrible rage, and his pupils dilated.

Vanessa steadied herself for his assault, but it never came. She opened her eyes.

Karyl stood still, staring at the entrance. The throng in the mosh pit stopped jumping and pushing. Faces turned. The singer in the band lost his words and stared at something in the audience.

The crowd stood still. Something bigger than the full-speed rock hysteria had taken hold.

"What's going on?" Catty asked.

"I don't know yet." And then Vanessa knew. "It's Serena and Jimena."

Serena and Jimena walked into the crowd, strides long and seductive. Jimena wore a silver bustier and capris with matching sandals. Her hair was rolled on top of her head with glitter and jewels. Curls bounced with each step. Her face gleamed; her full lips sparkled. The tattoos on her arms seemed iridescent. She whooped and squealed and gave Serena a high five.

Serena had moussed her hair so it stood on

end. Streaks of orange glitter shot from her temples into her hair. She wore a yellow tulle skirt over a sheer, clingy red dress and looked like a walking flame.

The strobe light flickered, making the entire room surreal.

"Non aliquis incipit convivium sine nobis," Jimena yelled.

"Nos sumus convivium!" Serena joined in.

Vanessa wondered if it was a curse or an incantation.

Their silver moon amulets caught the flashing strobe light and threw magic rainbows across the faces of the Followers. Cassandra squealed and put her hands in front of her eyes. Tymmie and Karyl glared.

"Hey, boys," Jimena said to the band and stood with her hand on a hip thrust to the side. "Where's the music? We came here to party."

The bass player smiled. The drummer nodded, and music crashed through the room. The velocity gained with each beat of the drum. The guitars sent metallic notes into the air like machine-gun fire. The corrugated walls of the warehouse vibrated. The mosh pit spun into slam dancing.

Vanessa felt a strange thrum against her chest. She looked down. The light from her own amulet was so strong she had to look away.

Serena gestured to Karyl and Tymmie, wiggling her fingers in an enticing way "Come on, bad boys, we're here to play. That's what you wanted."

Tymmie and Karyl smiled dangerously. Their power came like an invisible wave pushing against her. Vanessa took an involuntary step backward. The force of their thoughts didn't seem to affect Jimena or Serena.

"Well?" Jimena was expectant, head cocked to one side.

Cassandra joined Tymmie and Karyl. Her thoughts came like hellish screams. Vanessa grabbed her ears, even though she knew the piercing noise was inside her head.

Jimena and Serena stood perfectly still, as if the screams didn't bother them.

Frustrated, Cassandra lunged and swung. Jimena ducked. The nails missed Jimena's cheek by inches. Jimena shined the light from her amulet into Cassandra's eyes.

Cassandra grabbed her eyes and tumbled away. But it was something more than the amulet that had stopped Cassandra. Vanessa could feel it now, a dangerously benevolent power that billowed from Jimena and Serena.

Tymmie grabbed Serena and Karyl stared into her eyes. The pupils in Serena's eyes expanded. Vanessa could feel the force of their struggle. Her head pounded with the energy.

Finally, Karyl stumbled backward. Then Serena swung around and shined her amulet in Tymmie's eyes, but again Vanessa knew it was something more than the power of the amulet that made Tymmie look confused and stagger before he turned and ran.

Serena turned to face Karyl again. The skin tightened against his skull as if anger and hatred burned inside him. His power vibrated through Vanessa in an ominously exciting way, his thoughts sweetly seductive and irresistible. Her eyes drifted to him. She wondered if Serena was also drowning in his eyes.

Then Jimena touched her. She snapped back with a wrench of her neck.

"Take Catty and go outside to the car." She stood protectively in front of them.

Vanessa concentrated until she and Catty were as weightless as moonbeams. Then they drifted up and over the crowd. She glanced down at Stanton. She could feel his eyes saying their battle wasn't done. She looked away.

Outside fog had settled on the ground. She pulled her molecules together and slowly drifted back to earth next to Jimena's car.

Catty hugged her fiercely. She almost lost her balance. "Thank you, Vanessa."

"How did they catch you?" Vanessa squeezed Catty tightly.

"I was doing my leapfrog back to Saturday night. It worked," she said with excitement. "But Karyl, Tymmie, and Cassandra were following you that night at the Bowl. I got too close, and they grabbed me. I was so drained from all the time-twisting that I couldn't get away. They kept me prisoner. You can't imagine what it was like reliving time with them. I still can't figure out why they were following you."

"There's something I've been wanting to tell you," Vanessa began. "You're not a space alien."

"No?" Catty's voice seemed disappointed. "What am I, then?"

"A goddess."

"Yeah, right, would a goddess have trouble pulling a comb through her hair? Or get so many bruises?" She held out her arms.

"For real, not a space person, you're a goddess."

"A goddess," Catty repeated, as if she were tasting the word. "Yeah, I always knew."

"You did not." Vanessa laughed.

"Sure I did," Catty said, and then she was crying in Vanessa's arms.

Serena and Jimena ran out to the car, exhilarated and glowing.

"*¡Ándale!* Hurry," Jimena urged, "before they get to changing their minds and decide they want to fight some more."

They climbed in the car. Jimena turned the key in the ignition. The mufflers thundered.

As the car pulled away, a new worry filled Vanessa. She had promised Maggie she wouldn't meet Stanton, and now she had defied her. She was sure there was going to be a punishment. Would she take away her power? She didn't want to lose it now. Her stomach churned with apprehension.

Jimena stopped the car in front of Maggie's apartment and got out. She turned to Vanessa. "Maggie said we had to bring you back here after.

They walked up to the front door and pushed the security button. There was no answer.

"Push it again," Serena said.

Suddenly Maggie appeared, breathless, behind them. "Sorry I'm late. I had to take Vanessa's friend Morgan home."

"She's all right?" Vanessa asked.

"Of course."

Then Vanessa took a deep breath. She didn't know if she should try to apologize now, or wait until after Maggie told her what her punishment would be.

"Vanessa . . ." Maggie started.

"I know I failed," Vanessa cut in, and felt hot tears press into her eyes.

"Failed? No, not at all."

"I didn't fail? But you made me promise to do nothing. You said I had no choice."

"I had to test you, Vanessa," Maggie said. "Yes, I needed to make sure you were willing to risk everything to do what was right. Saving Catty was the right choice." She placed her soft hand on Vanessa's cheek. "You are one of those daughters upon whom Selene has bestowed great gifts. She has given you magnanimity of spirit, physical energy, and courage."

Vanessa felt a strange glow tremble through her. She glanced at Serena and Jimena and saw relief on their faces as well, and then she looked at Catty, who looked totally confused.

"Welcome, my last daughter."

Catty smiled. "You're the lady from my dreams. You're real! How cool!"

They went upstairs to the apartment. The room smelled of ginger and cinnamon and glowed from candles placed around the room. The table was set for tea. They sat down and Maggie poured tea as Serena and Jimena told her what had happened.

"You all did well tonight," Maggie praised

them. "And to think this is the Nefandus Moon, a dark moon special to the Atrox. Very good, my dears."

"They're not defeated," Jimena said.

"But they're been stopped on a very momentous night, and my daughters are still together."

Maggie talked quickly as she wrapped Catty's arms in bandages and applied a slippery goo to the cut on her forehead. She told Catty everything that she had explained to Vanessa about the Atrox and its followers. When she finished, she added something Vanessa hadn't heard before: "Your gift only lasts until you are seventeen, and then there's a metamorphosis. You have to make the most important choice of your life. Either you can choose to lose your powers and your memory of what you once were, or you disappear. The ones who disappear become something else, guardian spirits perhaps. No one really knows."

The girls sat silently, taking it all in.

Then Vanessa remembered the strange words that Serena and Jimena had spoken. "What were the incantations you yelled when you came in to rescue Catty and me?"

"Non aliquis incipit convivium sine nobis," Jimena said.

"Nos sumus convivium," Serena finished.

Maggie looked at them sternly. "That's what you said?"

Jimena nodded. "It means 'No one starts the party without us.'"

"Yeah, 'cause we are the party!" Serena grinned and then they were all laughing.

"But wait." Catty put her hand up and touched the poultice that Maggie had put over the bruise on her forehead. "How did you know where to find us?"

"That's easy." Serena looked at Jimena. "She had a premonition."

"Yeah, I saw you all dolled up in blue." Jimena smiled at Vanessa.

"But I didn't even know where I was going." Vanessa leaned back in her chair, bewildered.

"It's not like reading minds," Serena explained.

"I saw the warehouse." Jimena tapped the side of her head with her finger. "I used to be one of the girls who hung out there, so I knew where to go."

"So how did you fight them?" Vanessa asked.

"The amulets." Serena cupped her hand around hers. "They give us power."

"Now, I've told you that's not it," Maggie warned. "The amulets are only symbols. They mean nothing without your faith. It is your faith in yourselves to turn their evil away that makes you stronger than they are."

"But the amulets glowed," Catty pointed out.

"That was your power, my dear." Maggie spoke softly. "The amulet is only a reminder of the power inside you. Each of you has a special power to fight the Atrox. Jimena's premonitions will tell us when someone needs our help. Serena with her mind-reading will know when someone is being tempted by the Atrox. Vanessa's invisibility will enable her to go among the Followers unseen and tell us what they are planning. And Catty can travel into the past or future to confirm our suspicions so that the Followers cannot deceive us. Together you are an unstoppable force."

The girls looked at each other and smiled.

"Why does the dark of the moon give me the creeps?" Vanessa sipped the tea.

"Evil forces are stronger in darkness. I suppose some would blame Selene for the dark moon." Maggie turned her face away. "There wasn't always a dark of the moon, you know."

"What happened?" Catty asked.

"Selene was responsible for guiding the moon across the skies. One night Selene looked down and saw Endymion in the hills, the most beautiful man, a shepherd."

Vanessa thought of Michael. Then she blushed and looked around the table.

Maggie cleared her throat. "She fell in love. First sight. All that heart-flipping, adrenaline-surging wonder of it. She couldn't resist him. She crept down to lie beside him, abandoning her duty. Some say she asked Zeus to make Endymion sleep for eternity so she would always have him with her. But the truth is Zeus was so angered by the darkened sky that he punished Selene and made it so Endymion should sleep forever. But that didn't stop Selene from loving him. She slips away for a few nights each month to visit her sleeping lover and see if she can wake him."

"What would happen if she did wake him?" Jimena asked.

"After all these years I 'd hate to consider the consequences. She'd probably stay away for months, wreak havoc with the tides and weather." Maggie started laughing. "What would scientists think of their theories then? Gravity?" she said as if it were an absurd idea and laughed some more.

At sunrise, Catty and Vanessa walked home.

"Wow, what an adventure," Catty said. "Let's go back and do it again."

"No!" Vanessa grabbed Catty's arm. She looked at her watch. The hands were gratefully still.

"Just kidding." Catty laughed and hugged her.

CHAPTER TWENTY-SEVEN

WHEN VANESSA CREPT back in her bedroom, she found a red velvet pillow leaning against her other pillows on her bed. She picked it up. GODDESS was embroidered in deeper reds and golds on the front.

"Stanton," she whispered and stared at the pillow. She was going to toss it, but something made her hold it tight.

"Goddess," she read again, and smiled.

She took a long shower, letting the hot water wash the glitter and paint from her body. She crawled into bed and didn't bother to close the window. She sensed that she was safe, for now. She curled against the red velvet pillow and fell asleep thinking about Michael.

She woke later that day, a little stunned by all that had happened, and dressed. Catty had planned to spend the day in bed sleeping, but Vanessa had two things to do that couldn't wait.

At dusk, she walked down Fairfax Avenue carrying the lawn flamingo she had purchased at Armstrong's. She turned down Melrose Avenue and walked for several blocks, past boutiques named Street Slut and Wizard, then turned again. She found the house with the missing flamingo and set the new one in the ground.

She still had something important to do. It was risky, but she felt she owed it to herself. She walked over to Michael's house and knocked on the door.

"Vanessa," Michael said in surprise when he opened the door.

She pretended not to see his look of irritation. "I just wanted you to know that none of the things I did were ever about you."

He looked confused.

"I had something going on in my life. Something that made me act odd at times, but it's nothing to do with you. I really like you. And I wanted to kiss you and I wanted to hold your hand, but when you touch me, I get nervous and I feel all crazy inside and I act weird." She stopped. Was he smiling?

She started again. "And I'm probably never going to stop acting the way I do, because that's just who I am."

She looked back at him. Why didn't he say anything?

"Well, there, I said it. That's the truth."

He still didn't say anything.

"So I wanted to let you know that."

She bit her lip, shrugged, then turned and walked away feeling totally humiliated.

"Vanessa," Michael called.

Her heart flipped. She turned back. He was definitely smiling.

"You want to go to Planet Bang with me Tuesday night?"

"Yes." Did she answer too quickly? Her

molecules buzzed in a dreamy way, and she smiled back at him. "Yeah, I'd like that."

"I'll pick you up early, and we'll eat first."

She nodded. "That sounds great."

"You want to come in? I was just playing the piano."

She smiled mischievously and walked toward him. "No," she whispered and looked deep into his eyes.

"No?" he teased.

And then he reached out, and his arms were around her. She breathed in the spice soap smell of him. He bent his head down, and his lips pressed against hers. Waves of desire rose inside her. Her molecules swirled in pleasure, but they stayed together tight and strong. She let him kiss her again before she stopped him. Then she opened her eyes and looked at him.

"So I'll see you at school tomorrow," she said, and turned to leave.

"Tomorrow." He grinned.

"Bye." She blew him a kiss and hurried down the walk.

And then she was running back to Melrose.

She looked up and saw the crescent moon. She glanced behind her. The street was empty. She smiled and let her molecules go. Her spirits soared. She sailed beyond the neighborhood toward Hollywood. Catty was right. It was a gift. She wished she had used it more.

Soon she flowed above a boy selling souvenir maps to the stars' homes for eight dollars. The maps were years old. Most of the stars no longer lived at the addresses listed on the cover.

She concentrated. "Three maps, please," she said in a ghostly whisper.

The boy looked up and down, then turned completely around.

She laughed, a phantom in the wind, and caught the next breeze.

At Hollywood and Vine, a bus filled with camera-clicking tourists drove by. On a whim she funneled through an open bus window. Then, in her best Marilyn Monroe voice, she whispered, "Welcome to Hollywood, my fine folks."

The tourists looked bewildered, astonished.

"Don't be afraid," she said. "I'm just Tinsel Town magic."

The tourists clapped.

She spent twenty minutes being Marilyn's ghost and making tourists laugh. Then she spilled out the window to a burst of applause and waited for the next breeze.

The wind picked up and carried her away. She could stay invisible forever. She didn't completely understand her power, but she was beginning to understand who she was. *Goddess,* she thought, and her molecules formed a smile before she rode the breeze with arc-shaped leaps, like a dolphin, up and down toward home.

BOOK TWO

into the cold fire

PROLOGUE

In antiquity, Hekate was loved and revered as the goddess of the dark moon. People looked to her as a guardian against unseen dangers and spiritual foes.

All was well until Persephone, the goddess of spring, was kidnapped by Hades and ordered to live in the underworld for three months each year. Persephone was afraid to make the journey down to the land of the dead alone, so year after year Hekate lovingly guided her through the dark passageway and back. Over time Hekate became known as Persephone's attendant. But because Persephone was also the queen of the lower world, who ruled over the dead with her husband, Hades, Hekate's role as a guardian goddess soon became twisted and distorted until she was known as the evil witch goddess who stalked the night, looking for innocent people to bewitch and carry off to the underworld.

Today few know the great goddess Hekate. Those who do are blessed with her compassion for a soul lost in a realm of evil. Some are given a key.

CHAPTER ONE

SERENA KILLINGSWORTH stood on the shoulder of Pacific Coast Highway near the bluffs, waiting for her surf-rat brother to pull his surfboard from the back of the utility van. She stared out at the gray-green water and breathed in the briny smell of sea and kelp. Overhead seagulls circled with their shuddering *kee-yahs*.

"Awesome," Collin said behind her. "The waves are really pumped up."

Her thoughts had been on something more deadly than surf. Still she smiled when she turned to her brother. "Great set," she agreed.

Collin pulled his wet suit from the back of the van and snapped it into place. He was such a board-head that he ignored warnings about surfing alone, especially at night. Serena didn't question his swimming. He was strong. It wasn't riptides, sharks, or wipeouts that made her fear for his safety. She knew of other things that made a Los Angeles night perilous. And lately those dangers had become more menacing.

"Aren't you going out?" he asked, and motioned with his head to her board.

"No," she said, and tied her sweatshirt around her waist. She wore a long-sleeved bathing suit. She had planned to go out. But that was before something had happened at school. Now she needed time to think.

"Should," he said.

"I'll wait on the beach."

A wind blew at the incoming waves, holding them up and making them more hollow. Perfect for surfing.

"It's classic," he said. "You sure?"

"Sure."

The setting sun speckled his crystal-blue eyes with flecks of light and colored his long white-blond hair fiery gold. Nothing about the two of them looked similar. Her hair was dark, the roots almost black, the tips Crayola red. Pointy black shades hid her green eyes, and her tan was even darker than his because she loved the sun and hated the sticky feel of sunblock.

"So," Collin said, and pulled out his board. "How was school today?"

She stiffened.

"Well?" He threw down a towel and set his board on top.

She felt ambushed. "I guess you know already or you wouldn't be asking." There was no way he could know what had happened unless Morgan Page had told him. Morgan had a crush on Collin and used Serena as an excuse to talk to him.

"You're getting a flaky reputation," Collin warned. He grabbed a chunk of paraffin from the back of the van, got down on his knees, and started rubbing a thin layer of wax on the deck of the board.

Serena tried to swallow her anger. If he knew the facts, he wouldn't question her. She smiled to herself and fantasized about telling Collin what her true identity was. She imagined the surprised look on his face. Would he feel proud of her? Or frightened? For sure, he would never look at his younger sister the same way again.

"It's not funny," he said as if he could sense her smiling.

Her daydream slid away. "What did Morgan tell you?"

He stopped waxing the board and gazed up at her. A strange look crossed his face.

Immediately she realized she had made a mistake.

"I never said it was Morgan." Then his face relaxed and he chuckled, "You always know how to read my mind."

She breathed out. No need to panic this time. He'd gotten used to the way she sometimes knew what he was thinking. He thought it was because they had become so close after their mother left them. If he only knew.

"It was easy to guess," she said simply. "Morgan exaggerates so she'll have an excuse to call you."

He stood and threw the wax into the back of the van with a loud thump. "Did she say that?" A sly smile crept across his face.

"No," Serena responded. Then she caught the puppy-dog look in his eyes and whispered a quick prayer, *please, no.* Things were already difficult enough without adding Morgan to the mix. It would be a nightmare if Collin liked her. Serena had a mental flash of Morgan hanging out at their house, watching her, following her, nosing around her bedroom. It was bad enough she had to see her at school every day. Morgan seemed to suspect that something about Serena and her three best friends—Jimena, Catty, and Vanessa—was different. She had no idea how different they actually were. Still, some days she snooped disturbingly close to the truth.

She sighed. "You'd like to go out with her, wouldn't you?"

"No." He spoke too quickly. She didn't need to be a mind reader to know that was a lie.

"Yes, you would," she pointed out matter-of-factly.

"I'm just going to meet her for coffee." He took a thin plastic blade with a serrated edge and scored grooves into the wax on his board. "What's wrong with that?"

"She asked you to meet her to talk about me, didn't she? Like she wants to help."

"How do you know that?" He tossed the wax comb into the van and slammed the cargo door.

"I know Morgan. I thought you did, too. Did you forget? You always said she doesn't have boyfriends, she takes prisoners." Serena hated the nag in her voice.

"Morgan's changed." He was being annoyingly defensive.

"Not enough," Serena muttered and turned away. She couldn't tell Collin what had really happened to Morgan last month to make her change. He probably wouldn't believe her anyway. Even Morgan didn't understand what had actually been done to her. If she did, she would have been more frightened by those punks this afternoon. Morgan couldn't know how vulnerable she was right now. That was one reason Serena and Jimena had risked exposing themselves in order to protect her. Had Morgan seen them do anything strange this afternoon? She clicked her barbell tongue pierce nervously against her teeth.

Collin started to pick up his board but stopped. A look of astonishment crossed his face. Had she slipped? Given something away?

"What?" she asked.

"Your moon amulet." He reached for it. "It changed color."

She took a quick step back before he could touch it. She looked down at the amulet hanging around her neck and studied the face of the moon etched in the metal. The charm had been given to her at birth. It wasn't pure silver, but sparkling in the light of the setting sun, it cast back a rainbow of shimmering lights. Jimena, Catty, and Vanessa each had one, too. Serena never took hers off.

"Probably the setting sun." She clasped her

hand around it. The amulet resonated as if an electrical current passed through it. Did that mean one of them had followed her? She looked quickly behind her. Traffic continued down the highway, tires humming. She didn't see anything odd that should alert her to danger.

She wished Jimena were here. Normally, they were inseparable, but this evening Jimena had to do community service at Children's Hospital. She worked with children undergoing rehabilitation for gunshot wounds. She read to them, played checkers, and showed them how to macramé. Jimena had been in a gang and sentenced twice to a Youth Authority Camp for jacking cars. She would be there now, if a lenient judge hadn't sentenced her to do community service work instead. Jimena had been one badass homegirl before she understood her destiny. Their destiny.

Collin placed his hand on her shoulder.

Here it comes, she thought. She mouthed the words as he spoke behind her.

"I'm concerned about you. . . ."

But his next words took her completely by surprise.

"Maybe if you had a boyfriend—"

She spun around on him. *"What?"*

"Morgan says that's why you act the way you do . . . because you don't have a boyfriend. You never—"

"The last time I tried to have a boyfriend, you scared him away. You were always in his face." She couldn't tell him the real reason it was so difficult for her to have a boyfriend.

He shrugged it off. "You're older now. Maybe if you found someone—"

"A guy isn't the answer." Anger burned inside her. She was so annoyed at Morgan that she wanted to explode. But how could she be mad at Collin when she knew how much he worried about her?

Collin spoke softly now, sensing her anger. "She said she was flirting with these guys, and you and Jimena came up and started talking gibberish."

"It wasn't gibberish. It was Latin," Serena snapped, and immediately wished she hadn't.

"Latin?" Collin repeated in disbelief. "No one speaks Latin. It's a dead language." He looked at her curiously. "When did you learn Latin, anyway?"

"Just did." Again she wished she hadn't mentioned the Latin. It was one more secret. She had been born with the ability to speak Latin and ancient Greek. She just hadn't known it until she had learned about her destiny.

"Morgan said you were really upset. What did they say in *Latin* to get to you?"

She sighed. *"Foeda dea."*

"What does that mean?"

"Ugly goddess."

"Goddess?" He seemed to think that was funny. "That upset you?"

"Forget it." She started walking toward the beach.

"Morgan says kids at school call you the Queen of Bizarre."

She whirled around.

"Morgan," she corrected. "Only Morgan calls me the Queen of Bizarre. Everyone else likes me."

At least she thought they did. They seemed nice enough to her, all except Morgan, who seemed to have some personal vendetta against her that she didn't understand.

"Well, it's a little odd you made those guys get away from her," Collin said.

"It wasn't like Jimena and I didn't have a reason for doing what we did. But Morgan didn't tell you about that, did she?"

"What was it?"

"Those guys were bothering her. I don't know why she told you she was flirting with them. Morgan's never liked hard-core punkers. She likes jocks. She was telling them to get away from her and they wouldn't. I mean, the guys were wearing chains with padlocks and they each had five hoops piercing their lips."

Collin gave her an amused look.

"Okay, I've got piercings, but these guys have faces that look like pincushions, jailhouse tattoos for time spent, and a major attitude."

"Punkers who speak Latin?" He looked doubtful.

Why had she mentioned the Latin? "Yes."

"That's not how Morgan described it."

"Of course not," Serena said with frustration. "She wanted an excuse to call you and she couldn't tell you that Jimena and I rescued her, because then she might look bad. She's lucky Jimena and I were around." Morgan didn't know how lucky. She never had the best judgment about people. Then another thought came to her. What if Morgan had tried to set it up to see what she and Jimena would do? Could she know that much?

Collin smiled broadly. "So you and Jimena rescued Morgan? Chased the bad boys away?" He hugged her and she could smell the neoprene rubber of his wet suit. "Cool. My sister and Jimena Castillo, sophomore vigilantes of La Brea High."

That was closer to the truth.

"So don't worry about it," she said.

But he was already looking back at the ocean. The waves called. Morgan was forgotten.

"Let's go." He picked up his board and started walking.

They slipped through a narrow opening in a

fence. She took off her blue sandals and walked down the spongy ice plant that covered the sandy slope, then followed Collin to the shoreline. Sand squeezed through her toes. She kept glancing at her moon amulet. It was no longer glowing. She wondered what it had picked up earlier.

At the water's edge Collin slipped the Velcro strap around his ankle that leashed him to his surfboard. A wave fanned across the sand and Serena felt the cold water gather around her ankles with a shock.

"Damn," Collin muttered.

She looked at the sets rolling in. Two other surfers rode the waves. Collin liked time alone.

"Be careful," she said.

"No fear," he whispered. He hesitated a moment as if he were uttering a prayer to the great Kahuna, the only true surf god. Then he charged into the waves, slipped the board into the darkening water, slid on top, and paddled over the next wave.

She waited in the foam and backwash until he caught his first wave. The setting sun glowed through the wave and silhouetted him. He was phenomenal. Hanging ten was his specialty. It wasn't easy. To do the move he had to abandon the usual sideways stance that made it easier to control the board. He stood on the tip of the nose, all ten toes hanging over, knees slightly bent, arms balancing out to his sides. Sometimes crowds gathered and watched his nose-riding.

She walked along the wet sand over broken clam and cockle shells. The soft roar of surf and the constant hum of traffic on Pacific Coast Highway were a pleasant relief from the noise that usually filled her mind. The water rolled over her feet and the backwash pulled the sand beneath her steps back to the ocean.

She wished she could tell Collin the truth. She hated keeping so many secrets from him. If only he knew, then her behavior wouldn't seem strange. But would he believe her even if she did tell him she was a goddess, a Daughter of the Moon? And that she was here to protect people from the Atrox, an evil so ancient it had tempted Lucifer into his fall? He'd probably think she'd become a druggie or gone mental.

She glanced back at the waves. Collin caught another, then kicked off as the wave broke into frothy whitewater. What would he do if she did tell him? It wasn't as if she couldn't prove to him that what she said was true, because she also had a gift. She could read minds.

She hadn't understood her power when she was little. She only knew then that she was different from everyone else. Sometimes in the excitement of playing, she'd forget her friends weren't speaking and she'd answer their thoughts. Even now, if she became too happy or excited, she'd answer people's thoughts as if they had said them out loud. That was one reason it was difficult to have a boyfriend. It wasn't just Collin who had freaked out the last guy. She'd done a good job of that herself. She had been sitting in his car, listening to him say all these nice things about her. She had nodded her head and said *thank you* and *I like you, too.* Then she had looked at his face and known immediately from his puzzled expression that he hadn't uttered a word; she'd been answering his thoughts. It had definitely been bye-bye time after that. She had been too embarrassed to see him again. She still blushed whenever she saw him in the hallway at school.

She climbed over barnacle-covered rocks exposed by the low tide and walked around a pile of yellow-brown kelp. The seaweed had washed to shore and now smelled like the fish trapped in its ropy coils and strap-shaped blades.

She gazed up at the first-quarter moon. She loved the pallid luminescence. She arched her back and slowly opened her arms to receive the moon's light. So much had happened to her. It was still hard to believe. Who she was had remained a mystery to her until she met Maggie Craven, a retired schoolteacher with magic of her own.

"Tu es dea, filia lunae," Maggie told her at their first meeting. "You are a goddess, a Daughter of the Moon." Maggie had explained that in ancient times, when Pandora's box was opened, the last thing to leave the box was hope. Only Selene, the goddess of the moon, saw the demonic creature

lurking nearby that had been sent by the Atrox to devour hope. Selene took pity on humankind and gave her daughters, like guardian angels, to perpetuate hope. Serena was one of those daughters. Then Maggie told her about the Atrox. The Atrox and its Followers had sworn to destroy the Daughters of the Moon because once they were gone, the Atrox could bring about the ruin of humankind.

The words still stunned her. How many people even believed in the mythical world? She had read a few myths in sixth grade, but she didn't think goddesses really existed. And if they did, they wouldn't look like her, funked-out in her great-grandmother's pointy-framed sunglasses, a green stud piercing her nose, a stainless-steel barbell through her tongue, and a hoop through the skin over her belly button. Maggie had laughed and said people judged too much by looks anyway. It was other things that made a goddess, like magnanimity of spirit, courage, and a deep willingness to put one's safety aside to save others. Maggie assured her that Selene had bestowed many gifts on her, but Serena had a bewildering feeling that a darker goddess had also gifted her.

The punkers who had been bothering Morgan today were a new kind of Followers. They weren't like the ones in Hollywood who tried to conceal their identity. These flaunted their allegiance to the Atrox. They were punks with pierced lips, rat's-nest hair, and goat tattoos on their left arms. They used mind control, sucking hope and dreams from their victims. Worse still, they liked blood sports.

She'd ask Maggie about them when she saw her on Thursday. Maggie had become her mentor and guide and Serena loved her like a grandmother or a favored aunt. Before she met Maggie, she had been like a receptor, receiving random thoughts. Sometimes she went days without hearing anything. Other times it felt like there were three radios turned full blast in her head with everyone's thoughts jumbling inside her.

Maggie taught her how to go inside a person's mind. It wasn't easy. The first time she'd tried, she and Maggie had walked over to the

Beverly Center. They sat in the food court at the top of the mall, eating California wraps. Maggie pointed to a young boy and told Serena to concentrate, and in her mind's eye to ease her way into the boy's head.

She did as Maggie had told her and suddenly she was inside the boy's thoughts.

His mind was cluttered. Baseball, soccer, and video games played around her in a dizzy swirl. Then TV shows, movies, and a golden retriever name Harry. Just when she wondered if she was going to be lost forever inside the boy's head, she felt Maggie's hand clasp hers and she was back in the mall, her wrap poised near her mouth.

"Wow" was all she could say.

"That's just the tip of the iceberg." Maggie had smiled. "Wait till you see what you can do."

Even now, when Serena practiced reading a person's mind she would sometimes get caught in their thoughts like a fly in a gluey spider web and panic, thinking she was going to be trapped forever in another person's psyche.

Maggie thought she had mastered her

mind-penetrating skill, not perfectly, but well enough to go on to the next level of power. Now Serena was learning how to take a thought and tuck it deep inside a person's mind so they wouldn't remember it. She called it zapping.

Serena felt a chill and realized she had been wandering aimlessly down the shore for a long time now, enjoying the phosphorescent beauty of the waves. She hurried to a seawall, climbed it, and looked back. She could no longer see the stretch of highway where they had parked the van. She turned to go back when a wave hit the wall and splashed over her. If she went back the way she had come, the incoming tide would cut her off near the rocks. She didn't want to get caught in an unexpected wave, especially in the dark and fog, so she decided she'd better find a way up the bluffs.

By the time she found a path, the fog had pushed into shore, wet and cold. She set down her sandals, untied her sweatshirt, and pulled it over her head. It did little to stop her shivering. Her back ached from the cold and her bare legs were covered with goose bumps. She trudged slowly up the hiking trail through the chaparral. The scrub oaks took on a twisted, haunted look in the darkness.

She walked with care, her uneasiness quickly turning to alarm. She had gone only a little way when she heard a sound as if someone were running in the path ahead of her. The fog was too dense to see.

"Hello!" she yelled.

She cautiously stepped forward.

That's when she heard voices, faint and far away, like a church choir. Singing? No, more like chanting.

She walked quickly now, wanting more than anything to be out of the cold and back in the glare of city lights. Ahead she could see a glow in the fog, and stepped faster. Soon she could make out the cloudy images of people standing around a fire in a clearing ahead. She couldn't imagine anyone having a campfire party on a cold night like this one, but she was grateful she had found them.

Only a few more steps and she could see the fire clearly, with about thirty kids standing in a circle around it. She'd get warm, then ask them the way to the highway. As she walked around the group, no one seemed to notice her. There was a strange tension in the air, as if something important were about to happen.

A girl with long blond hair stood too close to the fire. She wore a low-cut, iridescent black dress; the flowing sleeves reached the tips of her fingers, a gold boa circled her neck, and glittering bracelets curled around her arms. She looked more like she was dressed for a prom than an outdoor party. Flames radiated from the fire and seemed dangerously close to her. Her skirt kept flapping into the blaze.

No one seemed alarmed.

Then the girl smiled, turned, and stepped into the fire.

CHAPTER TWO

NONE OF THE KIDS standing near the fire seemed concerned. Were they all blasted on forties or high on 'shrooms? Why wasn't anyone doing anything?

Serena dropped her sandals and barreled through the crowd. Her heart raced as adrenaline pumped through her.

The girl's dress billowed, then whipped around her as if she had been caught in a maelstrom. Flames screamed, wrapped around her long hair, and carried it skyward as a log rolled to the edge of the fire with a hiss.

The kids stepped away from the rolling log, but no one made a move to help the girl.

Serena was close enough to the raging flames to hear the crackling logs, but she still couldn't feel the heat. She should have been able to feel its warmth by now.

And then she saw something that made her stop abruptly. Flames seethed around the girl's arms and face in wild delight, but she wasn't burning. She didn't even look like she was suffering. She looked euphoric. Awestruck, Serena stepped closer. It had to be her imagination, but the air seemed colder near the fire.

She hesitated, then brushed her hand through the fire. It flared up. Flames licked the tips of her fingers, and it felt like ice. She pulled her hand back and brushed a thin frost from her skin.

A cold fire? That was impossible. She stared in wonder at the girl in the inferno.

The girl lifted her head to the night sky, spread his arms wide, and smiled.

"Lecta! Lecta! Lecta!" the others were chanting. Was that the girl's name?

The flames flickered around the girl's face. She inhaled the fire, then opened her eyes. They shone, phosphorescent. The blaze screeched into the night sky and the girl stepped out.

Serena felt a thrum against her chest. She didn't need to look down to know her amulet was radiating a white light. Its power was like an invisible wave pushing against her in warning. She took an involuntary step backward and quickly looked around. She had stumbled into a gathering of Followers. But why hadn't her amulet warned her earlier? And why weren't they trying to destroy her? They weren't even trying to use their mind control.

That's when she saw Karyl on the other side of the fire. He smiled at her through the sparking flames. Even at this distance she felt something creepy about him, the way he looked at her. The last time she had seen him his mind control had come screeching at her in hellish waves as she faced him in battle. That was the night Karyl, Tymmie, and Cassandra had tried to destroy Catty and Vanessa and steal their powers. She and

Jimena had almost been too late to rescue them, but in the end they had saved the other girls.

She turned and bumped into Tymmie. He was tall, his hair dyed white-blond, the black roots showing. His lips curved in a crooked sort of way. His nose hoops reflected the orange-and-red flames.

"Hey, Goddess." He stepped aside. His thin face still looked haunted but didn't pose a threat.

Cassandra stood on the other side of him, her eyes reflecting the fire. She was wearing stretchy black capris under a black tulle skirt, and silver studded cuffs with a black tank top. Thin white scars on her chest made an S, a T, and an A. She had been madly in love with Stanton, the leader of the Followers, and had tried to slice his name on her chest with a razor blade.

Cassandra looked Serena over. "Cute outfit," she said sarcastically.

Serena glanced at the kids standing around her. They were all dressed as if it were prom night.

Cassandra gave her another venomous glance, then ran her fingers through her maroon-colored hair and stared back at the fire.

Serena backed away, more shaken than if Cassandra had slapped her.

She felt bewildered. She had battled these people once. So why didn't they challenge her now? Was this some kind of trick? A trap?

Then she saw Stanton walking around the fire toward her. He was handsome in a dangerously sexy way in his silky black tuxedo. She knew not to stare into his blue eyes, but there was something compelling that made her eyes linger. Maybe it was the reflection of the fire that made his eyes sparkle with such tenderness. Usually there was a darkness and faraway coldness about them that threatened to drag people into his evil world.

Before she was even aware of it he stood beside her, his eyes inviting and seductive.

"I'm glad you came," he said softly, and stroked her hair sensuously. His eyes held hers. It wasn't terrifying, but comforting and lovely, and that was more frightening than if he had tried to push into her mind and control her.

Her heart began to race painfully in her chest. She staggered backward and stood precariously close to the fire. The smoke billowed around her. She breathed it in. The pungent smell made her dizzy and a little sick to her stomach.

She grabbed her moon amulet and felt an immediate comfort. Maggie had told her that she would always know intuitively what to do, especially when the moon was full. The moon wasn't full, but at least it wasn't a dark moon, which was when she was most vulnerable. Her powers were weakest during those three nights when the moon is invisible from the earth. She tried to clear her mind to think. She felt like running.

A baffled look crossed Stanton's face. "Serena, are you all right?"

"How do you know my name?" she asked as new apprehension filled her. He had never used her name before. He had always called her *Goddess,* the way someone spits out the name of an enemy.

"You told me," he said and circled closer to her. He reached out to touch her again when panic took over and she ran.

"Serena!" he shouted after her.

She crashed through the kids standing near the fire.

Stanton kept calling her name. His footsteps pounded the ground behind her.

It was dangerous to run so near the edge of the bluffs. She ran anyway. Terror shuddered through her and her breath came in rasping draws. Her hands were still quivering, but not from cold now. She was dripping with perspiration. She tried to think. Most of the Followers standing around the fire were probably initiates. Kids who had turned to the Atrox, hoping to be accepted into its congregation. They would want to prove themselves worthy of becoming a Follower. They would have some powers of hypnosis, but her skills were far greater than theirs. They would be no threat, unless a large group of them caught her.

Tymmie, Karyl, and Cassandra had been accepted by the Atrox and were apprenticed to Stanton, learning to perfect their evil. She might be able to fight them off, but Stanton was another matter. He could read minds, manipulate thoughts, and even imprison people in his memories.

She ran more quickly now, arms pumping at her sides. The footsteps behind her were gaining.

That was the last thing she remembered.

Serena awoke with a start on the beach near the seawall. She looked around her, astonished. A moment ago she had been running on the bluffs above the water and the next she was on the beach, lying in the sand. "Stanton?" she called with dread. Her hands were shaking and she felt unbearably cold. When he didn't answer her, she stood slowly, feeling dazed.

She looked in the wet sand. She saw only her own footprints. Could she have fallen asleep and dreamed about the cold fire? She didn't remember resting or even sitting down. She lifted her hand to brush back the hair hanging in her eyes and felt a sharp pain. Her palms were raw and scratched. She stepped down to the water and let a wave wash over them. The salt water stung. Could she have fallen over the bluff, tried to grab hold of something, then slipped and lost consciousness when she hit the sand?

She started walking down the beach. After some distance she heard music coming from Collin's van radio. Relief flowed through her. Never had his irritating, bad-to-the-bone surf guitar music sounded so heavenly.

She turned toward the music and ran up the sand, kicking through discarded cans and the charcoal remains of a long-ago beach fire.

Strong hands grabbed her.

She let out a startled cry.

"Serena?" Collin said in a bewildered voice. His flashlight shone in her eyes, then away. "Where've you been?"

"What do you mean? Why did you stop surfing so early?"

He pushed his waterproof glow-in-the-dark watch in front of her. She stared down at the face of the watch in disbelief. Two hours had passed since the sun had set and she'd left Collin.

"I've been looking for you for almost an hour," he scolded.

She continued to stare at the watch.

"What happened to you?" He took off his jacket and placed it around her shoulders. It was warm from his body heat and she gratefully snuggled into it.

"You're shivering and—"

"And what?" She tried to push into his mind to see what he was seeing but her own mind felt sluggish.

"How'd you break your glasses?"

She took them off the top of her head. The lens was missing from the right side.

"I don't know." She hated the tremble of fear that had crept into her words.

"What do you mean *you don't know*?"

She shrugged.

"Did you fall on the rocks?"

She shook her head, even though she knew he couldn't see her in the dark.

"You didn't try to climb up the cliff, did you?" he asked.

"Maybe." She tried to force herself to remember. "I must have fallen."

"You know how dangerous that is!" He sounded really upset.

They walked back toward the van in silence, following the bobbing beam of his flashlight. Soon streetlights from the highway cast a dim light over the beach.

Finally she was able to steady herself enough to speak without the strange twitch in her words. "I don't know what happened," she said. "I thought I was on top of the bluffs, but then I woke up in the sand like I had fallen asleep."

He opened the van door and the dome light came on. She glanced up and saw the worry on Collin's face. She wondered what he was seeing on her own face, because he held her hands tightly.

"Are you sure you're all right?" And in the same breath he said, "You're lucky paramedics aren't scraping you off the rocks."

He opened her hands and looked at the palms. They were scratched, as if she had fallen and tried to grab hold of something.

She closed her hands into fists.

"Let's get out of here," she said and slipped into the passenger side of the utility van. She pressed her bare feet into the carpet. What had happened to her blue sandals? She touched the top of her head and squinted, trying to remember. It only made her feel dizzy. The fire seemed hazy now, like a dream. The more she tried to pull it into focus, the more it drifted away.

"Serena."

She became aware then that Collin had been talking to her.

"Do you want to go to the hospital?"

"No," she said.

"Sure?"

"Yeah."

She felt his hand touch her head and then she looked at the tips of his fingers. A single drop of blood sat on the top of his index finger.

"You must have hit your head," he said. "Maybe we should go to the hospital."

"I'm fine." She tried to sound convincing as she pulled down the mirror on the visor. She examined the small scrape. "It's not deep."

"Promise me that you'll stay away from the bluffs," he said.

"I promise." But she didn't think she had fallen. She would remember slipping, trying to hold on, the freefall.

"Home?" he asked. The concern in his eyes made her feel guilty.

"Yeah, turn on the heat," she said and pulled the seat belt around her. She hated the unclear feeling inside her head. She clasped her arms around her for warmth. Even the familiar smells of surf wax, zinc oxide, and suntan oil didn't comfort her the way they normally would. She wanted to be away from this beach that had once been such a place of solace.

Collin jumped behind the wheel and turned on the engine, then the heater.

She turned and looked toward the cliffs, hoping to see the faint glow from a fire through the fog. She didn't see anything. Maybe Collin was right. Maybe she had fallen.

He pulled into the fog-locked traffic and turned the music higher.

By the time they merged onto the Santa Monica Freeway, her heart rhythm had returned to normal.

"How was it?" she asked finally.

"The skeg was humming," he said. A skeg was the tail of the surfboard and humming was the whistle the skeg made cutting at high speed through the water.

Her mind felt less fuzzy now and she gently pushed into Collin's mind to see if he had seen anything that might give her a clue about what had happened. She didn't find anything unusual, but twice he glanced at her as if he could feel her sorting through his thoughts. What would he do if he found out she could read his mind?

CHAPTER THREE

SATURDAY MORNING, the aroma of baking muffins filled Serena's warm kitchen. Her pet raccoon, Wally, paced near his food dish, his nails clicking impatiently on the floor. Serena sipped her now cold coffee and finished telling Jimena about the night before.

"And then I woke up on the beach by the seawall," she finished.

"That's it?" Jimena asked.

"It."

Jimena leaned against the cupboard, deep in thought, and raked her hands through her long black hair. Her hooded, zip-front sweater hid the tattoos on her arms, remnants from her days in a gang, but the tattoo on her belly peeked over the top of her hip-huggers.

"That's some bad stuff." Jimena shook her head. "Feed Wally while I think."

Serena filled a bowl with grapes, then mixed a can of cat food with some baby food on another plate.

Jimena helped her set the food on the floor, then she sat on the counter and swung her long legs in and out of the sunlight cascading through the windows. "It had to be a dream," she decided, and counted on her fingers. Her nails were long and painted turquoise. "First, I would have had a premonition, *sin duda,* if you were going to meet up with a group of Followers."

"Probably," Serena agreed.

That was Jimena's gift. She had premonitions about the future. She was almost always forewarned if one of them was going to have a serious run-in with the Followers. It was creepy to think that she could see the future, especially because she had never been able to stop any of her premonitions from coming true, no matter how bad they were.

"Second, no one can stay in a fire that long and survive. If the Followers could, Maggie would have told us."

Maggie had introduced Jimena and Serena a year back. At first it had been a very reluctant friendship. Jimena had been deep in a gang, jacking cars and hanging out with her home girls. No way was she going to be friends with a wimp like Serena. Serena had liked that Jimena never played games the way most girls did, saying one thing and doing another. That made it easy for Serena to respect her. The first time they had fought a group of Followers, Jimena had changed her mind about Serena. Serena had never backed down. Now Jimena trusted Serena with her life.

"Third," she said as Serena pulled the muffins from the oven, "the fire felt cold. That's dream stuff."

Serena took the muffins from the tin and set them in a basket.

"What's fourth?" Serena had caught Jimena's thought. She carried the muffins to the table and set them next to the butter and a carafe of coffee.

Jimena jumped off the counter and followed her. She sat down and buttered a muffin. Steam curled into the air as the butter melted. "Fourth, you wouldn't be here if you'd met up with a gang of Followers."

Serena nodded, but the explanation didn't feel right. She knew there was more, but she couldn't seem to work her mind around it. She slumped back in her chair. "Stanton chased me."

"You told me."

"I think he caught me." Serena slipped Collin's cozy sweater off her shoulder. She showed Jimena the bruises on her arm that looked as if someone had grabbed her hard.

Jimena touched the four round bruises near her shoulder.

"You must have done it yourself on the rocks," Jimena assured her. "You'd remember if someone grabbed you."

"Maybe," Serena said. "Remember last month when the Followers caught Morgan and stole her hope?"

Jimena nodded.

"She was all dazed," Serena continued. "And didn't know what had happened to her. Maybe that's what happened to me."

"Followers don't want *your* hope. They want you, *Serenita.*"

"Still . . ."

"Don't worry about it," Jimena assured her. "Worry can't do nothing to protect you. Friends are for that, and I got your back."

"Thanks." Serena chewed the side of her mouth, thinking. "It's just weird not to be able to remember what happened for almost two hours. Maybe I should tell Maggie."

Jimena gave her a curious look. "You'll have to wait until Thursday, when we meet her for tea. She won't be back until then, remember?"

Serena started to answer when the back door opened and Collin walked in.

"Hey," he greeted them. He wore vans,

low-slung baggies, and a bad mood. He'd just come back from an early morning at the beach and hadn't bothered to wipe the zinc oxide off his nose and bottom lip.

"How was it?" Serena asked.

"Waves were awesome." Collin opened the refrigerator and pulled out a quart of milk. He stood in the open refrigerator, swallowed the milk, then tossed the carton in the trash and slammed the refrigerator.

From the scrape marks on the side of his leg, Serena figured he'd wiped out. He must have hurt himself to quit so early.

Suddenly, his nose drained. He tried to catch the water with the back of his hand, then grabbed a dish towel and wiped his chin and nose.

"Tienes mocos," Jimena laughed. "You are such a faucet nose."

Collin frowned. After a grueling surf session his nasal passages filled with sea water, and then drained at embarrassing times.

"I thought you never wiped out?" Jimena

added with a big grin. "Didn't you tell me a faucet nose was caused by having water forced up your nose during a wipeout?"

"Look, *ghetto*," Collin said with a burst of anger that wasn't like him. "You don't even know what a wipeout is." He started rummaging noisily through the cupboards.

"Oye, mocoso." Jimena stood, her chair scraped back. "Who you calling *ghetto*?"

"You." Collin slammed a cupboard door.

Jimena took her attitude stance and now the air prickled with rising tension.

"Over in El Monte, they call you the kook of Malibu." Jimena danced with her words, spreading the syllables long with a superexaggerated Mexican accent that normally she didn't have.

Serena shook her head. "Kook" was an especially derogatory term, meaning someone who lived inland and got in the way of real surfers by doing something impossibly stupid like abandoning a surfboard so that it caused a major wipeout for someone else.

Collin's eyes lingered on Jimena. "Yeah, well,

it was a fool kook who caused me to wipe out today, probably one of your ghetto friends."

"Please." Serena rolled her eyes. "Do you guys have to fight every time you see each other?"

Collin grabbed a muffin, eyes still focused on Jimena, and shoved it in his mouth as if he were purposely trying to gross her out by eating with his mouth open.

She shook her head. "I've seen blood and brains, little boy, you think you're going to gross me out with bad table manners?" Jimena cleared her throat as if startled by a memory that had been conjured up. She turned to Serena. "So what you looking for in the garage sales today?"

Collin tapped the edge of the table angrily. "Later," he said, and trundled out of the kitchen.

"Fringed poncho, maybe." Serena watched Collin leave the room.

"I want some of those psychedelic polyester shirts." Jimena sipped her coffee.

"We better go." Serena stood. She wished her brother and her best friend wouldn't fight so much.

They left the house and started walking over to Fairfax Avenue. They walked in silence for a while, then Serena spoke. "Can you believe what Morgan said about me needing a boyfriend?"

"That's her life." Jimena shrugged. "She can't live without a guy."

"It's not like it's exactly easy for us to have boyfriends," Serena said.

"Yeah," Jimena agreed. "Every time I meet some *reteguapo* guy, the more I like him, the more premonitions I get about him. The more premonitions I get about him, the more I don't like him. It takes the magic out when I see him sneaking around and doing things he doesn't even know he's going to do yet. Only Veto was true to me, but then he ends up dead." Her words turned hoarse.

"Well, at least none of them are calling you weird," Serena offered.

Jimena laughed so loudly that the people lined up to eat at Red turned and looked at her. "I wish I could have seen you sitting there, all pretty and *suavecita,* saying 'thank you' and 'I like you, too,' when he hadn't even said a word to you."

"But I never got mad at a guy for something he hadn't even done yet," Serena shot back.

"Yeah," Jimena considered. "Who wants a boyfriend anyway? Guys are a mess of hormones and sweat."

"Me?" Serena said weakly.

Jimena smiled at her. "*Yo tambien,* but different this time. I don't want to know all about the future with him. I don't want to see his death coming, or see him messing with some *ruca.* Someone like your brother. That's what I want."

Serena stopped suddenly, and two Hassidic men on their way to temple almost bumped into her. "You hate my brother!"

"I mean some *vato* like your brother but *not* your brother," Jimena corrected.

"What do you mean?"

"*Con tu hermano,* the only thing I ever see him doing in the future is riding a wave."

They were silent for a long time, then Serena spoke hesitantly, "You ever think that maybe we're not supposed to have boyfriends because of what happens when we turn seventeen?"

"I had Veto," Jimena whispered.

"And he died," Serena finished for her.

Jimena nodded. "Maybe we're not."

Their gifts only lasted until they were seventeen. Then, Maggie had explained, there was a metamorphosis. They had to make the most important choice of their lives. Either they could lose their powers and the memory of what they had once been, or they disappeared. The ones who disappeared became something else, guardian spirits perhaps. No one really knew. They didn't talk about it much. It was too frightening.

"Vanessa has a boyfriend," Serena added hopefully.

"Yeah, but she almost didn't," Jimena pointed out.

Vanessa had the power to become invisible, but when she became really emotional, her molecules began to separate on their own. When Vanessa had first started dating Michael Saratoga her molecules had gone out of control, and she had started to go invisible every time he tried to kiss her.

"There they are." Serena pointed down the street.

Catty and Vanessa were vamping it up on the corner of Fairfax and Beverly, in bell-bottoms with exaggerated lacy bells that they must have pulled from Catty's mother's closet.

Vanessa gave them the peace sign. "Feelin' groovy." She winked. She had gorgeous skin, movie-star blue eyes, and flawless blond hair. She was wearing a headband and blue-tinted glasses. Catty was forever getting Vanessa into trouble, but they remained best friends.

"Love and peace," Catty greeted them. Catty was stylish in an artsy sort of way. Right now, she wore a hand-knit cap with pom-pom ties that hung down to her waist, and her puddle-jumping Doc Martens were so wrong with the bell-bottoms that they looked totally right. Her curly brown hair poked from beneath the fuchsia cap and her brown eyes were framed by granny glasses, probably another steal from her mother.

"You like our retro look?" Vanessa giggled at all the cars honking at them.

“Yeah, but what’s that smell?” J[illegible]na sniffed.

“Mom’s aromatherapy.” C[illegible]rolled her eyes. “It’s lavender, so I won’[illegible]essed out.”

“When were you ever st[illegible]ut?” Serena hooted.

“Never,” Catty answered “Mom just thinks everyone is stressed.”

Serena smiled. “It doesn’t smell so bad.”

“I don’t think I’ll be borrowing it.” Jimena wrinkled her nose.

Maggie had brought them all together and was still showing them how to use their special powers to fight the Atrox and its Followers. According to Maggie, they were an unstoppable force, but that’s not how they felt. More often they felt as if their powers controlled them.

Vanessa waved a newspaper. She had circled and numbered the garage sales and brought a map.

“The first sale is only a block away.” She started in the direction of Fairfax Avenue.

Serena told them about the cold fire and the girl named Lecta as they walked down a side street.

"It had to be a dream," Vanessa said. "The fire was cold."

"If they were acting like they wanted to party, maybe you did some act of kindness to them so they couldn't hurt you," Catty said.

"I'm sure I didn't," Serena said. A Follower could never harm a person who had done a genuine act of kindness toward him or her. Serena looked at Vanessa. Once Stanton had trapped Vanessa in his childhood memories. While she was there she had tried to save a younger Stanton from the Atrox. For that he could never harm her.

"Do you know anyone named Lecta?" Vanessa asked.

"No," Serena admitted.

"It was a dream," Catty insisted. "The girl didn't burn."

"That's what I've been telling her," Jimena agreed.

"Yeah." Serena scowled. "But it felt so real."

"Haven't you ever had one of those dreams where you want to wake up but you can't, then when you finally do, you feel relieved what happened was only a dream?"

"Sure." Serena nodded. "But this was different."

"There's one way to find out," Catty cut in as they reached the first garage sale.

Serena picked up a jeweled necklace with a small drop pearl surrounded by garnets. "Which is?" She held the necklace across her forehead.

"Looks hot." Jimena admired it.

"Yeah, it's looks like a headache band like they wore in the twenties." Vanessa examined it.

"Excuse me," Catty interrupted. "But I had a terrific idea."

"What?" Serena pulled a dollar from her pocket to pay the lady holding the sale. She slipped the necklace into her pocket.

"It's easy." Catty smiled. "I'll go back in time and check it out."

Catty had the freakiest power. She could actually go back and forth in time. She missed a lot of school because she was always twisting time. But her mother didn't care, because she knew Catty was different. She wasn't Catty's biological mother. She'd found Catty walking along the side of the road in the Arizona desert when Catty was six years old. She was going to turn her over to the authorities in Yuma, but when she saw Catty make time change, she decided Catty was an extraterrestrial, and that it was her duty to protect her from government officials who would probably dissect her. She still didn't know that Catty was a goddess. Somehow it was easier for people to believe in space aliens than in goddesses.

"So who wants to go with me?"

"No, thanks." Vanessa shuddered. "I hate the tunnel." The tunnel was what she called the hole in time that Catty had to travel through to get from one time to the next. Besides Catty, Vanessa was the only one who had been in it.

"How 'bout you?" Catty elbowed Serena. "You're always bugging me to take you back."

Serena shook her head. "Not this trip." She had wanted to try it out even after hearing Vanessa describe the dank, burnt-cabbage smell of the tunnel and thrill-ride feel of the travel. She wasn't even afraid of the landings. Vanessa had told her that when they arrived at their destination, they fell back into time, which felt like falling on granite. Plus Catty was seldom accurate in her landings. They might land miles away, and near the ocean that could mean really bad news. Still, Serena would have been willing to risk it, if the memories of last night with the Followers hadn't been haunting her.

"I don't want to run into the Followers," Serena said simply. "Go someplace else and I'll go with you."

"*Please,* your landings are way off, and you'd have to land next to the bluffs and the ocean," Vanessa cautioned.

"Jeez, I've been practicing so much and you guys still don't trust me," Catty complained, and twirled the pom-poms on her cap, then looked slyly at Jimena. "You sure you don't want to go?" Catty's eyes began to dilate as if power were surging in her brain, and she reached out for Jimena's hand.

"Look, the trip only takes minutes for you," Serena said. "But the rest of us have to relive the whole night, and I know that's something I don't want to do." But it was too late. She could already feel the change around her, as if the air pressure were dropping. She glanced at Catty's watch. The hands started to move backward.

"Stop!" Vanessa yelled. Her hair stood out with a charge of static electricity.

When Catty didn't stop, Jimena grabbed Serena and Vanessa. "Hold your amulets."

They each grasped the moon amulet hanging around their necks.

"Meet you at Kokomo's," Jimena yelled before Catty disappeared in a blinding flash of white light. The air settled.

"Why didn't we go back?" Vanessa looked around, baffled.

"Maggie told me holding the amulet is a way for us to stay in the present when Catty travels back in time," Jimena explained. "I was supposed to tell you. Sorry. Forgot."

"Why did you see Maggie?" Serena asked.

"Premonition," Jimena answered. "I saw her just before she left."

It wasn't unusual for Jimena to have a premonition that she needed to discuss with Maggie, but this time Serena had an uneasy feeling that there was something more she wasn't telling. But she let her suspicion slip away. Jimena had never kept anything from her before.

Vanessa was thoughtful for a moment, then she spoke. "Catty says all time exists at once. We just experience it one day at a time because that's the way we've been taught to think about it. I guess she's right. We're here. She's there. Kind of freaky."

"It's freaky, all right." Serena thought of Catty back at the cold beach while they were safe in the warm sunshine. She wondered what Catty was seeing.

At the fourth garage sale, Vanessa's stomach growled. "I'm hungry, and Catty should be getting back by now."

Serena, Vanessa, and Jimena walked down Fairfax toward Farmers Market. Buses brought tourists to the open-air market for souvenir shopping and dining. There were so many places to eat that it was almost impossible to choose.

They found a table under an umbrella at Kokomo's and sat down.

A constant procession of tourists wove in and out of the tables at the small open-air restaurant and gawked at the glossy autographed photos of celebrities on the wall over the counter. The tourists peered at the girls, hoping to recognize someone famous. Vanessa, Jimena, and Catty were used to it because they had grown up in Los Angeles. Serena had come from Long Beach, and tourists on the *Queen Mary* weren't looking for movie stars.

Vanessa looked at her watch as the waiter came to their table. "Catty's taking too long," she whispered.

"We shouldn't have let her go," Jimena said.

"You girls decided yet?" the waiter asked impatiently.

"Give us a few more minutes," Vanessa answered.

The waiter went to the next table.

Suddenly strange currents shimmered like heat waves in the air and a change in air pressure made people look at the sky as if they expected to see a storm brewing. Serena could feel the hair on the back of her neck rise.

Catty fell in a heap on the blacktop walkway next to their table.

People around them turned and stared.

"Where'd she come from?" a woman with thick dark glasses asked.

"Must have fallen off the roof," a man commented.

The waiter looked at Catty as if he'd found a cockroach on the table.

"Hi." Catty stood. She was soaking wet. A long strand of kelp wrapped around her arm. Without missing a beat, she turned and faced the gathering crowd. "Don't forget to see *Ocean Deep,* coming soon to your local theater."

Tourists clicked pictures, and some applauded.

"Hollywood." Catty laughed even though she was shivering.

Vanessa, Jimena, and Serena gathered around her.

"What happened to you?" Vanessa pulled the kelp off Catty's arm.

"Yeah." Serena took off Collin's sweater and placed it around Catty.

"More important," Jimena said, "what did you see?"

"My landing was way screwed up," Catty explained. "I landed in the ocean and had to swim for shore."

"Why didn't you just come back right away?" Vanessa asked.

"I couldn't." Catty shrugged. "I panicked."

Serena pushed into Catty's mind. She saw the dark and felt the cold water draining Catty's strength as she swam toward the sound of the surf.

Vanessa hugged Catty. "You've got to be more careful."

Serena shivered and came back from the place in Catty's mind. "Let's go to my house," she suggested. "It's closest."

"Maybe we should go to my house," Vanessa said, too quickly.

"You always do that," Serena turned to face her. "Whenever Catty's with us you never want to go to my house. What's up?"

"That's not true," Vanessa said defensively.

"Yeah, it is," Jimena piped up.

"True," Catty added. "What's at Serena's house you don't want me to see?"

"Don't be silly." Vanessa waved them away. "You're just imagining it."

Catty and Serena looked at each other and nodded.

Serena crept inside Vanessa's mind and tried to find the reason Vanessa didn't want Catty to go over to Serena's house. She pushed around memories of Michael, peeked at the homework—she had no idea Vanessa studied so much—and then she found the memories of Vanessa's visits to her home, but she didn't find anything to give her a clue. She slipped back out.

Vanessa was staring at her. "That's creepy, Serena."

"What gave it away?" Serena asked.

"I was suddenly thinking about all my homework!" Vanessa laughed. "You must have accidentally pushed the memories to the front of my brain."

Serena shrugged. They turned down Beverly and soon they were in Serena's warm kitchen. Serena gave Catty a pair of clean sweats.

"You can change in the downstairs bathroom, it's right next to the washer and dryer. There's a shower, too, if you want."

"Thanks." Catty disappeared into the utility room next to the kitchen.

"She's lucky she didn't drown." Vanessa shook her head and took cocoa from a cupboard.

"We shouldn't have let her go." Serena placed a pan on top of the stove as Jimena pulled milk from the refrigerator.

That's when they heard Catty scream. They ran to the utility porch.

Catty bumped into them. "There's a wild animal in your bathroom!"

Serena pushed past her and ran into the

bathroom. Wally leaned into the toilet, meticulously cleaning a grape.

"That's just Wally." Serena lifted her pet raccoon from the toilet. She wiped his paws with a towel and carried him back to Catty. "I should have warned you, but I just thought Vanessa would have told you."

Vanessa got a strange look on her face. "Oops."

"That's it?" Serena asked. "You didn't want Catty to know about Wally? Why not?"

Before Vanessa could answer, Catty spoke. "I can't believe you took a wild animal out of its natural habitat and keep it as a pet. It's drinking out of the toilet!"

"He would have died if I hadn't taken him. His mom abandoned him. And he wasn't drinking out of the toilet," Serena corrected. "He was washing a grape."

Catty shook her head. "They have shelters for wild animals who are deserted." She turned to Vanessa. "I can't believe you didn't tell me. We've got to do something."

Vanessa rolled her eyes. "See?"

"So what are you going to do about it?" Jimena joked. "Turn Serena in?" She took Wally from Serena and handed him to Catty. The raccoon licked her ear, then started grooming her wet hair.

Catty petted Wally. "Well, he doesn't seem like he's suffering. I guess living with Serena is better than being dead."

"Thanks," Serena said sarcastically.

"Sorry." Catty smiled. "I didn't mean—"

Then Catty looked really serious. "Just don't anyone tell my mother. Ever!" She put Wally down and went back to the bathroom to shower and change her clothes.

A few minutes later Catty joined them, smelling of soap. They sat around the kitchen table drinking hot cocoa and Catty told them everything that had happened. "Once I swam to shore I hiked up the cliff near the seawall, but I didn't see anything. No fire. Not even a smoky smell."

"Then I must have fallen." Serena focused on

her memories of that night. "But it felt so real."

"We better tell Maggie anyway." Jimena looked around the group.

"When we have tea with her on Thursday," Vanessa added.

"Okay," Serena agreed, and tossed another marshmallow into her cocoa.

Catty picked up the deck of tarot cards that were sitting on the table and placed them in front of Serena. "Read our fortune. Do it for all of us at once." There was too much excitement in her voice, as if she were trying to lift the solemn mood that had settled over Serena.

"I don't know if it can work that way," Serena said.

"Try," Catty coaxed.

Serena shuffled the cards. "I'll just do a three-card spread. Everyone think of their question while I shuffle." She glanced up. They were all staring at her. She didn't need to read their minds to know they were all asking about the cold fire. "Okay, so now each of you divide the deck so that we have three stacks that are facedown. One for past, one for the near future, and one for the final outcome."

Each of them divided the cards, then Serena turned over the first card from the first stack. "The devil." She frowned. "Not a good sign."

"What does it mean?" Catty asked.

"It means that we've entered a negative cycle and our problems are going to multiply. We won't be able to see the whole picture clearly."

"Too weird." Catty was hushed.

"Go on." Vanessa nodded.

Serena snapped the card from the second stack and placed it on the table.

"The moon." Jimena smiled. "That's got to be a good sign for us."

"No," Serena whispered. "This card represents what is about to be. Things are not going to go smoothly because of some deception."

"Yikes." Catty's eyes widened.

"They're just cards," Vanessa reassured them. "They don't mean anything, really. Turn over the next one."

Serena did. "The high priestess." Her hand

started shaking and she quickly dropped the card and hid her hand under the table.

They all stared at her.

"Well?" Catty demanded. "What's the outcome?"

Serena scooped up the cards. "Let's try again."

She shuffled, then let them divide the stack. She took the first card, then the second and the third. The devil, the moon, and the high priestess came up again in the same order.

"Quit fooling around," Jimena scolded.

Serena sighed. "I'm not."

"What does the high priestess mean?" Vanessa wondered.

Serena tapped her finger on the card. "We're at a crossroads and the outcome will be different from what we expect."

"That doesn't have to mean anything bad," Vanessa said hopefully.

Serena cleared her throat. "Changes are taking place." She didn't like the way the high priestess card seemed to be warning her.

"Forget it." Catty stood up. "Cards can't tell the future anyway. Besides, I'm bored with cards. Let's practice dancing."

"That's a good idea." Jimena turned on the radio. "*Hay que ser muy desinhibida para esto,* Vanessa."

"What's she telling me?" Vanessa moved her feet with the beat of the music.

"You got to be uninhibited," Catty teased.

"How'd you know?" Vanessa asked. "You don't speak Spanish."

"'Cause you always freeze up! And if you want to impress Michael you're going to have to let your butt swing!"

Vanessa took a deep breath and followed Jimena's lead.

"Con más sensualidad." Jimena swayed her hips.

"I understood that one." Vanessa smiled.

Serena was still staring at the cards.

"Come on." Jimena took her hand and pulled her away from the table.

Serena fell in line behind Jimena but kept glancing back at the devil card. The creature drawn on the face of the card had the head and feet of a he-goat and the bosom and arms of a woman. "It's the tarot's mystery card," she whispered. "It's never good."

"Stop," Vanessa admonished. "We need to practice our new dance steps so our crew will look hot when Michael's band plays at Planet Bang."

"So *you'll* look hot," Catty corrected.

"Yup!" Vanessa answered with delight.

"All right." Serena tried to concentrate on dancing, but the cards kept drawing her eyes back, as if to warn her of something important.

CHAPTER FOUR

MONDAY AT SCHOOL Serena set her cello down and opened her locker slowly. Chopin's Sonata in G Minor was still on her mind. She would need to increase her practice time if she was going to be able to play the sonata perfectly for the winter concert. She could mark the measures with which she was having the most difficulty and begin with those, exercising her fingers until they ran smoothly over the fast runs.

She held the locker door open, pulled out her algebra book, and slipped her music back inside.

Someone nudged the locker door shut.

She turned sharply and took in a quick gulp of air.

Zahi leaned against the row of lockers. He had moved to California from France two weeks ago. His black hair fell in his eyes and he casually brushed it back. A gold stud glistened in his left ear. She loved his angular face, his clear brown eyes, his French accent and European charm.

"And how are you today, Serena?" He had the most wonderful accent she had ever heard.

She wished she could control the blush rising to her cheeks. "Hi." She tossed him an insolent smile. She might as well wear a neon sign: *Serena Killingsworth has a major crush on zahi, new boy at school, incredible looker who is also smart and speaks French and—*

"I heard that you can read my future in your tarot cards." He looked at her with open interest.

"Who told you that?" she teased.

"Morgan told me."

"Morgan, huh?" Serena tilted her head. They had been talking to each other a little more each day and she was sure that he liked her at least half as much as she liked him. Did he want her to read the cards so he would have an excuse to visit her? She glanced at his eyes. She couldn't pull away. The only other guy this good-looking at school was Michael Saratoga, and he was totally devoted to Vanessa.

"If you can see the future, should I be scared of you?" He rested his hand on the top of the lockers so that his arm was close enough for her to feel the heat radiating from his body.

"Maybe." She leaned toward him, daring him to put his arm around her. She loved the way he looked at her. "You don't have to be afraid of me." She spoke the words like an invitation. "It's just for fun. I'll read your spread for free." Did that seem too desperate? Guys usually couldn't get to her like this. What was it about him that made her feel so strangely wonderful?

"I'll read coffee for you."

"You mean tea?" she asked.

"No. Where I come from, the coffee is so strong that you turn the cup over when you are finished drinking it and read the dregs."

"I didn't know they did that in France."

"I speak French," he explained, "and my family lived in France, but we come from Morocco. I also speak Arabic." He whispered the last word and it brushed lazily across her cheek.

She picked up her cello and started walking.

He walked with her. "Do you find me at all interesting?"

"What?" She stopped and looked at him.

"Or maybe you belong to a very serious religious group? One perhaps that does not allow you to talk to the boys?"

"Why would you think that?"

"All this week I've been trying to get you to invite me to your house and so far I have had no luck." He let his hand run down her arm. She felt herself drifting at the sight of his lazy smile. She didn't move her arm.

"Well?" He stretched slowly, lifting his books over his head. His black turtleneck pulled up and she caught a glimpse of a sun tattooed around his belly button.

"Sure, you can come over." She cleared her throat and looked down at her fuchsia cashmere tube top and feather-trimmed zebra-print slacks, then smiled flirtatiously. "Would someone into a way serious religion dress the way I do?"

He laughed. The sound was full and rich and made her want to hug him. "That is why I wanted to meet you. You dress like a Christmas tree. I'm an artist. I love color and style. Look down the hallway—you would think they were winter birds, would you not? All black and gray and navy blue. You are from a tropical paradise."

She hadn't thought of it before. The sun was shining but the hallways looked dark. Then she glanced at him. He was wearing a tight black turtleneck, black jeans, black boots, and a thick black belt with a curious silver buckle.

"You should talk!" She laughed.

"I like the way you laugh." He pressed closer to her.

She pushed into his mind for one quick glimpse. She concentrated and was immediately filled with joy. His memories and thoughts were all in French and Arabic. Maybe she could finally have a real boyfriend. No way could she answer this guy's thoughts. She couldn't understand a word.

"Of what are you thinking now?" A slow easy smile crossed his face.

"I don't speak a word of French," she said. "Or Arabic."

"That makes you so happy?"

"Maybe." She tilted her head. "We'll see."

"Do you always smile so much?" he asked. "It is as if you have a big secret."

If he only knew her secrets.

"Yeah, I guess I have a couple secrets," she teased.

"Tell them to me," he whispered.

"Can't." She shook her head.

"I like your tongue pierce." He touched her bottom lip.

Her heart flipped. The way he was looking at her, the light touch of his finger on her lip . . .

His face suddenly turned serious and he

leaned forward. "I like you, Serena." His hands caressed her cheeks.

She wanted to kiss him, right there in the middle of the hallway with kids pushing all around them.

He fixed his eyes on her as if he could read her thoughts and he grabbed her free hand. "I want my invitation first."

"Zahi." She tried to say his name as if she hadn't practiced it in front of her mirror at home. "Why don't you come over to my house tonight?"

He leaned closer and she wondered if he was going to kiss her. Then she heard a commotion down the hallway, and the moment was gone.

They broke apart and turned. Morgan was walking toward them. She wore a leather maxi coat over a slinky short red dress, and black suede boots that came above her knees. Her hair was all sunlight and shimmer. Every guy turned his head and made a comment or gave a whistle as she passed.

Zahi stared at Morgan. He probably had a major crush on her, like most of the guys at school.

"Ah, Morgan," Serena commented dryly.

"You are prettier." He playfully touched her chin.

"I'm afraid that's not so."

"Yes, so," he insisted with a melting smile. "You have class and style that show you think for yourself. Morgan is a page from a fashion magazine." He touched her arm lightly. "I have to go on to my next class now. The teacher hates late arrivers. I will see you soon, no?" He ran backward, watching her, before he finally turned and sprinted away.

"Class and style," she whispered after him.

Jimena, Vanessa, and Catty came up behind her. "Why are you looking so dreamy?" Jimena studied her.

"Zahi," Catty answered with a sly smile. "It's only completely obvious she likes him."

"He's really cute." Vanessa looked him over appreciatively.

"Serena likes 'em brooding and tortured," Jimena added.

"He's artistic," Serena defended.

"How are you going to kiss him with that barbell through your tongue?" Jimena asked, pushing her playfully.

"Kiss him?" Serena hadn't really thought about the barbell getting in the way. Would it? She had never gotten to kiss her last boyfriend, and the only other kisses she had had were the awkward pecks from games of spin the bottle in sixth grade, long before she had ever pierced her tongue.

"Isn't that what couples do?" Vanessa smiled in a pensive kind of way.

"Unless they go invisible," Catty teased.

"That's not funny." Vanessa was still sensitive about the difficulty she'd had kissing Michael. Probably because she was afraid it could happen again.

"Just don't lick his face like they do in the movies," Jimena said. "Guys hate that."

"How do you know?" Catty joked. "Have you licked someone's face?"

"Listen to the voice of experience," Jimena bragged. "Don't lean in too fast—you'll chip your teeth. And if he shoves his tongue down your throat—"

"Gross!" Vanessa, Catty, and Serena said in unison.

"This is real life, *chicas*." Jimena crossed her arms. "You want to hear or not?"

Serena raised her hand. "Yeah, I want to hear."

"Me, too," Vanessa chimed in.

"If he jams his tongue in your mouth, pull away and smile at him. He'll figure it out if you keep doing that."

"What if he doesn't?"

"Then you stick the tip of your tongue into his mouth so he can see that a kiss is not supposed to require a Heimlich maneuver."

"You guys are pathetic," a voice said snidely.

They turned and Morgan was standing by her locker. "If you like someone it comes naturally."

"Maybe you always kiss guys who have done a lot of smooching." Catty grinned wickedly. "The rest of us date guys who aren't disease-ridden."

"That's *so* not funny," Morgan said. "Besides, when have you ever had a date, Catty?"

"No seas pesada," Jimena muttered in a low voice.

"What?" Morgan twisted her head around.

"She said don't be a pain in the butt, Morgan." Catty arched her brows. "You going to do something about it?"

Morgan glanced at Jimena.

Jimena held her head back and glared at her.

"Who's planning on getting kissed, anyway?" Morgan pulled a strawberry gloss from her locker and rubbed it on her lips.

No one answered her.

"It's not like I'm not going to find out," she said and eyed Jimena as if she were the enemy.

Jimena cocked her head and folded her arms over her chest.

Catty rolled her eyes. "Since when is it your business, anyway?"

Morgan pulled her books from her locker. "As if I really care." She looked at them derisively. "You going to be home this afternoon, Serena?"

"Yeah, maybe, why?"

"No reason." Morgan slammed her locker closed and slunk back down the hallway.

"Man, that girl gets on my nerves." Serena watched Morgan stroll away from them.

Vanessa spoke up. "You guys should give her a chance."

They all turned and looked at Vanessa in disbelief.

"She only, like, tried to steal Michael from you," Serena pointed out.

"And I bet she still would," Catty added.

The bell rang and they all ran for class.

Serena quickly forgot about Morgan and started planning for Zahi's visit. She wondered if she should bake chocolate chip cookies. She decided to stop on the way home and buy some chocolate chips at Ralph's.

Serena stared out the kitchen window. The smells of freshly baked cookies wafted through the kitchen. A pale gibbous moon hung in the sky, even though the sun hadn't set yet.

"These cookies are your best ever," Jimena said behind her and spread her khaki pants on the table. "We should start selling them. Seriously."

The back door opened and Collin walked in.

"Hey," he said. His nose and lips were still covered with white zinc oxide.

"*Oye,* Serena, a *payaso* just walked into your kitchen!"

"Don't you ever go home?" Collin looked annoyed. He scooped up a handful of cookies.

"Those cookies aren't for you," Jimena informed him. "They're for Zahi."

"Zahi?" Collin asked. "Who's that?"

Serena felt herself panic. Now Collin would know a boy was coming over. Would he play guardian as usual?

"Zahi is a friend of Serena's," Jimena explained.

Collin looked at Serena. "Have I ever met this guy?"

"No." Serena kept her voice light. "He just moved here."

Collin sat down at the table. "Maybe I'd better meet him, then."

"Don't you have a life of your own?" Jimena mocked. "If you got a girlfriend, you wouldn't need to play chaperone to Serena."

Collin glared at her. "Yeah, I need a pain in the butt like you."

Jimena's eyes sparked with fire.

"Would you guys *stop*?" Serena couldn't take it anymore.

Collin glanced at the clock. "Later," he blurted and left the kitchen.

"He's such a little—" Jimena started.

Serena interrupted her. "Do you ever think that the reason the two of you clash all the time is because you secretly like each other?"

"*Mira,* Serena." Jimena laughed. "You can read my mind, so you know that's not the truth."

The doorbell rang.

Serena ran to answer it, hoping to find Zahi. She swung the door open. Morgan stood on the tiled porch, looking at the faded ceramic frogs and trolls under the prickly pear cactus near the door.

"Morgan?" Serena couldn't hide her disappointment.

"A hello would work fine." Morgan walked in confidently.

"What do you want?" Serena hated the way Morgan kept looking around her trying to see inside.

Morgan waved a twenty-dollar bill. "I want you to read the cards for me." She was still dressed the way she had been at school.

Serena stared at her.

"Please," Morgan pleaded more softly.

Serena shook her head. "The psychic shop is closed." But she gently pushed into Morgan's mind to find out why she had really come over. It was a mess inside, with half-completed thoughts and lots of worries. She always expected Morgan to be serene on the inside. That's what she projected outward. But it was only for show. Serena pushed around the surface thoughts, going deeper, trying to find a thought to hold on to and follow. Big speech at the prep rally on Thursday. Shopping. Credit card limit. Credit card limit?! Serena didn't even have a credit card. Then she found what she was looking for. Morgan liked

Collin. She more than liked him. No way did Serena want Collin to become one of Morgan's trophies.

"Serena." The word came to her softly at first. Then someone was shouting in her ear. Reluctantly, she left Morgan's mind.

"What happened to you?" Morgan rubbed her temples as if she had felt Serena inside her head. "You looked like you were in a trance or something."

"Just thinking."

"Well, will you read the cards for me?" Morgan snapped impatiently.

"Sure." Serena closed the front door as a plan came to her. It was wrong. She shouldn't. But she had to keep Morgan away from Collin.

"It's dark in here," Morgan complained.

"So turn on a light." Serena started down the hallway. She didn't want Morgan to see the smile on her face and get suspicious.

Morgan flicked on a light switch. A blaze of light sparkled from the chandelier hanging over the entrance. She followed Serena down the unlit hallway and through the dark dining room, turning on lights. Finally they pushed through a swinging door and entered the yellow kitchen, which smelled of freshly baked cookies.

Wally was curled on the table near the khaki pants Jimena had laid out. She was cutting the legs open up to the crotch so she could sew the panels together to make a long skirt.

"That's so gross," Morgan commented.

"What?" Serena wondered if Morgan was talking about the skirt Jimena was making.

"The raccoon," Morgan said with disgust. "They have diseases, you know, ones humans can catch."

"I take him to the vet every few months."

"It's probably against the law anyway."

"So what you going to do about it?" Jimena put down her scissors and stared at Morgan.

Wally seemed to sense the tension between them. He climbed off the table and scuttled flat-footed toward Morgan. She backed up, fanning the bottom of her coat to shoo him away.

Jimena laughed and Morgan glared at her.

Serena took the plate of cookies to the table. "Here, have one. I just made them."

Morgan looked at the cookies as if they were rat-poison. "No thanks." She carefully brushed off a chair before she seated herself.

Serena sat on the other side and shuffled the cards four times. She set the deck in front of Morgan. "Divide the cards into three stacks with your left hand."

Morgan looked at Jimena. "This is private, all right?"

"Sure." Jimena gave her a fake smile. She picked up the pants and left the room.

Morgan divided the cards into three stacks, but her eyes kept glancing at the back door as if she expected Collin to walk in any minute.

Serena took the cards and wondered what Morgan would do if she knew Collin was upstairs. Probably find a reason to go upstairs and accidentally stumble into his bedroom.

Serena flipped the first card and didn't bother to look at the face of the card.

"You're here about a guy," she announced as if she had read it in the card.

Morgan smiled and seemed impressed.

"Oh, no." Serena gasped as she turned the next card over.

"What?" Morgan immediately leaned forward. How could anyone look so perfect?

"He doesn't like you." Serena shrugged apologetically. Did he? In reality she didn't know how Collin felt about Morgan.

Something changed in Morgan's eyes then. Was she sad? Morgan? Serena actually started to feel sorry for her. She pushed back into Morgan's mind to see and found something that surprised her. Jealousy. Morgan was jealous of her? Serena Killingsworth? She examined the feeling closely, surprised by how much Morgan admired the way Serena dressed, and how she wished she were talented like Serena. Serena softened a little. She slowly left Morgan's mind and turned the next card. She started to say there was still a chance, but before she could, Morgan spoke.

"You know, Serena," Morgan chided, "you really should do something about the way you dress. It's a complete embarrassment to your brother."

Serena's mouth fell open. Was it? Had Collin told Morgan that? Frantically, she shoved back into Morgan's head and pushed through her thoughts, trying to find a memory of a conversation that Morgan might have had with Collin when he told her that Serena embarrassed him. When she didn't find it, she stopped and pulled away from Morgan's mind.

Morgan looked at her strangely. "Do you have any aspirin?" she asked.

Serena searched through the cupboards, then came back with two aspirin and a glass of water. She handed them to Morgan.

Morgan tossed the aspirin in her mouth and sipped the water.

Collin came back in the kitchen. He had changed into vans and khakis and the vintage rayon Hawaiian shirt with palm trees and beaches that Serena had bought him at Aardvark's.

"Hi, Collin." Morgan's headache seemed to have vanished miraculously. She crossed her legs, exposing a nice slice of tan thigh above her boots.

Collin was surprised to see her. Unhappy? No. He looked at Morgan with real joy. "Hey, whatcha been up to?"

Morgan looked at Serena. "I guess your cards got confused."

"What?" Collin asked.

"Serena was just trying to mess up my life." Morgan stood and started playing with the buttons on Collin's shirt.

"I just say what the cards tell me," Serena lied.

Morgan shrugged. "Don't worry about it. I'm so used to your jealousy that it doesn't even bother me anymore."

"*What?* I've never been jealous of you."

"Oh, please." Morgan waved her off. "It's so obvious, the way you look at me."

Serena looked from Morgan to Collin. She expected Collin to defend her but instead he looked at her as if she had disappointed him.

She knew she shouldn't do it. Maggie had taught her never to use her gift to her advantage, especially when it could hurt someone. Too bad. She rammed into Morgan's mind again, searching until she found the speech she was supposed to give at the pep rally on Thursday. With one tiny zap, the speech Morgan had worked so hard on was pushed behind the memory of her sixth-grade Christmas party, when she had stuffed her bra with Kleenex. Serena hadn't perfected this part of her power yet, so Morgan would probably remember some of her speech. But no way was she going deliver it with the usual smooth Morgan confidence. Serena backed out, satisfied.

Morgan rubbed her temples.

"You okay?" Collin seemed concerned.

"Just a bad headache." Morgan eyed Serena suspiciously. "I never get headaches."

Serena tried to hide the wicked grin that was stretching across her face. She picked up a cookie and bit off a piece.

Morgan continued to rub her temples. "Let's drive down to the beach." She looked at Collin. "Maybe I need fresh air."

"Sure." He stepped forward.

"Shouldn't you practice your speech?" Serena offered, stifling a laugh.

"What speech?" Morgan seemed baffled.

"I heard you were supposed to give one at the pep rally on Thursday," Serena said innocently.

Morgan looked reflective for a moment as if she were trying to pull some thought into focus. "I can't think right now."

They left and Jimena snuck back into the room. "Okay, what did you do?"

"How do you know I did anything?"

"You were all squinting and zombied out. I knew you were in her mind."

"Do you think Morgan noticed?"

"She's too self-involved. So what did you do?"

Serena suddenly remembered Maggie. "I'm in big trouble." Maggie was going to be so disappointed in her. "I zapped her mind. Not big, but enough. Let's just say that the pep rally will be very different this time."

Jimena smiled. "I'm down with that. They're always so boring. I can't wait."

"I shouldn't have done it. It's just that she makes me so mad."

"Don't worry about her. She's a *rata*."

"*Rata?* A rat?" Serena said.

"A girl who hangs around waiting for guys. She's got no life." Jimena looked at her watch. "I got to get over to Children's Hospital so I can get in enough hours this month. Sorry I can't stay longer."

"See you tomorrow." Serena waved.

After Jimena left, Serena sat in a chair and set her cello on the end pin between her knees. She loved the way she had to hug the cello when she played. She dreamed of meeting her idols some day in a master class or onstage, someone like Yo-Yo Ma or Han-Na Chang. She picked up her bow and began to play. The music flowed around her, sad and filled with longing.

She had only been playing for a little while when she looked up and gasped.

Zahi stood in the kitchen watching her.

"I am sorry," he apologized. "But your back door was open and I heard the cello music." He smiled. “It drew me to you as if it were calling me. It is quite lovely.”

“Thank you.” She wondered why she wasn’t more upset that he had come into the house without knocking or announcing himself.

He pulled a chair up next to her. “I love the cello,” he said shyly.

“Me, too,” she agreed. “It communicates the way no other instrument can. It’s so sorrowful and theatrical. It seems almost human the way it expresses so many emotions.” She blushed and felt suddenly stupid for sharing her passion with him.

“It is you,” he whispered, his voice solemn. She felt as if he were talking to her from a very deep place inside himself that he seldom shared. “The cello is only wood and a bow. You are the real instrument. It is your deep emotion that I hear when you play.” He touched her cheek lightly.

“Thanks,” she said, again feeling thrilled that they had shared so much.

“Play again,” he asked. “Please.”

She leaned over her cello. She started to play

with a long strong note, making sure the sound was even through the whole bow.

Then her fingers worked a fast run and she stepped into another world. The kitchen and Zahi were no longer there, only her music swirling around her until she was lost in it.

CHAPTER FIVE

SERENA SAT ON A FOLDING CHAIR, put a Tootsie Pop in her mouth, and waited nervously. The gym had a stale smell left over from years of basketball games. Sneakers caught and squeaked on the polished wood floors as kids filed into the room and talked noisily, waiting for the pep rally to begin.

Finally, the lights dimmed and Morgan walked across the stage, smiling at the football players seated on chairs behind her. She wore iridescent paisley-print pants, a square-neck top, and lots of attitude. Serena hated to admit it, but she looked good.

Morgan stepped behind the podium and bent the microphone to her. Then she paused and nervously twisted a strand of hair. She cleared her throat. Finally she began her speech. "The day of my Christmas party in sixth grade was the worst day of my life."

Kids in the audience looked at each other and shrugged. The football team seated behind her shifted uneasily.

"That was the day I stuffed my bra with Kleenex," she said too loudly, and made the microphone shriek.

"Woo-hoo!" someone shouted.

Some kids began to laugh. Coach Dambrowsky hurried across the stage, his heavy footsteps making loud thuds on the wood floor.

"The Kleenex fell out when I started dancing," Morgan continued seriously. "One piece came out, and then another, until finally I ran to the bathroom and emptied my bra."

Morgan looked up at the stage lights as if something had just occurred to her. "So don't stuff your bras with Kleenex. You may think guys don't like flat-chested girls, but I found out that day they do."

Guys hooted and applauded.

She started to speak again, but her words trailed off as Coach Dambrowsky took the microphone. "I think that was an interesting speech, Morgan, but let's introduce the football team now." He handed the mike back to Morgan.

She smiled nicely and glanced back at the football players, who were stretched out in their folding chairs. They grinned devilishly back at her. Some waved.

She paused for a long moment as if she were trying to remember something else. "I should have used socks," she continued. "But I was afraid they might start smelling." She cupped her hands under her breasts. "I'm glad I no longer have to worry about that or have to put up with being wedged in those padded bras."

Guys howled and whistled. The football team applauded.

Coach Dambrowsky grabbed the mike again. "Thank you, Morgan," he said nervously. "Why don't you have a seat, and I'll introduce the players."

Morgan took a seat, and even from the back of the auditorium Serena could see her blush bright red.

The kids in the gym were still laughing when Jimena, Serena, Catty, and Vanessa walked out into the sunlight.

"Why was Morgan talking about stuffing her bra?" Catty wondered.

"What did that have to do with getting us excited about a football game?" Vanessa added.

Jimena couldn't stop laughing. "Yeah, it made sense." Jimena glanced at Serena.

"You promised you wouldn't say anything!" Serena scolded.

"Cool." Catty looked at her with admiration. "What did you do to her?"

"You didn't!" Vanessa's eyes were wide. "I always knew she had stuffed her bra. I remember the party."

"Take us back in time so we can listen to her speech again," Jimena begged Catty.

"Let's go back to the party!" Catty's eyes dilated as if a potent energy were building in her brain. The minute hand on her watch started turning backward.

Serena caught her wrist. "It's not funny. I feel really bad about it."

"You should feel bad." Vanessa was being nice as usual. "The whole school heard her confess. She's going to be so embarrassed."

"Why should Serena feel bad?" Catty asked. "Morgan deserved it after everything she's done."

Michael Saratoga appeared behind Vanessa and put his arm around her. His wild black hair hung in thick curls on his shoulders, and a barbed-wire tattoo circled his upper arm. He had strong angular features, a great smile, and soft dark eyes. "Hey, you guys. Do you know why Morgan's speech was so crazy?"

"No!" they all shouted in unison.

Michael smiled. "Just asking."

Morgan stomped over to them, her neck and chest still pink with embarrassment "You witch!" she screamed at Serena.

Everyone turned and looked at her. "I know you did something to me, Serena."

"What's your trip?" Jimena stepped up to Morgan and started to push her away.

Serena grabbed Jimena's hands and held them.

Morgan glared at Serena. "Like I would go up onstage and tell the whole school about the most embarrassing day of my life. You did something!"

"What could I have done?" Serena tried to seem as sincere as she could.

"You can tell fortunes," Morgan stated. "So I bet you do more. You probably put a spell on me because your brother likes me! How else could I have forgotten my speech? I mean I told everyone about the Kleenex—" Morgan stopped. She glanced at Michael and her face turned a deeper red.

Everyone laughed except Serena.

"No one can put a spell on you, Morgan," Michael told her. "You were just doing what you always do."

"What?"

"Being totally self-absorbed."

"But I never forget my speech." Morgan put her hands on her hips.

"If Serena did something to you, you should be thanking her," Michael added. "It was the best pep rally we've had all year."

Morgan tilted her head. "You're right." She smiled at Serena but her eyes looked vengeful. "What am I thinking? Just nerves from giving a brilliant speech." She twirled and stormed away.

"Wow." Michael looked concerned. "I've never seen her so upset. You think she's having a breakdown? Maybe we should tell the school counselor."

"She's all right," Vanessa assured him, and glanced at Serena before she and Michael walked away.

"Don't let Morgan get to you," Catty soothed. "It was really funny what you did."

Serena caught her thoughts and knew Catty was going to repeat the pep assembly over and over.

"I'll meet you later at Chado's." Catty walked off.

When she left, Serena looked at her watch. "I've got to go or I'll be late for my cello lesson."

"Yeah, see ya," Jimena called.

Serena picked up her cello from the music room, then walked over to Bella's house for her lesson.

She had trouble with the fast runs and could hear Bella click her tongue impatiently every time she stumbled. But it was the shaky long note that made Bella touch the bow gently, signaling her to stop.

"Serena." Bella spoke in her thick Russian accent. "Do you know you are playing a cello? Did you think maybe it changed into a drum?"

"Sorry." Serena felt embarrassed.

Bella sighed heavily and sat beside her, her arms wrapping around Serena to show her how to position her fingers to play the multiple stops with which she was having difficulty.

When her hands fluttered away, Serena could still smell Bella's lilac powder. Serena played the measure again.

"Perfect." Bella applauded. She sat on the couch facing Serena. "Having a student like you, Serena, is one of the great joys in my life."

"But," Serena added for her.

"*But* an artist must surrender to her work, day after day, even on days when she doesn't want to practice, days when her mind is on boys and dances and dresses. Talent alone . . ." Her shoulders slumped as she sighed heavily. "A person with less talent will have more success if they practice, but they'll never be able to touch the soul the way you can, Serena. You can make people feel and long and appreciate—but it takes sacrifice."

She walked over to the window as if she were suddenly alone in the room, and looked out. Then she turned and looked back at Serena. "Don't fail yourself, Serena."

Twenty minutes later, Serena walked into Chado's. She loved looking at the brown canisters of tea that lined the walls in the front room. She peeked into the lavender room where tea was served. The room was crowded already. Then she saw Maggie sitting in a corner near the window. She really looked like a retired schoolteacher. Her long gray hair was curled in a bun, her delicate fingers ran up and down the handle on her teacup, and she was smiling at nothing in particular. She lifted her cup and took a sip.

Serena walked over to her and set down her cello beside the table.

Maggie stood and gave her a warm embrace.

Serena started to smile and stopped. Maggie was looking at her strangely.

"What is it, my dear?" Maggie touched Serena's cheek. "You seem so distraught."

"I . . ." She looked down. Daughters of the Moon were never supposed to use their powers to hurt others, and Serena had definitely done so in zapping Morgan, even if Morgan did deserve it. How was she going to tell Maggie? She didn't want to disappoint her.

Before she had a chance to explain what she had done, Jimena, Vanessa, and Catty walked in the front door.

"Hi." Catty sat down. "Did you tell Maggie about your dream yet?"

"No," Serena answered.

"What dream?" Maggie lifted her teacup and took a long sip.

"It was a really weird dream." Serena spoke slowly. "It was about a fire."

"Yeah," Jimena added. "Only it was cold."

"The flames were cold, but it still burned the wood," Serena explained.

"But not the girl who walked into the flames," Vanessa continued for her. "What was her name? Lecta?"

Maggie looked up sharply.

"What's wrong?" Serena leaned forward. Maggie was too powerful to let anyone into her mind, but her emotions shimmered in the air like an aura.

"Serena, dear," Maggie began, her concern visible on her face.

Serena clasped her shaking hands under the table. "Tell me."

"I'm afraid you've witnessed an arcane

ceremony of the Atrox." Maggie looked at them solemnly. "I wanted to discuss the new Followers, but this seems far worse. *Frigidus ignis.*"

"What's that?" Jimena asked.

"The Atrox gives immortality to favored followers who prove themselves, and"—she paused—"to Daughters of the Moon who turn to the Atrox and become Followers. The chosen ones step into the cold fire and the flames burn away their mortality and bestow eternal life."

Serena was thunderstruck. "It wasn't a dream?"

"But I went back," Catty protested. "I didn't see a fire."

"You couldn't see the fire." Maggie sighed. "The Atrox wouldn't allow you to see it unless . . ." She looked at Serena and fell suddenly silent.

"What?" Serena demanded.

"Lecta wasn't the girl's name," Maggie told them. "*Lecta* means 'chosen one.' *Lecta,* or *Lectus* if it is a boy. It is a very high honor to be chosen from the legion of Followers to receive one of the highest gifts the Atrox can bestow . . . immortality."

"You'd think people would have heard about the fire and all tried to jump in," Jimena mused. "I mean, *damn,* to live forever."

"It's not quite that easy." Maggie looked grim. "The Atrox must invite you into the fire. If not . . ."

"What?" Catty sipped her tea nervously.

"If you attempt to enter the fire, even brush a hand through it when you're not the chosen one—you suffer a horrible death."

Serena began to shudder. She had brushed her hand through the flames. What did that mean?

"But why would the Atrox allow me to witness such a ceremony, and not Catty?" Serena tried to keep her voice calm.

Maggie paused and shook her head. "It's such an ancient ceremony. I didn't realize it was still practiced."

Serena couldn't ease the disquieting feeling that was growing inside her.

Maggie placed a warm hand on Serena's. "You must be careful. The Atrox and its Followers can be very seductive. They could trick you into becoming one of them without using their powers of will."

"Am I a chosen one?" Serena could barely get the words out.

"Perhaps," Maggie answered her. "Perhaps the Atrox has chosen you."

A shiver spread through Serena.

Jimena looked at her. "We've got your back. We're not going to let anything happen to you."

Serena shook her head sadly. "Remember the tarot cards? The devil, the moon, and the high priestess? The cards predicted my fall."

"No," Maggie declared firmly. "You must never be fatalistic."

"But you made it sound like the Atrox doesn't let you see the fire unless—"

"No," Maggie interrupted. "I said the Atrox is very seductive. One of the powers of evil is to make you think your destiny is inescapable, but things are never hopeless."

The waitress brought over tiered silver plates with little sandwiches and pastries.

Maggie poured tea for each of them and began to speak quietly. "You must be very strong now. This new group of Followers is somehow connected to the cold fire, even though it was Stanton and the Hollywood group who showed the fire to Serena. Remember that there is much competition among Followers for a place of power in the Atrox hierarchy."

She glanced around her to make sure no one was listening before she continued. "Because the Daughters of the Moon live in Los Angeles it is only natural that ambitious Followers should find their way here, hoping to win the biggest prize—the seduction of a Daughter of the Moon or the theft of her powers. The Atrox would award such a deed by allowing the Follower into its inner circle."

She took a bite of scone and resumed speaking in hushed tones. "The Atrox is ruthless. It may very well have tricked Stanton into showing the fire to Serena in order to make her more vulnerable to the one who will try to convince her to step into the flames."

Serena stared at her tea. Did Maggie think she would ever betray the Daughters of the Moon?

Jimena took her hand and held it tightly.

Maggie seemed to read her thoughts. "People once thought that Hekate had betrayed her role and become an evil force, but that wasn't true."

"Who's Hekate?" Catty asked.

"The goddess of the dark moon," Maggie explained, and sipped her tea.

"If she's the goddess of the dark moon she must be evil," Vanessa surmised.

"Why would you think that?" Maggie seemed astonished. "Someone has to reign over the dark. That's when people need help the most, isn't it?"

"So Hekate was good?" Jimena looked hopeful.

"She did some very good things," Maggie hesitated. "But then . . ."

"But then what?" Catty was becoming impatient.

"Oh, I don't know, maybe she lived in the darkness too long."

They all looked at Serena, even Jimena. Did they think she was going to reign over the dark? Become a Follower?

Maggie continued, "Hekate portrays most vividly the struggle between good and evil that is in each one of us."

Serena felt suddenly ill at ease. She needed to do something. Her muscles were too tense and her hands and feet too jittery to stay seated at the table. She jumped up. "I'd better go."

"Please don't," Maggie said and looked at her kindly.

Serena tried to smile, but hot tears brimmed her eyes. She picked up her cello case and hurried outside.

She didn't slow down until she was at the corner of Third and La Cienega, waiting for the light to change. She stared across the street at the Beverly Center. The parking structure was aboveground to prevent methane gas seepage, a potentially lethal chemical hazard that existed in this part of Los Angeles. The mall took its odd shape because it curled around a working oil rig in back.

Someone called her name.

She turned. Zahi waved.

"Serena, what are you doing?" He ran up to her. "Daydreaming? I am glad you were, it gave me a chance to catch up to you."

She glanced at the light. It had turned green. Now the yellow-orange hand was flashing, warning pedestrians to stop.

Zahi took her cello and they ran across the street. Cars honked impatiently at them.

"You seem upset." Zahi looked concerned. "Is something bothering you?"

"It's nothing."

"Maybe you would like to talk with me about it, no? You will feel better if you do."

He took her hand. His touch surprised her. She looked into his eyes, so clear and intently watching her, as if she were the only person in the world who mattered to him. Suddenly Maggie's warning didn't seem very important. It was hardly the first time Serena had been in danger, anyway. Only last month she and Jimena had had to rescue Catty and Vanessa from the Followers. She could handle the Atrox. Of course she could. Why was she worried when such a cool guy seemed to like her?

"Do you need to go home right now?" He didn't take his hand away.

She shook her head. "No, Dad will be late. He's working on a big case and Collin is surfing."

"Good. Then please go with me to Michel Richard's for a cappuccino."

"Sure," she responded, even though her stomach was already full with tea and scones. She wanted to be with him.

"Great." He smiled and kissed her lightly on the cheek.

She sucked in her breath, startled by the kiss.

That's when she heard Jimena call her name.

"*Oye,* Serena, wait up!"

She looked back.

Vanessa, Catty, and Jimena darted through traffic as the cars started to roll forward. A barrage of horns and squealing brakes filled the air.

Zahi stepped back. "But you have plans with your friends. I should leave, no?"

Serena wanted to go with him, but more than anything she hated girls who dumped their friends to spend time with a guy.

"Yeah." She made an effort to hide her disappointment. "I guess so." Zahi walked away.

"He's so cute." Catty elbowed Serena playfully. "I love his accent. I wonder what France is like."

And suddenly they fell quiet, thinking about their final destiny when they turned seventeen.

"Yeah." Serena spoke quietly. "I wonder, too." It scared her if she thought about it for too long. She didn't want to lose her memories of any of their adventures. She looked at her friends. Did they have similar fears? They were fifteen now. The change was only two years away.

Vanessa was the first to break the dark mood. "Let's go over to the Skinmarket and try on makeup."

"Yeah!" Catty whooped.

They ran to the escalators and rode up to the seventh floor.

Serena stopped at the two-tone false eyelashes.

"You'll look like a *payasa*," Jimena warned, and picked up a pair with tiny red feathers.

"What's that?"

"A clown." Jimena laughed and took the eyelashes with the tiny feathers up to the cashier. "But a totally cool one."

Catty squealed. They all turned. She was holding up a can of hair spray and a stencil. "Look at this. We can spray hearts and lightning bolts on our hair."

"Do me," Jimena begged.

A few seconds later Jimena had a silver lightning bolt on either side of her head.

"Wild!" Serena grinned and tried to remember why she had been so worried when she ran out of Chado's earlier. Everything was perfect. She had great friends and a guy who really liked her.

CHAPTER SIX

FRIDAY NIGHT, Jimena and Serena strutted up to the line of kids waiting to go inside Planet Bang. Serena recognized some of the kids and waved. The fast rhythm of the music thumped through the walls and undulated around them, making them move their heads with the beat, but other things made Serena's heart jitter. She looked around hoping to see Zahi. The new lashes made a strange shadow at the top of her vision.

"Scope it out." Jimena nodded in the direction of the crowd. "You ever seen so many *churrisimos vatos*?" A sultry smile crossed her lips as she caught the sideways glances of the guys in line looking her over.

"I'm only looking for one."

"You're going to knock him out with those lashes." Jimena was still scanning the guys. "They're awesome and you know it."

Serena let a sly smile cross her face. She knew she looked good. She never cared if a guy liked the way she dressed. She loved the lashes and the glitter waves she'd painted on her bare legs. She'd spent the afternoon in Freddie's having extensions added to her hair. Now her black roots with the red tips had gorgeous tight curls that reached to her shoulders.

"Do you see him?"

Jimena shook her head. "You've got it bad."

"I can't believe I'm so nervous." Serena took a deep breath.

"Hormones." Jimena laughed. "It's not nerves. It's anticipation. You're dying to get your lips on his." The stenciled silver lightning bolts shimmered in her hair when she moved.

They both wore wide cuffs of sequins.

Jimena wore silver and Serena wore gold, to match their outfits.

"Maybe he's inside already." Serena stepped forward.

"Calm down," Jimena soothed.

At the door they opened their purses for security. A security guard with a gold tooth smiled and waved them inside to the cashier.

They paid and walked into the large interior that had once been a ballroom. The pulse of the music made the floor vibrate as machines on either side of the stage released mist into the room. The vapors caught the light show. Blue and red lasers pierced the air in time to the punk-rock beat.

They walked around the crowded dance floor. Guys turned and stared.

"I don't know why you're so nervous about Zahi, anyway," Jimena commented. "You could have your pick of the guys."

"Maybe," Serena answered with a big smile. "But Zahi's not just a guy. He is total perfection."

Jimena laughed.

The music stopped and the deejay hopped back and forth on the stage.

"Come on, raise the roof!" he shouted into a microphone. "Throw your hands up. Come on, raise the roof!"

Kids stopped dancing and lifted their hands to the ceiling in time to his cadence. He built the energy high and then let industrial music pump against the wall. The music took over and everyone started dancing. Jimena and Serena stood on the edge of the dance floor. The music beat through them and they started to move.

"I don't see him." Serena could feel her heart beating rapidly with anticipation as she scanned the dark corners and the dance floor.

"He'll be here!" Jimena rolled her eyes. "Let's stand in the light. I want to see what people think of my outfit."

They moved over to the canteen where a big guy with a buzz cut sold soft drinks and pretzels.

"Okay, ready? Get anything?" Jimena posed and put a dollar down for a Pepsi.

Serena concentrated. "Most of the guys are

thinking you're hot, but they don't want to ditch the girls they came in with."

Jimena was wearing a shimmery silver skirt and a halter top. "All right, I'm going to go bikini now." She tugged, then pulled the skirt below her belly. Her tattoos looked good and the hoop in her belly button sparkled as she aligned the hip-hugging skirt with her hipbones.

"You got their attention now." Serena laughed. *"Do you ever."*

"Okay, dig deeper." Jimena smiled big. "Are any of them wondering what I like to read?" She moved one hand sensually down her hip and rested it lightly on her thigh.

"Ah . . . no." Then Serena stopped. She was picking up something. Impossible. It sounded like Collin. *Jimena looks really good tonight.*

She shook her head. Collin was surfing or at home, no doubt, but still she found herself involuntarily scanning the kids in the club, looking for him.

"What?" Jimena watched her closely. "Did you find him?"

"Sorry, you didn't find Mr. Perfect tonight," she stated finally.

Jimena shrugged. "Maybe tomorrow."

The deejay was going back and forth between sounds—top forty, house, disco, and techno—until he saw what the kids would dance to, then he'd stay with that. He started another song and the strobe light flashed, making the room jump with the strange flicker of old film footage.

That's when she saw him. Zahi was walking toward her. He wasn't bagged out like the other guys. He wore a black T-shirt under a black leather jacket, and his hair was slicked back and parted in the middle, the sides starting to fall into his eyes.

She squeezed Jimena's arm.

"You gotta chill," Jimena said.

"I can't."

"Yeah, you can." Jimena pulled her onto the dance floor. "You're a goddess, remember? One thing you got is cool. Like an iceberg." She put her hands on Serena's hips and they started dancing, bodies flowing with the music, hips swaying.

"Make him want you," Jimena whispered. "Let him spend long, tortured nights dreaming about you."

"Look and suffer." Serena let her hands reach for the heavens. The tips of Jimena's fingers touched hers, and then she felt other hands on her waist. Her lungs took in a sharp breath. Her heart raced. She turned slowly. The hands held her waist more tightly. Zahi danced slow and sensual next to her. His jeans rubbed against her bare legs, and he pulled her closer and closer until their breath mingled. His eyes lingered, taking in every bit of her. Her heart throbbed until she couldn't draw a breath.

Jimena giggled behind her.

"See ya." Jimena waved and then there was only Zahi. Even the music seemed far away.

"I was afraid you wouldn't come." Zahi murmured the words against her ear like soft, lazy kisses.

Something stirred with delicious longing inside her.

"I had to wait until Jimena could get the

car," she explained, wondering if he could even hear her above the music.

"You look beautiful tonight," he said. His finger stroked her bare back.

Adrenaline shot through her and her heart pumped crazily.

"I'm glad you're here with me." He nestled his lips against the curve of her neck. His soft breath tickled her bare skin.

She closed her eyes and let her arms slowly entwine his neck. She had never been this close to a guy before. She didn't know it would feel this good. His lips moved up her neck to her cheek, searching for her lips.

Finally, she was going to have her first kiss.

She turned her face to him, her lips parting when someone tapped her shoulder.

Go away, Jimena, she thought.

The finger tapped again, hard and urgent.

She opened her eyes and angrily turned.

Collin stood behind her.

"Collin?" she said in shock. "What are you doing here?"

"What are *you* doing, you mean?"

"You always said Planet Bang was a place for wanna-bes and gremmies," Serena reminded him.

"Obviously." He was looking pointedly at Zahi.

Morgan ducked from behind Collin. "Hi, Serena." Morgan smiled smugly. She looked incredible as always, in a slinky black camisole with shimmering white capris and sleek tiger-print sandals, hair glittered and curled.

She threaded her arm through Collin's and held on possessively. "I was just telling Collin how you hexed me."

"She didn't hex you, Morgan," Collin corrected.

Morgan shrugged.

"Hexed?" Zahi laughed and looked at Serena. "Is she calling you a witch?"

"I didn't do anything." Serena was feeling flustered with her lie.

Suddenly, Jimena was beside her. "Are you still playing that tune?" Then she glanced at Collin. "And what are *you* doing here?"

Before Collin could answer, Morgan spoke. "I know she did something to me when I was over at her house. I don't get headaches."

"You think Serena's a *bruja*? A witch?" Jimena asked dangerously.

"Those things are possible," Morgan replied. "Scientists have studied curses and they're real. Right, Collin?"

Serena watched Collin closely.

He ignored Morgan and looked at Jimena. "So you know about witches and spells, Jimena? I bet you cast a lot of spells on guys."

"Yeah, well, you'll never know, will you?" Jimena snapped.

Collin smirked. "What makes you think I'd want to know?"

"That's right." Jimena nodded to Morgan. "You like girls all shiny and smiley."

"What does *that* mean?" Morgan knew she had been insulted, but wasn't sure how.

"If you have to have it explained to you, you're more *tonta* than I thought." Jimena crossed her arms in front of her chest.

The music changed to a sultry beat.

"This music is banging." Jimena started to sway. "I'm going to dance." She strutted out to the dance floor and two guys quickly walked up to her.

Collin took Morgan's arm. "Let's dance."

"Aren't you going to talk to your sister?" Morgan said.

Serena glanced at Collin expectantly.

"Come on." Collin took Morgan out to the dance floor near Jimena. Morgan pouted and refused to dance until Collin coaxed her, running his hands up and down her arms. When they finally did dance, his eyes kept drifting back to Jimena.

Zahi curled his arms around Serena. "Why does she think you did something to her?"

Serena sighed. "It's a long story,"

"Let's forget about Morgan, then." He gently pulled Serena out to the dance floor.

Zahi drew her to him, his touch frighteningly tender, the heat from his body warming hers. Her skin suddenly became feverish and supersensitive. The caress of his hands on her bare back was making her dizzy. They danced to the luxurious feel of the song, their faces close as if they were sharing secrets.

A couple jostled into them and she fell hard against his body. His arms tightened and kept her there.

The music became more frenzied. Kids around them danced wild with the beat, but they stood motionless, holding each other.

He bent his head. He was going to kiss her now. She closed her eyes.

The music stopped. The sudden silence felt cruel, and then the houselights came on. She opened her eyes. Her lips, parted expectantly, were inches from Zahi's mouth. He didn't let her go.

The deejay introduced Michael's new band. The drummer started marking the beat, then the rhythm guitar and lead guitar began to play. The singer grabbed the microphone and the band went full tilt into smooth, feel-good music. Kids crowded the stage.

Jimena came running back to Serena and Zahi. "Where's Vanessa? I thought she wanted to dance when Michael played."

"I don't know!" Serena shouted above the music.

Michael played bass guitar and sang a song he had written for Vanessa. When he finished the crowd went wild. Most of the kids started dancing again, unable to resist the beat of the music.

Vanessa and Catty ran up to them. Like Serena and Jimena, they wore hip-hugging skirts, halter tops, and thick cuffs.

"Let's show them our moves," Vanessa said excitedly. She had been waiting to impress Michael with how well she had learned to dance.

Serena looked at Zahi questioningly.

"Please, I want to see you dance also."

"Wait for the next song." Jimena motioned to the band. "We need a different beat."

Then the music changed and the lead singer's voice belted a song with hungry desire. They were ready. They looked at each other, smiled, and melted together in a slow-moving swing that made everyone turn and stare, even Morgan.

Serena watched Zahi watching her; his eyes lingered, taking his time. She slid her body next to Jimena's, never taking her eyes off him. Then she bent lower, the long muscles of her thighs pulling tight. Rolling her hips with the beat, she placed her hands on Vanessa's shoulders.

Zahi smiled, his eyes half closed, and a jolt of pleasure shivered through her. She turned her head from side to side, moving as one with Jimena, Catty, and Vanessa. They slithered together. She turned back. Zahi had taken a step closer as if he needed to wrap his arms around her and hold her tight.

The music ended too soon. The lights came up and everyone applauded wildly. Girls bumped around Serena, crowding toward the stage to get autographs from the band members.

Serena continued to look at Zahi with sweet longing.

"Do you see that?" Vanessa asked with a flare of jealousy. "Look at all the girls who want autographs!"

The mood was broken and Serena turned slowly away from Zahi.

Catty giggled. "Don't look at the girls lined up for autographs, listen to the ones talking about you."

Girls were pointing at Vanessa and their voices carried over the crowd.

"That's Michael Saratoga's girlfriend," one said enviously.

"Isn't she pretty?" another added.

Vanessa beamed.

Jimena shook her head and laughed as more girls pushed toward Michael.

A girl lifted her sweater and asked him to sign her belly. He took a large black felt marker and scrawled "Michael" across her stomach. Other girls wanted him to sign arms and neck.

"Do you believe what he's doing?" Vanessa's anger flared up again.

"It's becoming a Michael-fest," Serena commented, and she felt Zahi's hand rest on her shoulder.

"You looked very good," Zahi whispered in her ear. "More than good."

"Thanks." Serena looked into his eyes.

Jimena nudged her. "Catch what's happening now?"

The next girl in line smiled coyly at Michael, then she undid the buttons on her blouse and stuck her chest out.

"What's she doing?" Vanessa's face was flushed.

Michael smiled sheepishly, then gripped the black felt marker and wrote his name over the swell of her breast. The girl touched the tips of his fingers when he finished writing and kept his hand there while she said something to him.

"What's she saying?" Vanessa asked.

"Forget about it," Jimena said. "You know Michael doesn't like her."

"What are they saying?" Vanessa insisted. Serena could feel Vanessa's anger like a sudden thunderclap resounding in her head.

"Just chatter," Serena lied. The girl was asking Michael to meet her later, but Michael said no.

"Look at me." Vanessa spoke tensely. "It's happening."

Serena turned. Vanessa was disappearing. Strong emotions made her lose control of her molecules. Her hands looked fuzzy.

"Help me," she whispered. Her greatest fear had always been that someone would see her disappear.

"Cover her," Jimena ordered. "She's going!"

Serena looked nervously at Zahi. Luckily he was staring at the commotion onstage.

"Relax," Catty coaxed, and swerved in front of Vanessa. "That girl's not his type. You're his number one."

Vanessa's hands and feet had vanished now and the side of her face had elongated into a funnel of dots. Her eyes were glassy and her voice sounded rubbery when she spoke, "How could he?"

"It's a guy thing," Jimena said. "Haven't you figured that out by now? You want to go invisible? Michael will see."

The girl turned and walked away from Michael, then looked back over her shoulder at him.

"He's still looking at her," Vanessa complained, but it was difficult to understand her now.

"Looking at her because he's so glad he's with you," Catty chattered on, trying to distract her. "Sing something, quick. It'll help you relax."

The girl waved to Michael, then blew him a kiss.

"That—" Before Vanessa could call the girl a name her voice left her.

"Do something," Jimena urged Serena. "See if you can zap her emotion. Quick! Go in and calm her!"

Serena had never tried to change someone's emotion before, but it was definitely going to be bad news if Vanessa disappeared and someone saw. She quickly pushed into Vanessa's mind. The anger was hot and thick and made it hard to enter. Her pinging molecules showered Serena like a barrage of searing needles.

Serena tried to calm Vanessa. Then she felt a crack in the anger and entered, hoping to pull a better emotion to the front of her mind, but behind the barrier of anger was a single thought that shocked Serena.

She burst from Vanessa's mind and took two staggering steps backward as if the thought had shoved her. She looked at Vanessa. How could one of her best friends think that about her? Did Catty and Jimena feel the same way?

CHAPTER SEVEN

ZAHI CAUGHT HER. "What is wrong?" he asked. "Are you feeling ill?" His brown eyes looked distressed.

"Nothing." She shook her head. But she was sweating now and couldn't stop her hands from shaking. Did Vanessa really think Serena would betray the Daughters of the Moon?

"You are shaking," Zahi whispered, and held her tightly.

She tried to pull away from him. "I'm not feeling very well," she said. "Maybe I should go home."

"Let me take you home, then," he offered.

"No." She spoke too sharply and pushed away from him.

He looked bewildered.

The houselights went down and the music started again. Kids crowded onto the dance floor and the strobe light flashed, making everything surreal. Michael ran to Vanessa and kissed her.

"Hey," Michael greeted her. "Seeing all those girls made me so happy I'm with you."

"Why?" Vanessa was still annoyed. He didn't seem to notice the way Vanessa's molecules had suddenly snapped back together when he touched her, or maybe he thought it had only been the lighting that had made her look so strange.

Serena watched them, her heart beating rapidly as she twisted into Vanessa's mind to see if there was more.

Michael smiled and answered Vanessa. "Because I know you'd never do something as crazy as ask a strange guy to sign your belly or . . . well, you saw, you know." He kissed her lightly.

"You didn't have to sign . . . where you signed," Vanessa said, but her anger was fading. Michael held her closely.

"I'm so glad I have you," he whispered. "You're not even jealous."

"Right." Catty winked at Vanessa.

Vanessa smiled, happy again, and her mind slowly closed, hiding her thoughts from Serena.

Serena tried to enter Catty's mind and see if she felt the same as Vanessa. Catty looked at her as if she sensed Serena's struggle to read her thoughts.

Serena stepped back, suddenly too dizzy and weak to stay inside. She turned back to Zahi. "I'm sorry, but I've got to leave. Jimena will give me a ride home."

His smile crumpled. He didn't bother to hide his disappointment or the concern he felt. "Call me tomorrow and let me know if you are feeling better."

She nodded and walked over to Jimena. "Take me home."

"What's up?" Jimena seemed uneasy.

"Can we just go now?"

Vanessa, Catty, and Jimena stared at her with worried expressions.

"Sure." Jimena didn't hesitate. They started walking toward the door.

Outside, she tried to push into Jimena's mind, but it was like a stone wall.

"What is it you don't want me to see?" Serena demanded.

"What do you mean?" Jimena dug the car keys from her purse.

"You know what I mean."

Jimena was silent. Her lips tightened.

"I thought you said we were always going to keep it real," Serena pleaded. "Always real between you and me."

Serena sensed that it was difficult for Jimena to tell her what was on her mind.

"I had a premonition," Jimena started slowly.

Serena waited. Her heart beat rapidly.

"I saw you standing in the cold fire," Jimena whispered. "That's what we've all been hiding from you. We didn't want you to worry."

"You should have told me." Fear trembled through Serena's body.

"We're watching over you," Jimena assured her. "We'll make sure it doesn't come true."

"But you've never been able to stop any of your premonitions from coming true."

Jimena was silent for a long time and when she finally spoke her voice broke. "I know," she said sadly.

CHAPTER EIGHT

SERENA LAY ON HER BED, twisting her leopard-print sheets around her and watching the slow-moving yellow globs in her purple Lava lamp. She tried to take in deep, soothing breaths, but her anxiety was like heavy stones crushing her chest and she couldn't expand her lungs. A deep cold had settled inside her. She tossed and stared at the corners of the room, wondering if another light might help.

When she was young she had believed in witches, vampires, and ghouls. After her mother left, she slept with all the lights on. That's what she had missed most when her mother had gone: safety in the night. Now her childish fears were back to haunt her, but with a new and real focus. Evil did lurk in the night and she could even name it. The Atrox.

There was no way she could betray the Daughters, was there? She couldn't imagine becoming a Follower.

Wally jumped on her bed, startling her. He snuggled his way under the covers and curled in a ball next to her.

"What do you think, fur face?" she said, and scratched behind his ear. His masked face stared back from beneath the covers as if he were trying to comfort her. She pulled him against her and finally she was able to drift into an uneasy sleep.

She awoke a few hours later with a start, her heart beating rapidly. If it had been a dream that awakened her, she couldn't remember it. She shook her head and sat up in the bed.

Wally scooted deeper under the covers.

Soft music came from downstairs. Maybe Collin was home already. She glanced at her clock.

It was only 11:45. She didn't think Morgan would release him that early. Still she jumped from bed, slipped into her furry slippers, and hurried into the hallway and down the stairs. She needed to talk to him. He had a way of making her feel safe and comfortable. She couldn't tell him the truth, but just talking to him would help ease the tension.

A light shone from under the door in her father's den, and music was coming from the CD player. She listened. She didn't think Collin would be listening to Mozart's *Requiem Mass.* Could her father be home? He said he'd be in San Francisco all weekend. Maybe the music was Morgan's idea of romance. Collin would be playing surf guitar music by Dick Dale and his Del-Tones.

Cautiously, she stepped forward and pressed her hand against the door. If Morgan was sitting with Collin on the couch, she was going to back away. She peeked into the den, then froze, gasping involuntarily.

Terrified, she took three quick step backward, turned, and ran.

CHAPTER NINE

STANTON LEANED AGAINST the leather sofa, leafing through a book on medieval architecture. His blue eyes glanced at her with hot energy, and a dangerously sensual smile slid across his face. He tossed the book aside and ran after her.

She ran back up the stairs, her footsteps thundering through the house. Where was all her goddess power? Normally her nerves would be thrumming and power surging through her. But tonight her mind was too jangled from everything that had happened. What could she do? A 911 call was a silly idea. What would she say?

His feet pounded on the steps behind her, gaining.

She could stop and face him, but she had to compose herself first. She rushed to her room, slammed the door and locked it. He smashed into the door.

She tried to calm herself and build her energy.

He continued to bang against the door, and then silence followed.

She glanced at the door. The doorknob started to turn. Then suddenly it snapped, the lock broke with a loud clank, and Stanton stepped into her room.

She took in a deep breath. Power gathered in her chest and then spread with force to the tips of her fingers. Her moon amulet cast a silvery glow across the room.

"Is that what you wear to bed?" Stanton smiled at her. "I had expected something a little more edgy."

"What I wear to bed?" She looked down at her pajamas, then glanced back at him and shook her head. This had to be a dream.

"You're not dreaming," he corrected her. The light from the moon amulet shot across his face. He blinked, then with a swiftness that seemed impossible his hand shot out and grabbed her.

She tried to pull free. When she couldn't, she pushed into his mind to stop him, but he had already invaded hers. He wasn't trying to battle her. He was soothing her, his calming words whispering around her anxiety and fear with the softness of angel wings.

"Serena." He repeated her name luxuriously as if he enjoyed the easy roll of it across his tongue.

"I can feel your heart beating fast," he continued. "But you don't need to be afraid of me. Look at me." The silky command in his voice made her want to gaze into his eyes. But that was too dangerous. He could trap her in one of his memories forever.

He pulled her to him with a gentleness she could never have expected from someone so evil. A delicious craving ran through her. She should hate his touch, but it was somehow drawing her to him.

And then against her will she opened her eyes. Had he made her do that? No, she had done it on her own. She was remembering something that was far away and she couldn't bring it into focus yet.

"I'm sorry." He spoke in hushed tones. "I know this is frightening for you. Every time I warn you, Zahi erases my warnings from your memory."

Confusion rolled through her. "Zahi?" She pulled back and stared into his soft blue eyes, even though that was the most dangerous thing she could do.

"Yes."

He had to be telling her lies to bring her defenses down, and then when she was no longer protecting herself he would attack.

She let her power build.

A lazy smile crossed his face. Couldn't he feel her preparing for battle? Wasn't he going to defend himself?

He spread his arms to his sides, smiled broadly, opened his mind to her, and waited for her attack. Another trick?

"You have the power to look into my mind and see if I'm telling the truth," he offered.

She watched him, not sure what she should do.

"I'm waiting."

What would she find if she penetrated his mind? She took a deep breath. Would he ensnare her? She plundered in and was met with a memory of the two of them walking along the beach on a chilled and foggy night, talking. It was the night of the cold fire. He held her hand. She pushed in farther and found a jarring memory of her fall from the bluff, the terrible seesaw sensation of teetering on the ledge and his struggle to pull her up. He had saved her. And finally she had willingly allowed him into her mind to remove the memories of the hour they had spent together so that he could find out who was stealing her memories and why.

She caught a glimpse of something else, but before she could examine it he jerked it from her with such force that she stumbled from his mind. The impact almost made her fall backward.

Stanton steadied her and they sat on the edge of her bed.

"That night at the beach." His words were soothing. "When you saw the cold fire. I came to you and you ran from me and fell off the bluff. That's how you broke your glasses and scratched your hands. You were caught on a ledge and I helped you up."

"The bruises on my arm?" she asked.

"From pulling you up," he explained. "I'm sorry." He touched her arm as if he were trying to take away the pain.

"You didn't trust me then, and you don't now." Stanton pulled something from his jacket pocket and handed it to her. Her blue sandals.

She looked at them. Spots of black tar stuck to the soles, and the purple-and-blue beadwork across the straps was covered with sand.

"That night at the beach, I knew someone was stealing your memories, so I erased the hour we'd spent together until I could find out who was stealing your memories and why. I suspected Zahi was pushing your memories deep into your unconscious so you couldn't remember my warnings."

"Zahi?" she asked in disbelief.

"Only the most powerful Followers can steal both memories and feelings."

"But why would you warn me?" She shook her head. This was impossible. "You'd want to see me destroyed."

"Zahi is my worst enemy," Stanton said with a flare of hatred. "And if he can deliver you to the Atrox, he wins a place of power above me."

She stared down at the carpet. If Stanton could deliver her to the Atrox he would also win a place of power.

"Yes," he answered her thoughts. "But I won't."

"How can I trust you and not Zahi if you're both Followers?"

"Because I haven't stolen your thoughts or memories."

"I don't know that." Could she believe him? Her sworn enemy was asking her to trust him, and she liked Zahi so much.

Stanton stood, suddenly full of rage. Or was it jealousy? She wasn't sure.

"Zahi is a master of deceit." He stomped back and forth across the room. He ran his hand through his blond hair. "He's like a chameleon. He can mold his personality to show you only the person you want to see. And he means to destroy you. I swear that is his only intent."

She chewed on her lower lip.

"I'll protect you," Stanton promised.

"I can't trust you," she insisted. "This is just another trick. You must have the same plans for me. Maggie told me about the Regulators. You wouldn't take such a risk."

Was it a look of surprise on his face, or fear? The Regulators were a small group who had the power to terminate any Follower who betrayed the Atrox.

"I haven't done anything to displease the Atrox," he said in a low voice, and then opened his mind to her. She couldn't believe what she saw there. Before she could be sure, the back door opened downstairs.

"That's Collin." She panicked. "He can't see you!"

"Don't tell me you're afraid of your own brother?" Stanton seemed to think that was funny. She hated the smirk that crept over his face.

She shoved him. "You want Collin to kill you? Hide."

That made him laugh louder. "Kill me?"

"Stop it," she warned him, "or he'll hear you."

"You think I should be afraid of your brother? I'm an immortal."

Collin's heavy steps filled the downstairs hallway. Her heart raced. Why was life so complicated?

His footsteps started up the stairs.

Stanton sat on the bed smiling at her.

"Please!" she begged. "He'll never understand."

Stanton didn't move.

"Serena?" Collin called from the hallway. "Are you still up?"

Her heart fell. How was she going to explain Stanton to her brother?

CHAPTER TEN

"I CAN EXPLAIN," Serena said quickly as Collin stepped into her bedroom.

"Explain what?"

"The guy. He's a friend from school," she lied. "He needed a homework assignment. I—"

Collin pushed around her.

"Don't hit him!" She grabbed Collin's arm.

"Who?" Collin looked back at her.

She turned and looked into the bedroom. The room was empty. Maggie had told her some of the Followers were shape-changers. Was Stanton one? She let out a long sigh, and just as quickly new anxiety filled her. Maybe it had only been a dream. It had felt like one.

Collin looked at her strangely and placed a heavy hand on her shoulder. "You know, sometimes your weird jokes aren't very funny." There was true concern in his voice and she could feel the beginnings of one of his brotherly lectures.

"Not tonight, Collin," she said. "I don't need a big-brother lecture right now. . . ."

"I'm just worried about you," he continued. "You know, maybe Morgan is right. I mean, if you're making up having a guy in your room, maybe you really do need a boyfriend."

She was too tired to deal with this right now. She poked into his brain, took his worries about her and pushed them behind his memories of the North Shore on Oahu. Then she pulled out, blinked, and glanced at him.

He looked a little stunned.

"You were saying?" she asked.

"Can't remember what I was saying."

"You were telling me good night." She gave him a sweet sisterly smile.

"Yeah." A dreamy look covered his face. "You think maybe dad will take us back to Hawaii for Christmas?"

"Maybe, if we both ask him," she offered.

"Mmmm." He started out the room. At the door, he stopped and turned back. "Hey, I remembered what I wanted to tell you."

Her heart sank.

"You looked really good dancing tonight. Everyone said so. You and Jimena were awesome."

"Thanks."

When his bedroom door closed, she shut her door and leaned against it.

Stanton emerged from the shadows.

"So your brother thinks you need a boyfriend?" he teased.

"Stop."

"I wish I could have seen you dance tonight." His dangerous beauty was hypnotizing. She felt sorry for him suddenly, remembering what Vanessa had seen when she had been sucked into his memories. His father had been a great prince of Western Europe during the thirteenth century and had raised an army to go on a crusade against the Atrox. The Atrox had stolen Stanton to stop his father. She looked at him now and sensed the young, frightened boy he had once been.

"I have one last question," she began. "Why did I stay so long with you if all you needed to do was warn me about Zahi?"

An odd look crossed his face. "Look," he pulled her to him again. "Look in my eyes and I will show you." His hand brushed her cheek and then he held her face tenderly.

Did she dare?

"Zahi has stolen more than my warnings," he continued. "He also stole the memories of all the times we have spent together."

The words hit her with the power of a lightning strike. "You said *we*? Of the time *we've* spent together?"

"Yes, *us*," he whispered. "Let me show you. Just one memory for now. Later the rest."

Against her will, she fell deep into his thoughts. His memories swept around her. She tried to pull her mind back, but part of her was rushing to meet him as if she had waited a long time to do this. The sudden eagerness frightened her. What was happening? He was her enemy. She had done battle with him.

Despite herself, she was sinking deeper and deeper into the memories. Suddenly, she was reliving the hour they had spent together walking on the beach and talking. How could she have spent time with Stanton and not remember? Could Stanton really like her, his sworn enemy?

He looked into her eyes. She knew she should stop him, but her body shivered pleasurably with the feel of his warm lips on her neck. She finally let herself go and breathed in the sweet soap smell of him. Her lips moved slowly across his cheek to meet his, her desire irresistible.

He stared down at her as if he needed to savor this forbidden moment. He didn't bother to hide the eagerness in his eyes. With his hands, he cupped her face, sending a delicious shiver through her. Then his eyes closed and he kissed her, his lips soft on hers.

Her lips parted as if they had kissed him

before and then his tongue brushed lazily across her lips.

Too many dangerous emotions swirled around her. She felt disgust with herself for wanting him so desperately. She tried to stop the aching need that spread through her body. It was her mission to protect people from Followers. From Stanton. She couldn't allow herself to like him.

She stopped abruptly and looked up at him.

"You can't fight it," Stanton said.

Did he too think she would betray her destiny? How could she trust him? In the past he had deceived and betrayed Vanessa.

Stanton looked at her and she knew he was reading her distrust.

"I appreciated the kindness Vanessa showed me, but I never felt the connection with her that I feel with you. I've liked you since the first time our minds met in combat. I've more than liked you, Serena." His hand touched her cheek.

She remembered that battle. How strange it had been. She had suspected even then that he had been teasing and playful, not really trying to destroy her.

She shook her head.

"I'm telling you the truth," he insisted.

She felt hot tears gather in her eyes. He was telling the truth. But their kind of relationship would always be forbidden.

"That night when we walked on the beach you told me you were willing to risk it. You promised to defy everyone to be with me."

She gazed into his eyes and knew he was still hearing the doubt in her mind.

He turned and left.

CHAPTER ELEVEN

MONDAY MORNING Serena and Jimena stood in line waiting to go through the metal detectors. The high school had just banned backpacks and messenger bags to stop kids from smuggling drugs and guns onto campus.

Security guards asked guys in bagged-out sweatshirts and jeans to lift their tops.

"Do they really think that if a guy is strapping he's going to hide the gun in his waistband? Get real." Jimena sniffed contemptuously. She wore the khaki skirt she'd made from her slacks, and a flirty, off-the-shoulder T.

Jimena took a sip of coffee from her Styrofoam cup. "Here. Want some?" She offered the cup to Serena.

Serena shook her head. She felt uncomfortably warm in her pink snakeskin jacket. The wooden platforms with the neon-green straps and rhinestones were already starting to cramp her toes.

"What's wrong?" Jimena asked finally.

"What do you mean?"

"You've been huffing and sighing all morning like you're still mad at me for keeping the premonition from you."

"No, it's . . ." She broke down and told Jimena about Stanton's visit, but she couldn't tell her everything, especially not about the memories of the time she and Stanton had spent together.

"Since when does a Follower care enough to warn one of us?" Jimena sipped the coffee.

"He said Zahi was a Follower."

Jimena laughed. "Zahi is about the sweetest guy I've ever met."

"Still. What if?"

"Zahi doesn't look like the new Followers. He's not all punked out. Look at his left arm. No tattoo. Stanton was playing with your mind. But if you're still worried, why not use your moon amulet?"

"I've looked at it. It doesn't glow when he's around."

A puzzled look crossed Jimena's face, and then it was her turn to step through the metal detector. She did and waited for Serena on the other side.

Serena passed through and then paused while one of the security guards went through her purse.

The guard handed the purse back to her and she caught up to Jimena.

"I'm talking about the power that Maggie just told us about," Jimena whispered. "The special one."

"What special power?" Serena asked as they walked toward their lockers.

"*De veras,* you don't remember?" Jimena sounded perplexed.

Serena shook her head.

"What's up with you lately? You were so psyched to try it out."

"Maybe it's the winter concert." Serena sighed. "Maybe algebra. My mind feels like mush."

"Maybe it's Zahi." Jimena giggled. "You're too in love to think about anything else."

"I don't know." Serena wondered what else she might have forgotten—or had pushed from her mind.

"Give Zahi your moon amulet to hold. If he's a Follower as Stanton says, then the moon amulet will leave a mark in his skin."

Serena clasped her amulet. How could she have forgotten something so important? She vaguely remembered Maggie telling them, but it felt far away and dreamlike.

"Here he comes now," Jimena said under her breath.

Serena turned. Zahi ran up to her. She took an involuntary step backward and smiled nervously. Could he really be stealing her memories?

The bell rang.

"Gotta go," Jimena called and ran off.

"Hello, Serena," Zahi said, and ignored the crowd of kids running to class. He wrapped his arms around her. "Let's leave school this afternoon, just you and me."

Serena hesitated. "You mean cut classes?"

"Yes."

A funny feeling crawled through her stomach. She glanced down at her amulet. Why wasn't it glowing? Or did it only glow when she was in danger? She couldn't quite remember. She looked into his warm brown eyes, then down at his perfect full lips.

"Sure," she finally said. "After algebra."

"I'll meet you at Borders in the coffee bar."

"Okay."

Two hours later, Serena hurried up the stairs in Borders. She sat in a chair next to the window and looked down at the traffic on La Cienega. She took a deep breath and leaned back. People were reading at the tables around her. Their thoughts combined into a soothing murmur, like the rush of water around stones in a creek. Her muscles began to relax. Only then did she realize how anxious she had felt.

Zahi came in and set his books on the table. "Campus security was watching the area between the gym and the music room. Sorry I'm so late. I'll get us something to drink."

He went to the coffee bar and came back with two steaming cups of chai tea and a chocolate chip muffin.

She breathed in the scent of ginger, clove, and cinnamon spices and looked through the steam across the table at Zahi.

Zahi reached over and took her hand. "I'm glad you came," he said and kissed the tips of her fingers. "You seem like a very serious student. I was afraid you wouldn't meet me."

She unhooked her moon amulet from the chain around her neck and handed the charm to Zahi.

"What is this?" He took it in his left hand. "A gift from another boy, perhaps?"

She laughed, all her doubts vanishing. "No,

not from a guy." She looked at his sweet smiling face. Zahi, a Follower? No way. How could she have ever suspected something so ridiculous? It seemed foolish to make him hold her amulet. Stanton's accusations felt more treacherous than true. She tried to remember what he had said exactly, but it was all so shadowy now.

Zahi rested his hand with the amulet under the table and sipped his tea. "So how is your practicing with the cello?"

"Okay." She started to feel at ease and more self-confident. "I'll have the sonata memorized by the winter concert."

"Good, I want to hear it. Promise to play it for me soon."

"I promise," she answered. The longer she was with Zahi, the farther the night with Stanton drifted into the unconscious layers of her mind.

"There is going to be a rave in the desert this Saturday night," Zahi said.

"I've always wanted to go to one." Serena smiled. "It sounds so cool, dancing all night."

"Go with me, then," he urged. "Can you

leave your house without anyone knowing?"

"I think so." She was getting excited. "Collin won't check on me, and Dad's working strange hours right now. Jimena will freak out. I know she's always wanted to go to one, too. I can't wait to tell her."

"Serena." Zahi was suddenly serious.

"What?"

"Without all your friends." He spoke softly. "They are very nice. I don't mean anything against them, but I want to spend time with you. Alone. Will you go out with me, Serena, alone?"

Her heart careened against her stomach. She hoped he didn't see how happy she felt.

He leaned across the table and whispered, "It should be a very romantic night. The moon will be full."

"Yes." She nodded. "I want to go."

"Good." He looked into her eyes. "I'll be at your house at seven, then, or do I need to meet you someplace?"

"No, come to the house. I'll get rid of everyone before you get there."

"Good," he said. Then he leaned completely across the table and kissed her quickly on the cheek. "I must go now." He stood and handed her necklace back to her.

She held it in her hand. She had forgotten that she had given it to him.

Serena quickly clasped it around her neck and immediately felt a sense of relief.

CHAPTER TWELVE

SATURDAY NIGHT, Jimena walked into Serena's room carrying a brown paper bag filled with cartons of takeout Chinese food. The aroma of green onions, garlic, and pork filled the room. Jimena set the bag down on the floor in front of the TV and flipped a video into the recorder.

Serena cleared her throat. "I . . . I think I'm coming down with flu or something,"

"You stay in bed. I'll sit on the floor." She handed Serena a white carton of chop suey and a pair of chopsticks wrapped in paper.

"I think I just want to sleep," Serena tried again.

Jimena took the remote and put the movie on pause.

"Sorry," Serena apologized. "Maybe you should go."

There was so much disappointment in Jimena's face that Serena almost told her to stay. Guilt weighed heavily on her now. She couldn't believe she was lying to her best friend over a guy. If she did tell Jimena about the rave, she'd probably help her dress in something really funky and not even feel jealous. So why couldn't she bring herself to tell her?

"I can tell you're not feeling well," Jimena finally said.

"How's that?" Serena asked.

"You don't seem like yourself. All week you've been, I don't know, distant or something. You got a fever?" Jimena touched her forehead and a peculiar look crossed her face.

"What?"

"Nothing," Jimena said quickly, but Serena

knew she was holding something back.

She tried to peek inside her mind, but the wall was up again.

"Tell me. What did you see?" Serena insisted.

"I said *nothing*." Jimena ejected the cassette from the recorder. She gathered the food and the videos together.

"Why are you upset?"

"I better go so you can get some sleep." Jimena left the room.

"Jimena," Serena called after her. She ran to the hallway but Jimena was already bounding noisily down the stairs.

She heard Jimena and Collin in the kitchen.

"Leaving so soon?" Collin asked.

"Yeah," Jimena said flatly. "You like Chinese?"

"Love Chinese," Collin answered. "Don't you want to share it?"

The back door opened with a squeak, and then Jimena yelled back as if she had stopped at the door remembering something.

"Check on your sister, okay?"

"Is she sick bad?"

"Just check on her," Jimena told him, and then the door banged shut.

Serena hurried back to bed and pulled the covers around her.

A few minutes later Collin's slow steps beat on the stairs. Finally he walked into her room holding a white carton and chopsticks. He picked a carrot with the chopsticks and tossed it into his mouth.

"You okay?" Collin asked.

"Sure, just a cold."

He sat on the edge of her bed. "Should I stay home and make you some chicken soup?"

"No, I'm just going to sleep. Go surfing. I'll be fine."

"Sure?"

She nodded.

He remained sitting on her bed eating chop suey as if he had something more to say. His words surprised her. "Has Jimena got a boyfriend?"

"No."

"Figures," he muttered and stood. "Get better. I'll check on you when I get home."

"No!" she said too loudly.

He turned and looked at her with concern.

"I mean, please don't. I need the sleep."

"Sure." He stood and left her room. She jumped up and waited by her bedroom door until she heard Collin leave through the back door. Then she ran to the window to make sure. She watched his utility van back out of the drive and turn down the street.

Serena went to the bathroom and locked the door. She stared at her reflection. Her eyes had a dark haunted look and the wide-eyed stare of an insomniac. Why wasn't she excited? Strange thoughts and feelings kept whispering across her mind. Was there something important she should be remembering? For some reason, her mind couldn't focus. She took foundation and dabbed it on the bluish circles under her eyes.

A picture of Stanton flashed across her mind with such startling clarity that she froze for a moment. He had visited her in her bedroom. Had that been a dream?

She put on mascara, pasted a bindi on her forehead, then pushed her hair back with a jeweled tiara. She liked the look with her new extensions.

She walked back to her room, looking for comfortable shoes. She could wear thick socks with her new Doc Martens. She found the shoebox under her bed and pulled it out. What she saw inside made her hands start shaking.

The Doc Martens had been worn. When had she worn them before? She clutched them close to her chest and stared out the window, trying to focus on the memories from the back of her mind.

The full moon started to rise and with it came another memory of Stanton. She was finding it impossible to concentrate on anything. Had he warned her about something?

Normally the milky light from the moon made her feel strong. But tonight the moon seemed an omen. Maybe she shouldn't go.

But there was something else. If she didn't go, she would always wonder what might have happened. Maybe it was better to follow Collin's philosophy. Why not try it? If you feel yourself falling, dive. No fear. Take it to the end. She'd go with Zahi.

She jumped off the bed, hurriedly pulled on sweats, then wrapped bright pink and purple boas around her neck. She was going to have fun. She was sick of all the baby games at Planet Bang and the La Brea High dances. This was going to be the big time.

As she spread glitter on her neck and face and her spirits soared, but when she accidentally touched her moon amulet, a prayer tumbled from her lips, *"O Mater Luna, Regina nocis, adiuvo me nunc."*

She sat back on her bed. What was happening to her? That prayer only came out during times of great danger.

She looked behind her as if she expected to see someone standing in the corner of her room.

Then the doorbell rang.

CHAPTER THIRTEEN

ZAHI LEANED AGAINST the doorjamb. He looked sexy and handsome, dressed in khakis and a sweatshirt. His presence had a calming effect on her. "You look wonderful." He admired her.

She hurriedly locked and closed the door, then and followed him out to the car.

"You have the directions?" she asked.

He smiled and opened the car door. "On the seat." She picked up the directions, sat down, and snapped her seat belt into place.

They drove up the Antelope Valley Freeway at breakneck speed, then took the Pearblossom

Highway through a forest of spiny Joshua trees and cactus scrub. Moonlight illuminated the desert, giving it a strange underwater glow. She rolled down her window and the sweet smell of desert sage filled the car.

"Look." Zahi pointed to the blue and pink laser lights piercing the night sky. Latticework towers on the horizon looked like a strange spaceship.

"Cool," she breathed softly.

As they drove closer the traffic became more congested. Then it stopped. Guys wearing walkie-talkie headsets waved flashlights and directed kids to a parking area. Some impatiently drove off the road into deep sand and got stuck half on, half off the road, adding to the traffic jam.

The wind shrieked in and out of the car, but when it stopped, the music was loud enough to carry across the desert.

"Let's turn back and walk," Serena said with mounting excitement.

"You don't mind the walk?" Zahi asked.

"I'm too wound up. The walk will give me time to calm down."

He leaned over and kissed her. "No calming down tonight," he whispered, then he spun the car, gunned the motor, and left a track of rubber on the two-lane highway.

He found a place at the edge of the highway that looked good and parked. They got out and started walking. The desert wind blasted around them, thrashing their hair and slapping their clothes against their bodies. Her boa followed after her like a flying snake.

Soon they were walking with other kids dressed like techno hippies in bright neon colors, carrying light sticks and Day-Glo flowers. Throbbing brass and machinelike sounds drowned out the howling wind. They passed a girl selling T-shirts with the rave culture's neo-hippie motto, PLUR, written on the front and underneath, in small letters, PEACE, LOVE, UNDERSTANDING, RESPECT.

Kids sold water, glow sticks, flares, smiley faces, Day-Glo plastic jewelry, and pacifiers from their cars.

They had gone about a mile when they

stopped and Zahi gave their tickets to a man wearing a floppy purple hat.

Serena stepped into the mix. The huge size of the gathering made her feel as if she was going to the county fair. The music beat faster than machine-gun fire, hitting 160 beats a minute. The energy pulsed through her as rapidly as the beat.

She held her arms out and started twirling. Zahi grabbed her around the waist and they twirled wildly together until they were both out of breath.

He kissed her lightly and then they started walking again.

The vibrations grew stronger as they pushed toward the towering speakers. The sound quaked through her chest, rocking ribs, heart, and bone. It felt excitingly weird and good. She tried to soak in as much of the delicious energy as she could.

Some of the kids leaned against the speakers, bathing in the throbbing beat.

Zahi took her hand and they walked through another group of kids, who were sucking on plastic baby pacifiers while they danced.

"Why are they doing that?" Serena asked.

"The pacifiers ease the teeth-grinding effect from the Ecstasy," he explained. "Don't worry. We don't need drugs for thrills." He leaned down and kissed the side of her head. "We'll enjoy a greater energy. I promise."

Up on the stage a deejay wearing thick gold chains over a black T ran back and forth between four turntables. Everyone was into the dancing.

Serena snapped her light stick and started moving, the beat too fast to catch. She waved her arms and head.

"Wait," Zahi mouthed.

She didn't want to wait.

"Dance," she yelled over the music, and hopped over to him. He pressed his body next to hers, his hand curling tightly around her waist. She looked into his eyes, so dark and reflecting the moon's silver light. He almost looked supernatural, like a creature of the night. Why hadn't she noticed how compelling his eyes were before?

She felt his breath on her lips. The desert

wind rushed around them as if it were trying to separate them.

"Wait for what?" she asked even though she was sure he couldn't hear her. She didn't want an answer; she wanted his kiss. His lips were inches from hers now.

"Promise yourself to me?" he said.

A deep blush rose inside her.

"Maybe." She wanted love, respect, and trust first. She wasn't in a hurry. She glanced up at him and boldly put her arms around his neck. She did want a kiss.

He smiled and looked down at her, taking his time and making her hungry with anticipation. He looked darkly beautiful, his eyes lustrous. Then he pressed his lips on hers. A jolt of pleasure rushed through her body. His hands traced up her back.

"Let's go over there." He pointed to a smaller group of kids on the steep rocky slopes of a nearby butte. The jagged rocks and sheer sandstone outcroppings were silhouetted against the indigo sky. The kids danced around a fire in some antic neotribal way. It looked like fun.

"Okay." She closed her eyes and lifted her face for another kiss, but he was already pulling away.

They shoved through dancers waving Christmas tinsel, boas, flags, flowers, beads, and light sticks.

When they reached the fire, Serena climbed on a bolder and started dancing again.

She whooped, glad she had decided to come. Then from the corner of her eye she noticed something strange. One by one the kids around her had stopped dancing and were staring up at her.

Their eyes glowed phosphorescent.

She stood motionless.

Punkers. Pierced lips. In the fire's flickering light, their tattoos looked like the he-goat depicted on the devil card in her tarot deck.

She jumped off the bolder. Why would Followers be at a rave? Even these newer aggressive ones? They feared the full moon, when their eyes turned phosphorescent and ordinary people could feel their evil.

Their eyes flashed with anticipation.

She stood in front of Zahi, ready to protect him.

The fire raged upward when she did.

"We've got a problem," she said to Zahi, hoping he could hear her. "We have to leave now. I can't explain why. Just trust me."

Suddenly, she was doubtful that she could fight so many of them by herself.

She turned to push Zahi farther away. When she did, he smiled and lifted his left hand. A glossy impression of her moon amulet glimmered on his palm.

She now understood why the devil, the moon, and the high priestess had shown up in the spread. The cards had been trying to warn her. Even as she reproached herself for being so incredibly stupid, she knew there was still part of her that wanted Zahi.

"You would not be the first goddess to join the Atrox," he said. Or was he speaking inside her mind? His words felt seductive and compelling. "You're smarter than the other goddesses. Even Maggie sees it. She's been trying to tell you."

He touched her and she backed away from him.

"The dark of the moon was sacred to the witch goddess, Hekate," he said. "It could be sacred to you as well. All you have to do is step into the fire and become immortal. Why do you need the Daughters of the Moon when you can become even more powerful and have eternal life?"

The flames twisted, the tips radiating a strange whiteness that seemed almost pure. Sparks burst into the air and continued to glow as they twirled up and up.

"Lecta," Zahi said softly.

The fire responded and flames shot toward them like searching arms eager to embrace her.

"Lecta." Another Follower joined in, and soon they were all chanting, *"Lecta! Lecta!"*

She could no longer hear the music from the mammoth speakers, only the cold fire calling to her.

The blaze reached higher.

"Make me proud," Zahi coaxed. "Live with me for eternity."

The flames roared with impatience.

"I won't," she finally spoke. "I won't go in the fire."

"No matter." Zahi smiled malevolently. "I will take you to it."

He grabbed her wrists and began to pull her toward the flames. The dark anger made his face even more perfect than it had been before, a purely evil beauty.

She tried to fight him with mental force, but his power was stronger and her head pulsed with the rhythm of his thoughts. Her temples throbbed as the pain inside her head became unbearable. Her vision clouded as his power cut through hers like shards of broken glass.

CHAPTER FOURTEEN

SERENA SAW THE FULL MOON through the wavering flames.

"O Mater Luna, Regina nocis, adiuvo me nunc," she whispered, chanting the prayer like a mantra.

"The prayer will not help you, Serena." Zahi smirked.

She was close enough to the fire to feel its sweeping coldness.

She continued to look at the moon through the turbulent fire. Suddenly she knew Zahi couldn't harm her. Even alone she was protected. She gazed at the moon's brilliance, breathed deeply, and felt power surge through her.

Zahi noticed the change. "Do you think the moon will protect you?" he whispered across her mind. "Look again."

Darkness crept over the edge of the moon.

"The moon is entering the shadow of the earth," he said. "There is a full eclipse tonight. For two and a half hours you will be without the protection of your moon."

Serena looked up as the edge of night began to cross the moon.

Her power ebbed.

Zahi grabbed her hand.

It took all of her effort to block him from controlling her. And then he broke through her mental barrier with an explosive force. His thoughts flooded through her and took control again.

She looked at the flames licking the night sky and felt a lethargy take over.

She hesitated, then took one step forward and another.

"Lecta," the Followers began to chant again.

The flames radiated out and encircled her wrists with terrifying coldness. She shivered. The cold penetrated her bones as she stood at the edge of the fire.

Her tears turned to small ice crystals that slid down her cheeks. Then Zahi's mind wrapped completely around her like protective dark wings, and her resistance died.

CHAPTER FIFTEEN

POWERFUL HANDS GRABBED her shoulders and suddenly yanked her back. Zahi left her mind with a suddenness that caused a painful jolt. She fell to the ground. She shook her head, the hypnosis over, and inched back as glaring, angry flames howled skyward, then tracked along the coarse soil trying to grab her and pull her back.

Stanton stood protectively over her.

The power emanating from Stanton and Zahi made the air crackle as if great electrical currents were flowing between them. The small hairs on the back of her neck rose and the air became too thick to breathe. She didn't have the strength yet to stand.

The Followers loyal to Zahi crowded around him. They could not attack without his order.

Stanton stood alone. Was he powerful enough to fight off Zahi?

The air became heavy with the smell of ozone, and then the air exploded violently with a roll of thick thunder. Stillness followed. She didn't know who had won. She took a deep breath and then another.

Stanton ran to her and grabbed her hand.

"Come on!" he said. "We have to get away before Zahi recovers."

She glanced back. Zahi appeared to be frozen in a trance.

She didn't want to stay with Zahi and his Followers, but at the same time she didn't completely trust Stanton. Why had he rescued her?

"Haven't you figured out yet that I was telling you the truth?" he snapped angrily. "Of course not. You don't remember because Zahi hid those memories from you again."

She tried to stand but her legs were too shaky. Her head throbbed. Seeing that she couldn't run, Stanton swung her up in his arms and carried her.

"Up there." He motioned with his head. "We'll hide in the rocks."

He ran into the rocky terrain of the butte, carrying Serena. Night predators scrambled away as he wound in and out of the rocks and shadows. The laser lights and cold fire created strange shifting shadows across the face of the sandstone outcropping.

Stanton tripped over a rock. They fell and he tumbled on top of her.

"Sorry," he said. "Are you okay?"

"No." Pain racked her bones.

She suddenly realized he was still lying on top of her, his body warm against hers. And she wasn't repulsed, not at all. Her hands moved against her will, curling up around the hard muscles on his back. She looked into his blue eyes, visible in the dark, so startlingly honest.

"Stanton," she whispered, and as she said his

name a deluge of memories flooded over her, swirling with tumultuous speed around her every thought. He wasn't pushing them into her mind. The recollections were forcing their way back from some dark hidden place deep inside her.

He touched her cheek softly as if he knew what was happening. She closed her eyes.

"I'm sorry." She spoke with deep penetrating sadness as she finally recalled how many times Stanton had warned her about Zahi. "I should have believed you."

"How could you?" he asked. "He only left you with bad memories of me."

She lay quietly beneath him, immersed in the memories. How could she feel this way about someone who had dedicated his life to evil?

She could tell by the disappointment on his face that he read her bewilderment and alarm. She looked away.

"It takes longer for the emotions to return," he said simply, and then he motioned for her to be quiet.

A shadow fell over them.

She looked up. A Follower stood nearby. His spiky orange hair and the hoops pierced through eyebrows, lips, and nose made him look edgy and hard-core.

She made her mind blank so that if this Follower had learned how to sense thoughts he wouldn't be able to pick up hers.

The Follower shook his head, then rubbed his eyes, and she knew Stanton was working his mind. He fingered his nose ring, looked in the opposite direction, and ambled away from them.

Stanton got off her and helped her up, then they peered from behind the boulder.

The Followers swarmed through the jagged rocks.

"It's only moments before another one finds us," Stanton whispered. "We're going to have to split up."

"Okay." She nodded and looked up the bluff. It was a steep climb but the only way she saw to escape.

Stanton touched her cheek and turned her head to face him. "If you have the power to read minds and steal memories, then you also have the power to cloud minds."

"I've never done that before." She shrugged. "I don't know if I can."

"You'll have to use that part of your power to protect yourself in case one of them finds you."

"But I don't know how." Usually she would practice her new skills with the other Daughters before trying them on anyone alone.

"I'm going to distract them," Stanton said. "Hopefully, Zahi will chase after me. He'll think you're the easier prey and come back for you later."

"Thanks." She shot him an angry look.

He almost laughed. "I said he'd *think*. He doesn't know you the way I do. Sneak back to the rave and hide in the crowd."

She realized suddenly that he was going to sacrifice himself to save her. Maybe he could fight off Zahi, but what about all of the other Followers?

She touched his hand. "Two together have better odds."

"No." He shook his head. "I can explain

stealing you from Zahi because the Atrox thrives on competition among its Followers, but I wouldn't be able to explain helping you escape."

"The Regulators," she remembered with a sudden chill.

"The Atrox has to believe that I stole you from Zahi for my own prize and then you escaped from me."

"Be careful," she whispered and looked at the shadows. They seemed natural enough, but the Atrox was always around, sending shadows like tentacles as its eyes.

"Don't worry," Stanton assured her when he saw her studying the shadows. "It's not here."

"How can you tell?"

"Centuries of experience," he said with a grim laugh, then he stood.

"Caprimulgus!" he yelled angrily.

She translated his Latin. "Milker of goats?" It would have been funny if her hands hadn't been shaking so fiercely.

"Trust me. It's a big insult," Stanton explained.

"Let's run up the butte and find a better place to hide," she suggested, worried for his safety.

"No," he said firmly. "Our chances are better if we separate."

Serena peeked around the corner of the boulder as Stanton hollered, *"Caper!"*

The word made Zahi furious. She flinched in anticipation, but nothing happened. Apparently his power wasn't strong enough to confront Stanton from a distance, because she didn't feel a change in the air.

"Caper!" Stanton yelled again.

She'd have to ask Maggie what *caper* meant. Stanton read her mind.

"I just called him a he-goat. That's the way people with an ordinary knowledge of Latin would translate it, but I really called him the smell of an armpit." Stanton looked at her doubtful expression. "Maybe you have to have been around for a few hundred years to understand."

He bent down quickly and kissed the top of her head. "Good luck."

Stanton darted over the rocks. The Followers ran after him. Stones and pebbles rolled down the butte behind him.

When the running footsteps were too distant to hear, she stood and looked around the rock outcropping.

A Follower grabbed her. The girl was trying to look deadly dangerous with her black lipstick, piercings, and partially shaved head.

"Goddess," she whispered fiercely into Serena's ear, and bent her arm back painfully. "Zahi! I've got her."

CHAPTER SIXTEEN

THE FOLLOWER HELD Serena tightly, but her mind didn't try to control her. She started to yell again, but before she could, Serena pushed quickly into her mind.

The girl's mouth closed and a whimper died in her throat.

She had no barriers against Serena's entrance. Her mind was frightenly dark and empty, all hope surrendered to the Atrox, no dreams, no plans for the future, only a vast desert of days stringing hopelessly before her. She was only an initiate, waiting to see if the Atrox would accept her as a

Follower. Serena relaxed. Someone who had recently turned to the Atrox was the easiest to save. Serena didn't need to stay in her mind to control her. She slipped back out.

"You're new, aren't you?" Serena commented, clicking her tongue pierce against her teeth.

The girl frowned.

"They haven't even told you anything about mind control yet. Don't they trust you?"

The girl didn't seem to understand.

"Sorry," Serena said. "You're about to displease your master." She let the power build inside her head and then she released the force.

The girl put her hands over her face. She leaned against the rock, then slid down its side. Still holding her head, she spread her fingers and looked dumbly out at the shadows in front of her, her eyes uncomprehending.

"You'll thank me someday," Serena told her, wondering if the girl had parents who were frantically waiting at home to hear from her. "The Atrox isn't going to allow you in now that you've let me escape."

Rocks tumbled down the side of the butte.

Serena looked up. Several Followers were running toward her, jumping over craggy rocks. Zahi stood at the top, his hair whipping around his face. She could feel and see the strength of Zahi's mind crackling through the night air, sparking off rocks and boulders, searching for her.

She turned to run but tripped over a rock. She tumbled and looked back.

"Stop!" Zahi yelled. She slowed, but only for an instant.

She glanced up at the moon, almost lost in the earth's shadow now.

She ran crazily, leaping over cactus shrubs and rocks, until finally she was pushing through the twirling, jumping, spinning bodies.

And then she saw Morgan dancing with two boys.

"Morgan!" she shouted, even though she knew Morgan couldn't hear her over the beat of the music. She ran to her.

Morgan had braided her hair with Christmas tinsel and strapped fluffy angel wings on her back. She'd never looked so funked-out and cool. The guys dancing with her wore yellow, pink, and violet glow hoops around their necks and arms, reflector tape on their jeans, and large floppy hats.

"Morgan," Serena called again as she drew closer.

One of the guys tapped Morgan and pointed to Serena.

Morgan stopped dancing, her fists on her hips. "What do you do? Follow me around? The cool doesn't rub off, Serena."

"I need to talk to you." Serena pulled her away from the boys.

"Why don't you go back to geek heaven with all your bizarre friends," Morgan snapped and yanked her arm away from Serena.

"This is way serious," Serena insisted. "I need your help."

"Right." Morgan gave her a spiteful smile.

"Remember what happened to you a month back with those kids who hang out with Stanton?"

Morgan took a sudden step backward and gave her a petulant look. "You can't threaten me. I'm not afraid of you."

"Why would you be afraid of *me*?" Serena demanded. "It's the others—"

"Please," Morgan said, and pulled on a gold chain hanging around her neck. A charm that looked curiously like a standing he-goat dangled on the end of the chain. "Zahi gave me this charm. He said it could ward off the evil eye and protect me from your black magic."

The charm looked demonic and evil.

"I think the charm is bad luck." Serena felt suddenly worried for Morgan's safety.

"Right," Morgan smirked. "I figured you'd say something like that. Did I mess up your plans? I guess you can't cast any more spells on me. What did you want to do? Get me to stay away from Collin? Have me make a fool out of myself again? I'm so on to you. You may be able to fool the others into thinking you're just a regular kid who likes to study and dress weird, but I know the truth and I'm going to tell everyone."

Serena looked quickly around. How soon before the Followers found them? Morgan was vulnerable because she'd already had a run-in with them. Serena didn't feel as if she had enough power to fight them all. She grabbed Morgan's hand.

"We're in danger here. We have to leave."

"I'm only in danger from you and your magic."

Someone grabbed Serena from behind.

She let out a cry.

CHAPTER SEVENTEEN

SHE TURNED, ready to fight Zahi.

It was one of Morgan's dumb boyfriends.

"Witch, huh?" the guy said in a teasing way and hung an uninvited arm over her shoulder. The brim of his floppy hat hit Serena's head. "You want to put a spell on me?"

"Get off me," Serena said and tried to push him away.

"Voodoo me," he leered and tried to kiss her.

"Go back to Morgan." She shoved harder.

He stumbled backward, then smiled stupidly at Serena and started dancing in weird jerking steps.

Serena started to walk away from them when he grabbed her again.

"I said leave me alone!" She turned, ready to punch him, but looked into Zahi's smiling face instead.

"Goddess." His eyes dilated and glowed.

Then the night air shuddered and his energy burst into strands of light that twisted toward her. She understood his power to control her now, the subtle way he hid memories from her. Before he pushed into her mind, she sent all her force out and tunneled into his. Maybe she could cloud his thoughts and use that moment to escape. He wouldn't be expecting her attack.

She thrust into his mind and knew immediately she had made a dangerous mistake. She felt his laughing embrace as his power sucked her deeper and deeper inside him. The rave fell away and she stood in cold darkness. She began to shiver. Something menacing hovered in the shadows around her.

The Atrox. The black night shadows snaked around her, caressing her with unmistakable tenderness and coaxing her forward. What did it want her to see? She took one slow step and then another, afraid of what she might see when the shadows cleared.

"Look, my chosen one," a steely voice commanded.

The shadows cleared and a mirror stood before her. She looked at her reflection. She was different, her green eyes as deep as newly cut emeralds, her skin flawless and glowing with a strange light. A shiver traveled through her as she felt her evil potential. She had an impulse to run, but where? She was trapped inside Zahi's mind.

"Look," the shadow whispered and cradled her. "Look at what I offer you."

She stared in the mirror again and her reflection changed. She held her cello, lovingly embraced between her knees, hand delicately pulling the bow across the strings. The picture was mesmerizing.

"Look deeper," the voice challenged.

She touched the gilt edges of the mirror, and suddenly she had no desire to flee. She was playing on a stage, a symphony behind her, the audience enraptured.

"You shall have that." The voice spoke with complete confidence.

How had the Atrox known her most secret dream? The dream she had been afraid to voice even to her best friend Jimena.

The music rolled over her in waves, her fingers so sure on the strings. Tears formed in the sides of her eyes. Yes, this was what she wanted more than anything, but she had been afraid she wouldn't . . . couldn't have the time to make it come true. And here it was. Success without the sacrifice. She would do anything—

Someone tackled her to the ground. The mirror shattered around her, bursting into vapor. Her chin hit the dirt and sharp pain spun inside her head.

CHAPTER EIGHTEEN

THE FALL RELEASED HER from Zahi's hold. Her head ached and thin lines wavered in front of her eyes as if Zahi were still trying to pull her back into his world of dark promise. She looked up.

Zahi stood over her and seemed as baffled as she felt.

She looked around, unable to grasp what had happened. Kids danced wildly, their feet stomping near her. The rapid pulse of the music beat through her.

"Jimena?!"

"Did you think I was going to punk out on you?" Jimena said, and helped her stand.

"Thanks." She took Jimena's hand and stood.

Zahi's eyes burned yellow, his power sweeping around them, but he didn't seem as invincible as before.

Jimena and Serena concentrated on pushing back his mental attack. Serena felt lost in her own power as it filled the air with an invisible force. Their moon amulets gleamed white and then shot blinding purple bits of fire into the air. Kids nearby stopped dancing and waved their hands through the air in amazement. Some jumped and tried to catch the purple embers floating in the wind like thick snowflakes.

Serena and Jimena released their power.

Zahi stumbled back.

"Come on," Jimena said, and grabbed Serena's hand. "You've done enough fighting for tonight."

Serena turned and bumped into Morgan.

Morgan screamed and jumped back. She

held out her he-goat charm pinched between white trembling fingers and pointed it at Serena as if it were a knife.

"Stay back," she yelled.

"Did Zahi do something to her?" Serena asked Jimena as they started pushing through the crowd.

"You were in a trance or something when Zahi had you," Jimena explained. "Then she saw what we did to Zahi. She's probably afraid you're going to put another spell on her."

"Another? I never put a first one on her."

"Don't waste energy trying to figure out Morgan, we've got to get away from here before Zahi and his band of Followers get after us."

Serena watched Zahi put his arm around Morgan. Morgan looked up at him with a coy smile and stared into his eyes.

"We've got to get Morgan." She started back and Jimena stopped her.

"Look again," Jimena warned.

Morgan lost the fast beat of the music. She entwined her arms around Zahi, still lost in his eyes. Her hips moved snakelike to music only she could hear. Zahi placed his hands on her waist and glanced back at Serena.

"Mine now," he mouthed, or maybe he had brushed the words across her mind, because she heard them clearly.

Serena darted back to fight Zahi.

Jimena grabbed her hard. "*No seas tonta.* You did what you could. He only took Morgan to get at you. You think you can fight him now?"

Zahi's punk Followers swarmed around him and glared at her.

She could feel Zahi's taunting laughter as she finally turned and followed Jimena.

They continued pushing through the dancers until they were running past the buzzing generators. The fumes from the generators drifted away, replaced by the aroma of desert sage. They slowed and started trekking across the desert through the spiked and twisted Joshua trees. The lunar eclipse threw an eerie reddish color across the moon's face.

Serena spoke first. "How did you know where to find me?"

"Over at your house, when I touched your forehead to see if you had a fever, I got a premonition so big it almost knocked me on my butt. I saw you at the rave with Zahi. Didn't take much figuring to know what had caused your flu."

"I'm sorry." Serena looked down. "But how did you know I needed help?"

"Because you'd never put some *vato* in front of your friends. And for sure you would never lie to me. So I got to thinking about what you'd said about Stanton."

"His warning to me about Zahi?"

"Yeah. Plus Zahi transferred to our school about the same time the new Followers showed up. That's when I knew he'd put a hold on you. So I blasted up to the desert like a rocket. I would have been there sooner but I had to park about a mile out."

"Thanks," Serena said, and hugged Jimena.

They came to a dirt road.

"Let's take this." Jimena pointed. "It should hook up to the highway."

Their feet crunched over gravel and dirt.

Without Joshua trees and scrub to shelter them, the wind battered against them in unrelenting whirls, driving dust into their eyes.

"I saw the Atrox," Serena said slowly. "At least I think I did. It wasn't so scary."

"Wasn't?" A look of surprise held Jimena's face.

Serena shook her head. "Do you ever wonder why we're doing this? I mean, we've got Followers always chasing us down and it makes a real mess of our social life. What happens if we tell Maggie we don't want to do it anymore?"

"We can't. It's our destiny. You know that." Jimena sounded concerned. "Besides, I figure there's something important waiting for us."

"But Maggie can't even tell us what's waiting for us. She should tell us what happens when we turn seventeen," Serena complained.

"Maybe she doesn't know," Jimena suggested.

"She knows," Serena said with sudden anger. "Maybe going with the Atrox is easier."

Jimena stopped and grabbed Serena's elbow. "You *loca*? What's got you?"

Did she dare tell her the truth? "I mean, why not become queen of the dark?"

"Because," Jimena insisted.

"That's not an answer. Why be good when we're in so much danger and we don't even know if we get a future? If the Atrox can give us so much, why not be bad?"

"I know bad." Jimena spoke quietly. "It's not the answer." She fingered the scars on her arm as if the return to her memories were making them throb. She caught Serena looking at her. "If you don't have the scars, then you didn't have the life."

Jimena was silent for a long time, the desert wind lashing her hair into her eyes. "I didn't go looking for trouble at first, but it was always there. I felt like I was caught in this hole and I kept digging, thinking I could get out, but the hole just kept getting deeper and bigger. Then one night at a party, this guy walks in and he takes an AK-47 from his coat and starts shooting. I mean, *damn,* I'd never seen so many people die. He killed two of my home girls. So the next day at school I got a gun. I walked over to him, sitting all alone in his car and I shot him. I kept pulling the trigger till his friends stopped me. That was the first time I got sent to camp."

"Did he die?"

"Lucky for me he didn't. His car got most of the bullets. But I was still going to kill him as soon as I got out."

"Did you?" Serena asked softly. Jimena had never told her this much about her life before. She had thought Jimena had gone to camp for stealing cars.

"I got out and that's when I turned evil," she continued. "I must have been evil to do the things I did before I got caught up again. I didn't care. I was jacking cars and taking all kinds of risks. Some days I even scared myself. But I couldn't stop. I didn't want to. Being bad and breaking all the rules can make you feel invincible. There's power in that . . . for a while . . . and then . . ."

"What?"

"There must be something deep inside people that doesn't like to be bad, because afterward I felt like I was all alone in the world and nobody could love me after the things I'd done. But I didn't want to give up the feeling of power I had when I was bad. I felt above everyone. Bigger. Better. A real hard-rock gangster."

They walked down the road in silence, listening to the haunting wind.

"I got caught again, went to camp—but this time—"

"That was right before I met you," Serena added.

Jimena nodded. "But this time something snapped and I lost my anger. I mean I got in there and I was waiting in the holding tank with these shackles around my arms and waist and ankles, staring at the gray wall and I thought, I do not want to spend my life this way."

"But how did you get community service?"

"That was after I got out of camp. My home girls did the throw-down. They took this old woman's purse, but the cops caught me. The cops wanted me to talk, but no way was I going to be a rat-head. The judge saw something different in my eyes this time. I could see it on her face, the way she smiled at me like she knew I'd finally learned my lesson. She knew I'd changed. I had. Used to be I wouldn't have even talked to someone like you, who followed the rules. I thought I was better because I didn't have to. Now we're kicking it like we've known each other forever."

Serena put her arm around Jimena.

"So maybe it looks good, what the Atrox showed you," Jimena continued. "But after, when you're alone, it won't look so good—won't feel good, either. It's worth nothing, 'cause that's what you end up with."

They reached the crossroads and stopped. A small house was nestled under a row of swaying cypress trees. Flames flapped furiously from four rusted oil drums in the front yard, making shadows jig and twist around the trees and house.

"Who'd live all the way out here?" Serena wondered.

"Doesn't matter," Jimena said. "Let's cut across the yard."

They stepped into the yard and a shadow

moved in the darkness under the cypress tree, then another stalked forward.

"What was that?" Serena asked nervously.

"Your imagination is in high gear." Jimena laughed.

Then three large black dogs charged from the shadows, teeth bared, ears back. Their paws and nails scattered dirt, pebbles, and desert dust.

"Ay!" Jimena yelled, and jumped behind Serena.

"Here, nice doggy," Serena crooned in a soothing voice, but the sound of her words only seemed to make the dogs angrier. Their snarls grew louder.

The first dog pounced as an old woman wrapped in a black shawl stepped out onto the small wood porch. The wind caught the tail of her shawl and whipped it up and around, tangling it in her long white hair.

Serena could feel the dog's hot breath on her face. She stiffened, too stunned to run, and waited for the teeth to bite into her cheek.

The old woman whistled.

The dog whimpered and turned back, its paws pushing off Serena's chest.

The other two dogs slid in the loose gravel, turning. Then all three ran back to the woman, who now stood in the yard in front of the porch.

Serena wiped the hot spittle from her cheek, then rubbed her hand on her sweats.

"Man, I can fight an ancient evil," Jimena muttered. "But give me a good ol' American dog and I turn to yellow Jell-O."

"I'm right there with you." Serena didn't need to turn around to know that Jimena was trembling as badly as she was.

The dogs pranced around the woman, licking her hand. The one that had attacked Serena now lay on his back in the dirt yard, begging for a belly scratch.

"Who is that woman?" Jimena whispered.

"I don't know."

"Let's get out of here. The crossroads are *peligroso*. They're dangerous, eh?"

But neither of them moved. There was something about the woman that held them. She wore three iron keys on a chain around her neck, and when she turned toward them the keys hit each other with a soft clanking sound.

"Who says the crossroads are dangerous, anyway?" Serena asked, unable to take her eyes off the unusual woman.

"My *abuelita.*"

"Girls," the woman called.

And they both jumped.

"Come here, please." Her voice seemed remarkably young and strong.

"Yeah, what?" Jimena shouted. "You got something to say, we can hear you from here."

Serena elbowed her. "She probably wants to apologize for letting her dogs scare us."

"She's a witch, a ghost, or *la llorona,*" Jimena said.

"How can you tell?"

"You got eyes."

"She's okay." Serena grabbed Jimena's elbow and pulled her forward. "She's just someone's grandmother living out here."

"Check her out."

"All right." Serena pushed gently into the woman's mind. She couldn't. There was nothing there. Impossible.

"You picking up anything?" Jimena asked impatiently.

"No." Serena shrugged. "I think I used up all my energy tonight. How 'bout you?"

"Yeah, but I don't need a premonition. It's common sense. Strange old woman. Living alone. I don't want to go inside and see all the dead rats and cats and kids in her refrigerator and watch her sing over the bones."

The woman started walking toward them. Her milky brown eyes were deep-set and filled with knowledge. "I've been expecting you," she said.

"That's it." Jimena threw up her hands. "I'm outta here."

Serena grabbed her arm and made her stay.

"Have you young women ever heard of Hekate?" the woman asked, and petted the dogs prancing around her skirt.

"What about it?" Jimena said.

"Why are you asking us about Hekate?" Serena didn't believe in coincidences.

"She protected people from going the wrong way at the crossroads," the woman began.

"We're not going the wrong way, *viejecita.*" Jimena crossed her arms. "My car's parked right over there."

"You'd be surprised." The woman's wrinkled lips turned up in another smile. Her crooked finger pointed in the opposite direction.

"Come on, Serena." Jimena started walking.

"I'm going to stay," Serena decided. She had a strange feeling this woman wanted to help her. "Get the car and come back for me."

"¿Estás loca?" Jimena was exasperated. "Haven't you had enough for one night?" She kicked the ground. The dogs growled and she stepped back.

"I need to talk to her."

"Whatever." Jimena shook her head and walked off.

Serena followed the woman inside. The dogs rushed around her and settled under a table in the middle of the room. The woman shut the door against a dust devil forming in the yard. The door rattled as the wind continued to rage.

Dozens of candles of differing shapes and colors lit the interior and cast a warm glow about the room. The air smelled of vanilla and pinecones.

The old woman sat down at the oak table in the middle of the room. Two plates, two cups, a dish of petits fours, and a teapot sat on the table as if she had been expecting company.

"Come in and sit down," the old woman offered.

Serena sat across from her. One of the dogs rested its head on her shoe, its nose cold against her ankle.

The woman poured two cups of tea, and in the candlelight her face looked sad.

"Did your electricity go out?" Serena asked, but she already knew the answer.

"No, I prefer the dark. You could say the dark is sacred to me."

"Why?"

"Because everyone must travel through the dark in order to reach the light. I suppose that means they must all come to me eventually for advice."

"You are Hekate?" Serena whispered.

"Hekate." The woman repeated the name as if the feel of the word on her tongue awakened something inside her. "No." She picked up the plate of petits fours.

"Are you lonely living all the way out here?"

"Some of us must bear more in life than others," the woman answered softly.

Serena braced herself to hear the woman bemoan her solitude.

"But that can be a blessing." She offered Serena the petits fours.

Serena took one and bit in.

"Some people want an easy life, they want the fame and fortune and none of the struggle." She stopped and looked at Serena. "I suppose you have a dream?"

"Yes," Serena answered as the wind shrieked

over the roof and pounded against the door, demanding entrance.

"I can see what you want and yet it's frightening to you, wondering if you can work hard enough to achieve it."

Serena nodded.

The wind screamed again under the door. The candles flickered and underneath the table the dogs whimpered.

"I love the wind," the woman said, looking behind her. "All women have the power of the wind inside them, deep in their souls. The problem is . . ."

Her eyes looked at the ceiling as the wind skated across the roof, lifting shingles. She smiled and turned back to Serena.

"The problem is most women let this force die out to a breeze when a whirlwind is needed. When her forces are gathered and focused, she can do anything. It's when the force is scattered that she fails."

The house shook and then the wind broke open the door, whirled around the room, and blew out the candles. Then it left as suddenly as it had come, leaving only the dark and the smell of candle smoke in the room.

"You see," the woman said, and reached under the table to pet her whining dogs. "It can be quite powerful when focused."

The roar of mufflers sounded outside. Then Jimena walked across the porch. The boards creaked under her feet. She peeked inside. "Serena?"

"Yeah?" Serena didn't move.

"Let's roll," Jimena said impatiently.

"Thank you." Serena stood and walked to the door.

The wind had become no more than a whisper now. The flames in the oil drums licked lazily toward the night sky and reflected off the blue fender of Jimena's car.

The woman followed them to the door, the dogs by her side. Before she closed the door, she spoke to Serena in Latin. *"Id quod factum est, infectum esse potest."*

"What do you mean?" Serena asked.

"Use it," the woman said, and lifted a chain holding one of the keys from around her neck and placed it around Serena's neck.

"What is the key to?" Serena examined it in the dim light.

"You'll know if you ever need it." The woman smiled, went back inside, and closed the door.

On the drive back to L.A., Jimena asked, "What did she say to you, anyway?"

"Id quod factum est, infectum esse potest."

Jimena thought for a moment. "What has been done can be undone. What does that mean?"

"I'm not sure," Serena said, and fingered the key. Then she thought about Zahi, and suddenly she knew what she had to do.

CHAPTER NINETEEN

THE NEXT DAY, Serena called Zahi and asked him to meet her near the Beverly Center.

The Sunday morning traffic was light, the air still, and a thin layer of gray clouds hung in the sky. Zahi walked up San Vicente, where she waited under the green awning of the Hard Rock Cafe.

"I changed my mind," she said when he reached her.

He placed his arm around her and whispered, his breath warm against her ear, "I knew you would." Then he leaned back and looked at her, his eyes filled with cruel delight and satisfaction. "Say it," he commanded.

She stared straight at him. "I'll step into the fire and become the witch goddess."

The wind whipped around them, spinning dirt, paper, and dried leaves from the gutter as if the Atrox had been listening and her promise had swept it into ecstasy. But then she caught the surprised look in Zahi's eyes and wondered if the whirlwind had come from a force inside her.

"Lecta," Zahi uttered with a slight tremor in his voice. "I will pick you up tonight. The moon rises at seven. I will be parked in your driveway at six-thirty."

"All right," she said, and walked away. He watched her as she stepped around the corner and walked past Todai and Ubon. She continued down the street to Jan's coffee shop.

Catty, Vanessa, and Jimena were waiting for her at a large booth in the back. It was warm and crowded inside and smelled of bacon, coffee, and fresh-squeezed orange juice. She slid into the booth. They had already ordered a Belgium waffle and a cup of coffee for her.

"You did it?" Jimena said.

Serena nodded.

"Did he say where you were going?" Vanessa asked and poured syrup over her waffle.

"No." Serena took a sip of hot coffee, hoping it would ease the chill inside her.

"It's dangerous." Jimena looked worried.

"It's the only thing that can be done," Serena declared. "We have to get rid of these new Followers. Zahi is their leader, and without him they'll be weakened."

"I'll go invisible and follow you," Vanessa suggested. "And then I'll come back and tell Catty and Jimena where you are."

"Hopefully, I'll get a premonition before then." Jimena took a deep breath. "We won't leave you hanging."

"If worse comes to worst," Catty added, "I'll take us back in time and then we'll just keep doing it until we get it right."

They all smiled, reassured, but Serena knew

it wouldn't work that way. They'd only have one chance. They seemed to understand.

"How are you going to fool Zahi?" Jimena asked.

"Yeah," Catty wondered. "What if he reads your mind and knows you're trying to trap him?"

"We should go talk to Maggie," Vanessa said. "She only lives a few blocks away."

"No." Serena didn't fully understand why she needed to do this without Maggie. "It's too late. I've made up my mind. Besides part of our mission is to find a way to release the Followers from their bondage to the Atrox."

"Yeah, but I don't think we're supposed to die trying," Catty pointed out. "Maggie's always helped us in the past."

"I agree." Vanessa pushed her food away. "It could be way too dangerous."

Serena looked at Jimena.

"I'm down for you." Jimena sighed. "But they're right. It's dangerous and I had that premonition of you standing in the cold fire."

"Look, you guys, you're either going to help

me or I'm going to do it by myself." Serena looked around the table. They each nodded their agreement.

That night Serena dressed to meet Zahi. She used a metallic green eye shadow on the top lids and the outer half of the bottom lids so that her eyes looked like a jungle cat's. Two coats of black mascara completed them, and then she smudged a light gold gloss on her lips.

She took a red skirt from the closet. The material was snakelike, shimmering black, then red. She slipped it on and tied the black strings of a matching bib halter around her neck and waist. She painted red-and-black glittering flames on her legs and rubbed glossy shine on her arms and chest.

Finally, she took the necklace she had bought at the garage sale and fixed it in her hairline like the headache bands worn by flappers back in the 1920s. The jewels hung on her forehead, making her look like an exotic maharani.

She sat at her dressing table and painted her

toenails and fingernails gold, then looked in the mirror. A thrill jolted through her as it always did. No matter how many times she saw her reflection after the transformation, her image always astonished her. She looked supernatural, a spectral creature, green eyes large, skin glowing, eyelashes longer, thicker. Everything about her was more forceful and elegant—an enchantress goddess. She couldn't pull away from her reflection. It was as if the warrior in her had claimed the night.

At last she took her moon amulet and placed it around her neck.

The doorbell rang. She grabbed the iron key and her high-heeled sandals, and hurried down the dark hallway, a faint rainbow light shimmering around her. Already she could feel Zahi's presence on the other side of the front door, his evil waiting to embrace her.

"Let him wait," she said softly to herself. She sat on the steps and slipped into her sandals. The ritual was complete now. She was ready for battle.

She stared down at the key in her hand. "Ready?" she whispered to Vanessa, who had been waiting invisible by the door. Then she slipped the key into her skirt pocket. She opened the door, waited for Vanessa to breeze past her, and stepped outside.

Zahi leaned against his car parked in the driveway, his legs crossed in front of him. When he looked up and saw her he gave an involuntary start and then a slow smile spread across his face. His deep brown eyes met hers and she saw the desire in them. She strolled over to him.

"I'm glad you changed your mind." He took her hand, turned it over, and kissed the palm. "Goddess," he whispered, and continued to hold her hand near his face, his breath warm on her skin.

She slowly pulled her hand away and worked hard to keep her mind blank. She could feel him softly treading through her thoughts.

He opened the car door. She climbed in and purposefully stretched her legs. Her dress rode up her thighs. She watched him watching her and didn't stop the stretch until she felt a chill brush across her back. Then she knew Vanessa was in the car.

"I'm settled in now," she announced coyly.

"Temptress," he said, smiling wickedly.

She took deep breaths as he hurried around the car and got in the driver's seat.

He turned the key in the ignition and the engine thundered. He backed the car from the drive with a squeal of brakes and headed toward Fairfax.

She let her head rest on the back of the car seat and smiled when she caught him casting sideways glances at her. Headlights, streetlights, and neon signs flashed light and shadow across the inside of the car.

"Your mind seems empty tonight," he said. His warm hand touched her knee, the fingers soothing.

"Oh," she started. "I—"

"You don't need to feel so nervous," he reassured her. The hand glided up her thigh.

"What happens after I become a Follower?" A flash of movement made her look in the back. Vanessa was crouched behind the driver's seat, slowly becoming visible. Her fear and nervousness were making her reappear.

"What?" Zahi's hand flew back to the steering wheel and he glanced at Serena suspiciously.

"I'll miss my friends," she said too loudly, trying hard to distract him and at the same time keep her mind empty.

"You will make new ones." He dismissed her worry and looked in the back. "What are you looking at?"

"Nothing," she whispered and ventured a glimpse into the back. Vanessa was invisible again. She breathed deeply and tried to relax.

They drove to the corner of Wilshire and Curson and parked near the Page Museum, where the La Brea tar pits were.

"Here?" she asked.

"Here." He got out of the car and then walked around the car, opened her door, and pulled her out.

He started to slam the door. She caught it.

He looked at her strangely.

"I felt dizzy for a moment," she said and

hoped he couldn't see the lie in her words. He had almost slammed the door on Vanessa.

"It will be over soon." His gleaming yellow eyes weren't even trying to hide his bold scrutiny of her body. "And then you will be mine for eternity."

Her heart beat more rapidly.

She felt a ruffle of air and knew Vanessa was out of the car. She slammed the car door. "Let's go."

They walked around the oozing tar pit, past the statues of the mammoths edging down to the water to drink.

As they continued around the Page Museum, blue and orange flames exploded into the night sky and sparkling red embers showered down on them like falling snow. An amber glow covered the park and the back of the L.A. County Art Museum.

She felt a light wind whisper through her hair and knew Vanessa was leaving to get Jimena and Catty.

They walked closer to the flames.

Zahi's Followers turned and smiled at her in welcome, their eyes yellow and needy. She thought she saw Morgan in the crowd, but the girl ducked behind two guys.

The fire seemed hungrily aware of her presence. Its cold flames shot out and curled around her, making her shiver. Patches of frost remained on her skin where the flames had caressed her.

"Step in," Zahi ordered.

She needed to wait until the other Daughters returned before she entered the fire. Otherwise her plan wouldn't work.

"Don't we party first?" She did her best to smile beguilingly at the other Followers, who seemed eager to do something more than look at flames.

Too late, she realized she had let her guard down. Zahi was in her mind, and now he understood her need to stall for time. Angrily, he tore the silver amulet from her neck, tossed it to the ground, and pushed her backward. She tripped and fell into the fire.

The flames shot up, and with a sudden roar,

sucked her into the middle of the fire.

She tried to breathe, but the bitter air felt too cold. Dancing flames surrounded her, and every time she turned to flee, more flames shot up until she was lost in the freezing inferno. Her bones began to ache from the cold. Her fingers grew numb. Frost gathered on her skin in crystalline snowflake patterns that glittered gold, then red. Her body throbbed, but just as the pain became unbearable, something sweet and longed-for penetrated her being. She gasped. Then with delight, she smoothed her hands down her body, over breasts, waist, hips, and thighs. The desire filled her, a wicked longing.

"Lecta," Zahi breathed, and the ceremony began.

CHAPTER TWENTY

SERENA STRUGGLED AGAINST the caressing flames, the fierce hunger working inside her. Then the crackle of the flames grew still and cello music played, filling her mind with sweet promise. She stopped fighting. The flames soothed her and gave her a sensation of power. Her worries burned away as her strength grew.

Through the veil of flames, Zahi smiled triumphantly.

Abruptly, she reached through the shroud of fire and grabbed his arm.

He hadn't been able to read her intentions

because the Atrox had filled her mind with music. A look of total surprise and soul-wrenching fear covered his face as she yanked him into the flames.

The fire howled in anger and exploded into a blinding flash. The center of the blaze became piercingly cold. Sparks cascaded onto the lawn and trees, setting new fires.

Serena held Zahi tightly against her. *"Id quod factum est, infectum esse potest."*

"No!" Zahi screamed.

As she repeated the words, the fire became a swirling vortex, its shrieking colors circling with ever-increasing speed.

"What has been done can be undone!" Serena continued to repeat the words as the flames lashed at her with stinging cold.

In the distance the sirens of fire engines filled the night.

Serena looked through the violently rotating flames and saw Vanessa, Jimena, and Catty running toward her. They looked like goddesses; Vanessa dressed in shimmering blue, Jimena in lightning-strike silver, and Catty in wild strawberry pink, their hair bouncing in silky soft swirls with each step.

A police car with its light bar flashing electric blue drove into the park. The siren wound down and the officers jumped from the car. Some of the Followers ran. Morgan was one of them.

Serena grabbed Zahi's left hand and looked at the palm. The glimmering tattoo from her moon amulet had vanished. Zahi was mortal again. Serena pushed him from the fire.

He stumbled out and Jimena grabbed him. His remaining Followers circled him with anxious looks. Then one by one they began to scatter and run.

The first fire engine arrived and parked, followed quickly by a second and a third.

Firemen in yellow soot-covered protective clothing with fluorescent strips and domed helmets jumped from the trucks and began pulling hoses toward the fire as others worked with wrenches to attach the hoses to the hydrants.

Serena started to step from the flames, but the fire held her with almost human hands, inviting her to stay. The show of color and sparks became spellbinding and Serena could feel her sense of herself slipping away, pulled down into an ice-cold abyss. She ceased to resist. She breathed the flames. Its cold reached into her lungs, curled inside her chest and lay there like ice-blue flowers.

Jimena, Vanessa, and Catty watched in horror, their moon amulets glowing.

Serena stepped from the flames and stretched her arms over her head, enjoying the luxurious feel of her body. What would it be like to live forever? To see the next millennium, and the next? She opened her eyes and knew by the shock she saw in Jimena's eyes that her own now glowed phosphorescent.

She remembered the promise the Atrox had made to her, but she had no interest in the cello now and wondered why she would ever waste her time on something so foolish.

The fleeing Followers hesitated as if they sensed her growing power. A few jumped over the fire hoses and ran back to her.

She picked up her amulet where Zahi had tossed it. It seared her flesh. She glanced down. The outline of the moon was burned into her skin. She dropped it and Catty picked it up.

She watched the confusion on the faces of her friends as the power of the Atrox continued to grow inside her. She cherished the anguish she saw.

"Goddesses," she sneered, and then whooped exuberantly and prepared to fight her once best friends.

CHAPTER TWENTY-ONE

THE GLOW OF THE FIRE flickered nervously over the faces of Catty, Vanessa, and Jimena. The fear in their eyes mirrored the change they now saw in hers. Even Zahi, sprawled on the grass, looked afraid of her.

Serena smiled contemptuously. She gave them a little mental shove to demonstrate her new power.

Vanessa took a step backward, shocked, but Catty didn't flinch. "I'm not impressed," she said.

Jimena had a different look, one she couldn't

quite read. "We've got to get Serena back into the fire, quick before the firemen drag their hoses over here and put it out."

"Why?" Vanessa asked with growing worry.

Jimena kept her eyes on Serena while she spoke to Vanessa. "So we can burn the immortality off her. You don't get immortality without one big commitment to the Atrox." She took a resolute step forward.

Serena laughed at the determination she saw on Jimena's face.

"I don't think she's going to go." Vanessa seemed apprehensive.

"We'll make her," Catty replied.

Serena taunted Jimena. "You still think you're the tough goddess?"

Jimena didn't answer.

Serena laughed and gave them another mental jab, but this time Jimena had prepared for it and it didn't penetrate.

"So we're battling now," Serena said with glee.

Catty joined Jimena.

Vanessa stopped them. "Serena is a *Lecta,* a chosen one."

"So what?" Jimena tossed her head impertinently.

"Serena was invited into the fire," Vanessa explained. "Maggie said if you're not invited into the fire, the flames cause a horrible death. If the fire touches either of you—any of us—"

There wasn't the slightest hesitation on Jimena's face. "I'm not afraid of her," Jimena said. "She's just a chump with an attitude and she's going back in the fire." With even more resolve, she strutted forward.

Serena hesitated for the slightest second, wondering what it was inside Jimena that made her willing to risk an excruciating death to save Serena. And then she let the power build inside her until the air rippled.

Jimena suddenly lunged through the thick air and grabbed Serena's arm.

Serena let the force gather inside her mind, then she shoved it out at Jimena—one sharp invisible bolt of pure energy. Pain registered on

Jimena's face, but she didn't drop her hold.

Then Catty broke through the waving air and took her other arm.

"No!" Serena yelled, and the scream scraped up her throat with wretched pain, the sound so deep and angry it frightened her. It wasn't her voice.

Catty and Jimena pulled her toward the flames.

A fireman stopped them, his face in shadows cast from his helmet. "What the hell are you girls doing here?" he asked from behind his fire shield.

They ignored him and continued to pull Serena toward the flames.

"Get back," he yelled and plunged ahead, dragging the hose. When he was only ten feet from the blaze, he lifted his fire shield, then stripped a glove from one hand and waved it in the air. A look of awe covered his face.

"Cold," he said. "It's cold!"

Before he could say more, two other firefighters ran up behind him and took their positions on the hose. Water charged through the hose with sudden force and shot into the flames.

The fire consumed the water, hissing violently, and grew into a billowing tower.

"We've got to act now." Jimena reached for Serena again.

A policeman pushed them away from the shooting flames into the crowd that had gathered behind a barricade. Overhead a helicopter shot a column of light over the chaos. News vans set up their antennae and newscasters spoke rapidly into microphones.

"Firefighters have changed their approach," the newscaster spoke into a microphone as kids behind her threw gang signs and waved at the camera's eye. She continued, "At first fire officials thought the fire was set by an extreme group of punkers. Now they have determined it is a crude-oil fire, possibly caused by a methane gas explosion or seepage from the adjacent tar pits. They are now spraying a synthetic film-forming foam over the fire and do not anticipate any danger to the County Art Museum or the Page Museum."

The camera turned to the firefighters covering the flames with foam. The flames dwindled. Smoke billowed gently into the air, gliding in and out of the bars of white-blue light cast from the police and television helicopters overhead.

Serena brushed her hands through her hair, then turned and looked at the Followers who had gathered around her. "You're going to have to do better than you did tonight," she scolded with a brazen smile. Then her eyes caught Zahi, standing next to Jimena. Was he trembling? She hissed at him. He backed away.

"I was worried about kissing you." She laughed in disgust.

Her Followers laughed and the sound filled the night air with a chill.

"Goddesses," she said. "Not tonight but soon—I'll have the pleasure of destroying you."

She started walking saucily away, and enjoyed the looks she saw in the faces of the men, old and young.

Then she turned back. “Be sure to tell Maggie thanks for all the extra time she spent training me to use my gift. I’m sure it will come in handy.”

Serena smiled maliciously and walked away.

CHAPTER TWENTY-TWO

SERENA HADN'T GONE FAR when something made her skin prickle. She turned as Vanessa ran in front of the TV camera and dissolved into a ghostly shimmer.

What was she doing? Vanessa's greatest fear had always been that someone might see her become invisible, and now she was flaunting it. Why? Vanessa danced away from the TV camera, billowed on a breeze to the firefighters, and then like a circus performer, she fluttered in and out of focus.

The firefighters stopped spraying foam. The

first one took an involuntary step backward and knocked into the one behind him.

Newscasters and camera operators ignored the police officers. They pushed through the barricade and ran to the fire to capture the impossible on tape. Pandemonium broke loose. Vanessa led the crowd farther and farther away from the dwindling flames.

During the confusion, someone tackled Serena to the ground. Jimena!

Before she could push her away, Catty slipped the moon amulet around Serena's neck. Serena tried to yank it off, but Catty held her hands. The silver moon burned into Serena's skin and the searing pain distracted her. She couldn't concentrate enough to use her power. Jimena and Catty pulled her into the few smoldering flames while the crowd watched Vanessa do her invisibility dance.

The flames seethed and hissed and tried to push Serena from the fire. But Jimena stepped into the blaze, clasped Serena tightly, and made her stay.

"Id quod factum est, infectum esse potest," Jimena

repeated, her voice becoming weaker and weaker.

The fire shrieked its protest. Cold spasms shuddered through Serena as the blaze began to burn away her immortality. Slowly, she returned from the wintry abyss into which she had been pushed. She saw a future again, not an endless string of days. Time seemed suddenly more precious, the night more beautiful. As the fire continued to consume her immortality, her allegiance to the Atrox retreated and her moon amulet no longer blistered her skin. Then she looked down and became aware of Jimena in the fire with her, writhing in excruciating pain.

"No!" she screamed.

She tried to step from the cold fire, but the blaze raged and refused to release her. The flames, like icy tendrils, twined tighter and tighter around her arms and legs. She concentrated, and when she did, her forces gathered and focused into a violent whirlwind that extinguished the blaze.

Serena pulled Jimena from the embers and smoke and knelt beside her.

Jimena was dying.

CHAPTER TWENTY-THREE

CATTY LEANED OVER HER. "Is she going to be okay?"

"I don't know." A hollow ache spread through Serena.

"Maybe if I take her back in time," Catty offered, her eyes wide as her pupils began to dilate.

"No," Serena whispered, but already the air had started to change as Catty readied for a trip back in time. Then Serena remembered the key. "Wait." She took it from her skirt pocket and placed it around Jimena's neck.

Catty knelt beside her. "What are you doing? I'll take her back to before she stepped into the fire and keep her from going in."

Serena shook her head. "It's too late for that."

Catty nodded. The air became still again. A tear rolled off her cheek and fell on Jimena's arm. "What will the key do?"

Serena held Jimena tightly. "I hope it will unlock the right door and bring her back."

A chorus of *ahh*s made them look up. Vanessa became completely invisible now. The show ended. Police officers pushed the crowd back behind the barricades. It was only minutes before paramedics would see Jimena and come running with their red metal cases. Serena knew intuitively that she couldn't let them take Jimena from her, not until Jimena found the door in the dark and used the key to unlock it and come back to the light.

"Look," Catty whispered.

Bluish arcs sparked around the key and then it vanished.

A moment passed, and then Jimena's eyes opened with a strange shudder.

"Hey." Jimena smiled weakly. "So I guess I showed you I'm still the tough goddess."

"You're bad, all right." Serena breathed out in relief. She squeezed Jimena. "I'm glad you made it back."

"Here they come," Catty warned.

Paramedics were running toward them.

"Let's get out of here," Serena said. "Can you stand?"

"If I made it through that, I guess I can stand," Jimena answered, but her legs were shaky and Serena had to help her up.

"Where's Vanessa?" Serena asked.

"She said she'd meet us back at the car." Catty grabbed Jimena's other arm.

Jimena, Catty, and Serena ran through the firefighters and news reporters to Jimena's car. Vanessa was waiting there, gasping for breath, her face red.

"You were great!" Catty said.

They scrambled into Jimena's car and she

started the engine. The tailpipes thundered as they pulled away from the curb.

"You sure were one bitch with an attitude," Jimena told Serena.

"I'm sorry." Serena felt that those words couldn't begin to make up for what her friends had done for her.

"I'm going to remember this forever," Catty announced. "You owe us big-time."

"I can't believe you took such a risk," Serena said to Jimena. "Going into the fire!"

"How 'bout Vanessa?" Catty added.

"Yeah." Serena turned and looked at Vanessa. "You were always afraid of having people see you go invisible."

Vanessa smiled triumphantly. "By tomorrow everyone will think it was an illusion caused by the fire and helicopter spotlights. No one would believe I actually became invisible."

"Not unless they're kissing you and see you go," Catty reminded her with a laugh.

"Vanessa's right," Jimena added. "Everyone will think it was some trick of the camera."

After a moment, Serena spoke slowly. "What was it like?"

"You mean when I was gone?" Jimena asked.

"Yeah, where did you go?" Catty was awestruck. "And how did you get back?"

"Hekate," Jimena mused. "She led me back. I had Serena's key, but she guided me to the right door."

Serena looked out the window. She was still feeling guilty.

Jimena glanced at her when she stopped at a red light. "You would have done the same for me," she said softly.

At home Collin was watching *Eyewitness News* on the television when Serena and Jimena walked in.

"What were you doing so near the methane gas explosion?" Collin asked.

"I've got to tell you the truth." Serena looked at Collin seriously. "I'm a goddess, and tonight I almost became the goddess of witches."

Collin stared at her oddly, then he broke into one of his great laughs and hugged her. "You've got the most bizarre imagination of anyone I've ever known, but that's part of what I love about you."

He let her go and turned to Jimena. "Are you a goddess, too?"

"Did you ever have any doubt?" Jimena bent her head to the side and gave him a sweet smile.

Serena loved the easy way Jimena could flirt.

"I guess I always knew." Collin shook his head. "So you two wanna make some popcorn and watch TV? There's a sci-fi marathon on tonight."

"Sure," Jimena said.

"Yeah, why not?" Serena looked from Jimena to Collin. She was happy they were finally getting along.

CHAPTER TWENTY-FOUR

On Monday, Serena saw Zahi in the hallway after school. He looked confused and embarrassed. He started to apologize.

"For what?" She touched his arm and looked into his eyes.

"Thank you," he finally said.

"You're welcome."

Zahi smiled tentatively and walked away.

Then Morgan strutted toward her, wearing tight black capris and a shiny snakeskin halter-top, the he-goat amulet proudly displayed on a thick gold chain. Serena had seen her running away with the other Followers the night of the cold fire and knew she was one of them now.

"I know what you did to him," Morgan accused in a nasty whisper. "But I'll get him back." She pinched the charm and dangled it in front of Serena in challenge.

"I won't let you," Serena warned.

Morgan gave her an arrogant smile. "It's official now, isn't it, Serena? Our clash is finally real."

"I never wanted to fight you, Morgan. You always started it with your attitude. I would have been your friend—"

"Right," Morgan sneered. "Try and stop me now." She turned with a snap of her heels and hurried down the hallway to Zahi.

"Morgan's one of them now," Jimena said flatly.

Serena turned, surprised that Jimena and Catty had been standing behind her. They looked at each other sadly.

"You think she'll bring Zahi back?" Catty looked anxious.

"Not with us around," Jimena said.

Serena shook her head. "I went into his

mind. I can't read his thoughts because it's all French and Arabic, but I wanted to see if I could feel anything. The Atrox is gone."

Morgan turned and gave Serena a wicked glare, then she walked backward, grinning at Serena in challenge. *Later,* her mind whispered before she turned and sauntered slowly away.

"What's up with Morgan now?" Vanessa asked as she joined them.

"She's a Follower," Jimena stated, her body tense with new anger.

Vanessa's face fell.

Serena clasped her shoulder. "We tried to protect her," Serena said.

"Yeah," Vanessa agreed and bit her lip.

"And you got Zahi back," Catty said to Serena "That was more important."

"We *all* got him back," Serena corrected.

Michael ran up to them, smiling. The air filled with his nice spice-soap smell.

"Hey." He slipped his arm around Vanessa and gave her a quick kiss. "What's up?"

"I'll see you guys tomorrow." Vanessa smiled

and walked off with Michael.

"I'm late." Catty looked at her watch. "I'm working for my mom this afternoon."

They waved good-bye and Jimena and Serena started walking down the hallway in the opposite direction.

"You wanna hang out?" Jimena asked.

"No, I got something I have to take care of," Serena said. "Will you feed Wally for me?"

"Sure. You need a ride where you're going?"

"No thanks. Got one."

Serena walked off campus and when she was sure no one was watching, she headed down a side street, then ran over to La Brea.

Stanton's car was parked in front of Pink's hot dog stand. Its sleek black metal reflected the late afternoon sun. He glanced up and smiled in recognition. He walked up to her and wrapped his arms tenderly around her. She pressed against him, enjoying his gentle touch. Then he kissed the top of her head and she looked up at him, her eyes now unguarded.

"Ready?"

BOOK THREE

night shade

PROLOGUE

Diana was the goddess of the hunt and of all newborn creatures. Women prayed to her for happiness in marriage and childbirth, but her strength was so great that even the warlike Amazons worshipped her.

No man was worthy of her love, until powerful Orion won her affection. She was about to marry him, but her twin brother, Apollo, was angered that she had fallen in love. One day, Apollo saw Orion in the sea with only his head above the water. Apollo tricked Diana by challenging her to hit the mark bobbing in the distant sea. Diana shot her arrow with deadly aim. Later, the waves rolled dead Orion to shore.

Lamenting her fatal blunder, Diana placed

Orion in the starry sky. Every night, she would lift her torch in the dark to see her beloved. Her light gave comfort to all, and soon she became known as a goddess of the moon.

It was whispered that if a girl-child was born in the wilderness, delivered by the great goddess Diana, she would be known for her fierce protection of the innocent.

CHAPTER ONE

JIMENA CASTILLO WALKED down the rain-drenched street as if she owned the night. And she did. This was her neighborhood, the Pico-Union District of Los Angeles. She passed Langer's Deli, held her face up to the cool rain, and crossed Alvarado Street against a red light.

A Ford Torino jerked to a stop, inches from her knees. Before the driver could honk, Jimena tapped the hood of the car. The man glanced up and her eyes warned him, *You're out of your neighborhood.*

He understood and settled back patiently as

if it were normal to stop at a green light in Los Angeles. Once Jimena had crossed the street, the car screeched away.

Jimena headed toward MacArthur Park. She was tired and coming down fast. The *tecatos* peeking from their makeshift tents might think she was on drugs. If they only knew what she had really done that night, what would they think? She wondered if her true identity would frighten them or make them ask her for help. She laughed, her voice as light as raindrops.

Jimena saw a movement from under one of the benches. Pieces of cardboard slipped off a sleeping body. She felt a sudden need to stop and confess. To sit on the bench above the poor homeless person and tell him everything. She didn't give in to the urge but hurried to the path around the lake. Rain made the wet asphalt look as slick as sealskin. The giant water fountain in the middle of the lake continued to spew water into the air as if it were working hard to send back the rain.

When she approached Wilshire Boulevard, her eyes automatically scoped out the street.

Traffic was light but the dangers were big. Wilshire was the boundary of her neighborhood. She had to cross enemy land to get to her grandmother's apartment.

At the corner near the bus stop, a *klika* of enemy homegirls waited impatiently in the shadows. They looked as if they had plans to throw down some old lady when she got off the bus. Maybe someone who cleaned the floors at Cedars-Sinai Hospital or worked the tables in a West Los Angeles restaurant.

Jimena didn't slow her pace. She walked steadily toward them, head high.

The girls glanced once, twice, then with slow casual steps they ambled away from the bus bench as if they hadn't seen her.

Jimena sensed their fear. That brought a smile to her face. Her reputation was still so big that even tough *enemigas* wouldn't face her down.

She strutted past them, her heels snapping loudly on the sidewalk. She enjoyed the feel of their admiring eyes, their sideways glances and the wonder she saw on their faces. Jimena wasn't choloed out in khakis, a tight T, and long, boyfriend-borrowed Pendletons. She wore a slinky dress and ankle-breaking high heels. The rain made the dress cling to her body, so they knew she wasn't strapping. No gun. Still, they were afraid to confront her.

This time she stopped for the red light, pausing to let the *chicas* know she didn't fear them. It felt good to be the toughest *chola en el condado de Los Angeles.* She was still down for Ninth Street, her old gang, but at age fifteen, already a *veterana.* A *leyenda,* her homegirls told her with pride. Jimena had been a real badass before she understood her destiny. She glanced at the scars and tattoos on her hand. What would the *klika*-girls do if they knew her true identity?

She turned back to toss them a grin, but they were already hurrying away down the boulevard.

The light turned green. Jimena started across the street as slow, lazy thunder rolled across the night and vibrated through the ground. She eagerly looked at the midnight sky. Thunderstorms were rare in Los Angeles, and she wanted to see a jagged flash of lightning. Another thunderclap rocked the air but again without a heralding bolt of light. The rain was heavier now and cold. Jimena walked faster.

A car splashed by, its tires humming on the wet street.

"Jaguar." The word came over the rain as soft as a secret.

She stopped and looked behind her. Only Veto had called her "Jaguar," and he had been dead a year now, killed in enemy land. Could it have been those homegirls? Had they somehow gathered their courage and decided to face her? She studied the rain-drenched shadows. The glossy shimmer of wet leaves reflected the pink-and-blue neon lights. But her mind wasn't on finding enemy homegirls. She thought about Veto. The ache of missing him surprised her. How could she miss him so much after a year? She yearned for the sweet kind of love she had known with him.

She had transferred to La Brea High School

less than six months ago, and the guys there never did more than smile or ask her to dance. She could feel them looking at her when she walked down the hallways, but when she caught their glances, they looked away. Perhaps they saw the gangster in her eyes or in the curl of her lips. Veto had said she was like a jaguar; her show of teeth was a warning, not a smile. She was probably scaring the guys away without even knowing it.

She walked slower now, ears sensitive to the slightest sound. Raindrops hit leaves, grass, and car roofs, but it was one voice she longed to hear. Memories of Veto echoed cruelly through her mind. She never understood why he had gone off to enemy territory the night he was killed. She felt bitter about his death. He'd been acting crazy, but going over to enemy land without his homeboys was even too *loco* for him. What had made him go?

"Jaguar."

She heard the word clearly this time, and turned. A lean muscular young man stood silhouetted in front of a security light. He started walking slowly toward her. A gust of wind blew his raincoat open and it flapped behind him like giant black wings.

When he stepped into the amber light of the street lamp, she gasped. "Veto?"

Veto stood in front of her, his face as bold and beautiful as his Mayan ancestors', with dark flashing eyes and high cheekbones. His blue-black hair was dripping rain as if he had been following her unseen for a long time.

Her heart pounded wildly. "Veto." She spoke his name slowly this time, enjoying the luxurious feel of it on her tongue and wondered if she were dreaming. She had dreamed about him so many times since his death, and sometimes even awoke thinking he had called her name.

He stepped closer to her. There was something different about the way he looked. Veto, but not Veto. His hair was longer than he had worn it before, his skin was paler, and he had lost weight. She studied his black eyes. They blinked as if the dim streetlights were too bright.

Even as part of her recoiled, her hand reached out to touch the tiny scar on his right cheek. His skin felt warm under the raindrops. Veto, alive? Her mind rushed to find an explanation. His casket had been closed at the funeral. She had never actually seen him dead. Could the police department and the coroner's office have made a mistake? Maybe some other homeboy had been buried in his place. She weighed the possibilities. Perhaps Veto had been put in the witness protection program. That would explain his crazy behavior, if he was intending to turn *rata.* And after his funeral his mother and three younger brothers had moved back to Mexico.

"What are you doing here? Were you in the witness protection program?" she asked, hating the air that separated them.

"No, Jaguar, I'm no rat-head." He tried to smile the way he had always smiled at her, but his lips seemed stiff and unused to it. Sudden sadness burdened her heart. Had Veto been someplace where smiles were dangerous signs of weakness?

"Then what?" She couldn't say more. Her bottom lip started quivering and the tears she had been unable to cry at his funeral a year ago rolled down her cheeks.

"Estás llorando?" Veto clasped his arms around her. His warmth seeped into her cold skin. "I never saw you cry before."

"It's rain," she lied, even now having to be the tougher one.

He kissed the tears.

She pulled back. "Where have you been?" The words came out with hoarse anger from missing him so much.

"Lost."

"Lost? What kind of answer is that?"

"I got back to you. That's all that matters. I always told you nothing was ever going to separate us."

"So you did make a deal with the cops? Who'd you rat out?"

He turned away, and then she knew. He had too much *cora* to rat out any of his homeboys. It had to be the guy who had been selling drugs to Veto's homeboys. Only Veto was strong enough to do that. That meant he'd gone up against someone big and needed to hide.

She nodded, understanding. "You're here now. Where are you staying?"

He didn't answer her.

"Are you hanging out with your homeboys?" He was probably living from one couch to the next. That troubled her. Why hadn't anyone told her Veto was back?

He started to say something, but thunder shattered the night and Veto jerked around. When he looked back at her, stark terror covered his face.

"I gotta go." His words came out with a nervousness she had never heard in his voice before.

"Don't," she said. "Come home with me."

But already he was pulling away from her. "No, I can't. I gotta be somewhere."

"Where?" She hated the look she saw on his face. Veto has never been afraid of anything. What could be so bad that it could scare him?

Another clash of thunder shook through the ground. The alarm in Veto's face made her heart race. "What is it? What do you see?" she asked.

"Nothing." His eyes betrayed the lie.

"Tell me," she whispered. "I got your back."

Veto started to run.

"Wait," she demanded.

He turned and ran backward, smiling at her. "I'll see you soon," he shouted through the rain. "When it's safe."

"Safe from what?" she yelled.

Then her legs acted on their own and she ran after him.

New thunder shuddered through the ground. Veto turned and sprinted down the sidewalk toward the park.

"What is it?" She splashed through puddles, calling after him, "What's wrong?"

He dodged the traffic on Wilshire. She had just started after him when a truck blew its horn. She jumped back on the curb. The giant tires sprayed her with water. After the truck had passed, she could no longer see Veto.

She crossed the street and circled the park, then stood alone in the storm until her body shivered with cold and her hair was pasted against her head.

Finally she turned and walked slowly back to her grandmother's apartment building.

There was so much she wanted to tell Veto. She glanced down at the triangle of three dots tattooed on the fleshy web between her index finger and thumb. The day she got jumped into Ninth Street, Veto had tattooed the dots into her skin using ink and a pin. Later, he had tattooed the teardrop under her right eye when she got out of Youth Authority Camp. The second teardrop was for her second stay in Youth Authority. She would have gone back a third time for firing a gun, if a lenient judge hadn't sentenced her to do community service work instead. She had fired the gun in frustration when she couldn't stop her homegirls from doing a throw-down. The cops had caught her, but she wouldn't turn *rata.* She was willing to go back to camp to protect her homegirls. That was the code. But the judge had seen something different in her eyes this time and let her off with community service.

Jimena had known about her destiny by then, and she had changed. It amazed her even now, if she thought about it. Who would have thought she was meant for something so important?

She looked back at the rain-soaked shadows. What would Veto do if he did know the truth about her? He was the one who had always said there was magic inside her. *Bruja,* he had teased. He had called her a witch because she could see the future.

Secretly, she had been afraid when Veto called her gift witchcraft, because she didn't think she was seeing the future. She thought she was making the dark things happen. The first time she had a premonition, she had only been seven years old. She had been outside playing with her best friend Miranda when a picture of Miranda in a white casket crossed her mind. Then Miranda had touched her, asking her what was the matter, and another picture had played behind her eyes. She saw Miranda walking down Ladera Street as a car sped by. Shots blasted from the car window and Miranda fell to the ground, dead.

The premonition had terrified her. She had tried to keep it from coming true and made

Miranda go a block out of her way each day when they walked home from school. But then one day Jimena had come down with the flu and had to stay home. That afternoon, she heard the gunshots, and she knew.

Jimena was scared that she had caused Miranda's death. After all, she had seen it happen. Sometimes even now it bothered her that she could see the future, especially because she had never been able to stop any of her premonitions from coming true, no matter how bad they were.

She stepped across the street and headed toward one of the brick hotels that lined this part of Wilshire Boulevard. The hotels had been converted into apartment homes for poor people, but the whirling pink-and-blue neon lights with the old hotel names still lit the night sky.

Maggie Craven loved the old neon lighting and had told Jimena stories about going to elegant parties in the hotel ballrooms. Jimena imagined Maggie dancing with some movie star. She loved Maggie as much as she could love anyone, even her grandmother. Maggie had been the first person to explain to her that she had a gift that allowed her to see things that were going to happen in the future. She wasn't a witch who made the bad things happen.

Now, Jimena didn't know what she would do without Maggie. But in the beginning it had taken her almost a year to believe what Maggie had told her about her destiny. Maggie had first appeared in her dreams, urging Jimena to come see her. When Jimena had finally gone to Maggie's apartment, she had been shocked to discover the woman in her dreams actually existed. Maybe that would have been enough to convince others that what Maggie said was true, but to Jimena, Maggie's words sounded like madness.

"Tu es dea, filia lunae," Maggie told her in Latin at their first meeting. "You are a goddess, a Daughter of the Moon."

Maggie had explained that in ancient times when Pandora's box was opened, the last thing to leave the box was hope. Only Selene, the goddess of the moon, had seen the demonic creature lurking nearby, sent by the Atrox to devour hope.

Selene took pity on humankind and gave her daughters, like guardian angels, to perpetuate hope. Jimena was one of those daughters.

Jimena had been stunned. Goddess? Did such beings exist?

Maggie also told her about the Atrox, the primal source of evil. The Atrox and its Followers had sworn to destroy the Daughters of the Moon.

"Me?" Jimena had responded.

"Yes." Maggie had explained that once the Daughters were gone, the Atrox could bring about the ruin of humankind.

The words still overwhelmed her. How many people even believed in the mythical world? She'd heard the *viejecitas* tell stories of other gods who lived in the jungles of Mexico and Guatemala. The old women swore the voices of those gods could still be heard in the ruins at Tikal and Chichén Itzá. But she'd never taken their stories seriously. She didn't think goddesses really existed and if they did they wouldn't look like a *chola* with two teardrops tattooed under her right eye.

Maggie had hugged her dearly when she expressed her doubts and told Jimena that a goddess of the moon had given her many gifts and that someday she would know the truth.

Jimena wished Veto had stayed long enough so she could tell him about her destiny. He had always seen her as someone special. Her gift never frightened him the way it had scared others. Thinking about Veto now made her mind turn back to what had happened tonight. Why had he seemed so terrified? Then an uninvited thought pushed forward. Suddenly she knew his appearance had only been an illusion. Perhaps the intensity of her memory of him tonight had made her imagine him so vividly.

She turned down the walk that led up to her grandmother's apartment building. Cement lions sat on either side of the porch steps, dripping rain. As she slipped the key into the lock a sudden dread filled her. Maybe she was sensing something about the future. Something so terrible that the only way she could deal with it was to project the fear onto Veto's ghost.

She unlocked the door to the apartment building and hurried inside. The enormous stairs of the old hotel led up to a gloomy ballroom, now used only occasionally for community meetings. Framed photographs and yellowed newspaper clippings in the entrance behind dusty glass told of the days when the hotel had been what Maggie called a swanky place.

Jimena turned back and stared out the side window. An ominous change had come over the night. She shuddered, but it was more a deep inner chill that caused the cold now. She knew trouble was coming.

CHAPTER TWO

JIMENA UNLOCKED THE door to her grandmother's small apartment. The air was warm with the spicy smells of baking *chiles.* She walked through the dark living room to the light in the kitchen. Her grandmother stood over the stove, making tortillas from chunks of cornmeal dough by slapping them back and forth between her hands and cooking them in a cast-iron skillet. A stack of warm tortillas sat on the counter near a line of casserole dishes.

Jimena's *abuelita* looked up. Her regal face started to smile, but the smile was lost in a look of astonishment. She dropped a half-formed tortilla on the counter. *"¡Parece que hubieras visto un fantasma!"*

"I did see a ghost," Jimena spoke softly. "I saw Veto."

Jimena fell into her grandmother's comforting arms. The old woman held her for a long time, and when she pulled away, her black eyes seemed anxious, as if there was something important she wanted to say. She wiped her hands absently with a towel and stared at the rain beating on the window over the sink.

"What?" Jimena asked and gently turned her grandmother back to face her.

"Cuando te caíste del cielo . . ." Her grandmother started, but then a look of astonishment crossed her wrinkled face.

"What?" she asked.

"Your moon amulet," she said, reaching for it. "It's shining." Her grandmother touched the face of the moon, then jerked her fingers back as if she had been shocked.

Jimena looked down at the amulet hanging

around her neck. It was glowing. Had the amulet been glowing before when she was with Veto? Could she have been too anxious to notice the electrical thrum her amulet made to warn her in times of danger? Maybe the apparition really had been Veto's ghost.

Her grandmother looked across the room at the small cross hanging on the eastern wall next to the picture of the Virgin of Guadalupe. "The night you were born . . ." Again her voice drifted away as if she couldn't find the right words to complete her sentence.

"The night I was born? *¿Qué?*" Jimena asked. Always when her grandmother started to tell her about the night she was born, she stopped before telling her the whole story. "Does it have something to do with what happened tonight, with seeing Veto? Tell me!"

Her grandmother opened a drawer in the cupboards, pulled out a book of matches, and walked over to the tiny table covered with flowers, candles, and the icons of saints. Her hands trembled as she lit the candle for *La Morena.* She crossed herself and was silent a moment, as if she were praying to the beautiful Madonna of the Americas to give her guidance.

Finally she came back to the table and sat down. She motioned for Jimena to take the chair across from her.

Jimena did so. She felt tense with apprehension about what her grandmother was going to say.

"Maybe seeing Veto has something to do with that night," her grandmother finally confessed. Her tiny black eyes stared at Jimena. "It never surprised me that you can see into the future, because something very strange happened the night you were born."

"Tell me." Jimena moved the casserole dishes aside so that she could lean closer to her grandmother.

"I never told anyone before, because I was too afraid no one would believe me."

Jimena's heart raced. What was the secret that her grandmother had kept all these years? She laid her hand on top of her grandmother's cold fingers.

"Your mother and I were crossing the high desert, coming into California from Mexico so you could be born in *Los Estados Unidos.* We had to hide from *la migra* and when we did, your mother went into labor early, miles from any doctor. I was sure I was going to lose you and your mother. *Venías de nalgas,* a difficult birth, and then . . ."

Her grandmother paused and looked back at the picture of *La Morena.* The candlelight flickered across the face of the Madonna, and seeing her tranquil face seemed to give her grandmother courage.

When she continued, she spoke in a voice so low, Jimena had to pull her chair closer to hear.

"A beautiful woman, like *una diosa,* came from nowhere. I thought she was a saint who had come to take you and your mother back to heaven, but then I knew she was going to help us. She didn't open her mouth, but in my mind I knew what she was saying. I could feel her words as if she were speaking. *Un milagro.* It was a miracle. She gave you the moon amulet that you always wear."

Jimena looked down at the silver amulet hanging around her neck and studied the face of the moon etched in the metal. It seemed to sparkle back the kitchen light in a rainbow of shimmering colors. Her best friends Serena, Catty, and Vanessa each had one. Jimena never took hers off.

"*La diosa* said that as long as you wear the amulet, you'll be protected." Her grandmother touched the face of the moon lightly with her crooked index finger.

Jimena clasped the amulet and wondered what would happen if she ever took it off.

"So when you were a *niña* and you told me you feared for your best friend Miranda, I warned Miranda's mother to be careful. I knew you had gifts. I knew you were different from other children."

"Abuelita," Jimena started. Did she dare tell her the truth? What would her grandmother do if she knew who Jimena really was?

"So maybe seeing Veto is part of your gift. Maybe you can contact the departed. *Los difuntos*."

She stared at her grandmother. It was easy for her grandmother to believe that the dead were always around us. Each year during *Los Días de los Muertos,* her grandmother made an *ofrenda* for her grandfather, piling it high with marigolds and her grandfather's favorite foods.

But, Jimena wondered, if seeing the spirits of *los difuntos* was part of her gift, then why had she never seen her grandfather's ghost? She loved him as much as Veto.

She looked back at her grandmother. "Do you know who the woman was? *La Diosa?* Did she tell you her name?"

"Yes." Her grandmother nodded. "Diana. I asked her her name and in my mind I knew they called her Diana. I told your mother we must name you Diana, but she insisted we name you Jimena, after me."

Jimena smiled back at her. "I'm glad she did."

After a moment her grandmother continued, "So don't be worried that you saw Veto. It's all part of who you are. If we still lived in Mexico you'd be a strong *curandera* healing people."

"Or a *bruja*." Jimena laughed.

"Una bruja nunca." Her grandmother shook her head. "No, your gift is for good. I know this *con todo mi corazón*." She placed her hand over her heart.

Jimena wanted to tell her grandmother everything then, to let her know that she was fighting an ancient evil. Her heart beat rapidly, and she started to open her mouth to speak, but before she could, her grandmother spoke. "There, I've said too much already. I sound like one of those old women rambling at the bus stop to anyone who will listen."

Her grandmother glanced at the clock and the moment was lost. "Tomorrow the *señoras* from the nice suburbs will come on their way home from church and buy the *moles* to serve for Sunday dinner. I still have too much to do."

"I'll help you," Jimena offered.

"You take a warm shower and put on dry clothes first. I should have made you change your clothes before I spoke but . . ." She shrugged and changed the subject. "It's easier when your brother is here." Sometimes Jimena's brother delivered the food and collected the money, but now he was in San Diego helping their uncle open a restaurant.

Jimena nodded. It was easier for her, too, when her brother was home, because he let her drive his car even though she didn't have a driver's license yet. She'd learned how to drive when she was twelve so she could jack cars. It surprised her even now when she thought about the risks she used to take back in her old life. She felt guilty, knowing how much the arrests had hurt her grandmother.

Her grandmother bent over and opened the oven, then took a pot holder and pulled out a tray of black and blistered chiles. She removed the tray from the oven and shook the chiles into a paper bag to steam. She handed a pair of yellow rubber gloves to Jimena. "Hurry. Take your shower, then come back and peel the chiles for me, *m'ija*."

Jimena stood.

Her grandmother winked, picked up a chunk of masa and began slapping it back and forth.

"This is the last night of doing this."

Jimena nodded. Her grandmother was going down to San Diego to help with the restaurant.

Her hands stopped. "Only if you'll be all right alone. I'll stay if you need me."

"Go," Jimena answered.

"Maybe Tuesday then."

Jimena nodded.

"Now take a shower," her grandmother ordered.

Jimena hurried down to the bathroom. She bathed, put on a T-shirt and sweatpants, then came back, slipped on the rubber gloves, and sat at the table. She worked to remove the skin, ribs, seeds, and core from the chiles as her grandmother made the tortillas.

The smells of the *moles* bubbling on the stove and the rhythm of her grandmother's slapping relaxed her. Veto drifted back into memory and the ache and longing of missing him took its place in her heart.

CHAPTER THREE

JIMENA WAITED AT a bus stop on Melrose Avenue. The late-afternoon crowd pushed around her, sipping lattes and bottled water. Kids stopped to gaze at the punk paraphernalia in the shop behind her. Others tried on the trendy sunglasses that a street vendor was selling from a blanket stretched across the sidewalk.

When she saw Serena walking toward her, swinging her cello case, Jimena waved. Serena was wearing red cowboy boots and a lacy yellow sundress.

Jimena had admired Serena since the first

day Maggie had introduced them almost a year back. She would never have admitted it then because she had still been kicking it with her homegirls and putting on the *máscara* of a tough gangster. She had laughed when Maggie had told them they would be battling Followers together. There was no chance Jimena was going to let a wimp like Serena watch her back; that was one sure way to get killed. But Jimena had quickly changed her mind the first time they fought a group of Followers. Serena never backed down. Now Jimena trusted Serena with her life.

Serena sat on the bus bench, and brushed her dark hair away from her face. Her nose ring glistened in the late afternoon sun.

"So what are you *haciendo*-ing this afternoon?" Jimena asked.

"Music lesson." Serena carefully fit her cello case between her legs. "You hear the earthquakes Saturday night?"

Jimena nodded. "All that rumbling sounded like thunder to me."

"Me, too." Serena pulled the cello case closer

as an old woman sat down beside her. "The newspapers are calling it quake thunder."

"Could be. I didn't see any lightning." Jimena thought a moment. "But I can't believe those rumblings actually came from the ground and not the sky."

"The seismologists at Caltech are scaring everyone the way they're calling it an earthquake swarm. They're saying it could be a prelude to the big one." Serena pulled her student bus pass from her messenger bag.

Jimena nodded. "I don't want to be around when the San Andreas fault breaks."

An old woman sitting beside Serena leaned into them. "Earthquake weather," she whispered. "Look at the sky."

Jimena looked up at the gray cast and shook her head. "Those are just rain clouds."

Serena looked at the fast-moving clouds. "What's earthquake weather?"

"Just superstition," Jimena answered. "The old ladies where I live say they can tell when there's going to be a big earthquake because days before the sky turns gray and the air feels still and heavy on your skin."

"It's earthquake weather," the woman insisted with a crooked smile.

Jimena continued, "But the same *viejas* say you can't have an earthquake when it's raining and it was definitely raining Saturday night."

A bus pulled up to the curb and the woman hobbled onboard.

"Where were you yesterday, anyway?" Serena changed the subject. "I tried to call you to make sure you got home okay but no one answered the phone." Serena didn't need to say she had been worried. Jimena could see it from the look in her eyes. Serena glanced around to make sure no one was listening. "I thought maybe the Followers had caught up to you."

They had gone over to Hollywood Saturday night and run into Cassandra and a pack of Hollywood Followers.

Serena continued. "Then you weren't at school."

"I was at school. I just got there late. I had to

help my grandmother with the food on Sunday and then I had things I had to do the rest of the day." How could she tell Serena that she had spent Sunday looking for a dead person? She had gone to all the places where she and Veto had hung out, hoping his ghost might reappear to her. She shrugged. "And this morning, I overslept."

"What is it you're *not* saying?" Serena asked with a sly smile.

That was Serena's gift. She could read minds. Like Jimena, she hadn't understood her power when she was little. She only knew then that she was different. Sometimes in the excitement of playing, she'd forget her friends weren't speaking and she'd answer their thoughts. Even now, if she became too happy or excited, she'd answer people's thoughts as if they were saying them out loud.

"Tell me," Serena coaxed. "I know something else is on your mind."

Jimena needed to talk to Serena about Veto, but embarrassment made her hesitate.

"What?" Serena urged.

"Saturday night, I . . ." But as she started to tell Serena about seeing Veto, her amulet resonated against her chest with an electrical hum.

They both looked up, alert to danger.

Cassandra was shoving through the crowd, walking toward them. She wore stretchy black capris with a low-cut, black tank top and too much silver jewelry. Thin white scars formed a crooked S T A on her chest. She had been wildly in love with Stanton, the leader of the Hollywood Followers, and tried to cut his name into her skin with a razor blade before Stanton had stopped her. She might have been beautiful once, but evil had made her features harsh and pinched. She stopped in front of Tattoo You, a small storefront shop where kids got piercings and tattoos.

"What does she want now?" Jimena wondered.

"I told you she's been following us," Serena sighed.

"Why's she so desperate to get into a *pleito* with us?"

"Followers always want to get in our faces."

Serena tried to make light of Cassandra's sudden appearance but Jimena knew her well enough to know it troubled her.

"You'll lose," Cassandra whispered—or had she let the words slip across their minds? She was too far away for them to have been able to hear her. Jimena shuddered. She hated the way Cassandra had so easily entered their minds. She glanced at Serena, who seemed more than irritated.

"Steady," Jimena warned. "Don't do anything yet."

Cassandra had been accepted by the Atrox and apprenticed to Stanton to learn how to perfect her evil. Already she could read minds, manipulate people's thoughts, and even imprison others in her memories, but, unlike Stanton, she didn't have immortality.

"What's she up to?" Serena was upset.

Jimena shrugged. "You'd think I'd have had a premonition." She was almost always forewarned if they were going to have a serious run-in with the Followers.

"You know how she felt about Stanton," Serena said. "Maybe she suspects that I'm seeing him."

"You shouldn't be," Jimena scolded, as she had a dozen times before. "It's forbidden. If the Atrox finds out, it'll send Regulators to terminate Stanton."

"Like I don't know that?" Serena didn't take her eyes off Cassandra.

"Is he worth it?" Jimena felt apprehensive. If Regulators were powerful enough to destroy an immortal like Stanton, then Serena didn't have a chance against them. What if they caught Stanton while Serena was with him? "You're risking your life—and besides, it doesn't feel right keeping secrets from Vanessa and Catty."

It was more than that. She didn't know how Serena could trust Stanton so completely. Once Stanton had trapped Vanessa in his childhood memories. While she was there, Vanessa had tried to save a younger Stanton from the Atrox. After that act of kindness he could never harm Vanessa, but Serena didn't have the same guarantee. There was too much competition among Followers for a place of power in the Atrox hierarchy. Stanton could be using Serena. After all, the biggest prize for any Follower was the seduction of a Daughter of the Moon or the theft of her special power. The Atrox awarded such a deed by allowing those Followers into its Inner Circle.

But Serena cared for Stanton. Sometimes she actually felt sorry for him. His father had been a great prince of Western Europe during the thirteenth century and had raised an army to go on a crusade against the Atrox. But the Atrox had kidnapped Stanton to stop his father.

Serena nudged her. "Now look who's here."

Karyl left Tattoo You and joined Cassandra. He turned and smiled at them. He reminded Jimena of a lizard, the way his beady eyes darted up and down her body with frank sexual interest. That wasn't the only thing creepy about him. He looked their age, but there was something about him that seemed old and made her think he had been alive for hundreds of years.

Jimena turned slightly so that she could

watch Karyl more closely. "It's creepy the way he's just smiling at us."

"Hideous," Serena agreed. "It's as if he and Cassandra have something big planned."

"I know, but what?" Jimena knew Karyl's power. She had faced him in battle the night Karyl and Cassandra had tried to destroy Catty and Vanessa.

"They're acting weird," Serena said.

Cassandra had always been vindictive, but something was different about the way she strutted toward them now. Maybe she did know about Stanton and Serena. She stopped a few steps from them.

"Enjoy the nice weather while you can," Cassandra warned. "You won't be seeing many more days."

Behind her Karyl laughed. He opened the door to Tattoo You and Morgan stepped out and joined him. She wore a skimpy black dress and shiny black boots. A new gold hoop pierced the flesh above her eye. The skin looked bright red and sore. Jimena wondered what Morgan's parents would do when they found out what had happened to her. They'd never fully understand, but they'd see the change. Jimena didn't feel guilty about it the way Vanessa did. Serena and Jimena had risked exposing themselves in order to protect Morgan, but in the end the Followers had claimed her.

"Nice pierce," Jimena said. "You just get it?"

Morgan gave her a quick angry look and touched the gold hoop. It was something she never would have done before.

"Can you even believe that?" Serena spoke in a low snickering voice.

"Don't laugh." Jimena nudged her.

"I can't help it." Serena clapped her hand over her lips.

Jimena shook her head. She wasn't sure what she saw in Morgan's eyes now. Sorrow? Remorse? Rage? Morgan had always had an attitude that had made it impossible to be her friend, but now that she had become an Initiate she was even more edgy. Initiates wanted to prove themselves worthy of becoming a Follower. Morgan had a trace of hardness in her face now in spite of her perfect angelic features.

Cassandra's head whipped around, and she took a step backward.

"What now?" Serena asked.

"It's Catty and Vanessa," Jimena answered.

"Maybe she feels outnumbered," Serena suggested.

Jimena sighed with relief. "Good, I feel low on energy today."

Catty and Vanessa joined them on the bus bench. Vanessa had gorgeous tanned skin, large blue eyes, and shiny blond hair. She was wearing a pink slip dress and beaded slides. Michael Saratoga's jacket hung on her shoulders.

Catty was forever getting Vanessa into trouble, but they remained best friends.

"What's up?" Vanessa looked nervously down the street at Cassandra.

"Looks like the usual." Catty tried to say the words in an easy manner, but Jimena saw the way she had shuddered when she had first observed Cassandra, Karyl, and Morgan.

Catty took off her yellow slicker and leaned against the bus bench. She was stylish in an artsy sort of way. She wore a split tube top that showed off the piercing in her belly button and a pink hip-hugging skirt with an asymmetrical hem. She had let her perm grow out, and now her straight brown hair billowed in the afternoon breeze.

"Why is she following us?" Vanessa spoke in a hushed tone and fingered her hair nervously.

"We were asking the same question," Serena said.

"Oh look, it's Vanessa," Morgan called in a mocking voice.

Vanessa shook her head sadly. "I hate that we're going to have one more Follower to worry about, especially someone who used to be our friend."

"Speak for yourself." Catty made a face. "She was never my friend. You just don't remember how bad she was when she was normal."

Vanessa ignored Morgan's stare and concentrated on Cassandra. "Do you think she could suddenly have enough power to be a threat to us?

I mean she acts like she's got some big secret plan. Maybe I should follow her, you know, invisible."

Jimena smiled at her bravery. That was Vanessa's gift. She could expand her molecules and become invisible, but when she became really emotional she lost control and her molecules began to act on their own. When Vanessa had first started dating Michael, she had started to go invisible every time he tried to kiss her.

"Don't do anything yet," Jimena cautioned. "Not until we know more."

Vanessa nodded.

Serena started to stand. "I guess we're not going to fight them today."

"Is that what you're reading from them?" Catty asked.

"No, my bus is coming." Serena picked up her cello case.

"I'm going with you." Vanessa dug into her purse for her student bus pass.

"To my cello lesson?" Serena looked bewildered.

"No." Vanessa hesitated as if she wasn't sure

she wanted to tell them where she was going. "Okay, I'm going to see Michael. He's been a little too possessive lately, and I want to talk to him about it after he practices with his band today."

"A little too possessive?" Catty asked. "I thought you liked the way he was so attentive."

"I feel like I can't breathe." Vanessa looked down. "I just want time for myself."

The bus pulled up and Serena and Vanessa climbed on.

Catty watched the bus pull away. "I wonder if I'll ever have a boyfriend. It seems so unfair. You had Veto, and Serena had that guy last year. I'll probably never have someone."

"At least you're not one of those desperate girls who's willing to date some mutt just so she can go out."

They started walking through the crowd.

"I still wish I had a boyfriend even if it ended in total disaster. I feel so left out and lonely. Maybe I should go back a few years and trick some guy into falling for me," she giggled.

"You don't need to do that." Jimena punched her arm playfully.

Catty had the freakiest power of all. She could actually go back and forth in time. She missed a lot of school because of it. Her mother didn't care, though, because she knew Catty was different. She also wasn't Catty's biological mother. She'd found Catty walking along the side of the road in the Arizona desert when Catty was six years old.

"You'll find someone," Jimena tried to cheer her. "Next time we're at Planet Bang, stop watching your feet and look at all the guys who are looking at you."

Catty smiled.

Jimena turned back and looked at Cassandra, Karyl, and Morgan before they turned the corner.

The grim look on Cassandra's face brought on a premonition. Jimena gasped as the picture struck savagely. She saw Veto clearly, but she couldn't tell if it was nighttime or day. He was standing in MacArthur Park looking at Jimena. Then suddenly Cassandra came out from behind

Jimena, her hands reaching for Veto. Turbulent emotions came with the picture and Jimena clutched Catty for support. Was Cassandra embracing Veto or shoving him? Either way, the mental picture of the two of them together frightened her. She knew Cassandra was going to do something horrible.

CHAPTER FOUR

A ROLL OF THUNDER woke Jimena. She sat up in bed with a jerk, remembering the earthquake warning they had issued on TV. She glanced at her venetian blinds. They hung motionless. How could the thunder be an earthquake? Even the smallest *temblores* made her blinds sway, and there had been no pop and crack of the wooden door frames that always foretold the shaking of the earth. Maybe she had slept through those sounds, but she didn't think she could have. The Northridge quake had made all Angelenos supersensitive to unnatural nocturnal sounds.

She stretched, then cuddled her pillow. The air felt chilly, and she tried to fold herself deeper under the covers. Rain hit the side of the apartment with a sudden gust.

She turned over and looked at the clock on her dresser. It read 3:00 A.M. There wasn't much chance she was going to go back to sleep now. Maybe a glass of milk would help. She tossed the covers aside and trundled down the dark hallway to the kitchen.

The apartment seemed too cold. She rubbed her arms and started to turn on a light to check the thermostat, when a sudden sound made her cautious. She flattened against the wall and held her breath. The soft clanking repeated.

She crept soundlessly down the hallway and peered into the kitchen. The window over the sink was open. The curtains billowed out and the wind drove the slanting rain inside. Her grandmother was too careful to leave a window open. Jimena looked carefully around the room. The neon signs outside cast eerie colored light into the room, and the undulating curtains made shadows roll over the table and cupboards.

She didn't see anything. She stepped onto the cold linoleum and started across the kitchen to close the window, when something moved in the corner of her vision.

She held her breath and froze. On the other side of the table, someone was bent over, going through a bottom cupboard.

A *tecato* maybe. It wouldn't be the first time some drug user had crawled up the rusted fire escape and broken inside looking for something to sell quickly for drug money.

She took a quiet step backward, grabbed a cast-iron skillet from the stove, and wrapped her fingers tightly around the handle. She held it up as a weapon and with her free hand turned on the overhead light. For a brief moment the glaring white glow blinded her.

Then the person turned. Jimena drew in her breath with a gasp.

Chapter Five

"JIMENA." VETO STOOD slowly, eyes blinking. He seemed uncomfortable. "Turn off the light."

In the brightly lit kitchen, she could see him more closely than she had the night before. She had the oddest impression that he was embarrassed to have her see him dressed the way he was, in a tight black T-shirt, too-long rumpled jeans, and tennis shoes that were obviously too big for his feet. She could smell detergent and fabric softener, and she had the inexplicable impression that he had stolen the clothes from a Laundromat or stripped them off a clothesline. The clothes dangled peculiarly on his body and looked unlike anything Veto had ever worn before.

He glanced at the frying pan raised in her hand, squinted, and tried to smile. "Still the tough one?" He didn't wait for her answer. "I didn't mean to scare you. I was going to wake you. I should have, but I remembered your grandmother's cooking. Her *tamales* are the best in the world." He pointed to the empty corn husks piled on the kitchen table.

Crumbs covered the slick oilcloth. A jar of *jalapeños* sat open next to a dish filled with her grandmother's chunky sauce of tomatoes, cilantro, onions, and peppers. A ghost couldn't eat, could it? Surely that was proof he was real.

"I was just looking in the cupboard for something to clean up the mess I made." He stepped closer to her.

"You should have gotten me up." Her voice sounded angry, but she felt more hurt than angry. Since when did he need food more than he needed her?

He took the frying pan from her hand and set it back on the stove with a soft clank, then reached behind her and switched off the overhead light. The kitchen was bathed with the throbbing pink-and-blue neon lights from outside.

Veto's arm stayed behind her as he pressed her against the wall. He was still wet from the rain, and the sudden damp cold hit her with a sweet shock. His closeness made her forget all the questions she had wanted to ask him as her body filled with the delicious reality of holding him tight against her. She closed her eyes. If this was a dream or a fantasy, she didn't care. She didn't ever want it to stop.

After a long moment, she whispered against his ear, "Veto, I missed you so much. You have to tell me where you were."

"I missed you, too, baby." He rested his lips on her cheek.

"I hate you for leaving me alone." The words were spoken before she could stop them, but the tone with which she said them was more a confession of love.

"I know," he murmured and kissed her neck as if he were trying to kiss away her pain.

They were silent, enjoying the closeness of their bodies.

Veto spoke first. "I know how bad I hurt you."

"How? Were you watching me?" Her fingers trembled, unsure, as they worked their way up his arms to his shoulders.

"Every day." The words tickled against her ear.

"Why couldn't you have told me you were alive? You could at least have sent me a note." She couldn't say more. Her words were suddenly caught in the tumultuous emotions that tightened her throat.

"I was away."

She swallowed and forced her words out. "Away? Why'd you make us all think you were dead?"

"I'm sorry. There wasn't any other way. If there had been—"

"How can I believe you?" More than anything

she wanted to believe him. "You know how much I liked you." She had started to say *loved you,* but her hurt wouldn't allow her to say such a powerful word. She closed her eyes. Maybe it was a dream, only a dream, and he would fade away soon.

Veto pulled back and traced his fingers up her arm and across her shoulder to her lips. "Why are you smiling?"

"I'm laughing at myself," she answered without opening her eyes. "Because I'm wasting all this anger and pain and longing on you and you're probably nothing but a figment of my imagination."

"Can a dream do this?"

He pressed his lips on hers and the warm touch sent a jolt through her. She took in a quick breath, then slowly let her lips open. His tongue traced across her mouth and he pressed hard against her. His arms worked around her back and held her tight.

He pulled away and spread his fingers through her hair. "I promised you I'd never let anything separate us. You remember when I told you?"

She nodded and held up her hand. She still wore the thin gold ring he had given her that day. That was the day she had promised that she would be his someday.

He kissed the tips of her fingers. "I kept my promise. It was just hard to get back to you."

"From where?" she asked again. Wasn't he ever going to tell her? "Let me know what happened to you."

Thunder hammered across the night. The sound made the china vibrate in the cupboards. Jimena drew back and looked over Veto's shoulder. The curtains weren't swaying, and the leaves on the plants weren't bobbing.

"It can't be an earthquake," she said, more to herself than to Veto. Then she glanced at Veto. Even in the dim light she could see the look of sudden fear on Veto's face.

"What is it?" she asked, feeling her own heart race.

"Nothing." He tried to cover up his fear. He

put on his stone cold *máscara* as he'd always done in the old days when he faced down enemy gangsters, but he couldn't hide what was in his heart.

"You've never been afraid of anything—" she began.

"I'm not afraid—"

"Don't lie to me. I know you too well. I saw your face."

He hesitated. "It's the *temblores.* Since *el* Northridge I can't stand them. They make me crazy."

She could feel the falseness of his words. "You're lying to me," she repeated accusingly. "We never lied to each other before."

He tried to pull her back to him. "*Terremotos* have always scared me. You know they have."

She shook her head. "How come you feel afraid now?"

His hands dropped to his side, defeated. "I know what fear is now." He spoke the words so softly, she could barely hear them.

"Everyone knows what fear is! You think I'm *tonta*? Why'd you give me such a stupid answer?"

"I gave you the truth."

Another roll of thunder broke through the night.

"I gotta go." His words came out with a staccato quickness and his eyes darted around as if he were expecting someone to appear suddenly.

She clutched his arm tightly.

He looked at her oddly. "I have to leave now."

"Don't." Jimena held on to his arm, but already she could feel him pulling away from her. "Why are you running away just like the other night? Is someone after you?"

"Don't worry about it." He turned.

"Wait." She didn't want him to leave. She was afraid that if he did, she would never see him again. "I can help you. Tell me."

"I can't now. No time."

"Why don't you spend the night here?" She was frantically searching for a way to make him stay. Her voice sounded desperate.

He shook his head.

"Then promise me you'll meet me at school

the way you used to meet me at my old school, so I can show you off to my new friends."

"Where are you going to school now?" His eyes looked distracted and nervous. He kept glancing behind him at the open window. What was he looking for?

"La Brea High." She grabbed his hand. "Promise you'll be there."

"I promise."

A flood of light from the hallway filled the kitchen. She turned around as her grandmother walked into the room and turned on the overhead light. Jimena blinked and let her eyes adjust to the brightness.

"Jimena, who you talking to so late at night?"

"Veto," she started to say, but before the word left her mouth she turned back. The kitchen was empty.

Her grandmother walked across the small room and slammed the window, then grabbed a rag from under the sink and began wiping up the puddles on the floor before Jimena could see if there were any footprints in the water other than her own.

"What were you doing up?" Her grandmother's long braid fell over her shoulder as she worked.

"I guess I was walking in my sleep." Jimena looked at the window. Did she expect Veto to appear at the window and smile back at her?

She touched the side of her head. It was still wet from his hair. Or had that only been part of a dream?

"Let me fix you some cocoa so you can go back to sleep." Her grandmother stood and threw the rag under the sink. "I need some, too. Those *temblores* make me a bundle of nerves."

"You think the scientists are right?" Jimena sat down slowly, still dizzy from all the thoughts spinning through her head. "It didn't feel like an earthquake."

"It didn't feel right to me either." Her grandmother shrugged and started heating the water. "But scientists say so and I guess they know."

Her grandmother set a mug in front of her

and one on the opposite side of the table for herself.

"Maybe I shouldn't go down to San Diego tomorrow?" Her grandmother threw tablets of chocolate into the water and began stirring.

"I'll be fine," Jimena answered the look of concern on her grandmother's face.

"You come with me, *m'ija.* Your grades are good now. You need time away from Los Angeles and you could help."

"I can't," Jimena lied. "I've got too many tests coming up."

Secretly she was glad her grandmother was going to San Diego. She felt that things with Cassandra and Karyl were going to become dangerous, and she didn't want to have to worry about her grandmother on top of everything else.

"All right, then." Her grandmother nodded. "I'll take the early Greyhound to San Diego tomorrow. I've been worrying about what your uncle has been doing to my recipes for a long time now. Better to act, eh? I'll go down there and see for myself."

"Better to do something than to worry," Jimena agreed and started making plans of her own. She'd wait for Veto tomorrow. She needed to know if he was real or not. She rubbed her head. Were her feelings for Veto so strong that she was conjuring up his ghost?

CHAPTER SIX

GEOMETRY CLASS SEEMED to drag on forever. Jimena kept glancing at the clock until Mr. Hall scowled at her. "Do you think you can help the clock move faster by watching it, Jimena?"

"No, sir." She stifled a yawn and looked at Catty.

Catty drew a chain of entwined roses and hearts across her notebook. Jimena thought she was a talented artist.

Vanessa still took notes, her pencil scratching across the paper at an impossible speed. She eagerly raised her hand to answer Mr. Hall's questions.

The desk in front of Vanessa was empty. Serena had cut afternoon classes. Jimena wished now she had gone with her. She needed to talk to her about Veto, but she had a suspicious feeling that Serena was meeting Stanton. Jimena felt nervous about it. She worried that whatever Cassandra was planning involved Stanton.

She tried to quiet her apprehension by listening to the steady tap of rain against the windows. The weather forecast said it would clear by this afternoon. She hoped so. She didn't want to wait in the rain for Veto.

The bell rang and she jumped.

Catty looked up and stretched as slow as a cat.

Vanessa had a satisfied grin and carefully tucked her notes inside her geometry book. "You guys want help with the homework?" Where did she get the energy?

"No," Catty and Jimena answered together.

Vanessa winked. "All right, but if you change your minds . . ."

"No!" Catty and Jimena shouted and followed Vanessa outside to the hallway.

"Look who's there." Catty pointed, then pulled on her yellow slicker and opened an umbrella. "I thought you asked him for breathing room?"

Michael leaned against a bank of lockers. His black hair was pulled back in a ponytail, accenting his strong, angular features. He smiled when he saw Vanessa and his dark eyes seemed to light up. No girl could resist looking at him. Vanessa had liked him since the beginning of the school year when she first met him in Spanish class. Jimena didn't understand why she suddenly felt like she needed more room. Michael didn't seem like the smothering kind of guy.

"I was hoping we could talk some more," he said to Vanessa. Without asking he took her books so that she could pull on her trench coat, then he put his arm around her and started guiding her away from Catty and Jimena.

"I'll see you guys later," Vanessa called over her shoulder.

"Can you believe she's got such a gorgeous guy and she's going to throw him away?" Catty opened her locker and put her geometry book inside.

"She's not throwing him away. She just wants more time for herself."

Catty nodded. "Still."

"I know . . ." Jimena agreed and longingly watched Vanessa and Michael walk away. "They look so in love."

"She's a dope if she lets him go." Catty slammed her locker.

"Sounds like you're a little *celosa.*"

"A *little* jealous?" Catty grinned. "I'm crazy jealous. That's the one thing I want, and I don't ever think I'm going to get it." Catty looked down at her watch. "I'm late. I'm watching the shop for my mom this afternoon."

Catty's mother owned the Darma Bookstore on Third Street. Business had been slow recently, and Kendra had started teaching extension courses at UCLA. Catty's mother was a Latin scholar and had even worked once translating medieval manuscripts. She taught Latin and Classics. Jimena had been impressed when she met her. Kendra didn't seem the type to have done so much studying.

"So, you want to hang out at the store with me?" Catty asked. "We could make some tea and watch videos. It's never that busy. I think everybody in L.A. has their supply of Buddha beads." Besides prayer beads, the bookstore also sold candles, incense, crystals, and essential oils.

Jimena slipped into her coat. "No, I have something I have to do."

They waved good-bye, and Jimena walked out to the edge of campus, carrying a pile of books and an umbrella.

She sat on a cement bench that faced the street. The storm had started to clear, and blue sky peeked between swift moving clouds. A light breeze brought the smells of wet dirt, eucalyptus leaves, and drying cement. She lifted her hair and stretched, enjoying the feel of the clean air.

After an hour had passed, the sky had cleared completely. Jimena had missed one bus already, and when the next one approached she felt a need to run to it. Instead she let it roll by and decided to walk down to Beverly Boulevard and grab a bus there. She gathered her books and started walking.

She had only gone a little way when she felt a car pull up behind her. She turned expectantly, hoping to see Veto's smiling face, and was immediately let down.

Serena's brother, Collin, waved from behind the wheel of his utility van. Jimena had really disliked Collin when she first met him. Their constant bickering had upset Serena, but they got along okay now.

She stepped to the van and looked through the passenger-side window.

"I'm looking for Serena. Have you seen her?" His face was sunburned, his nose peeling and his lips still had traces of white zinc oxide. Lines from dried salt water traced around the back of his deeply tanned neck. Wind whipped through the driver's side window and blew his long white-blond hair into his blue eyes. He looked like something from a kid's comic book.

"I haven't seen her," Jimena answered.

"You haven't?" He looked surprised.

"Maybe she had a cello lesson," Jimena offered, even though she knew that wasn't true. Serena was keeping her relationship with Stanton a secret from Collin. Her brother was overly protective of his little sister, and that meant he tended to scare boyfriends away. Although, Jimena couldn't imagine anyone frightening Stanton.

"You want a ride then?" Collin leaned over and opened the passenger-side door.

She hesitated. There was still a chance she could meet up with Veto.

"Come on," he coaxed.

Finally she handed him her books and crawled in.

He smiled broadly and waited for her to hook the seat belt before he pulled away from the curb. His surfboard was in the back of the van wrapped in towels.

"Why aren't you surfing?" she asked. Collin was a total board-head. Waves were the only thing he ever had on his mind.

"Heavy rains bring pollution." He shrugged. "They closed the beaches."

During heavy rains, raw sewage filled with bacteria spilled into the ocean, threatening swimmers with hepatitis. But Jimena knew that not all of the beaches were closed. She had heard kids at school talking about the six-foot swells down at Huntington Beach.

"Too bad, storm surf is awesome." He mused. "You want to stop at Farmers' Market?"

"What for?"

"To get something to eat. Aren't you hungry?" He smiled and turned the wrong way. "Let's go down to Philippe's and grab a sandwich."

She shook her head. "Thanks, but I need to get home." The day felt so over for her. She just wanted to change into her sweats and go over her geometry while huddled in bed.

He continued driving toward downtown.

"You'll need to turn back," she reminded him. "I really don't have time today. Sorry."

He seemed disappointed. Maybe he hadn't eaten all day.

"Take this street back to Wilshire." She pointed and he took a quick right.

When they drove past MacArthur Park, Jimena thought she caught of glimpse of Cassandra.

"Pull over!" she yelled.

"Here?" Collin seemed surprised, but he was already aiming the car to the side of the road. "What's up?"

"I think I saw someone," she answered and unhooked her seat belt.

As the car slowed she jumped out and ran through the gridlocked traffic to the park. She hurried around people selling homemade food from large white kettles and darted past vendors' displays of brightly colored plastic toys, beaded jewelry, and silver watches.

She stopped near a man selling balloons and cotton candy in plastic bags.

Morgan and Karyl sat on a park bench near the lake, watching Cassandra step onto one of the paddleboats.

The wind twisted Cassandra's frilly lace skirt tightly around her.

Jimena started to go closer to investigate, when a commotion made her turn back. People were spilling from the sidewalks into the street, stopping traffic near Collin's van.

She glanced back at the water.

Cassandra sat down in the paddleboat, and Karyl and Morgan waved good-bye to her.

A shout made Jimena whip around and look back across the street. A young lanky boy climbed on the hood of Collin's van. He jumped up and down and waved his arms as if he had just won a soccer game.

She took one last glance at Cassandra. She was pedaling the boat out to the middle of the lake.

Then Jimena turned and sprinted back across the park. When she got to the other side of Wilshire near the van, she shoved through the crowd. She recognized some of the faces of the boys who were bothering Collin. Two lived in her grandmother's apartment building. They were acting bolder than their years, taunting Collin with lewd hand signs.

Collin leaned against the side of his van, legs crossed in front of him. He didn't seem worried. He was actually smiling at the boys.

The boys weren't Ninth Street and that was the problem. She thought they might belong to Wilshire 5. She had seen their graffiti in her grandmother's basement.

Collin didn't move. He was making no attempt to get back in his van and drive away. Didn't he know how dangerous this could be? Their spindly arms and legs might make them look like elementary school boys, but if he pushed them they would have to make a big show of their daring.

"Hey," she let the word come out hard and severe.

The three boys turned slowly and faced her. Their shaved heads made them look too young for the violence that was on their minds.

"Hey, what?" the lanky one said.

Then all three boys moved as one, close together toward her, emboldened by one another's bravado.

Jimena shook her head and smiled. "You think the three of you make a *vato* strong enough to take me on?" She folded her arms carelessly over her chest.

The fat, dark boy with the long Lakers T-shirt and huge Nikes glared at her.

She knew instinctively that to win she had to act crazy. She let her hand reach inside her coat. She no longer carried a knife or a gun, but her hand remembered the motions of reaching under a shirt, and resting fingers on the cold heavy metal of a gun. That was dangerous. The boys could be strapping. Twelve- and thirteen-year-old kids could buy guns, or steal guns as easily as they could find a way to get a pack of cigarettes.

"Where you from?" The larger boy held his head up in challenge.

She laughed. "*Nueve. ¿Y qué?* I'm Ninth Street and so what? What do you think the three of you are going to do about it?"

The boys hadn't expected her to be ganged up. They were too young to remember the time when everyone knew Jimena.

For a moment the boys had a strange look on their faces and they exchanged tense glances. Jimena knew that they saw something menacing and *peligroso* in her eyes.

The larger boy stepped back. "Come on," he ordered. "*La chica no vale la pena.* She's not worth it."

The smaller one spit near her shoe before he turned and slowly followed his friend.

"Bitch," the lanky one mumbled under his breath. He turned and bumped against the people circling the van as he walked away.

Once they were away from Jimena, they sprinted across the street to the park. They stole a soccer ball from a group of younger boys and started to play a hard game to undo the humiliation that a *verdadera* gang member had just inflicted on them.

She looked at Collin and shook her head.

He was still smiling. Those boys probably couldn't have driven his car, but the posturing, pretending to be able to do it, was what amused them. Other twelve-year-old kids in her neighborhood were fighting a war. She remembered the helpless feeling of hearing gunshots and seeing the white flashes from the back of cars and diving for cover. That had been in the old days of drive-bys. Now gangsters got their 9-millimeters, walked uninvited into parties, and shot at point-blank range.

She knew what a bullet could do, and she suddenly felt angry that Collin hadn't gunned the motor and fled.

"You think this is so funny?" she snapped. Before she could say more, thunder rippled through the air.

People in the park glanced up and looked at each other with astonished faces. Some laughed with nervousness, but no one ran because there hadn't been a tremor.

She scanned the lake for Cassandra. The boat was gone, and Morgan and Karyl were no longer sitting on the park bench. She checked the rest of the park. She didn't see them, but in the commotion they could have seen her and hidden. If they were doing something for the Atrox, they wouldn't want her to know about it.

"Doesn't seem like a quake to me," Collin said beside her.

She couldn't forget her anger that quickly. "Why'd you stay and mess with those 'hood rats?"

Her anger took him by surprise. "What do you mean mess with them? They accosted me."

"You know what I mean," she said. "You should have gotten the hell out. You think you can face down a gang of little punks? They get out of control and have to show the others that they got what it takes even if they don't. It's like these punks can't wait to build a big reputation so everyone will know their name."

"Is that what you did?"

That caught her by surprise.

"Yeah," she whispered in a hoarse voice that seemed to travel over all the memories of the things she had done. She gathered her books from the front seat of his van.

His eyes had a new look for her. Was it pity,

embarrassment, or understanding? She pretended not to see, and went on, "Maybe one of them even had a gun." She turned and started walking toward her grandmother's apartment. "Why am I wasting my time? You've had a nice easy life, so there's no way you can understand."

"And you don't understand my philosophy." He walked along beside her.

She glanced up at him. "Your what?"

"No fear," he whispered.

"What's that supposed to mean?"

"If I had given in and run like you'd wanted me to, then fear would have taken hold inside me." He shrugged. "Then it starts to grow until you're afraid of every little kid who comes up to you dressed like a gangster."

"Maybe you *should* be afraid of those little kids." She held her books tight against her chest.

He shook his head. "Once you're afraid of something, you attract it into your life. I know."

"Don't be stupid."

"Yeah, you try to avoid it," he explained. "And you try to get away from it, and because you're trying so hard, you're always concentrating on it, and the more you concentrate on it, the more you pull it into your life."

She looked at him and wondered what he had feared that had made him develop such an odd philosophy. He seemed to read her thoughts.

"When I was younger my mother kept threatening to leave us." He looked away from her then. "I was afraid she would. The fear became huge inside me. Every day I ran home from school. Every day I cleaned my room. All I could think of was her leaving. I tried everything I could to make her stay, and then she left. That's when I decided to stop being afraid."

"You were just a kid then."

"So was Serena," he added. "But I knew from that day that fear is a wasted emotion. It never stops anything bad from happening."

"Do you know where your mother is?" Jimena asked quietly.

He shook his head. "Who cares? That was more than ten years ago." But she knew from the tone of his voice that he did care.

She stopped at the walk that led up to her grandmother's apartment building. "I don't know where my mother is either."

He glanced down at her.

"She never threatened to leave," Jimena added. "One day she was just gone. Drugs made her go."

"I'm sorry," he murmured.

"My grandmother told me that some people can't overcome their addictions and they should be pitied and prayed for and loved all the more—"

He interrupted her. "But you can't forgive her?"

She nodded. "It's worse than that. Even now, if I think about her, I can't remember her face. I only see the photographs my grandmother has shown me and instead of remembering the time I spent with her, I remember the stories my grandmother has given me to go with the photos."

"At least you had a reason for her leaving." Collin didn't seem to be speaking to her but to himself. "I wish I knew why mine left."

"Did your dad ever tell you?"

He laughed, but it was a dry unhappy sound. "Yeah, he said she wanted to be a movie star."

He walked her slowly up to the steps between the two cement lions. He stopped her before she put the key in the lock.

"That wasn't fair what I said, about how at least you know why your mother left. It had to hurt as badly as mine leaving." He touched her hand. It surprised her and brought on a premonition so strong that she uttered a small cry and fell back off the step.

He caught her arm. "What?" he asked. "Are you okay? Why are you looking at me so strangely?"

She had seen herself kissing Collin. And it hadn't been a brotherly peck on the cheek. The kiss was long and passionate. She brushed her fingers across her lips. Collin? Why would she ever kiss Collin?

"Sorry," she said and fumbled with the key. It kept sliding across the lock. "I don't know what came over me."

He took the key from her, inserted it into

the lock, turned the knob, and handed the key back to her. "Maybe it hurt too much to talk about your mother."

She started to go inside. "No, that was okay. Sometimes it's good to talk about the bad things. It makes them hurt less."

He nodded and she closed the door, then stood to the side, and watched him walk back to his van.

She needed to see Maggie. Something had to be wrong with her power. First she had seen Cassandra with Veto and she wasn't even sure if Veto was alive or dead. And now she had a premonition of kissing Collin, her best friend's brother. She supposed it was possible for her power to mess up. It had happened once when she had a head cold and lost her hearing and sense of smell. Maybe standing in the rain had given her some kind of illness that had affected her.

This was definitely an emergency. She turned abruptly and ran up the stairs to her grandmother's apartment. She felt too impatient to wait for the elevator.

She unlocked the door, dropped her books on the floor, and picked up the phone. She had just started to dial when someone grabbed her from behind. She turned around, swinging.

CHAPTER SEVEN

VETO STOOD BEHIND HER, holding his jaw. "You hit hard," he teased.

"Veto! You scared me to death." She wanted to be angry with him but she felt too happy to see him. "How did you get in here, anyway?"

"The kitchen window." He handed her a single red rose.

She took it, sniffed the sweet fragrance, and made a mental note to nail the window shut.

She tilted her head in a flirty way and looked Veto up and down.

He wore a black leather jacket over a plaid

button-up shirt and khakis. A gold earring glistened in his ear and he had gotten a haircut. He smiled as if he knew she was admiring the way he looked.

"I couldn't meet you at school." He touched her chin lightly. "I had things to do."

She rolled her eyes. "What else is new?"

He took her hand and pulled her toward the door. "But now I have time. Come on. This is the first time it hasn't been raining. Let's go to the park so I can tell you everything."

"Everything?" She looked up at him, expectant.

"Yeah," he said as he opened the door. "*Todo*—and I'll answer all your questions too."

She set the rose down and grabbed her keys.

As they walked toward the park, Jimena felt as if a terrible worry were being lifted from her shoulders. People smiled at Veto and said hello. Three little boys ran up to him and asked if he wanted to buy candy bars for their Little League. There was no doubt in her mind now that he was real. She leaned against him as they walked down the crowded street. She wondered how she could have ever thought he was a ghost.

"When are you going to tell me?" she murmured.

"Soon," he promised. "Wait till we get to the park. Right now I can't get enough of this sunshine."

"I know." She lifted her face to the sun and enjoyed its warmth.

Children in bathing suits and shorts jumped in the rain puddles that shimmered gold.

They crossed the street through the gridlocked rush-hour traffic and entered the park. A *tecato* drifted toward them, his heroin-thin bony hand shaking a cup at them. His few begged coins rattled at the bottom.

Veto stared at the addict, then shook his head sadly. His reaction surprised Jimena. In the old days he might have yelled at or lectured the man.

Jimena turned and looked up at Veto. There was something different about him but she couldn't quite put her finger on it.

A woman wrapped in a *rebozo* sat on a beach chair with a bag of mangoes between her feet. Veto handed her a dollar. She took a knife, cut the mango into six easy slices, dropped the slippery yellow pieces into a sandwich bag, and handed it to Veto.

He gave one to Jimena and took one himself.

Veto took a bite and the juice ran down his chin. He didn't try to wipe it away but closed his eyes and held his face up to the sun. "This is heaven, you know. Sunshine and mango and you." His eyes opened and he looked at her in a strange way as if he were trying to memorize every thing about her.

"Kiss me," he whispered.

She leaned over and kissed his sweet lips.

"Let's go watch the old men play chess." He took a handkerchief from his back pocket, wiped his hands, and gave the hankie to Jimena. She wiped the sticky juice from her hands and face.

Veto took her hand and pulled her to the corner of the park where the old men had set up chairs and tables. They were hunched over, concentrating on the checkered boards. In the old days Veto liked to come here and watch the men play and then whisper their mistakes into Jimena's ear.

They stood behind an old man wearing a *tandito* and Stacy Adams shoes. His tattooed hand hovered over the castle. Age had blurred the letters written in his skin.

Veto studied the board.

Jimena felt a change in her moon amulet and looked up. Her breath caught. Karyl and Morgan were five feet away, their backs to her. They apparently hadn't sensed her presence because they were concentrating on the lake. Were they waiting for Cassandra? She shielded her hands against the glare on the water. The geyserlike fountain in the center continued spraying water, but she didn't see any paddleboats. The pedalo boat ride looked closed.

"Oye," Jimena whispered to the old man with his hand on the chess piece. "When do the boat rides open?"

The old man looked up at her, annoyed.

"Domingo, solamente domingo." He looked back at the chessboard.

"You want to go for a ride?" Veto asked. "The boat rides are only open on Sunday, but I can steal one."

Had Cassandra stolen a paddleboat?

She glanced back at Karyl and Morgan. She didn't need a premonition to know they were up to something bad. Her moon amulet vibrated against her chest in warning.

Veto could always read her emotions. Already he was scanning the park, trying to see what she saw. He put his arm around her and pulled her closer to him. "What? You see something? Wilshire 5?"

"I don't bang hard anymore. It's something else. You wouldn't understand." She caught the look on his face. He didn't like being excluded from her thoughts.

"*Dime.* Tell me."

The two men playing checkers sensed the command in Veto's voice and looked up.

"Nothing." She tried to make her voice

sound carefree. "I'm just getting a headache maybe from all the sun."

Veto recognized the lie. "*La verdad,* Jaguar. Tell me the truth. I've seen too much now for you to keep anything from me. *Ojalá,* more than you'll ever have to deal with or see." His eyes looked tired now. "Anything that's bothering you, you can tell me."

"I see some people I don't like." That was true, even though it wasn't the complete truth.

"If they give you trouble, I'll take care of them," he promised. "You know I will."

"This is a different kind of trouble," she whispered, her voice low with warning.

"*No hay nada* I can't handle." He spoke it like a solemn oath.

She nodded. There had been a time when that was true. Was it still? Could he help her find out why Karyl and Morgan were waiting by the lake? Maybe he could go over and talk to them, distract them while she had a chance to get in closer, and see if they were doing anything. But that was too dangerous. She would never risk Veto.

"So forget about them," Veto nudged her. "You're safe with me. Come on. I have important things I want to tell you. Let's go sit on a bench."

She started to follow him when thunder roared from the ground like a diesel truck bearing down on them at full speed. The ground shook and the vibrations traveled up her leg and through her back.

Veto grabbed Jimena and held her tightly against him.

All around them pandemonium broke loose. People ran away from trees, cars, and buildings, fearing this tremor might be the prelude to the big one.

Jimena glanced at Karyl and Morgan. They weren't running like the others. They stood and slowly walked to the edge of the lake. They were smiling as if the earth tremors had somehow made them happy.

The earth stopped shaking, but her heart was still beating wildly.

The water in the lake lapped at the sides and spilled over onto the asphalt path.

People laughed nervously. The two old men were picking up chess pieces and returning them to their chessboard.

"Ha, you'd do anything to get out of a losing match," the man in the *tandito* teased his friend.

The other old man smiled and picked up a knight from the dust.

Jimena remember how Veto had become so frightened before when he heard the earthquake thunder. She glanced up at him. He didn't seem afraid this time. She started to ask him why, but stopped.

The afternoon suddenly collapsed around her and she was filled with a cruel sense of déjà vu. Veto was standing exactly as he had stood in her premonition. She swirled around looking for Cassandra, afraid she was suddenly going to appear.

She shuddered. "Leave, Veto."

He looked confused. "I wanted to explain things to you."

She shook her head. "Go." The memory of Cassandra reaching for Veto closed in tight and she started to tremble.

"What?" Veto asked with true concern. "What's wrong?"

Everything seemed to move in slow motion around her as utter panic took hold. She looked behind her. How could she tell Veto about the premonition and make him understand how dangerous Cassandra was? Even if she could explain who Cassandra was, Veto would want to stay and fight.

She started to speak but her mouth felt too dry and she had to clear her throat first. "Things around here aren't the same as you remember them. There are other dangers."

He looked at her oddly, but he was still standing as he had been in her premonition.

Why wouldn't he go? Or at least, move. She shoved him hard, and still he didn't move.

"Jimena?" He reached out for her, filling her with an absolute sense of doom.

She felt suddenly trapped in a horrible dark hole even though she was standing in full sunlight. The sun now felt cold on her skin. She heard the stealthy snap of a footstep behind her and turned quickly. It was only a child trying to sneak up on a pigeon. She looked back at Veto.

"Veto, if you ever liked me, just do it. Just go. Please."

He took slow easy steps backward spreading his arms. "*Ya me voy,* all right? I'm going." He paused. "Where do you go with your friends?"

"What do you mean?" she said in a dry voice.

"Where do you hang out?" he continued as he took impossibly slow strides away from her. "Tell me so I can come see you."

"Friday night I'll be at Planet Bang."

"I'll see you there."

She nodded.

Jimena watched Veto run from her with a sigh of relief. He was far from her now, and she felt that he was safe again.

At last, she looked back at the lake. Karyl and Morgan were gone now. She scanned the park, but she didn't see them anywhere.

The sun was low on the horizon when she

finally walked back to her grandmother's apartment. She was going to call Maggie right away.

Jimena had picked up the phone and started to dial Maggie when someone knocked on the door.

She went to answer it. As soon as she opened the door, Serena, Vanessa, and Catty rushed inside with worried looks. Serena's tongue stud clicked nervously against her teeth.

"What?" Jimena looked from one to the other. She couldn't tell if they were angry or frightened or both.

Vanessa spoke first. "Tell Jimena what you told us."

Serena cleared her throat. "Stanton gave me a warning."

Catty kicked off her clogs and paced in chunky-striped socks that crawled up her pink tights. "I still don't understand why he would tell you. It has to be a set-up."

"Let her speak," Jimena broke in.

Serena stretched on the couch and cuddled a pillow.

"Because," Vanessa started to explain. "He uses us whenever someone threatens his position. I believe him. This isn't the first time he's told us something."

Catty walked over to the couch and fell on it. "I don't trust him."

"Tell Jimena," Vanessa coaxed Serena. "She can make up her own mind."

Serena began slowly, "Stanton told me that Cassandra has suddenly become favored by the most powerful Atrox Followers, the Cincti."

"Cincti?" Jimena translated the Latin. "Encircled? I don't understand."

"Cincti is what Followers call members of the Inner Circle," Serena explained.

Catty shook her head. "This is too much to believe."

Serena continued softly, her words heavy with concern, "In all the centuries that Stanton's been a Follower, he's never heard of anyone who is not an Immortal being allowed to visit the Inner Circle."

"Why would they choose Cassandra then?" Jimena asked. "She's definitely not an Immortal."

"That's my point exactly." Catty leaned forward. "Why Cassandra? I think Stanton's setting us up."

"I don't." Vanessa argued. "I think he uses us when it's to his advantage. And it's definitely to his advantage if we can stop Cassandra."

"He needs us to stop Cassandra," Serena said. "If Cassandra succeeds, then her place of power will be higher than his." Serena hesitated now as if she were trying to regain a measure of calm. "Cassandra wants revenge."

"She probably wants to get even with him for those ugly letters she cut into her skin." Catty nervously picked at the funky snake designs on her nails.

Jimena looked at Serena. Serena wasn't telling Catty and Vanessa the really bad news. Stanton had jilted Cassandra to be with Serena. Jimena could only imagine how much Cassandra wanted to get even with them both . . . if she knew. Maybe that's why the Regulators hadn't come after Stanton and Serena. Maybe Cassandra hadn't told the Atrox, because she was planning revenge on her own terms. Jimena shuddered and looked at Serena.

A worried look crossed Serena's face, but her voice was steady as she continued. "Stanton said she's been allowed to visit the Inner Circle because she has a fail-safe plan to stop the Daughters of the Moon."

"To stop *us.*" Vanessa repeated the words for emphasis. "That's why she's been acting so nasty."

"Does Stanton know what her plan is?" Jimena asked.

Serena shook her head.

"Go on," Vanessa urged. "There's more."

Serena pulled a tube of lip balm from her pocket and rubbed it across her lips before she went on. "The Cincti have allowed her to go back into the past to change one event so she can start her plan in motion."

"Has she gone already?" Jimena's fingers went automatically to her amulet. She pressed it into her palm.

Serena nodded. "Whatever they changed, they've changed it already."

Jimena looked from Catty to Vanessa and back to Serena. "Does Stanton know what event she changed?"

"No." Serena shook her head. "But whatever it was, it worked, because she was able to set her plan in motion."

"That's one reason I don't believe Stanton," Catty put in. "You can't go back and change something unless it was always meant to be."

"What do you mean—you can't change time?" Jimena asked. "They already did."

"Because," Catty explained. "Time isn't like a river with one day following the next. We just think of it that way because that's the way we've been taught; everyone talks about tomorrow or yesterday, but really all time occurs at once."

"Yesterday and tomorrow happen at the same time?" Vanessa rolled her eyes. "That's impossible."

"No. How else can I go back and forth in time?" Catty asked. "It's because time is like a huge lake—it exists all at once. We just experience it one day at a time. That's why I can never do anything to change what has happened in the past. Because if I were going to change something, it would already be part of our experience. See? So Cassandra couldn't have changed something. It was something that was always meant to be."

They all stared at her dumbly.

Jimena thought a moment. "So you're saying, if Cassandra changed something in the past, because it is already *past,* as far as we're concerned it's not something that has been changed, because it already happened to us."

Catty smiled. "Yup."

"I'd still like to know what she did," Jimena said.

"Me, too," Vanessa agreed.

"So just supposing that what Stanton said is true, what are we going to do?" Serena asked.

"I can't believe you're buying into anything that a Follower said." Catty stood. "You got anything to eat? All this talk has made me hungry."

Soon, they were sitting around the table in the kitchen dipping fried tortillas filled with melted cheese into a pot of homemade salsa.

"So we need a plan," Vanessa said finally.

"Let's go see Maggie," Catty suggested.

"We always do that." Serena took another *quesadilla.* "Let's at least try to figure something out by ourselves first."

"Well," Jimena started. "I saw Karyl, Morgan, and Cassandra in MacArthur Park today."

"What were they doing this far from Hollywood?" Catty wondered.

"Do you think it has something to do with Cassandra's plan?" Serena asked.

"I don't know," Jimena answered. "Earlier today when I saw Cassandra she was stepping onto one of the paddleboats. That was odd, because the boat ride is closed on weekdays. It's only open on Sunday. And when I went back later, I didn't see Cassandra, only Karyl and Morgan. And remember the earthquake this afternoon?"

"It didn't feel like a quake," Catty put in.

"When we had the tremor, Karyl and Vanessa didn't get scared like everyone else, they seemed—" Jimena thought, trying to find the right word for the expressions she had seen on their faces.

"What?" Serena licked her fingers.

"They seemed happy or maybe excited, but not in a bad way," Jimena answered. "Everyone else was running and screaming, but they smiled as if they'd been looking forward to it."

"Could they have discovered a way to make an earthquake?" Vanessa didn't hide the amazement in her voice.

"Impossible." Catty rolled her eyes. "They were probably just hoping someone would get hurt."

"Still the Inner Circle would be really powerful. . . ." Serena let her words trail off. "Do you think?"

"Maybe we should stake out the park," Jimena suggested. "And see if we can discover what Cassandra is up to."

Serena nodded in agreement.

"That's a good idea," Vanessa said. "I'll bring a flashlight so we can study."

"Please." Catty playfully punched Vanessa. "Why do you have to ruin every adventure?"

"We have to get into a good college," Vanessa reminded her and then stopped.

Catty looked down at the table. "It seems kind of silly to study unless . . ."

"Unless what?" Vanessa asked.

Catty stared at her. "Unless you've already made your decision."

Vanessa blushed.

The girls looked at each other. Their gifts only lasted until they were seventeen. Then there was a change, a metamorphosis. They had to make the most important choice of their life. Either they could choose to lose their powers and their memory of what they had once been, or they disappeared. The ones who disappeared became something else, guardian spirits perhaps. No one really knew. They didn't like to think about it.

"Let's not start worrying about that now," Serena broke in.

"Yeah," Jimena agreed. "Let's concentrate on the present."

"Okay, so let's start tonight," Vanessa suggested. "We'll camp right out there with all the drug dealers, addicts, and homeless people."

"Sounds like fun," Catty laughed.

"What else can we do?" Serena asked.

No one had an answer.

CHAPTER EIGHT

FRIDAY NIGHT, Serena was the first to arrive. She wore a slinky one-shoulder black dress with a plunging neckline and a beaded gold belt slung low on her waist. She carried a fringed bag, and Jimena suspected that her dangling earrings were a gift from Stanton.

"Wow," Jimena squealed, as she let Serena into her grandmother's apartment. "You're dressed to kill."

Serena seemed breathless with excitement. "What about you? I love that halter top with the split up the middle."

"Thanks." Jimena hurried back to the bathroom. She hadn't finished putting on her makeup yet.

A sly smile crossed Serena's face as she sat on the edge of the white porcelain tub. "Why are you fixing yourself up so special tonight? Are you meeting some hottie you haven't told me about?"

"I do this whenever we go out." Jimena rolled mascara on her lashes.

"You always look good, but tonight you look extra special. Maybe it's the glow of love," Serena teased.

Jimena bit her lip. She had been dying to tell Serena about Veto all week, but the right time never came. It seemed that Serena was always running off with Stanton, and if she and Serena had a moment together, Catty and Vanessa always showed up.

Jimena turned and faced her. "There is someone."

Serena gasped with delight. "I knew it. I've been picking up these dreamy thoughts from you all week of kissing and hugging, but I couldn't see who you were with."

"No fair reading my mind," Jimena said with a smile as she snapped crystals into her hair.

"Who are you going to see?" Serena stood.

Jimena looked back at the mirror and saw a blush rising to her cheeks, then she glanced at Serena's reflection.

Serena appeared perplexed. "Veto?! How?" Then her face became serious. "How are you going to meet Veto at Planet Bang? Are you having a séance?"

Someone knocked at the door.

"I'll explain later." Jimena hurried to answer the door.

Serena followed her. "Tell me."

"His ghost is still haunting me," Jimena teased mysteriously. She didn't have all the answers yet herself, so how was she going to explain Veto's sudden reappearance to Serena? "Let's talk later."

She opened the door and Catty and Vanessa pushed inside. Catty wore an iridescent hot green mini and matching eye shadow. Vanessa had covered herself with an ultrafine glitter. It looked really hot with her gold halter top. Her skirt hung across her flat stomach and hugged her hips.

"Tell her she needs to pierce her belly button if she's going to show off her body like that," Catty said as if she were continuing an argument they had started on the bus.

Vanessa ignored Catty. "Are we still planning to go to the park again tonight? It feels like such a waste of time. We haven't seen Cassandra all week."

"I think she knows about our plan and that's why we haven't seen her," Catty said.

Vanessa stared at Serena. "Did you tell Stanton that we were planning to stake out the park? He might have said something to Cassandra."

"I can't believe you'd think I'd tell Stanton our plan," Serena answered and toyed nervously with her new gold earrings.

"It's just strange Cassandra never showed up." Vanessa sighed. "I guess we should go to the park one last time."

"Dressed like this?" Catty asked.

"No one will see us if we're careful." Serena started toward the door.

Jimena followed her. "Yeah, and if some *tecato* does see us he'll just think he's having a heroin dream."

Vanessa stuck her hand into her gold velvet bag and pulled out a lipstick. She brushed it across her lips. "It's Friday already, and it just seems that if we haven't seen Cassandra once all week we're not likely to see her tonight. Besides, the moon is full. Do you really think she'd do anything during the full moon?"

The Daughters were more powerful under the steady glow of a full moon, but Followers were betrayed by the same light; their eyes turned phosphorescent and even ordinary people could sense their evil during that time.

"You just want to get to Planet Bang because you've made up with Michael again," Serena said accusingly.

"Would you stop reading my mind!" Vanessa tossed the lipstick back in her purse.

"What was all the big deal about needing breathing room?" Catty badgered.

Vanessa beamed. "We gave each other

breathing room, but then we missed each other too much."

"You mean you were afraid he'd get interested in someone else," Catty put in.

"Maybe." Then Vanessa looked at Jimena. "Seriously, do you think it's worth staking out the park one more time? Maybe we should just go on to Planet Bang."

"I think we should try one last time." Jimena opened the door.

"Yeah," Serena agreed. "Then we'll go see Maggie tomorrow."

The night was warm, with a gentle wind. They walked up Wilshire Boulevard under swaying shadows cast from the palm trees. As they neared the park Jimena noticed how each of them became quieter and started glancing at her moon amulet.

They hadn't gone far when they passed a guy removing the hubcap from his car. He looked suspiciously at Jimena, then stood and with the skill of a magician, swapped a small plastic bag for the bills wadded in the trembling hand of a man standing near him. Only someone who knew would have seen the transaction. Others would have thought the drug dealer was shaking the hand of a friend who had come to help him change a tire.

The full moon hung low in the eastern sky as they strolled into the park. Homeless people were starting to make beds for the night, laying out pieces of cardboard and claiming shelter under park benches.

Vanessa kicked aside a used hypodermic syringe. "I don't know what Followers could do to make the park worse."

Catty agreed. "What would they want to do here anyway?"

"It doesn't make sense, when they usually hang out in Hollywood." Serena added.

Jimena looked around. "The park's different during the day, when the old men and street vendors and children are here. It's a nice place then."

"Yeah, maybe the Followers have always claimed it at night," Catty suggested. "That could explain all the bad stuff that happens here after the sun goes down."

They stopped near the edge of the lake. Jimena's amulet began humming softly against her chest. "Look," she whispered.

Cassandra walked toward them, her hips swaying with practiced ease, and high-heeled boots clicking nicely on the asphalt path. A breeze blew through her long maroon hair as she tossed her head. She wore tight, low-cut jeans and a skimpy studded top. Silver chains dangled low on her hips. Under the moon's steady glow the jagged STA scars on her chest seemed to luminesce against her skin. Her eyes burned yellow.

A homeless man started to ask her for money but then drew back as if he had suddenly sensed her evil.

Jimena, Catty, and Vanessa quietly stepped into the shadows. Jimena had to pull Serena after them. Jimena felt a kind of nagging fear at the back of her mind as she watched silently. Her nerves tingled with anticipation.

Cassandra stood at the edge of the lake and

waited for a paddleboat to drift toward her.

"How did she do that?" Vanessa wondered. "The boats are all tied together."

Jimena shook her head "Maybe she didn't do it. Maybe the boat just got loose." But she knew that wasn't the case. She sensed that more was happening than they were seeing. She could feel the change in the air, something electrical and alive.

Cassandra stepped into the boat.

"Why's she doing that?" Catty asked in a low voice.

"That's what I saw her do that first day," Jimena whispered back. "The boat ride was closed, but she somehow found a stray boat and stepped on."

Cassandra rode the bobbing boat toward a geyserlike fountain.

Jimena was filled with frustration. Her muscles felt tight. "We can't see her if she goes behind the jet of water."

"I'm going to go invisible and follow her." Already Vanessa's molecules were starting to separate and she looked like a dusty cloud. The cloud swirled with a twinkle of gold, and then she became completely invisible.

Jimena could no longer see her, but she could feel a soft breeze as Vanessa flowed up and over her and headed toward the lake.

They waited impatiently in the shadows. Then a thought rose inside Jimena and she knew Vanessa was in danger. Her hands clasped into fists, and she started to run toward the lake as the ground began to tremble.

Thunder crashed through the air and the earth shook.

Jimena stopped. She glanced up and saw a golden burst of light over the lake. The light quickly became a dense form.

"Vanessa!" Jimena shouted with alarm.

Vanessa was visible again and tumbling quickly toward the water.

"Come on. Let's go help her!" Serena yelled, but Jimena was already running to the other side of the lake.

Just as Vanessa was about to hit the water,

her molecules separated into long strands and she became invisible again.

"She caught herself just in time." Catty panted as she came to a stop.

Serena slowed her pace. "Something bad must have happened to make her lose her concentration. Do you think Cassandra did something to her?"

"I hope she's all right," Jimena whispered.

A whirlwind whipped around them and then molecule by molecule Vanessa pulled herself back together until she was standing whole in front of them.

"What happened?" Catty asked.

"Cassandra disappeared." Vanessa caught her breath.

"What do you mean disappeared?" Jimena felt baffled. "How could she just disappear?"

Vanessa smoothed her hands over her body, straightening her halter and skirt. "Just that. She was there one minute and the next, both she and the paddleboat were gone. I wasn't expecting it, so I lost control and started falling toward the water."

The girls stared at each other.

"Does she have a special power like Vanessa's?" Catty wondered.

Serena shook her head. "I've never heard Maggie mention it. She would have told us. Some of the Followers are shape-changers, but those are all Immortals."

Vanessa interrupted. "You didn't let me finish." Her hand clasped Jimena's wrist. Her fingers were ice-cold.

"There's more?" Catty's eyes widened.

Vanessa nodded. "It didn't look like she became invisible. I would have understood what was happening if I'd seen her molecules spreading. It was just that she was there and then all of a sudden she was gone. As if she and the paddleboat had passed into another dimension."

They stared out at the moon's reflection on the lake.

Catty broke the silence. "So now we've seen Cassandra in the park, but can anybody figure out what she was doing?"

Vanessa shook her head.

"What we do know is that she's doing something odd here and that it involves the lake," Jimena said.

They all turned back and watched the shooting fountain in the middle of the water.

Serena nodded and stepped to the edge of the lake. "What's so important about this lake?"

"Beats me," Catty answered.

"The land here used to be a swamp," Jimena explained. "But the swamp was drained a long time back, and now the red-line subway tunnels under it, so the lake's bottom is actually the subway's roof."

Vanessa looked perplexed. "That doesn't sound like enough of a reason for Cassandra to be interested in it."

"Maybe it's what you said," Catty put in.

Vanessa turned to her, confused. "What?"

"Maybe she goes into another dimension. . . . Maybe there's a door or tunnel into another realm," Catty suggested.

"Could be," Vanessa answered.

"We can ask Maggie tomorrow," Serena suggested.

Finally, Jimena took a deep breath and sighed. "We might as well go on to Planet Bang. We're not going to get anything done here."

The girls started walking away from the lake. They didn't noticed the empty paddleboat bobbing back to the shore.

CHAPTER NINE

BY THE TIME CATTY, Vanessa, Serena, and Jimena arrived at Planet Bang their mood had lifted. The music was loud and the resounding beat made them forget Cassandra.

"Look at the line," Catty moaned.

Kids were crushed against the building in a line four deep, waiting to be checked by the security guards before they went inside to buy their tickets. The line continued down the block.

"Forget the line." Jimena started walking quickly. "Follow me."

Serena hurried after her.

"Come on," Catty cried to Vanessa and grabbed her hand.

They ran past the security guards.

"Hey!" someone shouted.

They hurried inside and shoved into the crowd of kids waiting to pay their entrance.

A security guard yelled after them, "Come back here."

"We better go back." Vanessa glanced nervously behind her.

"Don't look back," Serena warned. "They'll see your face. They won't come after us and risk having that mob of kids break loose and run in here. You think they want a riot?"

"Still, it was wrong what we did," Vanessa sulked. "What if the security guards look for us after?"

"Loosen up, Vanessa," Catty laughed and paid her entrance fee. "With everything going on, do you think they really care that four hot chicks pushed past security without letting them dig through their purses?"

Vanessa smiled. "The line looked a mile

long. I really didn't want to wait in it."

"Now you've got it." Serena paid and they hurried inside.

The breakneck rhythm thumped through the walls and pulsed around them. Their bodies felt the need to move and they started to dance close, hips in line, the way they had practiced. Jimena scanned the crowd, searching for Veto.

"Hey, guys." Michael Saratoga came over to Vanessa and kissed her cheek. She smiled and followed him to the dance floor. Catty stopped dancing and watched them go.

Serena stopped, too, and peeked at her watch, then around the room. "I have something I have to check on." She didn't bother to wait for their reply but hurried off.

"Who's she trying to fool?" Catty asked.

"What do you mean?" Jimena stared after Serena as she disappeared into one of the dark corners where lodos and stoners hung out. Had Catty figured out why Serena was always disappearing and who she was meeting?

"I mean, it's so obvious she's meeting a guy."

Catty put her hands on her hips. "Don't you think? I mean, why doesn't she want us to see him? Is he some complete nerd or something? I've even thought that maybe she's seeing someone's boyfriend."

"She hasn't said anything to me." Jimena hated lying.

Catty looked at her suspiciously, then sighed. "When is it going to be my turn? I mean, you've had a boyfriend. Vanessa has too many guys who like her anyway, and now Serena's always running off to meet some secret hottie."

Jimena laughed.

"It's not funny." Catty pouted.

"Yeah, it is." Jimena started dancing. She took Catty's hand and danced with her back to the dance floor. "It's funny because you haven't bothered to check out what's around you."

"What do you mean?" Catty started moving, facing Jimena this time.

"Move your hips, wild one," Jimena teased. "And I'll show you."

"What?" Catty seemed baffled.

"You are way too cute to think you're never going to get a boyfriend." Jimena placed her hands on Catty's hips. They danced close, facing each other. Jimena glanced around. "Okay, now look at the guys watching us."

"I see them," Catty complained. "They're all looking at you."

"Not." Jimena laughed. "Now I want you to take a good look around and pick the one that you like."

Catty turned and studied the guys. A cryptic smile slowly blossomed on her face. She smoothed her hands up over her waist, up and around her neck, then slowly through her hair, as if she were testing her power over the guys.

Suddenly, she turned back and faced Jimena. She was blushing and breathless with excitement. "I sort of like the one with the spiky hair." Catty motioned over her shoulder with her chin.

Jimena looked around. "Chris?"

"Yeah." Catty smiled.

Chris was new at La Brea High. He was a sweet-looking guy with a sizzling smile, but

Jimena was surprised that he was the one Catty would pick from all the *rompecorazones* and golden boys who were staring at her. He wore extra-large long shorts that came to the tops of his white socks and a heavy-metal red leather belt with spiky studs. A large suede cuff was buckled around his wrist. His head bobbed to the music and his red leather Reeboks bounced up and down.

Jimena sighed. He looked . . . well . . . strange. She shrugged. "Okay." Then she danced Catty over to Chris.

He smiled shyly and pointed to his chest as if to say "Me?" When Catty nodded, his smile stretched into a look of happy surprise, and he started dancing with her.

Jimena watched them for a moment, then closed her eyes and let the music take her away. She lifted her hands over her head and swayed. Someone bumped into her. She didn't bother to open her eyes to see who it was, but continued moving with the beat.

This time the person pressed against her.

Warm hands snaked around her bare waist.

A pleasant nervousness rushed through her. She turned and started to murmur Veto's name, but his name caught in her throat. "Collin!" What was he doing at Planet Bang?

"Hi, Jimena."

She stared at him. There was something different about him. Then she knew—it was the first time she had seen him without traces of zinc oxide on his nose and lips. His sunburn had turned a deep bronze and his blond hair wasn't windblown, but combed and silky. She had never seen him look so good. Then the premonition of the passionate kiss flashed uninvited into her mind. She blushed and backed away from him.

He grabbed her hand and pulled her back. The air was fragrant with his tangy soap smell. "You want to dance?" She took a deep breath. She was filled with dizzy confusion. Why would Collin want to dance with her? He smiled. Was he flirting with her?

She shrugged and wished she had worn a sweater over her revealing top. She could feel his belt buckle pressing against her stomach. She couldn't catch her breath.

"Why do you look so surprised?" he asked.

She glanced up at him. Why hadn't she noticed how handsome he was before?

He held her close, his hands firm on the small of her back. She placed her hands on his chest and tried not to look in his blue eyes. Normally his eyes were rimmed with red from too much time in salt water, but tonight they were clear and deep.

He looked down at her, but she quickly looked away. Why couldn't she look into his eyes when it was usually so easy to look in the eyes of other guys, tilt her head, and tease them?

She continued dancing with him but felt uncomfortably aware of the closeness of their bodies, the scratch of his khakis on her bare legs.

His hands moved up to the exposed skin on her back and he leaned down, pressing his cheek next to hers. She didn't know what to do with her hands, which were awkwardly crushed between them, a barricade.

Someone tapped her shoulder. She turned quickly, grateful for an excuse to pull away from Collin. Her face felt flushed and she drew in air.

Catty spoke into her ear. "Thanks. Chris is so cool. Isn't he adorable? I'm really psyched."

Catty went back to Chris, and Jimena turned back to Collin. He smiled sweetly, but even with the crush of kids dancing around them, Jimena felt too alone and isolated with him.

His hand was pulling her back to him when she caught Veto's face through the strobe lights. She almost ran to him. But something in the way Collin was touching her so tenderly made her hesitate.

She took in a deep breath and watched Veto walk toward her.

"You know him?" Collin asked from behind her.

She nodded. Veto looked incredibly sexy. His black hair gleamed in the flickering lights. His eyes were black and piercing. Every girl around her was staring at Veto as if he'd already broken her heart.

Veto stopped in front of her, took her hand, and pulled her away from Collin.

Collin was trying to smile, but Jimena could see the twitch in the corners of his mouth. It surprised her how much she cared about hurting him.

Veto put his arms around her and her worries slid away. He pressed her close against him and danced her slowly into a dark corner.

"None of the guys at Planet Bang are good enough for you, baby," he whispered into her ear. "They're all a bunch of wimps."

She laughed and smoothed her hands up his chest. She locked them behind his neck and gazed into his eyes. "All the guys are afraid of me," she confessed. "They never do more than look. But I know they like to look."

"The surfer's not afraid of you," Veto accused.

"Collin?" She glanced back. Collin was still staring at her. "Collin is my best friend's brother. He's like *mi hermano.* He just felt sorry for me, seeing me dancing by myself."

"Chale." Veto looked back at Collin. "I see his eyes. I know what he's feeling for you."

She looked at Collin, then at Veto. Was Veto jealous of Collin? He had always been *celoso.* Jimena cuddled tight against him. "Don't worry about the surfer. *Tu eres mi todo.*"

She could feel Veto's lips against her ear. "I'm not worried," he whispered, and then his lips were trailing kisses across her cheek. She turned her lips to kiss him when Catty and Vanessa came up to them.

"Hey, Jimena," Catty squealed, pulling Chris behind her. "Introduce us to your friend."

"Yeah," Vanessa said. "Everyone is talking about him."

Veto seemed embarrassed.

"This is Veto," Jimena said.

Catty paled and Vanessa took a step backward.

"What's wrong?" Jimena asked, then she remembered. She whispered to Veto, "They think you're dead."

Veto laughed loudly. It was a hearty, full

laugh. "Do I look dead to you?"

Vanessa and Catty exchanged uneasy looks.

"There was a mistake." Jimena's words came out with a nervous twitter. How could she explain that a person who was dead *wasn't* dead any longer? "He's been alive all along. Just somewhere . . ." Her words trailed off. That was all she really knew. Veto hadn't told her where he had been.

Veto interrupted her and spoke with cool charm. "It's a long story, but basically, I had to fake my death. The casket was closed at the funeral and my family moved away right after for their own protection." He put his arm around Jimena and nuzzled her hair. "But I'm back now."

Vanessa and Catty seemed reassured, but Jimena wasn't. She had known Veto long enough to know when he was lying. A strange uneasiness filled her stomach.

Catty tilted her head quizzically. "You mean you were in something like the witness protection program?"

Veto grinned slyly. "Something like that."

"Cool," Catty said. "Wow. I want to hear all about it."

Jimena looked from Vanessa to Catty. It was easy for them to believe. And why not? Veto was standing before them obviously alive. But the small seed of doubt inside her was starting to grow. Where had he been?

Vanessa stepped back beside Michael. "We should celebrate after. Let's go to Jerry's."

"That's a celebration?" Catty rolled her eyes.

"I'm hungry," Vanessa clasped Michael's hand and started moving her feet. "We want pastrami sandwiches."

Catty shrugged. "All right."

"Sounds good to me," Chris said before Catty pulled him back to the dance floor.

Veto took Jimena's arm. "Come on. Let's get out of here."

"Don't you want to stay and dance?"

He shook his head. "I can't believe you're hanging out with such kids. They never would have been your friends before. They're the kind of people we used to laugh about." He seemed angry, but underneath the anger she understood his hurt and fear.

"You'll always be everything to me, Veto," she said when they were outside and she was sure he would be able to hear her over the music.

He studied her face to find the lie, but she stared at him and didn't shrink back. His face mellowed, as if he had suddenly become ashamed of his own jealousy.

He put his arm around her and nodded his head slowly, as if he understood that she had seen deep inside him and accepted his failings.

He glanced at the full moon. "Remember how you always liked the full moon?"

She glanced up at the sky. "Still do."

"Yeah, we spent a lot of nights sitting on your grandmother's fire escape staring up at the stars." He bent down and kissed her lips lightly, then whispered against her cheek. "Let's go someplace where we can be alone."

They walked away from Planet Bang and turned down a side street into a residential neighborhood. The fragrance of night jasmine wafted into the air and the purple blossoms from the jacaranda trees floated lazily around them.

"I didn't want to share you with the world tonight," he confessed. "It's been too long since I've been able to talk to you and I got a lot I need to tell you." He rested his arm on her shoulder.

They stepped across the street. Jimena was filled with dreamy anticipation, anxious for Veto to stop and kiss her.

Veto started to speak again, but something made him stop. She could feel his muscles tense. His eyes cautioned her and told her not to make a sound. He squinted into the darkness. A breeze tossed oleander branches back and forth and made dim moon shadows swirl across the lawn.

Veto eased away from the sidewalk to the side of a house, pulling Jimena with him, his movements furtive and silent. "Come on," he whispered. "We'll cut through the backyard to the alley."

She glanced at him. She didn't see fear in his eyes, only caution.

"You worried about enemy gangs?" His

alarm was making her uneasy. Veto had always been able to sense the presence of enemy gangsters and *la chota.* What was he sensing now? "We're not in anyone's territory. The neighborhood around Planet Bang is like City Walk. It's open to everyone."

He didn't answer her. He studied the layered shadows in the alley, then pushed her protectively behind him. "You don't know what lives in the night."

She started to answer *I do,* but a phantom shadow moved near the back of a garage and made her suddenly watchful. She strained to catch another glimpse of what she had just seen. Whatever it was seemed to have hopped to another shadow near an evergreen. The movement wasn't the frantic rhythm of wind rustling branches. It had been too solid and purposeful, like someone trying hard not to be seen.

She felt the need to protect Veto now and wondered what he would do if she told him the truth about who she was. Would he even believe her?

Veto took two steps toward the drooping branches of an evergreen, his feet crunching softly on the gravel, and froze again. "Did you hear that?"

"What?" her voice was low. She had only heard his footsteps. She looked down at her moon amulet. It was glowing. Now her body thrummed, wary and vigilant, as if something ominous were about to happen.

She touched Veto lightly. "We'd better go." She took a step backward and tried to pull him away.

"There," he whispered in a harsh, angry voice.

A figure formed in the shadows and slowly Stanton appeared before them, his dangerous eyes so blue they seemed luminescent.

Serena had told her that Stanton was a shape-changer; he could turn into a shadow and drift for miles, then reappear. She wondered if he also had the power of a vampire to shift into a bat or wolf.

She looked at Veto and her body filled with

new anxiety. Stanton's ghostly arrival hadn't startled him. Couldn't he sense the danger? Jimena tensed.

Stanton stood aside and Serena stepped from behind him. "That was way cool," she exclaimed in a happy voice.

Stanton's long fingers touched her lips tenderly and silenced her. "We have company."

Serena looked up and stopped short. "Jimena!" Serena walked over to them. "Introduce me to your friend."

"Yes," Stanton added, his voice as soft as the night. But there was something more in the way he spoke, as if he knew a secret. "Introduce us to your friend."

Jimena hesitated. "This is Veto."

"Veto?" Serena seemed alarmed. "I thought you were only teasing about Veto haunting you."

Jimena knew it had been a big mistake not to confide in Serena, but before she could offer an explanation, Stanton spoke. "Jimena also thought Veto was dead, but *voilà*—there he is as solid and warm as you or me."

Then he spoke directly to Veto, mockingly. "Everyone thought you were dead, Veto. What did you do?"

A cold knot tightened in Jimena's stomach. Why did Stanton seem to know Veto? And why wasn't Veto afraid of Stanton?

Stanton smiled, eyes fervent. "He's not afraid of me, Jimena, because he's a shade. Isn't that right, Veto?"

"Come on, Jimena." Veto grabbed her hand and tried to pull her away. "You want to waste the night listening to some *vato loco* who uses magic tricks to entertain his girl?"

Stanton laughed—a dangerous sound. It made Veto stop and look back.

"You don't want your girlfriend discovering the truth?" Stanton said. "I don't blame you. She probably wouldn't want to date a shade."

Serena looked at Stanton. "What's a shade?"

"A shade is like a ghost—"

Jimena interrupted him with a nervous laugh. "Veto isn't a ghost. He's no more dead than me or Serena."

"Of course, if he were only a shade he would feel as thin as vapor, but . . ." Stanton stared at Veto.

Veto didn't back down and he still didn't seem afraid. He held his head up and looked straight at Stanton in challenge.

Stanton continued. "Veto has been animated by the Atrox."

Serena looked at Jimena, then back at Stanton. "How can you say such a thing? That's not even funny. If he were animated by the Atrox, then he'd talk. The Atrox would know about you and me and send Regulators after us."

A derisive grin slowly spread across Stanton's face. He pushed back the blond hair that had fallen into his eyes. "He wouldn't, not Veto, because he doesn't even understand completely what has happened to him."

Veto didn't respond.

He's dead. Jimena could feel Stanton tickle the words across her mind. *And there's a part of you that has known the truth since you first saw him, but you wouldn't let yourself believe it.*

Jimena felt anger surge inside her. She turned and faced Serena. "How can you trust Stanton? Don't you know how risky it is to keep seeing him? He's an Immortal. What evil things did he do to get that status?"

Serena touched Stanton's arm. "He's changed."

"Changed? Maybe he's telling you he has, but he's also a master of lies and deceit. Can't you feel right now how he's feeding on the bad emotions between us?"

"I don't have any bad emotions toward you." Serena eyed Jimena curiously. "Why are you upset with me?"

"If you'd bother to get in my mind and read what I'm thinking, you'd know," Jimena said.

Stanton gently turned Serena's face to him. "Don't argue with your friend. She has to believe this on her own."

That was worse than if he had coaxed them to fight.

Stanton's slender fingers slid down Serena's neck and rested on her shoulder. They stared into each other's eyes. Jimena knew they were having a mental conversation.

Ugly emotions overwhelmed her. How could she be *tan celosa* of her best friend? She felt the jealousy take over. "I'm tired of covering for you and lying to Vanessa and Catty about your relationship with Stanton!" she yelled, immediately regretting that she had let her anger out. But instead of apologizing, she whirled around and started walking away.

Then another premonition hit her hard.

She lost her balance and fell to her knees as a picture swirled behind her eyes and came fiercely into focus. She saw Veto standing in MacArthur Park. She couldn't read the expression in his eyes. The earth ripped open behind him, exposing a bottomless pit, and Veto tumbled backward into the abyss. She watched helpless as he fell and the earth closed around him.

When the picture vanished, she looked up and saw Serena leaning over her.

"What did you see?" Serena asked with concern.

"I saw Veto." Jimena couldn't control the shaking in her hands. "I couldn't save him."

Serena looked around. "Where is he?"

Jimena turned her head. Veto was gone. Panic rose inside her. "I have to warn him! I don't want to lose him again."

Serena looked up at Stanton. "Jimena needs me. I'll see you tomorrow."

Stanton faded back into shadows and left.

The perfumed breeze blew across them, bringing the night jasmine with it. Stanton whispered a warning—"Be careful"—and his voice left a chill in the air.

CHAPTER TEN

THE DAUGHTERS MET at Serena's house. It was late and Jimena was still upset about her premonition.

Wally, Serena's pet raccoon, sat on the kitchen table. He stood up on his hind legs when Catty and Vanessa entered through the back door with a grocery bag. They sat down and opened a quart of chocolate ice cream. Catty took a spoon and dug in, then handed the carton to Vanessa, who dripped a long string of chocolate syrup into the carton.

"What's wrong with Jimena?" Catty asked.

"She had a premonition," Serena said. "About Veto." She didn't need to add that Jimena had never been able to stop her premonitions from coming true.

Jimena slowly told them what she had seen.

When she finished, Vanessa was the first to speak. "Maybe this premonition isn't as bad as it seems. Maybe Veto fell into a construction ditch and a rescue team pulls him out."

"Or maybe it was water," Catty put in. "Maybe he just falls into dark water that could look like a bottomless pit."

Jimena shook her head.

Serena shuffled her tarot cards. "Maybe Vanessa is right. There could be another meaning. Let's look at the cards and see if we get a clue."

Jimena hesitated. "I don't know."

"Let's try," Catty put her hand on the deck. "We'll all put our thoughts into it and see what comes out."

"Yeah, let's try." Vanessa tapped the deck with her knuckles, then dug her spoon into the ice cream.

"Okay," Jimena reluctantly agreed.

Serena shuffled the cards and set them in front of Jimena. Jimena picked one and handed it back to Serena.

Serena gasped. "The death card."

Vanessa dropped her spoon. It hit the table with a loud clatter.

"Yikes." Catty looked worried.

They were silent for a long time, each lost in her own thoughts.

Finally, Vanessa spoke softly. "The death card can mean the end of a relationship, right?"

Serena nodded.

Vanessa continued. "Then I think the card is for me. It's telling me my relationship with Michael is over."

They looked at Vanessa.

Vanessa bit her bottom lip. "I told him tonight that we should start seeing other people."

"But I thought you'd worked everything out?" Catty stared at her in disbelief.

"Yeah," Jimena added. "You were so cozy at Planet Bang."

Vanessa shrugged. "I know. I like him so much, but he's going on tour this summer."

"So?" Catty said.

"So . . . what kind of summer will that be for me? I mean, I like him and I know I'll miss him, but I can't allow myself to be defined only as Michael Saratoga's girlfriend. Besides he'll meet zillions of girls."

"You're crazy." Catty shook her head. "Michael is perfect for you."

Serena looked down at the table. "The death card can definitely mean the end of a relationship." Her words were so mournful that everyone stared at her. "The card isn't for you, Vanessa." Serena looked up and her words trailed away.

"Go ahead and tell them," Jimena urged. "They'll understand. You've kept it a secret too long."

"What?" Catty and Vanessa said together.

"I have a confession to make." It took Serena a long time to say the words. "I've been seeing Stanton, not just seeing him, but *seeing* him."

"Seeing?" Catty's eyes were wide with disbelief.

"As in, dating?" Vanessa couldn't hide the shock in her voice.

Serena nodded. "For a long time now we've been meeting secretly and . . . I really like him but—"

"But that kind of relationship is forbidden." Vanessa looked from Serena to Jimena. "You knew about this?"

Jimena nodded.

"And you didn't tell us?" Catty seemed angry. "You should have told us. Serena could have been putting us all in danger."

"It's just that I like him so much," Serena offered. "And he's different with me. He treats me nice. He's so sweet and—"

"What about the Regulators?" Vanessa asked.

"I know." Serena nervously clicked her tongue piercing against her teeth. "If I stop and think about the Regulators I get terrified because I know the Regulators would destroy us both. That's why I had to keep it a secret . . . from everyone."

"And how could the Atrox not know? Since it hasn't sent Regulators after you, aren't you concerned that Stanton's relationship with you is part of a bigger plan?" Catty asked. "Like Cassandra's plan?"

"I don't think so," Jimena defended her. "I've seen them together. I think he really cares about Serena."

"That time he trapped me in his memories," Vanessa started. "He didn't seem all bad. I actually felt sorry for him."

"Please," Catty interrupted. "This guy has tried to destroy us, and you're telling me you feel sorry for him?"

"I was deep in his consciousness," Vanessa argued. "And it just felt like part of him wanted to be free from his bondage to the Atrox."

A hush fell over them.

Finally, Jimena picked up the death card. "Maybe it's something else. Maybe the card is warning us about Cassandra. She's our immediate threat."

"You're right," Vanessa agreed.

"First thing in the morning we should go see Maggie," Serena added.

Jimena set the death card in the middle of the table and stared at the skeleton dressed in a knight's armor. End, transformation, change, and loss. Those were the words most commonly associated with the death card. She had heard Serena say them enough. None of those words boded well for their futures. She looked around the table and had a sudden feeling that they were all in inexplicable danger. It wasn't a premonition, exactly, but the odd feeling carried an inkling of foreboding that made her hands tremble.

CHAPTER ELEVEN

JIMENA PUSHED HER sleeping bag aside and waited for her eyes to adjust to the dimness in Serena's bedroom. Serena and Catty were sleeping on the floor at odd angles. Vanessa had fallen asleep on the bed.

Jimena wondered what had awakened her. If it had been a dream, she couldn't remember it now.

A clatter came from a distant part of the house.

"Veto," she whispered and stared out the bedroom at the dark hallway. Had he somehow followed her here?

The same sound came again. She was confident it had come from the kitchen.

She slowly stood and reached for her robe. Serena had rolled on top of it. Jimena gently pushed her off and pulled it out from under her. Then she crept into the hallway.

She tread softly over the carpet, her ears alert to any sound. When she reached the top of the stairwell, another thought came to her. Maybe it wasn't Veto who had made the sound, but Cassandra and Karyl. She took one slow step and then another until she was at the bottom of the staircase.

Her breathing sounded jagged and she wondered if her body had sensed some danger that her moon amulet hadn't picked up.

As she approached the kitchen she could hear the noises more clearly. The person wasn't trying to be quiet. Then she remembered Wally. She felt a sigh of relief. He had probably gotten into a cupboard and started digging through a bag of potato chips.

She pushed through the kitchen door.

Collin stood over the stove, bare-chested, wearing low-slung baggy sweats, his blond hair looking pale white against his darkly tanned back. He turned, and when he saw her, a broad smile crept across his lips.

"Hey, you couldn't sleep either?" He greeted her. "I'm making hot chocolate. Want some?"

She shrugged. "Might as well."

He pulled a bar stool from the center counter over to the stove and she climbed on top. Collin glanced at her bare legs, then quickly away. She shifted uncomfortably. She had spent the night with Serena many times and Collin had seen her in all kinds of strange pajamas, so why did she suddenly feel embarrassed now? He was like a brother to her. She pulled the robe closed more tightly.

Collin took more milk from the refrigerator and poured it into the pan.

"Did you have a bad dream?" she asked and watched his hand stir chocolate mix into the milk.

"The best dream and the worst dream." He chuckled.

"How's that?"

"I was surfing Jaws in Maui. The waves are so powerful you have to be towed by a Jet Ski to go fast enough to catch them." He took two cups from the cupboard. "It was the best dream. The waves were glassy and the ride was awesome. But then I looked up and saw this five-story wave towering above me. The peak broke over me and it became the worst dream. I couldn't breathe." He started stirring the milk again. "That's always when I wake up; right before I drown. I have to catch my breath just as if I'd been under the water. I don't go back to sleep after that."

"Sounds scary," she agreed.

He smiled at her. His eyes dropped and moved slowly over her body, then, as if he were embarrassed that she had caught him, he turned off the burner with a snap and poured cocoa into the cups.

Jimena started to take hers.

"Wait," he ordered.

She set her cup down.

"You have to have whipped cream and cocoa

sprinkles." He hurried to the refrigerator and came back shaking a canister of whipped cream. He turned it over and pressed his finger on the side of the nozzle, but only air came out.

"You're doing it wrong." Jimena took the canister. Her finger slipped and she sprayed two inches of whipped cream on Collin's chest. She burst out laughing.

"You did that on purpose." He didn't look upset, though. His eyes looked—Jimena stopped—what was that look in his half-closed eyes?

She wiped off the whipped cream with the tip of her finger and glanced up. Had he moved closer to her? She could feel the warmth radiating from his body.

"Jimena—" He started to say something, but his words fell away.

His hand rested on her shoulder and then he looked at her as if waiting for permission. Had her eyes said yes? His hand glided down her back, and closed around her waist.

She drew in a quick gasp of air, surprised

and intoxicated by the feel of his hand on the small of her back.

He leaned over her. Was he going to kiss her? She hadn't realized until that moment how much she had wanted him to. Her hands lightly caressed his arms, undecided and hesitating, but only for a moment, then they slid up to his shoulders and she became aware now of how close they were standing to each other. She enjoyed the delicious feel of his breath mingling with hers and parted her lips slightly in anticipation.

Then she remembered her premonition of the passionate kiss with Collin, and just as suddenly another premonition hit her with a horrific punch. She saw Veto tumbling into the bottomless pit.

She drew away quickly.

"Jimena? Are you all right?" Collin looked concerned.

"Yes," she snapped, and ran from the kitchen as if she were trying to run from the tumbling image of Veto.

"Jimena!" Collin called. She could hear his

bare feet padding on the floor after her.

He grabbed her before she reached the stairwell. “I’m sorry—” He started to apologize, but she jerked away from him and ran up the steps.

At the top of the stairs, she turned back and pretended not to see the hurt look on his face.

CHAPTER TWELVE

LATE SATURDAY AFTERNOON, Jimena walked up to the security panel and buzzed Maggie's apartment. Serena, Vanessa, and Catty waited impatiently behind her.

A metallic voice came over the intercom. "I've been expecting you." A loud hum opened the magnetic lock and Serena swung the door open.

Jimena followed everyone into the mirrored entrance. She glanced at her reflection. She had odd bluish circles under her eyes from not sleeping and her forehead was pinched in a frown.

"Come on." Catty held the elevator open for her.

Jimena jumped on. The metal doors closed and the elevator trundled up to the fourth floor.

"Why do you suppose Maggie said she'd been expecting us?" Vanessa asked. "Did one of you call her?"

Serena shook her head. "It means something's going on and she thought she'd see us before now."

"I bet it's about Cassandra," Catty guessed.

Vanessa sighed. "I knew we should have come to see Maggie sooner."

The elevator doors opened.

They walked down a narrow balcony that hung over a courtyard four stories below. Jimena plucked nervously at the ivy twining around the iron railing.

Maggie waited at the door to her apartment. She was a thin, short woman with long gray hair curled in a bun on top of her head. She hugged each of the girls and hurried them inside.

"So much has happened," Maggie murmured,

as she led them down a narrow hallway to a living room and kitchen. The windows were open and curtains billowed into the room.

Simple haunting music of four notes played from stringed instruments. Jimena looked around the tidy room. She had never been able to identify the source of the music. She knew it didn't come from a sound system because Maggie didn't believe in electricity. She thought it destroyed the magic in the night.

Maggie sat down. "So now, you're here about the thunder, correct?"

The girls shook their heads.

Maggie seemed surprised. "No? Surely, you've heard it?"

"We've all grown up with earthquakes," Vanessa offered.

Catty shrugged. "Yeah, it's not like an earthquake warning from Caltech is big news to us."

"Earthquakes?" Maggie seemed completely baffled. "You think earthquakes caused the sound?"

The girls nodded.

"We're here about Cassandra," Serena put in.

"Cassandra and Veto," Jimena added.

"Well, tell me then." Maggie looked at Jimena and waited. Her warm, caring eyes always gave Jimena the feeling that Maggie was inspecting her soul.

"Veto," Jimena began slowly. "I thought he was dead, but he isn't. I was so happy to see him again, but then I started having premonitions about him. In the first one I saw him with Cassandra. I'm not sure if she was reaching out to embrace him or to push him."

Maggie covered Jimena's hand with her own, encouraging her to continue. But before she could speak, Serena added, "Stanton saw Veto and said he was a shade."

"What's a shade?" Catty asked.

"It's very simple really," Maggie began. "The ancient Greeks believed that after death, the spirit keeps the same appearance it had during life so that relatives and friends who die after will be able to recognize it."

"You mean, a ghost?" Vanessa questioned.

"Not exactly. It's not the spirit of the person, but an airy ghostlike image of the person."

Jimena felt relief flow through her. "Veto's not a shade then. He didn't feel like empty air. I mean, I kissed him. He was warm and solid."

Maggie's hand clasped her arm tightly. "But . . ." she began.

"What?" Panic seized Jimena.

"If Stanton recognized Veto as a shade . . ." Maggie's words came out slowly, as if she were still considering what this could mean.

Jimena rushed for an explanation. "Stanton could have lied."

"If Stanton recognized him as a shade," Maggie continued, "then it could be that the Atrox animated Veto for some evil purpose. If so, then he would feel as real as any one of us."

Serena looked at Jimena. "Remember? Stanton said Veto had been animated by the Atrox."

Maggie nodded. "Veto's appearance could also explain the strange thunder I wanted to talk to you about."

"What about the thunder?" Jimena's heart was beating wildly. She rubbed her chest, trying to calm it.

"Land thunder," Maggie whispered and looked off to the side as if she were remembering something. "It's the sound Tartarus makes when it opens. I suspected that Tartarus was opening and if so, then that could mean that the Inner Circle was allowing someone of high importance to visit." Her eyes fell on Jimena again. "Or to escape."

"It's Cassandra," Vanessa whispered and looked to Serena. "Tell her what Stanton said."

"What about Cassandra?" Maggie asked Serena.

"Stanton said that Cassandra had suddenly gained favor with the Inner Circle, the Cincti he called it."

Maggie nodded. "Yes, the Cincti, those closest to the Atrox."

Serena went on. "Stanton said Cassandra had been allowed to visit the Cincti."

Maggie frowned slightly. "If this is true, it is very bad for us because it means that she has come up with an evil plan. And it must be a very good one for her to be allowed an audience with the Cincti."

"We'll stop her," Serena said confidently. "We've battled her before."

Catty twisted a strand of hair nervously. "Stanton also said that she had been given permission to go back in time and change one event."

Maggie didn't seem surprised. "That must have been part of her plan. But whatever she changed is already part of your past now. What worries me is that she must know something about one of you, something that could make one of you vulnerable. That vulnerability could put all of you in jeopardy."

Maggie became silent. She appeared deep in thought as she studied each of them.

"Tartarus," Jimena repeated the word slowly. She wondered if the name had filled the other Daughters with as much dread as she was feeling now.

Vanessa looked worried. "What is Tartarus anyway?"

Maggie's voice was solemn. "Tartarus is a dark abyss far below the surface of the earth."

A cold fear gripped Jimena's chest as she remembered her premonition of Veto falling. Was he falling into Tartarus? She shook her head, trying to rid herself of the picture.

"Tartarus is surrounded by a thick layer of night." Maggie glanced around the table. "It's a place of damnation where its residents suffer endless torments. Some say it is where the Atrox resides and, of course, we know that the Inner Circle meets there." She shook her head. "Someone being allowed to visit the Inner Circle, someone who is not even an Immortal. This is a big event."

Jimena clutched the table. She was afraid to let go for fear her trembling hands would reveal the depth of her concern. One desperate thought played through her mind. She had to find a way to keep Veto from falling into the bottomless pit. When she was finally able to speak, her voice felt shaky and the words tumbled out in a strange pitch. "I had a second premonition."

"Yes, dear," Maggie encouraged her to go on.

She waited a moment, taking deep breaths before she continued. "I saw the earth opening behind Veto. A huge bottomless pit. He fell backward. It seemed like forever, and then the earth closed over him."

Maggie began, "It is possible that Veto has been deceived by the Atrox and—"

"No, Veto is too smart for that," Jimena interrupted. "He wouldn't let anyone game him."

"The Atrox and its Followers can be very seductive," Maggie went on. "It's possible that Veto has been animated by the Atrox without even understanding what has happened to him. To be alive again—think of the joy he must feel if it is true . . . to be able to see you again."

An iciness shot through Jimena with a sudden shock. "Veto would never allow himself to be used that way!"

"Maybe he doesn't know," Maggie said. "And that what you saw in your second premonition was his return to Tartarus. The Atrox would demand it."

"Maybe he's part of Cassandra's plan," Serena suggested.

"Not Veto." Jimena could feel anger brimming in her chest. "How can any of you believe that about him? Besides, we're all basing it on things that Stanton has said and Stanton is an Immortal who owes his allegiance to the Atrox. So how can we believe him? If anyone is deceiving us, it's Stanton, not Veto. Stanton is probably part of Cassandra's plan and he's telling us lies to distract us from what is really happening."

Serena glanced at Maggie and blushed.

"That's possible," Maggie agreed. "But not probable. The sudden appearance of Veto at the same time as the land thunder leads me to believe Stanton."

Jimena took a deep breath, trying to control her anger. Why were Catty and Vanessa and Serena looking at her with such sadness? Had they already decided that Veto was a shade? She could tell from their faces that they felt sorry for her. That was worse than if they had been angry with her for protecting Veto.

She stood. Her legs felt wobbly. "Veto could never do anything that would harm me." She hated the way her voice sounded weak and rasping. "No one has given Veto a chance to speak. I'll ask him point-blank the next time I see him."

"But you must be careful," Maggie warned.

Serena looked up at Jimena. "If the Atrox has animated Veto, we'll help you find a way to free him."

"Of course we will," Vanessa added. "We're all here to help."

Jimena didn't want their sympathy. She glanced at her watch. "I got to go."

"Please stay," Maggie said.

"I have to go to Children's Hospital," Jimena answered. "I need to get my hours in or I'm in violation of a court order." She tried to control her voice when she spoke but she knew they heard the anxiety in her words.

"I'll go with you," Serena offered.

"No," Jimena answered, too quickly.

Serena looked at her oddly. Jimena hadn't meant for the word to come out so harshly. She hated the distress she saw in Serena's eyes.

"I need time alone to think."

Maggie nodded knowingly. "Come back tonight after you've had a chance to take all this in."

"Yeah," Serena said. "We'll wait here for you."

Vanessa and Catty nodded their agreement.

"Will you come back?" Maggie asked.

Jimena chewed her lip and nodded. "I will." But she couldn't look in Maggie's eyes. She knew that if she did, the warmth and concern she would see there would make her break down and cry.

She hurried outside to the balcony, down the fire stairs, and out into the afternoon. Tears shimmered in her eyes and she brushed them away with the heel of her palm before they could fall down her cheeks.

It couldn't be true. It wasn't true. Veto was innocent. But even as she was trying to deny it, another part of her mind was recalling Veto's strange appearance the first night she had seen him.

She ran down Robertson toward Beverly Boulevard, as if distance could somehow lessen the effect of Maggie's words.

Tartarus was another name for hell, and Jimena knew Veto didn't deserve to go to hell, no matter what bad things he might have done. He was good deep inside, and he never would have done the things he had if he hadn't had to take care of his younger brothers and his mother.

And then a thought came to her that made her slow her pace. Maybe it had been fear that had made them do those things. The thought grew inside her like a terrible weight. Perhaps they had acted so tough and violent because they were afraid that if they didn't, people wouldn't respect them. It was easy to be popular in the 'hood when you had a big reputation and everyone was afraid of you. What would their lives have been like if they had been regular kids? She stopped. Perhaps Veto would still be alive.

She turned the corner as the bus pulled away from the curb. Normally missing the bus wouldn't have bothered her, but this evening it felt like a terrible omen of what was to come. She looked at the eastern horizon. The moon hadn't risen yet, and the sky seemed empty and alien.

She paced back and forth behind the bus bench. This time the tears were stronger than her will to hold them back and she let them fall. She didn't know if she was crying for Veto or for herself.

If it were true that Veto had been animated by the Atrox, then did that mean she would eventually have to fight him? She didn't think she could. She wouldn't. She had to find a way to free him.

CHAPTER THIRTEEN

THREE HOURS LATER, Jimena finished her work at Children's Hospital and rode the bus home. Visiting with the children always had a calming effect on her. She could almost forget her problems when they smiled at her from their hospital beds and wheelchairs. She sighed and looked through the graffiti-scarred side window at the moon. She felt embarrassed for the way she had acted at Maggie's, but she was too tired to go back there. Tomorrow would be soon enough to apologize. Right now she wanted a warm shower and a long night's rest.

At last the bus passed Alvarado Street. She grabbed the handrail and walked to the front as the bus pulled to the curb. She jumped off and had started home when someone called her name.

She whirled around. Veto leaned against the metal beam supporting the weather shelter over the bus bench, his legs crossed in front of him, exactly the way he had waited for her only a year back.

"Hey, Jimena." His words were lazy, his look sultry.

She took two quick steps back to him and slapped his cheek.

A slow, steady smile crossed his face. "I guess things are back to normal."

"How did you get back to me, really?" she demanded.

His eyes looked confused, and he reached for her.

"You know what Stanton said about you?" she continued. "He said you were a shade." She studied his face for a reaction but the light on Alvarado had turned green, and now traffic was moving swiftly down Wilshire Boulevard. The car headlights rushed over Veto, and the whirling light made it impossible for her to read his face.

"Shade?" Veto shrugged, his lips frozen in a grin. "I'm Ninth Street. *Puro* Ninth Street."

"Not a gang!" she shouted. "A dead person."

His eyes seemed to quiver and she saw the slightest droop in the corner of his mouth, but those could have been illusions created by the headlights.

"Come on." He pulled on her arm. "Let's go over to Langer's for something to eat. I told you I wanted to explain everything to you."

He darted into the street, pulling her with him. They dodged traffic. Angry horns honked behind them. One car skidded to a stop as they jumped on the curb and ran across the grass into the park.

"Veto." She called his name sharply and he stopped. "You didn't answer my question."

"What?" He acted as if he didn't understand. He had learned to hide his emotions from years of being in a gang, but she knew him well enough to detect the slightest nuance. And without the interference from the car lights she read his face clearly. Her heart sank.

"It's true, then," she said sadly.

"What's true?" He put his arm around her. "You're letting your imagination run away from you. I told you I was going to explain everything to you, but you won't give me a chance."

She stared at him, not even blinking when she spoke. "Don't play any games with me. I need to know the truth."

A nearby homeless man tossed in his sleep and looked up at them through his stained pink blanket.

She pulled Veto away and they began walking toward the lake. The rain had started again, and Veto took off his jacket and put it protectively around Jimena's shoulders.

"I know what you've done." Her words came out in a whisper. "You let the Atrox animate you so you could come back. You don't understand what the Atrox is, and now I have to find a way to free you."

He walked quickly ahead of her, then turned back and punched his right hand into his left palm. "I'm proud of what I've done. Why can't you be proud of me? No one has ever dared to do what I've done for love. I tricked the Atrox so I could be with you again."

Jimena stopped. "Do you believe that?"

"The Atrox is no match for a homeboy from *el Nueve*."

"No one can trick the Atrox." Her anger matched his now and their voices echoed around them. "No one!"

"Why can't you believe me?"

"The Atrox is using you, Veto. There's too much you don't understand."

"It's you who doesn't understand." He held his face up to the rain as if it could cool his temper. When he spoke again his words were slow and sure. "Didn't I promise you that nothing was ever going to separate us? Not even death? I'm just keeping my promise to you. My homies always said that I could trick the devil. Even you used to laugh and say it was true. So I did." He turned away from the rain and looked at her. "I tricked the Atrox. I did."

Jimena knew he was telling the truth as he believed it, but was it even possible to trick the Atrox? "Veto, the Atrox is using you, and it's my fault because I'm . . ." Her words trailed off and she started again. "It's my fault the Atrox did this to you, because it wants to hurt me and my friends. I'll do everything I can to free you from its control."

He touched her arm. "Free me? *¿Por qué?* Feel glad for what I've done. I'm with you again, and you know with your heart that I'd never let anything bad happen to you. The Atrox can't hurt you with me around. I got your back."

She shook her head sadly. "The Atrox is probably going to use you to hurt me."

He chuckled. "If I were working for the Atrox and going to harm you, wouldn't I have done it already, before tonight, before you found out how I got here?"

He put his arm around her and pulled her close against him.

"I risked everything to be with you again," he whispered against her cheek. "I risked my soul."

A chill spread through her, and it wasn't from the rain drizzling down her back.

"Has any *vato* every done so much for love?" he continued, his voice caressing and convincing. "I did it for you, baby. For us."

"Veto." All the old ache and loneliness came back. "It was wrong what you did and dangerous. How am I going to save you?"

"You got the power."

She looked at him surprised. "You know about me? Who I am?"

"What about you?" He touched her moon amulet with the tip of his finger. "I'm talking about this. What are you talking about?" Veto lifted the amulet. Rain beaded on the moon etched into the silver.

Jimena breathed a sigh of relief. At least he couldn't be a Follower or even a danger to her. If he were, the amulet would have burned into his flesh. He balanced the amulet on the tips of his fingers.

"What about my moon amulet?" she asked.

"It can keep me alive without the animation of the Atrox," he explained.

Was that true? She believed in the power of the amulet, even though Maggie had tried to dissuade her. Maggie said the amulet was only a symbol of the power inside Jimena.

He played with the chain as if his fingers were searching for the clasp. "All you have to do is let me wear it."

"I never take it off." That's what she said, but she had the urge to take it off now and see what would happen. "Since you've been gone, Veto, I learned something about myself . . ." If she did tell him the truth, would it change anything? Or would he laugh and tell her she was tripping?

Veto interrupted her thoughts. "If you let me wear it, it breaks the spell of the Atrox and I stay alive."

"Why do you believe that?" she asked.

"Because . . ." He looked behind him to make sure no one was listening. She couldn't image what he was going to say now if the other things he had declared had not pushed him to caution. "An angel came to me the first night that I found a way to sneak out of the earth. She was beautiful and glowing. She told me to get your moon amulet."

Jimena wondered if it was the goddess who had come to her grandmother the night she was born.

"Yeah, *es verdad.* She helped me find clothes to wear . . ."

Jimena held her hand up, signaling him to be quiet so she could think. If the amulet was only a symbol, as Maggie said, then she supposed it would be all right to take it off and let Veto wear it. And maybe it had powers that Maggie didn't know about. Perhaps it could break the spell of the Atrox.

She pinched the amulet nervously.

"Come on. Just let me try it on for a minute to see what goes on. Then I'll take it off and give it back to you. What can happen? There's no one around here but homeless people and *tecatos. Vamos a ver.*"

She started to unclasp the amulet. As she

did, she remembered her grandmother's warning. The goddess had told her grandmother that Jimena would be safe as long as she wore the amulet.

When she fastened the chain around Veto's neck, the amulet began to glow, filling the dark around them with a peculiar white light. Almost immediately Jimena felt the intrusion of another mind in hers, and something more, a pain twisting inside her like currents of electricity.

She jerked around.

Cassandra stood behind her, eyes dilated, her features sharp as her face grimaced in total concentration.

Too late to defend herself, Jimena realized that Cassandra had been hiding nearby and was now in her mind, reaching into the depths of her being and ripping her power away.

Karyl stood beside Cassandra, but it was clear that she was acting on her own.

Jimena focused her powers and tried to block Cassandra from going deeper inside her mind, but it was too late.

She looked at Veto. "You betrayed me." The words took all her energy. The pain inside her was complete now. She fell, disoriented, to the wet asphalt path.

Cassandra and Karyl gathered around her.

"Goddess." Cassandra smirked.

"Destroy her now," Karyl whooped.

"Give me time to enjoy my victory." Cassandra beamed and walked full circle around Jimena, her heels tapping a staccato beat in the puddles. Her long black cape flapped around her and swirled over Jimena.

Finally, Cassandra stopped and took a deep breath. When she spoke, the satisfaction in her voice was high. "Finally it's done."

CHAPTER FOURTEEN

"JIMENA." SHE HEARD someone calling to her from a great distance. Her eyelids fluttered and then her vision cleared. Veto was bent over her now, trying to protect her from the rain. She must have blacked out for a few minutes, because she didn't remember him kneeling next to her. She saw the intensity of the fear in his eyes and the hard set of his mouth and knew immediately that he hadn't betrayed her.

"I'll be all right," she muttered, but even that didn't ease the look in his eyes. Why was he so scared?

She tried to twist her head to see what was happening. Veto knelt closer to her and tried to keep her still. She glanced at him and when their eyes met, she knew. He was afraid of losing her.

Veto edged closer, eyes watchful. "What did she do to you?" he whispered.

"She took my power from me," Jimena answered.

"Power." Veto seemed confused. "What power?"

"My ability to see the future and fight the Followers."

"Followers?"

"People like Cassandra and Karyl," she answered. "They're Followers of the Atrox."

He seemed to understand.

"I told you." Her whisper felt hoarse. "The Atrox wants to destroy me. Since you've been gone I learned my true identity. I'm a goddess, a Daughter of the Moon."

Cassandra giggled behind her—a cold and evil sound. *"Were,"* Cassandra corrected her. "You once were a goddess, but no more. I took care of that."

Jimena saw the anguish in Veto's eyes. He understood now that he had been deceived. He started to unclasp the moon amulet that hung around his neck.

Cassandra stopped him. "Too late, Veto. It won't be any good to her now. You might as well keep it as a souvenir."

Karyl laughed. "Come on, destroy her!"

"Patience, Karyl," Cassandra murmured as if making the moment linger somehow made it better. "Besides, Morgan will want to see. Where is she?"

Veto tightened his grip on Jimena's arm. His eyes were staring at something across the park. "That's the angel I told you about. The one who helped me that first night."

Jimena turned her head. Morgan rushed down the asphalt path toward them, a spray of water splashing beneath her knee-high boots, her red mini wet and clinging.

Karyl snickered. "You did good, Morgan."

Morgan walked over to Veto. "You shouldn't believe everything a gorgeous girl tells you. Glitter makeup can make anyone glow."

That made Karyl and Cassandra laugh.

Then to Jimena she added, "Angel is such a natural role for me."

"Dark angel," Karyl corrected.

"My mind-control helped," Cassandra added. "It was easy to make Veto think he was seeing an angel."

Veto put on his stony *máscara* and held his head up and back. Jimena could feel his muscles tense. His hands formed into fists.

"Don't do anything," Jimena warned. "You don't understand what you're up against."

He stood. As he threw a fist at Karyl, thunder shattered the air. The ground around them shook and the earth ripped open behind Veto.

Veto balanced precariously on the edge of the precipice, his arms swinging wildly as he desperately struggled to keep from falling. Finally, he took a faltering step forward and smiled in relief.

Suddenly, Cassandra seemed to appear from nowhere. She walked quickly toward him and shoved his chest exactly as she had done in Jimena's first premonition. Veto lost his balance and as he started to fall backward, he turned with his last effort to face Jimena. His eyes held hers as he fell over the edge.

Jimena screamed, but the sound came out more a mournful groan. She dragged herself to the edge of the chasm and watched Veto tumble into the ink-black abyss, precisely as she had seen him fall in her premonition.

"Why did Tartarus open now?" Morgan's voice sounded worried.

"The Atrox must sense our success." Cassandra gloated. "And it wanted its puppet back."

Karyl's eyes fired with savage delight. "You think Veto will like it in Tartarus, Jimena?"

Jimena suppressed her tears and rose slowly, her legs barely able to support her. She took one halting step forward. Her voice was full of conviction when finally she spoke. "You haven't won, Cassandra."

Cassandra hesitated for only a second, her ice-blue eyes unsure, and then she laughed, the sound lifeless and pitiable.

"You're done, goddess." Cassandra's eyes began to dilate.

Jimena waited for her to strike, but Cassandra stopped and touched her temple as if she were feeling something strange. Jimena knew from the look on Cassandra's face that she was having a premonition.

When it was over, Cassandra smiled strangely. "This power stuff is a knockout."

"Did you see something?" Karyl asked.

"Yeah, wham, like a movie played behind my eyes." Cassandra's words rushed out in her excitement.

"Well." Morgan seemed impatient. "What?"

A satisfied look crossed Cassandra's face. "We defeat the Daughters in the biggest way."

Morgan whooped.

Jimena wondered what Cassandra had seen.

She listened carefully, hoping to hear a clue.

Karyl nudged Cassandra. "So tell us."

Cassandra started to walk away, smug. "I told you that if you steal the power from one of them, the rest will tumble."

"Yeah, like dominoes," Karyl agreed.

"My plan is working." Cassandra's pace quickened.

"Where are you going?" Karyl asked. "You're not going to get rid of her?"

"No, the premonition showed me a better plan," Cassandra said with alacrity.

Karyl seemed hesitant.

"I've seen the future, Karyl." She lifted her arms to the rainy night, and swirled suddenly around. Her black cape seemed to take flight. "Jimena is going to bring all the Daughters to the edge of Tartarus!"

Karyl smiled broadly.

"And I'll be part of the Inner Circle." Cassandra turned to leave, with Morgan and Karyn following close behind.

Jimena watched them go. She had never been

able to stop any of her premonitions from coming true. Did that mean she wouldn't be able to stop Cassandra's premonition from coming true either? She felt heartsick. Could all the Daughters be doomed because of her stupidity?

CHAPTER FIFTEEN

JIMENA WAS BREATHLESS when she finally reached Maggie's apartment and pressed the security button.

"It's about time," Serena's voice came impatiently over the speaker. "Where have you been?"

Jimena tried to speak, but her throat was too dry to utter a sound.

"Jimena?" Serena sounded worried now. She must have sensed trouble, because the magnetic lock buzzed. Jimena opened the door and hurried inside.

Serena was waiting for her on the fourth-floor landing when the elevator doors slid open. "What happened?" Serena asked.

"Cassandra and Karyl . . ." Her words fell away when she saw the way Serena was looking at her. What did Serena see in her eyes? Could she tell just by looking at her that she no longer had her power of premonition? Or was it something else?

Serena put her arm around Jimena. "What did they do to you?"

Jimena couldn't find her voice.

"Come on," Serena helped her along the balcony. They entered the apartment as Maggie came back from the kitchen, carrying a tray with a tall glass of water. "Drink this, Jimena, and don't say a word until it is finished."

Maggie sat down and Jimena drank. She knew immediately it wasn't water, but a cold herbal mixture that tasted of sweetened barley. The liquid soothed her throat.

"Now, dear," Maggie began. "I assume from the way you look that your last premonition has come true."

Jimena nodded. "How can I go down to Tartarus and rescue Veto?"

Maggie studied her for a long time. "The way down to Tartarus is easy, but to retrace your steps back to the world above is impossible."

"I'm willing to try," Jimena pleaded.

"It's too dangerous." Maggie shook her head. "I cannot let you do it."

"I have to do something!" Jimena felt confused. She had thought Maggie would have a plan.

"I know you're concerned for Veto," Maggie spoke sternly, "but perhaps you should be more concerned with what has happened to you. I have warned you time and time again to be careful. If the Followers can stop one Daughter . . . eliminate her, then the power of all the Daughters is greatly weakened. Perhaps you should tell your friends what has happened."

Vanessa leaned forward with a nervous expression. Catty twisted a strand of hair between her fingers, her eyes expectant. Only Serena seemed to know already. She looked crushed.

"Cassandra stole my power," Jimena confessed. "I was careless."

"Tell them the full truth," Maggie coaxed.

"I took off my moon amulet and let Veto wear it." She hated the look of shock and sorrow on the faces of her friends. "But I know Veto is innocent. He was deceived, just as I was."

"Yes," Maggie agreed. "And now all your powers are weakened."

"Why don't we act now?" Serena suggested. "If we know where the Atrox is, then we should go now and strike first."

"Yes." Vanessa seemed suddenly animated. "Why do we always need to wait for the Followers to do something? Let's attack and get it over with. I hate all this waiting and anticipation."

Maggie shook her head slowly.

"Vanessa's right," Catty put in.

"We should be like a gang," Jimena added. "If you hear your enemy is gunning for you, then you strike first and hard."

Maggie sighed sadly. "I've told you. Daughters can never use the tools of evil to fight the Atrox."

Jimena finally voiced something that had worried her since Cassandra had taken her power. She spoke hesitantly, the other Daughters staring at her. "Without my power of premonition, am I still a Daughter of the Moon?"

Maggie hesitated too long. That was more answer than if she had voiced the words.

"Then I know what I have to do." Jimena stood and pushed back her chair.

"No!" Maggie cried sharply, as if she had read her mind and knew what Jimena was going to do. "Evil only feeds evil."

"You keep our hands tied," Jimena accused. The other Daughters watched her, amazed at her anger. "We should have done something before now. If you had let us act on our own a long time back, then maybe Cassandra wouldn't have been able to trick me and steal my power. Because we would have already destroyed her. Why do we have to act like monks?"

"You need a cup of tea," Maggie offered. "Something to settle your nerves. You're not the first Daughter that this has happened to, and you need to have a clear mind."

"I've had enough," Jimena said in a low voice. She could feel her body automatically assuming a threatening pose. She held her head back and looked at the others. "Are all of you going to sit around waiting for Cassandra's next move?" When they didn't answer, she continued. "Maggie knows nothing about fighting evil."

Serena looked away from her. Catty frowned and Vanessa seemed frightened.

"Leave it to a homegirl." Jimena stepped back. "I'll fight Cassandra and win."

She turned abruptly and started to leave.

"Jimena," Maggie called after her. "You mustn't do this!"

"But I'm not a Daughter anymore, am I?" Jimena asked. "Now that Cassandra has stolen my power. So it doesn't matter what I do, does it?" Her heart was racing. More than anything, she wanted Maggie to tell her what she had said wasn't true.

But Maggie only looked at her sadly.

CHAPTER SIXTEEN

JIMENA WALKED WITH purposeful steps toward the door. Her hands trembled as she clutched the doorknob. No one called her back, not even her best friend, Serena, and that hurt. Was it so easy to let her go?

She yanked the door open, and then she was running down the balcony to the fire stairs. With each step she could feel the *locura* returning to her, that impossibly crazy-wild feeling she had had before when she was living *la vida loca.* Nothing could stop her. *Just do. Don't think.* She felt invincible again.

She hurried outside and started to run.

Someone called her name. She stopped and turned.

Collin jumped from his utility van. His hair was combed back in a ponytail, and he was wearing a Hawaiian shirt, baggies, and thick sandals.

"Hi." His smile was flirty and it annoyed her. "I'm waiting for Serena."

Sudden rage ripped through her. She resented that Collin's life had been so easy. It wasn't fair.

"Don't put your moves on me." Her voice sounded threatening.

Collin had been walking toward her and now he stopped abruptly. "What?" he asked with a baffled expression.

"You heard me. I know you're waiting for me and I don't have time to chat it up with some *gabacho* surfer. You go worry about your waves, pretty boy, I have things to take care of."

"What's your problem?" His words filled with anger of his own.

She looked at him thoughtfully. "You. That's my problem. Go find some perky girl who's all flirty and blue-eyed and doesn't understand what life is about."

Too late he tried to hide the startled look on his face.

She hurried away from him.

"Jimena!" This time when he called her name, she did not stop.

She had to figure out what she was going to do. She knew a gun wouldn't help against the Atrox, but a bullet would stop the Followers. Cassandra, Karyl, and Morgan weren't Immortals yet. A sly smile crept across her face. Wouldn't they be surprised to come face-to-face with her while she was holding a gun? Daughters had to live up to that goodie-goodie front and never use violence to fight the Atrox. But a homegirl . . . her fingers twitched, anxious for the heavy weight of a gun.

"You're going down, Cassandra," she whispered to the night. The need for revenge filled her heart and made her walk faster.

She could go to her homies. They would be happy to see her back and excited to go on a mission with her, but she didn't want to get them involved with the Atrox. She still felt as protective of them as she had in the years back when she was running wild with them and watching their backs. Maybe she could break into the gun shop on Alvarado Street . . . but that felt too close to home. She was sure someone would recognize her.

Then another idea came to her. She knew where to find guns. Lots of guns. In enemy land. It was dangerous, but it also felt like the perfect solution, and she liked the risk. Her heart started to race as it used to do before a mission. She could go to the abandoned house where she knew her old adversary, Wilshire 5, hid their guns and ammunition.

Forty-five minutes later Jimena hopped off a bus and hid in the dark shadows of a jacaranda tree as the bus pulled away from the curb.

She moved stealthily around the tree and scoped out the street. She knew where the Wilshire 5 liked to kick it. All she had to do was sneak past them in the shadows. Her heart found a faster rhythm, and she started forward. It had been a long time since she had gone on a mission. She liked the rush of adrenaline, the dry feel in her mouth, the hot nerves in her muscles. She wondered if this was the way the jaguar felt slinking around its jungle.

She had gone only a block when the solid beat of gangster rap boomed into the night. She clung closer to the shadows, eyes more watchful. A garage door was open and kids were dancing inside, knees locked together as they caught the beat and became one with the music. In front of the garage, silhouetted figures leaned against a wire fence, drinking forties and blowing cigarette smoke into the night air.

As she got closer she could see the *vatos* with their stubble-short hair and serious, alert eyes. The tattoos declared their allegiance to Wilshire 5. Some held 9-millimeter pistols. She wondered briefly how many times children had been caught in their crossfire. Had any of the kids she played with at Children's Hospital been shot by their stray bullets? She shook her head to erase the thought and glanced at the girls.

The girls had the same serious eyes as the guys, but most of them looked sad at the same time. They dressed in tight, low-slung jeans or too-short skirts and revealing Ts, advertising their sex, their *maquillaje* perfect and almost *payasa.* It made Jimena ill, the way some of the girls let the guys own them.

Only a few of the girls were warriors like Jimena. She recognized the hungry look in their eyes and the way they dressed differently from the other girls; in loose clothes so they could run fast, hit hard, and hide guns in their waistbands or taped to their legs. Those girls knew what a bullet could do to flesh and their eyes were as tense and watchful as the guys'.

Jimena hurried across the next street and let the shadows swallow her.

She passed a chain-link fence with razor wire curled around the top. A guy and girl leaned against the mesh, sharing secrets and kisses. She slipped around them and cut across an alley. She had only gone a short distance when she heard someone walking. The steps seemed furtive. She listened. The steps didn't continue. Maybe the night was playing tricks with her, but her gangster instinct told her she was being followed. Cautiously she slipped into the velvet blackness between a house and a garage and waited.

Finally she started again, eyes wary, looking around her.

She passed a long line of houses with boarded-up windows. Boxlike letters spray-painted on the walls warned the passerby to beware; they walked on Wilshire 5 territory. She slipped into the side yard, trampled through weeds, and hurried to the back of the old boarded-up house, then silently crossed the back porch.

She paused. Nerves tingled in her back. Long experience told her that someone was behind her. She held her breath and waited for a sound to give the person away.

At last, she decided it must be a dog or homeless person, and she brushed the wispy spiderwebs away from the door, turned the knob slowly, and walked inside. Wilshire 5 never kept the house locked. No one in their neighborhood would dare steal a gun from them. They never considered the possibility that someone from *el Nueve* would try such a dangerous thing.

A dank, moldy smell wafted up to her as she entered the deserted house. She listened intently for any sound. Wilshire 5 could come storming into the house at any moment. Some old grudge might suddenly be remembered after too many forties and send them for their guns, so they could go on a mission of revenge.

She stepped quickly, her footsteps pounding heavily on the wood floor. She reached the first closet. It was too dark inside to see, but already she could smell the bore cleaner and knew guns were hidden there and clean. She felt along the walls above the doorjamb until her fingers came across cold, chrome-plated steel. Her fingers worked quickly to take a gun off the nails. It was small and felt like a toy, probably some foreign special stolen from an old woman in a throw-down. She slipped the gun into her jeans pocket and felt in the dark for a heavier model.

A sound made her stop. Alert, she held her breath and listened.

Furtive footsteps stepped quietly across the floor. Whoever it was, he or she was trying hard to hide their approach. Had one of the kids at the party seen her? Or could it be Cassandra? Cassandra had stolen her power. Did that also mean that she now had some intuitive connection with Jimena and knew her whereabouts?

Jimena quickly removed the second gun. It felt heavy, hard, and cold in her hands. She liked the feel and was proud of the way she knew how to hold a gun. She was never going to kill a baby like some of these *vatos locos* who got a gun but never learned how to fire it. Working from memory, her fingers pulled the magazine from the gun. She held it in her hand, then, satisfied it was loaded, she slipped the full clip back inside. The metallic *click-clack* would alert the person on the other side of the door to her whereabouts, but she was ready.

Let them come, she thought, the jaguar in her smile. Her gun was loaded. She leaned back against the wall and waited.

The prowling footsteps stopped near the closet door.

Jimena made her wrists stiff and aimed the gun, even though she knew she was violating her probation and going against everything Maggie had taught her. Those rules no longer applied. She was the jaguar again and she was taking down the Atrox tonight.

She heard a hand brush against the door, then squeeze the doorknob. It turned slowly. She couldn't see it move in the dark but she could hear the soft ticking of metal as it turned.

She tensed and pulled back the trigger.

When the closet door opened, she fired.

CHAPTER SEVENTEEN

WHITE FIRE LICKED the ends of the barrel and a deafening explosion filled the closet. At the last second she had turned her wrist, and the recoil made the gun buck and hit her face.

"Collin?" His name wheezed from her lungs. She had expected Cassandra and Karyl, even some enemy gangster, but not Collin.

"Are you crazy?!" Collin shouted at her.

Pieces of plaster were still falling as Collin dropped to the floor beside her.

"Lucky for you I was able to twist the gun at the last second." Her head was throbbing from the recoil and her wrist felt like it was on fire.

"Lucky for me," he repeated in a thin voice.

Jimena took a deep breath. She was disgusted with herself. Maggie was right. Guns made violence too easy. How could she almost have gone back to *la vida*? Her hands worked automatically in the dark, taking the gun apart. The parts fell to the floor with dull, heavy thuds.

She shook her head. "You don't belong here, Collin. So why are you here?"

"No fear," he whispered.

"Yeah, right, no fear. Don't tell me you weren't afraid when I fired the gun, because I hate liars."

"Sure, I was terrified. But that's not the kind of fear I'm talking about."

"What is, then?" She tried to catch her breath.

His words seemed to resonate in the closet. "When you busted my act back in front of Maggie's apartment, I felt stupid for lying to you, saying I was there waiting for Serena. The truth is I had been hoping to see you, then when I lied to you and you rushed off, I realized I had lied because of fear."

"Fear?" she asked.

"Yeah, fear you'd tell me you liked me like a brother but didn't want to date me . . . you know the lines. I knew I had to find you and explain things to you."

"Explain what?" She was getting anxious to leave. The gunshot would have alerted Wilshire 5, and maybe even the cops. A police helicopter could be heading for them right now.

Collin continued. "I've liked you for a long time and that's why I've been following you around, going wherever I thought I could see you. Because I was afraid to just tell you the truth." He paused. "So?"

She didn't have time to consider her emotions right now. "So we got to get out of here before those *vatos* from Wilshire 5 come running to check out the gunfire." She stood.

Footsteps echoed hollowly across the floor.

"Too late," she whispered and cautioned Collin to stay down.

Karyl walked into the room, the bobbing beam of a flashlight in front of him. He shone the light in Jimena's eyes, then his light found Collin. Tymmie and Morgan came in after him, each holding a flashlight. They concentrated their beams on Jimena and Collin.

"Come with us," Karyl said flatly.

"You've got to be kidding," Collin answered.

"Do what he says and don't look in his eyes." Jimena grabbed Collin's hand and pulled him up. She didn't know what she was going to do. She had to protect Collin. There was no way she was going to let them turn him into a Follower.

Morgan stared contemptuously at Collin. She had had a huge crush on him once.

"Morgan, is this some kind of stupid high-school initiation?" Collin asked.

"This is dead serious." Jimena nudged him. "Just follow them."

"What kind of trouble are you in?" he muttered to Jimena.

"You wouldn't believe me even if I told you."

CHAPTER EIGHTEEN

KARYL AND TYMMIE walked them out to a battered Ford and pushed them into the back. The inside smelled of onions and old French fries. They stepped over McDonald's wrappers, and the remains of a Taco Bell burrito.

"What's going on?" Collin asked as Karyl slid into the driver's seat and turned the ignition. The tailpipes rumbled.

"No time to explain," Jimena whispered. "We've got to think of an escape."

Morgan crawled into the front next to Karyl. Tymmie pushed into the passenger's seat beside her.

Tymmie was tall, with white-blond hair and black roots. Three hoops pierced his nose and one pierced his lip. The hoops briefly caught a light from outside as he turned his head back to the front.

The car screeched away from the curb, and the sudden motion tumbled Jimena into Collin.

Morgan looked over her shoulder at Collin. The skin around the new piercing in her eyebrow no longer looked red. "I am so over you, Collin. I can't imagine why I ever liked you."

"Morgan," Collin answered. "Next time just send me a note, okay?"

Morgan's eyes narrowed to slits in anger. She didn't seem to like his answer, but she recovered quickly and smiled slyly. "No next time, Collin."

That made Karyl and Tymmie laugh.

Morgan turned back and Collin leaned closer to Jimena. "This is serious, isn't it?"

She nodded.

"We have to do something, then," Collin whispered. "If you're a victim of a crime and the criminal takes you to another location, you're probably not going to live."

"It might be worse than that," Jimena answered.

"Worse?" Collin looked totally confused.

Jimena sighed. "I guess there's a lot that Serena and I should have told you."

"Like what?" Collin asked.

Jimena looked into the rearview mirror and caught Karyl's smile, his eyes filled with desire. Then she remembered the second gun, the small one she had stuffed into her jeans pocket. Should she use it? Before she had time to consider what she should do, Collin nudged her. She looked at him.

"No fear," Collin whispered and glanced at the door handle.

Jimena understood immediately. Karyl was driving the car recklessly fast. He had already gone through one red light, blowing the car horn, and swerving around cross traffic, but he had to slow down sometime.

Jimena waited impatiently. Finally, the car started to slow at they approached a crowded intersection.

Jimena reached for Collin and held his hand, then opened the car door. Before Tymmie could grab them, they bailed.

They hit the pavement and skidded, scraping skin and jarring teeth. Cars swerved to avoid hitting them. Jimena could feel the heat of the car engines as they raced around her. She sat up, dazed, and looked at Collin.

Blood trickled from the corner of his mouth. He wiped at it with his tongue.

"No fear," he mouthed, and his eyes seemed lit with fire. "Now you know what a wipeout feels like."

She looked back at him with a wicked smile. "Now you know what living the life feels like."

"You're crazy," Collin told her, but she knew he meant it as a compliment.

"I know," she answered. "So are you."

"Yeah," he said with pride.

The Ford screeched to a stop and started backing up. Burning rubber smoked from the tires. The passenger-side door opened, and

Tymmie had one leg out, ready to jump after them.

"Come on," Collin yelled and took Jimena's hand. They dove into a yard, climbed over a fence, and ran across a backyard.

She could hear Karyl barking orders to Morgan and Tymmie. "Cassandra wants her now!" he yelled. His words echoed into the night and then slowly faded.

Finally, Jimena felt safe enough to slow their pace. They walked the rest of the way to Collin's van. Collin kept pinching his nose and checking for blood.

She looked at Collin with new admiration. Was she falling for him?

"So what were the things you should have been telling me?" he asked finally.

She bit the side of her cheek. Should she tell him? Would he even believe her?

"You remember that night Serena and I came home and told you we were goddesses and you thought we were teasing?"

His head jerked around and he studied her.

"Are you trying to tell me you weren't teasing?"

"Well, that's kinda true."

He started to smile and stopped. His eyes widened only slightly, and she knew he was ready to hear the truth.

CHAPTER NINETEEN

BY THE TIME THEY reached his van, the street was deserted and a calm had settled over the night. Collin opened the passenger-side door and waited for her to climb in.

Jimena hesitated. "I've got some things I have to do still."

He nodded and slammed the car door. She walked with him to the driver's side.

"One more thing." Jimena touched his hand lightly. "Let me talk to Serena before you tell her you know."

He opened the car door and climbed behind

the steering wheel. "Are you sure you don't want me to stay and help?" She shook her head and was grateful when he didn't try to convince her to let him stay. He turned the ignition and she watched him drive away.

She wasn't concerned that she had told Collin about the Daughters of the Moon. It didn't really matter now that he knew her true identity, because she didn't think she would survive the night. And if Serena didn't want Collin to know, she simply had to enter his mind and hide Jimena's confession behind old memories so he wouldn't be able to remember what Jimena had told him.

Jimena walked down the street to MacArthur Park. The hour was so late that even drug dealers had deserted the park. Jimena circled the lake, listening for the land thunder and searching for a possible entrance to Tartarus. Then she slipped silently into the shadows and waited.

She leaned against a tree trunk. The wind blew, scattering the leaves overhead and revealing the cold face of the moon. Jimena looked up and a simple prayer spilled from her lips, *"O Mater Luna, Regina nocis, adiuvo me nunc."* Normally the prayer was only said in times of grave danger, but this felt worse to her. She would gladly face any danger, but she couldn't allow Veto to spend eternity in the tortures of Tartarus because of her stupidity.

"Please," she whispered.

She heard something behind her and turned without making a sound. A glow filled the darker shadows. A woman stepped toward her, walking three large slender dogs. The beam from her key-chain flashlight ran swiftly over the grass and then across Jimena's leg.

The woman stopped in front of Jimena. Her dogs balanced on their hind legs, straining against their leashes as if ready to pounce.

The woman flicked off the light. Her hair was as black as midnight and flowed down her back. Her face seemed lit with the moon's radiance. A semicircular piece of white cloth was draped softly around her body and she wore sandals. She had a conspiratory grin. "Out rather late, aren't we?"

Jimena shrugged and stared at the lake. She didn't need conversation with a lonely woman tonight.

"Why are you in the park so late tonight?" The woman was trying to be friendly.

"I'm waiting for the earth to open," Jimena said matter-of-factly. Maybe if the woman thought she was crazy or high on drugs she'd go away and leave her alone.

But the woman looked her straight in the eye. "You want to go to the house of death."

A chill passed through Jimena. She had a strange feeling that the woman wasn't who she seemed to be. She was either Maggie in one of her many disguises or maybe even the goddess who had helped her grandmother the night she was born. "Is your name Diana?" Jimena whispered at last.

"Have we met?" the woman asked, and leaned against the tree next to Jimena.

"You helped my mother the night I was

born," Jimena said breathlessly.

"Do I look that old to you?" The woman restrained her dogs. They whimpered impatiently, finally circled and lay beside her.

Jimena shook her head slowly. She had never seen a woman look so lovely.

"And how do you plan on appeasing the spirits of the dead if you do go to the land of the dead?"

Jimena looked at her strangely. Was she serious? "What do you mean?"

"You're going to their house. What do you have to offer them so they will let you leave?"

Jimena thought a long moment. What could the dead possibly want from her? And then she remembered her grandmother's *oraciones* for her grandfather. "My prayers."

"Prayers?" Jimena could sense the woman's disappointment. "I remember a time when blood sacrifice was made. People slaughtered the pride of their herds."

"I don't have any cattle or sheep," Jimena offered. "I live in the city."

The woman snorted. "No one really believes in the mythical world anymore. Once people poured libations for the dead."

"Libations?"

"Milk and honey, mellow wine, and water sprinkled with glistening barley. Prayers? Well, I guess that is a modern equivalent. I suppose prayers will have to do."

"I could say them in church every day for a year," Jimena promised.

The woman considered that, then very carefully she spoke. "No one has ever been able to rescue a loved one from the world below." The woman looked up at the night sky. "Orpheus tried."

"Tell me," Jimena urged.

"Beloved Orpheus went to the underworld to rescue his wife after she died from a snakebite. Hades and Persephone agreed to let his wife leave because Orpheus had shown such proof of his love, but they set a condition. He was to return to the world of the sun without looking back at his lovely wife during the entire journey."

"And?"

"Eager to kiss his wife and afraid that she might not still be there, he looked back, and right before his eyes she died a second time."

Jimena considered the story. "I can do better. I will." She turned to the woman, hoping to convince her. "I only need someone to show me the way down."

The woman nodded sadly.

Thunder quaked through the ground, jolting through her bones. Jimena felt her heart race.

A soft lapping sound made her look across the lake. An old homeless man poled one of the boats toward her.

Jimena followed the woman to the asphalt path. The dogs strained against their leashes.

The woman gave Jimena a sorrowful look. "Every day you'll pray?"

Jimena nodded.

Finally the boat reached the lakeside and stopped. The old man had fierce eyes that seemed lit with a passionate fire. Filthy clothes hung shapeless on his skeletal frame, and he smelled foul. Jimena wondered how long it had been since he had washed his knotted hair and beard.

"Step into the boat," the woman said.

Jimena would have refused, but then she remembered the odd way she had seen Cassandra step onto the paddleboat. She raised her foot.

"Stop there," the man cried.

She paused.

"Tell me why you've come," he ordered. "It breaks the law of the gods for my Stygian craft to carry a living person."

"Nonsense!" the woman huffed, and handed him a gleaming coin. "I say she goes."

He took the coin with gnarled, dirt-caked hands and stuffed it into his clothing.

The woman nudged Jimena forward. She stepped onto the boat, almost losing her balance, then dropped into the seat, rocking the boat violently. The man balanced himself on the nose covering the bow until the paddleboat was steady again.

"Quae tibi nocere possunt, etiam te adiuvare possunt," the woman said.

"What?" Jimena turned back, but the woman and her dogs had already disappeared.

She repeated the words. *"Quae tibi nocere possunt, etiam te adiuvare possunt."* She thought a moment. "What can harm you, can also help you."

The old man grimaced and poled the boat toward a rolling mist that had gathered on the water. Jimena heard cascading water and wondered if the fountain in the middle of the lake could possibly make that much noise.

They entered the mist and suddenly the earth opened before them.

The old man grinned at her. "This is the river over which no soul returns."

They plummeted down a waterfall into darkness.

CHAPTER TWENTY

THE BOAT SETTLED at the bottom of the waterfall and headed forward into a wide-mouthed cavern. The air became sulfurous and thick and impossible to breathe. The churning waters turned opaque with mud, then still and dead.

Whispering cries surrounded Jimena, and she could feel something in the dark touching her like wispy cobwebs. In the distance dogs were barking constantly. When her eyes adjusted to the dusky light, she realized it was the ghostly forms of shades who were touching her, their sad faces begging her for release.

The man poled the boat toward shore and signaled for her to step off. Her foot slipped as she stepped into gray-green moss. As soon as she was on shore, countless drifting shades surged around her. She supposed she was in Tartarus now.

She recognized Veto's dim form in the dark. He looked angry. He floated to her. "Why did you come?" His voice was no more than a dry whisper.

"I couldn't let you stay here," she answered. Now that she was here, she wondered how she was going to free him.

"Go back," he ordered. "Save yourself."

"I won't go. I'll stay unless you go with me."

Then she felt a coldness and saw silken black shadows moving toward her.

"Is that the Atrox?" she asked warily.

"It's a spirit from the Cincti," Veto whispered, as the frenzied shadow pushed through the shades, then charged, twisting with tumultuous fury and howling. Jimena struggled to stand against the force, then froze. Terror tried to rise up inside her and push her to move, but a strange torpor had taken hold. It had been a crazy idea for her to come down here. She felt doomed. Why continue to struggle? Give up. Make it easy. Was she thinking those words, or were they being put into her mind? It didn't matter. She surrendered.

Veto tried to grab her, but his touch was more like a rustling of air. "What are you doing?" His voice had faded to a dry hissing noise.

A sweet lethargy had taken over and she didn't answer him. She wanted more than anything to sleep. She lay down on the dirt as an abnormally dark shadow eclipsed the others. It seeped into her lungs with complete coldness. She let it in and felt herself drifting in a lazy way.

Veto stripped the moon amulet from around his neck. "Save yourself," he tried to yell but his words were barely audible. "Leave."

She shook her head.

He clasped the amulet around her neck.

"It's only a symbol," she said in a drowsy kind of way. "Only a symbol of the power inside me."

"Then feel that power," Veto urged.

She glanced at him. It was too late.

But as she continued to stare into Veto's fading eyes something happened. She realized instinctively that the real power had always been inside her. It was something no one could steal from her. She could feel her energy building, pulsing through her like a jaguar in the night. Her gift of premonition and the amulet were only symbols. She understood now that Maggie had wanted her to realize this for herself; she had never stopped being a Daughter of the Moon. If Maggie had simply told her that she had the ability to stand against evil without using violence, or her gift, then she never would have found the self-confidence and faith that she felt rising in her now. She gasped for air, then coughed and spit.

The shadow whipped angrily about her. She stood and concentrated all her power on forcing the phantom creature out of her lungs and away.

"Go," Veto told her.

"I can't leave without you," she answered. "I won't."

She pushed his dim form forward. The shadows swirled and gathered force and chased after them.

Above them she heard rumbling. Was that the earth closing over them, or opening to release them from the land of the dead?

CHAPTER TWENTY-ONE

THE SHADOWS THAT had chased after Jimena and Veto with such fury stopped suddenly. The following silence was more terrifying. It hung heavily around them with the promise of something worse to come.

Jimena glanced up. Overhead she could see the crack in the earth's crust.

"The rumbling must have been the earth opening," Veto said.

Jimena felt hope rising, but just as suddenly her optimism vanished. Maybe the Atrox had opened the earth to allow them to escape because there was more to its plan.

They continued up a narrow path through rocky terrain covered with silt and sliding mud. The soft glow of moonlight shining through the rip in the earth illuminated Veto's ghostly image. He seemed to float more than climb as he led the way up.

Then they heard a crash of thunder.

Jimena looked up. The earth closed over them. All hope was lost. In the pitch-black darkness that followed, Jimena tried to climb forward but she lost her grip and slid down over craggy outcroppings, ripping her palms. Finally, she caught herself on a slab of stone. She waited in complete darkness, trying to capture her breath.

"Don't worry," Veto whispered beside her.

She hadn't even been aware that he was with her until he spoke.

"I'll show you how I've been sneaking out of Tartarus to see you." His words sounded sure.

He started forward again, up through a cramped cavern. It was dark and misty inside. A pale greenish light seemed to emanate from the churning mists. Jimena crawled after him. She kept imagining movement in the darkness around her. Something brushed against her cheek and then was gone.

A terrifying shriek filled the passageway.

She stopped, her heart slamming against her rib cage. The cries sounded like three dogs howling in terrible distress. Their wailings pierced her ears and filled her with an uncanny fear. She had never been afraid of dogs before.

"What is it?" she asked Veto, her voice shaky.

"A dog guards the entrance," Veto explained.

"That's only one dog?" she asked and started to turn her head.

"Don't look back," he cautioned. "You don't want to see."

She didn't look back. She didn't want to know what kind of dog could make such a terrifying sound.

A few minutes later, they crawled from the narrow passageway and stood.

"Careful now." He led her along the thin and

crumbling bank of a vast underground river.

Veto's body seemed more dense now. He took her hand to guide her, but his flesh felt too soft and she had the strange feeling that if she grasped his hand too tightly she would press completely through it.

They edged along the bank. Mud and dirt gave way beneath their footsteps and fell into the water below.

The murmuring flow of the underground river was starting to make Jimena drowsy. She pulled away from Veto, cupped her hands and scooped them into the water.

Veto pulled her up and away. "What are you doing?"

"I was getting sleepy," Jimena answered. "I thought some water would wake me up."

"Not here." Veto nudged her forward. "The souls of the dead drink these waters to forget their lives on earth."

She stared down at the water, her tongue dry and her desire to lap the waters huge.

A channel of gray light struck her eyes. She

squinted. She was sure it wasn't an illusion, but light from the outside.

"Stay here," Veto ordered. He pulled himself up. Dirt spattered down on her, then his hand reached for her. She took it. His skin felt warm and solid now.

She scrambled out after him, surprised to find herself standing in the middle of MacArthur Park. Traffic moved slowly down the wet streets surrounding the park, headlights reflecting off the pavement. She gratefully held her face up to the rain and let it wash the dirt from her face.

"See, easy." Veto smiled triumphantly.

"Too easy." She shook her head sadly.

His smile fell.

"Our escape was too easy," she warned him. "It has to be part of some larger plan." She sensed that the Atrox was still planning to use Veto to destroy her. They stood in the rain, trembling and unsure.

"If it's still planning to use me," Veto said, "then let's show it that it can't. Risk it all, Jimena. The Atrox hasn't won yet."

She clasped her moon amulet, thinking. There had to be a way to free Veto from the Atrox, but how?

"We need to find someplace safe." She grabbed Veto's hand and pulled him.

"What?" He followed after her. "Where are we going?"

"We have to hide," she answered.

They ran across the park, sloshing through rain-soaked grass. She thought of heading to Maggie's. Maybe she would know how to protect Veto, but that journey required the use of a bus and she felt intuitively that they didn't have that kind of time.

"There," she said suddenly and pointed to a church.

Veto rushed ahead of her up the wide steps and reached for the door. When his fingers touched the metal handle, a bluish flash of lightning struck his hand and he tumbled backward.

Jimena understood at once. Veto was denied entrance into the church because he was still animated by the Atrox, the primal source of evil.

"Go inside. Protect yourself," Veto ordered.

Jimena dropped to the ground beside him. "I can't abandon you."

The air around them changed. The rain stopped suddenly, and she knew the Atrox was coming.

CHAPTER TWENTY-TWO

AN OVERWHELMING CALM filled the air.

Jimena looked around her, expectant, knowing the Atrox was about to attack.

Then a strange sureness came over her and for the first time since Veto had returned to her, she knew what she had to do. She stood and opened the church door. Holding it propped against her foot, she reached for Veto. "Come on."

"I can't go inside." His eyes looked with

longing into the interior of the church.

"Yes, you can. Part of you is still Veto." She motioned with her head. "Hurry. The Atrox can't reach you there."

He stood up tentatively as if a great weight pressed down on him. He bit his full lips in a grimace when he tried to take a step forward.

"Hurry!" She could feel an unnatural storm building around them.

Without warning a gust of wind ripped the door from her hands and screeched around her in wild triumph. The door banged closed and she staggered backward.

Veto's face was a mask of fear.

She struggled against the wind. This time it took all of her strength to move the heavy wooden door.

"Go inside!" she yelled, but she doubted Veto could hear her. His eyes seemed touched with something unfamiliar.

Wind hammered down on her in cold gusts. She could feel her strength ebbing. She felt afraid, not for herself, but for Veto. A huge force seemed to be controlling him now. He started to walk down the wide steps that led up to the church, his eyes staring back at her with pure hate.

She was filled with utter and complete despair. She couldn't bear to lose Veto this way.

"No fear," she whispered. The wind ripped the words from her lips but not the power she could feel building inside her.

She battled against the wind to open the door, using her body as a wedge to force the door against the building. When she had it propped open, she charged down the steps to Veto, grabbed his hand and propelled him inside.

A tortured scream left his body as he stumbled over the threshold.

The wind slammed the door behind them.

Immediately Veto began to weaken and fade, but he didn't seem afraid any longer. He looked peaceful and happy.

She helped him sit on a back pew.

"I promised you nothing was ever going to separate us," Veto said softly, his words only whispers. "Not even death. I tried, Jimena."

"I know." She knew that she was watching him die a second time.

"I'm fading—I can feel it," he explained.

"It's going to be okay." She touched him reassuringly and wondered what emotions he must be feeling.

"I'm scared," he started again in a low voice. "It's from loving you so much and not wanting to lose you."

"Don't be afraid, Veto." she cradled him in her arms. "You won't be alone. Part of me is going with you. That's how it feels anyway. Part of me will always belong to you."

He smiled but it seemed to take all of his strength. "Go light a candle for me. Pray to *La Morena* to beg God to take back his fallen angel."

Afraid that he might slip away before she had one last look at him, she hesitated, then bent down to kiss his cheek. It was like kissing air. His hand reached for hers but was unable to clasp it.

"I'll light the candle." She started to go to the sanctuary, but Veto stopped her.

"Go with that punk *gabacho,*" Veto said. "He'll love you fine."

Unable to speak, she nodded, but she didn't think she could ever love someone again.

She stepped slowly to the sanctuary, took a wooden match from a tin container and lit a small white candle. The flame flared as she felt, more than heard, Veto speak to her. "I'll always be with you."

She was afraid to turn back and see what she knew was true. When she finally did, he was gone. She walked to the back of the church and sat on the pew, still warm from Veto's body.

When the flood of tears finally subsided, she remembered what the woman in the park had told her. *"Quae tibi nocere possunt, etiam te adiuvare possunt."* She thought a moment. "What can harm you, can also help you." And she made a decision.

She wiped her face on her sleeves, then stood to leave, but stopped abruptly. The rain beating against the stained-glass windows didn't sound like the workings of a normal storm. She hadn't noticed the way the wind screeched around the roof while she was crying, but now she did. The storm seemed malevolent and alive and waiting for her.

She decided to spend what remained of the night in the church. She stretched out on a pew, ignoring the angry sounds of thunder that seemed to shake the very foundation of the small church, and soon fell asleep.

When she woke up, soft gray light filled the sanctuary and rain was gently tapping against the stained-glass windows.

She stepped outside. Soft rain sprinkled her face. She started walking back to her grandmother's apartment. She had only gone a little way when she saw Serena running toward her, a red umbrella sheltering her from the rain.

Serena ran up to her and held the umbrella protectively over Jimena. "I've been waiting at your apartment all night. I'd just about given up hope. Collin came home—"

"I told him."

"I know. I was so worried about you. I knew you were going to try to go down to Tartarus to rescue Veto."

"I did."

"I would have gone with you," Serena told her.

"Thanks," Jimena answered. "But it was something I needed to do alone."

"Come on." Serena started walking quickly toward the bus stop. "Catty and Vanessa have been looking for you, too. We're meeting back at my house."

Jimena followed after her.

CHAPTER TWENTY-THREE

BY THE TIME JIMENA had finished showering and blow-drying her hair at Serena's house, Catty and Vanessa had arrived. They looked up when she entered the kitchen, then ran to her and hugged her.

Even Wally, Serena's pet raccoon, seemed happy to see her. He climbed off the table and scuttled flat-footed over to her and stood in a begging posture.

"Don't ever do that again," Catty warned. "You can't go off without us."

"That's right," Vanessa added and offered Jimena a cup of hot cocoa. "We're a team."

Jimena sipped the sweet chocolate. It tasted like the best she had ever had.

"Well," Catty asked impatiently. "Did you go down to Tartarus?"

Jimena nodded.

Serena sat down next to her, holding Wally on her lap.

After Jimena told them what had happened, she carefully explained her plan to take her gift back from Cassandra. When she finished she looked around the table.

Catty nervously pulled at a strand of hair. "It's risky, especially if Cassandra is anticipating your plan."

"How could she be?" Jimena asked.

"She stole your gift. Maybe the two of you have some kind of intuitive connection now."

Jimena nodded. She had already considered this. "If we did, then I think she would have been waiting for me in the park when Veto and I escaped."

"All right then." Catty seemed satisfied.

Vanessa bit her lip. "I don't know if I have enough power to keep both Serena and Catty invisible for so much time. I've only made Catty invisible before, and I didn't have much luck with that."

"You'll have to try," Serena said. "That's the best any of us can do."

Serena set Wally on the floor. "We really don't have a choice. It's the only plan we have."

Jimena studied her friends and hoped that her plan didn't fail. She remembered Cassandra's words. Cassandra had told Karyl that she had seen Jimena bringing all of the Daughters to the edge of Tartarus.

Jimena shuddered. She had to make sure that they met Cassandra as far away from the park as possible.

CHAPTER TWENTY-FOUR

THE NEXT DAY Jimena cut classes again and spent the afternoon looking for Morgan in Hollywood. Low-hanging clouds misted over the Hollywood sign and the day grew steadily colder. She knew Morgan didn't have enough power yet to be able to read her mind and discover her plan, but she was confident that Morgan could set up a meeting for her with Cassandra.

Finally, she found Morgan strutting past the Egyptian Theatre, holding an umbrella, her shiny black boots splashing in the puddles.

"Morgan!" Jimena called.

Morgan turned sharply. Jimena wasn't sure if it was a look of fear or disgust that crossed her face.

"I need your help." Jimena walked toward her.

Morgan took a step backward, unsure. "What do you want from me?"

Jimena tried to act humble. "I want you to persuade Cassandra to meet me tonight in front of the Pantages Theatre."

"Why?" Morgan's eyes narrowed suspiciously and her fingers touched the gold hoop pinched through the skin around her eyebrow as if it still felt tender.

"I want to talk to her about getting my power back." Jimena tried to make her voice as sincere as possible.

"*Your* power? It belongs to Cassandra now." Morgan smiled shrewdly. "But if you really want to see her, she'll meet you tonight in MacArthur Park."

Jimena felt her heart race. She didn't want the meeting to take place anywhere near the entrance to Tartarus. "Let's meet here in Hollywood," she suggested.

Morgan twirled her umbrella nervously. "You only live a few blocks from the park." She tilted her head coyly. "Why would you want to meet here?"

Jimena didn't have an answer. "All right. The park, then."

Morgan seemed too happy with her response. "Tonight in the park," she repeated. "Be there."

As Jimena watched Morgan walk away, a new worry took hold. Instead of trapping Cassandra in *her* plan, she wondered if Cassandra had now trapped Jimena in a plan of her own.

Back at the apartment, Jimena called each of her friends and told them to meet in the park tonight.

Then she went to her grandmother's bedroom and unlocked the trunk that sat at the foot of the bed. She lifted the lid, and the smell of mothballs filled the air around her. She dug through the clothes packed in the trunk until she found the blue halter top and black jeans she had been wearing the night Veto died. She wasn't sure why she had saved them, but she was glad she had, now. She was going to wear them tonight in honor of Veto.

She carried them back to her room, stood in front of the mirror over her dresser, and slipped on the gold earrings that had been a gift from Veto. Then she started to dress. She rubbed glitter lotion over her arms and painted black lines on her eyelids. She rolled on mascara, then stood back.

She studied her reflection. There was one last thing she needed. She wasn't sure there was enough time, but she knew she wasn't going to the park until it was done. She couldn't do it by herself, but she was sure Catty could help her.

She started to leave her grandmother's apartment but stopped at the door, remembering the smaller of the two guns she had stolen from Wilshire 5. She hesitated. She knew it was wrong, but it might also be the only way she could save Serena, Catty, and Vanessa. She hadn't told them about Cassandra's premonition, and she was worried that they were meeting Cassandra in the park.

Finally, she ran back to her room, took the gun, and slipped it into her jeans pocket, then left.

The rain had stopped, but clouds still covered the sky and reflected the city lights, giving the night a peculiar illumination. Jimena walked along the curb until she found a taxi. She took it over to Catty's house. The driver kept glancing suspiciously at her in the rearview mirror. She wondered if he saw the determination and fearlessness in her eyes. When he finally pulled the cab to the curb in front of Catty's house, he seemed relieved.

Jimena paid the driver, then hurried up the walk and rang the doorbell.

Catty opened the door, looking surprised, then quickly cautioned her to be quiet. "I thought we were meeting in the park," Catty whispered, glancing back over her shoulder as if she were afraid the doorbell might have awakened Kendra.

Jimena stepped inside. "I want you to tattoo me."

"Tattoo? I don't know how."

"You draw," Jimena explained. "That's all you need to know to do a jailhouse tattoo. I'll tell you the rest."

An hour later the tattoo of a crescent moon and star was bleeding on Jimena's arm.

"It looks good," Catty said with pride.

"Yeah." Jimena stood in front of the mirror and admired Catty's work. Excitement ran through her when she looked at herself. She glanced at Catty and knew she was feeling the same. They stared at each other's reflections.

"You look . . . like a goddess," Catty said, smiling.

Jimena remembered she no longer had her gift. Could she even call herself a goddess now? With rising self-assurance, she knew it was her rightful title. The power was inside her.

"Ready?" Jimena asked.

Catty nodded.

They tiptoed down the hallway, past Kendra sleeping in her bedroom, and out into the cloud-covered night.

CHAPTER TWENTY-FIVE

JIMENA PACED BACK and forth in the park near the lake, holding the moon amulet in her palm, anticipating its warning. She wondered why Cassandra hadn't arrived yet. Maybe Morgan had been unable to convince her to come.

Then she caught glimpses of someone moving in the shadows, and her amulet began to pulse.

"Jimena." The word hit her as Cassandra, Karyl, and Morgan suddenly appeared, walking toward her.

A breeze flapped open Morgan's long coat. It seemed to float behind her. Karyl was dressed in his usual black, his eyes glowing and ready.

Cassandra wore her cape and impossibly high-heeled boots. Under the eerie reflection of city lights from the clouds, her pale skin and hard, black eye makeup made her look more nightmarish than pretty, but, Jimena thought, that was probably the look she wanted. When her ice-blue eyes locked onto Jimena's, a huge force pressed Jimena down. Even at this distance she could feel herself start to fall into the depths of Cassandra's endless blue eyes.

Jimena winced and pulled back.

Morgan laughed, but her laughter no longer sounded human. It was edgy and evil. She smiled derisively. "Hello, Jimena, we're here for your meeting."

Karyl's eyes widened in anticipation, then wandered slowly over Jimena's body before returning to her face.

Cassandra pushed into her mind again, and Jimena felt her will draining from her. She flinched at the feel of anger, hate, and fear that Cassandra twisted into her thoughts, but in the same moment she was overwhelmed with pity that such ugly feelings were Cassandra's constant emotions.

She knew from Cassandra's sudden grimace that she had read Jimena's thoughts and that her pity had sent Cassandra into a violent rage.

You'll suffer, Cassandra promised. The words echoed painfully around Jimena's mind.

The awful pressure remained, coming at her in waves. Jimena let Cassandra slide completely into her mind. It was the only way to distract her so that Serena would be able to sneak into Cassandra's mind, and steal Jimena's gift back. It was also the most dangerous thing Jimena could do, because Cassandra could gain complete control over her, discover the plan, and destroy Jimena. *What can harm you, can also help you.*

A current of air flowed over her. She hoped that it wasn't just the wind, but Vanessa, Catty, and Serena nearby and invisible.

From someplace deep inside her Jimena

fought to keep her plan hidden. She kept repeating the words the goddess had spoken, "*Quae tibi nocere possunt, etiam te adiuvare possunt.* What can harm you, can also help you."

"Failed goddess," Karyl smirked. "A prayer won't help you now."

Suddenly Cassandra's head wrenched backward in shock. A distressed scream came from her twisted mouth as she fled from Jimena's mind.

Jimena took three stumbling steps backward, then looked around. She hoped Serena had been successful.

Vanessa, Catty, and Serena suddenly became visible.

Morgan seemed surprised, but Karyl and Cassandra smiled.

"I told you they would come," Cassandra said smugly.

Serena quickly entered Jimena's mind and Jimena could sense her gift of premonition returning.

"Thank you," Jimena said, as the power inside her grew, feeling stronger than it ever had.

It pulsed through every cell, gathering energy. "Now let's get out of here."

"Don't you want us to stop them?" Morgan asked.

Cassandra shook her head. "No need to."

A booming noise came roaring from the earth and the ground trembled.

Jimena fell to her knees as the earth ripped open in front of her. She tried to stand again and stagger backward, but she lost her balance and sprawled inches from the edge of the bottomless abyss. The sulfurous air from the land of the dead seeped into the night air around her.

Vanessa tumbled precariously close to the edge. Catty fell next to her.

Serena keeled over the edge. Jimena leaped forward and caught her. She clasped Serena's hand and held tight.

Jimena squirmed farther over the ledge, reached down, and grabbed Serena's other hand, straining, muscles pulling tight across her back as she tried to haul Serena back.

Immediately Cassandra's words flowed into

Jimena's mind. *You wanted a meeting to talk about getting your gift back? Do you think I'm that stupid? You fell right into my plan. I knew your friends wouldn't let you come alone.*

Too late Jimena knew she had been overly eager to face Cassandra in the park. As Cassandra sensed victory, her sapphire eyes flashed with hellish triumph.

"Hang on," Jimena said to Serena. "I won't let you fall."

Morgan peeked over the edge. "You can't hold on forever," she jeered.

One of Serena's shoes slipped off and fell into darkness.

"We'll save her," Catty cried. She and Vanessa scrambled backward and latched on to Jimena.

Cassandra whooped behind them. "My premonition," she yelled with glee. "Coming true exactly as I saw it."

Jimena could feel the earth giving way beneath her.

"You've never been able to stop any of your premonitions from coming true," Vanessa said with urgency. "Is it the same for Cassandra's premonitions?"

"I don't know," Jimena answered helplessly, as a mound of dirt beneath her crumbled and tumbled into the pit.

Rain started to fall. Three large drops fell on Jimena's hand and rolled down to her fingers. Serena's hand started to slide away.

CHAPTER TWENTY-SIX

THE RAIN MADE IT impossible to hold on to Serena's hands. Jimena had to do something and quickly.

"I'm going to let go of your right hand," Jimena warned her, "so I can grab your left wrist. Ready?"

Serena nodded.

Jimena released Serena's right hand and grabbed her left wrist. Her hold felt firm again, but she knew it couldn't last for long. She strained and tugged hard.

At the same time Vanessa and Catty pulled her farther away from the edge.

Serena dug her toes into the sides of the cavern.

Cassandra whispered across Jimena's mind, urging her to let go of Serena's hand. Then another voice pushed Cassandra's aside and scraped around Jimena's mind, the tone taunting and so different that she turned and glanced back at Karyl.

"Don't look at him," Vanessa yelled.

Karyl walked to the edge of the chasm and looked down at her.

"Ignore him," Catty urged and tugged hard on her legs.

Listen to him, Cassandra breathed the words softly into Jimena's mind. *He has something important to tell you.*

Jimena ignored them and glanced back at Serena. "Brace your feet against the side and try to walk up."

Serena did and was able to take one faltering step.

Jimena wiggled backward.

Karyl leaned down, closer to Jimena and spoke contemptuously in her ear. "I'm the *vato.* I'm the one who came to Veto the night he got shot. I lied to him and told him you needed his help. I led him into enemy land. He thought he was going to rescue you."

Jimena could feel anger rising inside her.

"Don't listen to him," Catty said.

"They're trying to get you to attack so you'll forget about Serena," Vanessa warned.

"Like I don't know that?" Jimena yelled back at them.

Jimena strained and pulled hard. Serena took another small step, digging her toes into the fissure wall.

Large clumps of dirt fell over the side.

Jimena had to worm backward to keep from falling. Her hands were on fire but she managed to smile reassuringly to Serena. "You're almost safe now."

She yanked again and moved backward as Serena took another small step. Catty leaned forward and grabbed Serena's other hand.

More dirt and grass gave way, but this time they pulled Serena up and over the edge.

"Hurry," Vanessa warned behind them.

They fell back as the ground slumped and large pieces of earth gave way.

Karyl smiled at Jimena with his strange, hungry eyes, and Jimena knew intuitively that she didn't want to hear his next words. She turned to face him, her moon amulet casting an extraordinary white glow over his face. He didn't seem intimidated by the power building inside her.

"Cassandra gave me the power," he bragged, his eyes burning. "The power from the Inner Circle to go back in time and change one event."

Jimena stood and stepped closer to him.

"But a big one," Cassandra added with a derisive grin as she stepped next to Karyl to face Jimena.

Karyl started to speak and Jimena interrupted him, her voice low and rasping, her anger complete, "You went back in the past to lure Veto into enemy territory?"

"To his death," Karyl said.

The air trembled with Jimena's power. She pulled the small gun from her pocket and pointed the muzzle at Karyl.

Morgan screamed and took quick steps back, but Cassandra didn't flinch.

Vanessa let out a long hiss of air and grabbed Jimena's arm. "Don't, Jimena. Remember what Maggie told us. Evil only feeds evil. We never use the tools of the Atrox."

Jimena jerked her arm away and cocked the hammer on the small gun. She kept Karyl in its sights. "Maggie doesn't know anything about fighting evil."

She let an indolent smile cross her face and then spoke to Karyl. "You're not Immortal yet, are you, Karyl? Too bad. A bullet can kill a Follower, right? You ever see what a bullet does to flesh?" She could feel the jaguar awakening and padding through her veins.

But Karyl didn't seem afraid, he seemed elated. So did Cassandra.

"Stop," Serena yelled, and then she was half-running, half-limping to Jimena's side. "The

Followers grow stronger when people use violence to fight them. You're only going to put us all in jeopardy."

Karyl sneered. "Veto thought he was going to rescue you, Jimena. His concern for you killed him."

"They'll be invincible if you use the gun," Catty cried.

Jimena gripped the gun with both hands. "He can't survive a gunshot."

"You're a force of good." Vanessa tried to convince her.

"Too late." Jimena smiled and pulled at the trigger.

CHAPTER TWENTY-SEVEN

JIMENA FIRED THE GUN into the ground beside Karyl. At the same time she concentrated and sent all her mental power twisting at him. The night filled with a strange, pure whiteness. Sparks burst into the air and continued to glow as they dropped slowly to the ground. Jimena felt lost in her power. Her nerves thrummed with excitement while her body felt exhausted from the effort.

Tiny tendrils of static electricity swept around Karyl in diminishing circles. His eyes turned blank, then dark. Without their scary luminescence, his eyes looked tortured.

Jimena pitied him now and felt sick in her heart when she considered how truly lonely and separate the life of a Follower must be. She wondered how they came to terms with the life they had chosen. Looking at Karyl now as he lay on the ground, she suspected that they never did.

"You didn't use the gun to hurt Karyl." Cassandra's words were filled with amazement and disappointment.

Jimena faced Cassandra. "Of course not, Cassandra, we don't use the tools of the Atrox. The gun was only to distract you." She threw the gun over the edge of the abyss.

Karyl whimpered with a low animal whine, then pulled himself up, and took two tottering steps backward. He stopped and looked around him as if he didn't know which way to go.

Cassandra rubbed her finger nervously over the scars on her chest.

Vanessa, Catty, and Serena lined up next to Jimena and faced Cassandra.

Morgan looked at them, then back at Cassandra and Karyl. She suddenly turned and ran.

Thunder crashed through the air.

Jimena turned quickly. The ground quaked, but this time the earth seemed to be closing.

Cassandra trembled and a low wail came from deep inside her.

"What's going on?" Serena wiped at the mud streaked across her face.

"I think Cassandra has displeased the Atrox," Vanessa said.

Cassandra cowered as if she expected a bolt of lightning or something worse to annihilate her. Her low pathetic cries were filled with fear.

"Do you think we should try to save her?" Catty's face was covered with raindrops.

"I don't think we can," Jimena mused. "She looks like she's in deep communication with the Atrox."

Cassandra let out a cry, then turned and slowly walked away.

The ground shook and roared with thunder. The earth closed completely and Jimena knew they had won for tonight.

CHAPTER TWENTY-EIGHT

AFTER SCHOOL ON Monday the girls met at Pink's. Jimena was late because she had stopped at church to keep her promise to the goddess. Her grandmother was proud of the way she now prayed daily for the souls lost in purgatory. Jimena liked the quiet and dark and peace inside the church. She had told her grandmother about her promise to the goddess. She didn't tell her everything about that night, but her grandmother had smiled and said she suspected that God had many good spirits to help keep watch over the people of earth.

Jimena bought three chili dogs and joined her friends, who were already sitting around a table in the back. They didn't look like they were enjoying the late afternoon sun or their dogs.

Jimena sat down. "So what's up?"

Serena was the first to break the silence that held the table. "Stanton's disappeared."

Vanessa lifted her sunglasses, then looked around to make sure no one was listening. "The Atrox probably sent Regulators after him."

"Are you sure he's disappeared?" Catty took a bite of hot dog and spoke with her mouth full. "I mean, how would you know if he disappeared or was just doing what Followers do."

"Trust me," Serena answered with a glare. "I know. Something's wrong. It's like he's vanished. I'm going to go looking for him again."

"You have to be careful," Vanessa warned.

"Let's talk about something else." Serena tried to act as if she wasn't bothered, but she kept raking her fingers through her hair and glancing at her watch.

"What time is it?" Catty asked finally.

"Almost four." Serena took in a deep breath. "I gotta go."

"Do you want me to go with you?" Jimena asked.

Serena shook her head. "No. This is something I need to do alone."

Vanessa shrugged, but Jimena could tell she was unhappy with Serena's decision.

Serena started to leave.

"Remember we're here for you if you need us," Vanessa said.

"Yeah, don't think you have to be like me," Jimena added. "And do it on your own."

"Wait." Catty stood. "I have to leave, too."

"Where are you going?" Jimena asked with a sly smile.

Catty seemed to blush. Maybe it was just the heat of the sun. "I got a study date with Chris."

"Study?" Vanessa's smile was huge. "Since when do you study?"

"And on a date," Jimena teased. "You must like Chris a lot."

"I like him." Catty smiled contentedly.

"Let's go," Serena added impatiently.

"Jimena, do you want to come with me to my ballroom-dancing class?" Vanessa offered. "It'll be fun."

"No." Jimena smiled back at her. "Go on," she insisted. "I need time to think, anyway."

"You sure?" Vanessa asked.

Jimena nodded. She waited until Vanessa had left with the others, then she got up and strolled through the alley behind Pink's and started walking down Melrose. She hadn't gone far when a horn honked. She turned. Collin's utility van pulled up to the curb.

"Hey," he shouted. "You need a ride?"

She shifted her head to the side. "Are you making a career out of following me around?"

"Maybe," he answered.

She glanced at him and wondered why she felt so happy to see him.

"You want to go down to the beach?"

She shook her head, but then she looked into his clear blue eyes and the wrong word came from her mouth. "Okay."

"Great." He jumped from the van, came around to the passenger's side and opened the door.

She hesitated. Why had she said okay? She didn't want another relationship. It would hurt too much when it was over. Besides, a dull ache for Veto still filled her heart.

"Maybe I shouldn't," she said, but even as she spoke the words her feet betrayed her and she walked toward the van.

They parked the van, then walked down Colorado Avenue and onto the Santa Monica pier. Twice Collin tried to hold her hand, but she pretended she had an itch on the side of her face that needed to be scratched.

"Let's walk along the shore," he suggested.

They took off their shoes and walked in the sand at the water's edge.

Collin looked out at the water. "I'm glad you and Serena finally told me the truth."

"Yeah?" A breeze ruffled through her hair.

Collin took her hand. She hadn't anticipated his touch and a sweet excitement rushed through her.

"It explains a lot." He smiled, then he looked at her oddly.

"What?" she asked.

His arm slipped around her. "I've never kissed a goddess before."

She pulled away from him and stepped quickly down the beach.

A sudden gust pushed against her. She stopped. The wind swirled, making her clothes flap around her, and in the circling wind she thought she heard Veto telling her to go back to Collin. *He'll treat you fine.* The wind died to a caress of air across her cheek. Then it was gone.

Collin walked up to her. "Do you want me to take you home?"

She shook her head and rested her hands on his chest. "Not yet," she answered.

He didn't move to kiss her but stared at her, unsure.

Her anticipation made her desire grow and when his warm lips finally touched hers, her body filled with happiness. He kissed her long and slow, the way he had in the premonition. And as the kiss continued, warm and intoxicating, a stream of swiftly moving pictures filled her mind, all showing her with Collin. She smiled to herself, knowing that her premonitions always came true.